GLORIOUS ANGELS

GLORIOUS ANGELS

JUSTINA ROBSON

Copyright © Justina Robson 2015

The right of Justina Robson to be identified as the author
of this work has been asserted by her in accordance with
the Copyright, Designs and Patents Act 1988.

First published in Great Britain in 2015
by Gollancz
An imprint of the Orion Publishing Group
Carmelite House, 50 Victoria Embankment,
London EC4Y 0DZ
An Hachette UK Company

This edition published in Great Britain in 2016
by Gollancz

1 3 5 7 9 10 8 6 4 2

A CIP catalogue record for this book
is available from the British Library

ISBN 978 0 575 13403 4

Typeset at The Spartan Press Ltd,
Lymington, Hants

Printed and bound by the CPI Group (UK) Ltd,
Croydon, CR0 4YY

The Orion Publishing Group's policy is to use papers that
are natural, renewable and recyclable products and made
from wood grown in sustainable forests. The logging and
manufacturing processes are expected to conform to the
environmental regulations of the country of origin.

www.orionbooks.co.uk
www.gollancz.co.uk

FOREWORD

WHY THE WAR IN THE SOUTH MUST END
By Tralane Huntingore, Professor of Engineering,
Glimshard Academy of Sciences.

The war in the south has already consumed our soldiers, our money and our interest in its outcome. Daily it costs us more tax revenues than the entire Sun City District. The news reports regarding it have slowed to a trickle of inaccurate supposition and death tolls or lurid recollections.

Mercenaries gather at our gates, eager for the high wages paid to career warmen, including fighters from groups historically and politically opposed to the Empire and sympathetic to the indigenous tribeswomen of the south whose lands we have invaded, willingly or not, in our march to claim the Southern Fragment. Those tribes fight a righteous war against an unsympathetic occupier.

Refugees fleeing the front have collided with related blood families along the Karoo forest and drawn them into the conflict so that now what began as a simple crossing of territory has become an attempt to hold an impossible line, hundreds of miles long.

Counteragents and sympathisers have come to the Imperial diaspora and burned crops, looted homes and murdered villagers

1

in shifting bands that are almost impossible to hunt down. They have allied with our ever-present agitators on the Steppelands and cannot be pursued even this close to home due to lack of manpower.

If this were not enough those countries bordering the Empire who have long envied our wealth and prosperity now see a chink in our armour as we lose guard patrols, civilian militia organisations and our attentions to our lands in order to fuel the conflict far beyond our natural reach. It has also lately been attested in several vivid journals, published lately by Hollow Victory Presses, that use of powerful mage weapons in battle has roused the Karoo of the southern forest and drawn them into the conflict. They are a combatant we cannot win against in our current depleted state.

With the greatest personal regrets I must advise the immediate closure of the Southern Fragment Expedition and propose extensive peacemaking diplomacy be carried out before we lose not only our dear sons and daughters but our beloved city and Empire as well. Is any scientific discovery, no matter how potentially significant, worth the price we are paying?

CHAPTER ONE

ZHARAZIN

Against a gunmetal grey sky a small plane was flying. Barely bigger than a hang glider, its two wings tilted and juddered in the force of the winds that tossed it this way and that. So violent and erratic was the progress that, seen from afar, it could easily have been mistaken for a leaf. But then a streak of light caught the edge of one of its propellers and flashed a regular code of brilliant motes that betrayed its mechanical nature.

Zharazin Mazhd, frozen almost into insensibility on his precarious perch, felt his heart catch at the sight. The slight increase of motion made him wobble and he felt the leather harness holding him against the icy stone slip a little as it took his weight. The pain of being forced to maintain one position for hours was outstanding and the cold had numbed his hands and feet in spite of their fireweave wraps.

As the plane battled closer, a figure could be seen sitting inside the light framework of the craft's delicate body, arms and legs working hard at various controls. The head was covered in a black leather helmet. Its full glass faceplate reflected the stormclouds. Beneath this an air tube curled down like a slender black trunk to the tanks behind the single seat. Wrestling hard with levers, one leg thrusting forwards, the other braced, the pilot struggled and cajoled the tiny craft in steady corrections towards the overgrown deck below Zharazin's ruined tower. The bees of the engine became a furious tiger and the underside of the wings lit with a burst of arcane energy in pale purple as the pilot applied maximum power in an attempt to stall their excessive speed. Success brought a sudden new series of terrifying angles of descent and the plane zigged, yawed and pitched as it dropped from the sky.

Zharazin put down the glasses for a moment and quickly wiped their lenses again, to be sure he would not miss the essential moment. Their heavy brass frames were cold and rigid against the bone of his eye sockets as he replaced them and the shaking of his hands made him bang them clumsily so that pain shot through one cheekbone but he found the airplane easily again, huge and out of focus in his vision. He spun the dials as it flitted closer to the platform where its landing circle was marked in weeds bursting through the stones, their lines vivid green against the yellowed streaks where the rest had been sprayed dead.

A gust of wind almost knocked him off his perch and he clutched and gasped with a moment of sudden terror. The glasses fell heavily against the strap on his neck. He swore, swore, swore, fumbling with his gloved, dead fingers until he had them back in place. For a second, the view wavered crazily and he lost sight of his quarry, but then he found the small shape, the violet glows already dying back until it was barely more than a silhouette against an ever-darkening sky.

There was a moment when the tiny craft was suspended in the air above the deck, so still that it might have hung there for ever, propeller whirring, insectlike, fragile. Then, with the sudden relenting of the wind, it dropped like a stone to the burst pavement of the runway and landed heavily with a thud that Zharazin felt as well as heard. He found his heart in his mouth. He'd thought the pilot was surely going to die, the plane

4

smashed into matches, although identifying an unprotesting corpse might be easier than the lengths this had forced him to.

His right lens was misting up again but he daren't clean it now. Now was the moment to which all his painful effort and machination had led. The pilot taxied forwards to the green circle's centre, stopped the plane, stopped the engines. They undid their harness and turned in place to operate a crank that wound in the singing wires of the crystallograph which sat behind them on the fuselage, mounted in an iron box and protected with an alder wood frame. That done they slithered to a position on the edge of the cockpit itself, reaching for the crystallograph again.

One, two, three, four – into the grey anonymity of a mail satchel went the crystals from the 'graph box. They looked like nothings now, shards of coloured rock, clouded with salty faultlines but he knew these to be the final components for Minister Alide's Chaos Gun, the weapon which would disintegrate anything that came within the range of its entropy beam. But they still looked like nothing, the crystals. As he watched they were covered in cotton wadding, strapped up tight and then their manager, the pilot, with minimum care, hoisted their bag free. With a movement more redolent of joy than fear they kicked their legs up over the side of the craft and jumped down to the ground.

Without their weight the wind buffeted the fragile plane and made it move. It slid a few feet. The pilot put one hand out onto the wing, avoided the still-lethal whirl of the propeller with ease and gave the mailbag a hefty underarm swing before letting it go. It sailed across the deck and into a bush. The pilot gave a nod of satisfaction that said clearly they were glad to be rid of it, however temporarily. It was heavy, so there was no chance it would be blown over the edge... Zharazin could not think about the edge. If he did he became aware of what was at his back and that was not worth contemplating. All the tower's safety mechanisms were long since dismantled or weathered away. It was a direct drop of six hundred feet to the city streets, and if the wind caused him to miss them it was a thousand more to the humble roads and fields of the farmlands.

He made himself not blink. His eyelashes bent against the glass.

The pilot was doing things to their craft Zharazin didn't understand but after a moment or two he watched in surprised admiration for the ingenuity of the machine as the wings were folded up and rolled in, the tail pushed up, and then, with a good shove, the entire thing was wheeled across to the one remaining whole hangar, gently eased through the door and locked in. If he hadn't seen it happen he would never have noticed the hangar itself – little more than one rotting workshop among many – nor believed something like that would fit in what was essentially a toolshed with a large door. The gale rattled the doors as the pilot heaved them to and sealed their mouldering green with a heavy bar. Then – yes! – they walked forwards to the bush and the bag with a strong, swinging stride, clearly high on the early evening's dangerous activity.

Zharazin had only seconds left before they would be gone. He tried not to get his hopes up. After all, he'd been here more than fifteen days in a row, and on none of those days had the pilot taken off their faceplate within viewing distance. The Infomancy demanded to know for certain who it was, and so he had no choice. There were not many candidates but guesswork was not something his mistress engaged with. He wondered if his own hopes had anything to do with the race of his heart.

The wind sucked at his boots, caught his scarf and tried to use it as a sail to pry him off his cliff.

And then it happened. The hands went up, the clasps were flicked free, the headcover pulled off and aside in one smooth gesture as the pilot, inexplicably, ignored the bag to turn and face the coming storm. A stream of black hair flagged out suddenly, long and thick, as they hung the mask on their belt and then pulled off their gauntlets too and flung out their arms to the sky in a lover's embrace.

'Turn, turn, turn,' Zharazin repeated under his breath, starting to curse the gods he'd been praying to a second before. It seemed the devils preferred him. His thundering heart stood still, waiting.

The pilot ran their hands through their hair and shook it out. Fresh spots of rain, cold, heavy and ominous began to land. They spattered the grey stone black in front of Zharazin and dashed themselves to death on the left lens of his glasses. One big breath … Then, finally! At last the exhilarated pilot turned and Zharazin got a clear look at their face for a single, perfectly lit moment.

Zharazin dropped the binoculars. They hit the rail before him and cracked a lens with a sharp retort, which made him start. There was a brief, awful moment in which he knew he was dead and his feet briefly paddled air. He grabbed for the balustrade's remains in front of him as he felt himself tip sideways. On his waist his rope harness creaked and the binoculars suddenly dragged on the back of his neck as they fell to the length of their strap – if not death by a fall then a hanging. For a few moments he was a scrabbling, panicking animal until his hands became sure the stone in front was not leaning, but strong, and his feet found the pitons he'd taken such pains to drill into position. He pressed his cheek to the cold rock, eyes closed, and saw behind the lids that revelatory moment once again; the triumphant tearing away of the headpiece, the self-satisfied shake of the head releasing all that coiling black hair, the utterly unexpected but hoped-for familiarity of that face.

Tralane Huntingore. Heiress of an ancient but defunct line of mages. Eccentric, erratic, renowned as a scientist, in the prime of her beauty at thirty-eight, mother of two daughters, the one slight, fair and scholarly the other dark, fierce and curved like a violin. Tralane Huntingore, a woman he had seen once in the street and never forgotten because seeing her had made him walk into a wall.

7

All this time he had guessed the pilot was a man, just because only a man could be risked on such a mission and Minister Alide, who authorised and banked the gun project, favoured men of the army for all tasks. Instead he had just witnessed the Matriarch of Huntingore complete a daring feat of skill that any Prime would be ecstatic to survive, and all to gather materials for weapons of mass destruction. She'd been jaunty about it too, for an outspoken pacifist who had written and distributed pamphlets against the very war in which the Empire was presently engaged, who harboured known dissenters in her household and who was, if rumour and research be believed, verging on bankruptcy.

The rock bit his forehead but he let it. He hoped the pain would clear a path in his mind and let him see what to do with this information, which he had fully expected to solve his problems but which had now entirely turned them on their heads and inside out. He didn't want to reveal her identity, but how could he not? The rock had no ideas, it seemed, because his forehead only hurt. The coming rain splashed on his wrapped hands further numbing them as their magic fought the bitter air and the water and lost. He had to go before it got too slippery and his nerve failed.

He straightened and looked across the crumpled ruins of the tower deck with naked eyes. Viewed this way the figure of Tralane was toy-sized and indistinct as the clouds reached the city proper and darkened the early evening into a menacing gloom. She grabbed up the mailbag of crystals with careless exuberance, walked across the empty reaches of stone to the black shadows where various stairs and elevators led down into the tower's guts, and vanished from sight there, the bag swinging from her shoulder and the mask jouncing at her back. A single ray of weak light reflected from her visor, the sky winking at him as if they shared her secret.

Suddenly cold beyond enduring and fearful of the climb,

8

Zharazin became aware of how far he was from anything resembling safety. It was only with the greatest determination that he was able to unclip his carabiners from the webbing wrapped around the spire and clip them instead to his ropes. He fumbled, but the webbing he had used to make himself an anchor on the fragile spire of rock was thoroughly bedded in place and would not come free. He began to get his penknife out to cut it, tuning the blade to the correct frequency just by experience, but just then a gust of freshening wind and a patter of rain warned him that the clouds were dropping fast. He made the cut but fumbled the knife as he turned the dial again and it fell from his hand. He watched it tumbling over and over until he couldn't see it at all against the thin mist and the gathering gloom. He heard no result as he prayed briefly that it not kill someone, grateful the mist utterly ruined any kind of view. Try as he might he couldn't think of it as anything but ominous bad luck. The sky winked. The mist consumed his knife. On the flight deck far below the weeds bent flat, bowing before the storm.

Moving jerkily with fear of this brewing spell he made himself climb out of the slender notch in the rock. He was stiff from sitting so long without moving and his legs and arms complained all the time about their weeks of climbing but he managed, little by little, thinking of the reputation and reward he would get for his information, and then when that failed of some other kinds of fortune to which he could aspire with his knowledge – many layers and systems of knowledge, not only this sliver – and these fantasies spiralled up around him in a cloud of dissolute protection and allowed him to creep down. He should take all the traces of his work with him, but he was too alarmed. He promised himself he would come back for them when the weather was more clement, knowing it for a lie. After all, nobody had been up here in decades and there was no reason for them to come here again. Zharazin was a good observer and the Array was a derelict artefact of no interest to anyone any longer. He could count the surviving members of the families that had once kept it working on the fingers of one hand and he knew the position of all their files in the Memoriam, including Tralane's. It was this diligence, observation, patience and a lot of luck which had let him work his way up in the world from thieving guttersnipe out on the hills to a rank within the Infomancy. Even if he hadn't been attempting to snake his way into the Empress's elite by hook, crook and bootstrap he might have tried to discover the identity of the crystal recorder's owner for the professional pride of the thing. Making an identification had seemed an obvious demonstration of his tenacity and determination, and his superiors would be glad to know where the Gleaming's supply of weapon-grade crystal shards was coming from: a matter that the Minister of Defence had kept from them for some time. But now this grand plan was spoiled. He wouldn't be selling information, he would be selling Tralane Huntingore. He wasn't convinced he would ever be ready to do that.

It amused him to know that this wretched surveillance had in fact mimicked one of his dearest daydreams: all the miserable, terrifying, arduous days and nights since midsummer Zharazin the ambitious spy and the mystery daredevil pilot and crystallomancer, Tralane, had been alone together, far from the eyes of the world. And if the pilot didn't know he'd been there and he didn't tell, then there was even less reason to come and rip out the pitons that betrayed his daring path up the face of the tower. But he felt like he ought to. Leaving them felt like leaving a signature behind. Glimshard was a city of mages, one of the Eight, and that was a dangerous place in which to be complacent, on any front. He still felt off balance and a little sick as he finally put foot to flat roof tile at the tower's base. He couldn't think what to do or how to turn just yet, so he gathered up his gear instead and carefully made his way home.

TRALANE

Tralane stood in the darkness at the top of the Diligent Stair and listened briefly to the sound of her breath and the blustering work of the storm. She felt sure that as she had been fighting the wind to land there had been a flash towards the left side of the collapsed flight tower. Lightning, had been her first thought, with a grab in the stomach and renewed strength as she muscled the ailerons into position. Flits didn't react well to lightning. They were made of lacquered paper, bent wood and charms, and thus tended to burn up almost instantaneously – their one drawback – so landing had suddenly become even more imperative as if the wind was not enough. However, the lightning hypothesis did not hold as there was no thunder and when she looked again she'd seen nothing, it being too dark. She wondered if she'd imagined it, but when she closed her eyes after touching down in a moment of relief there had been a dot of dark blue behind her lids. Unlikely as it seemed, her limbs sank with the sensation of cold dismay at having been seen. Possibly. Maybe. One could drive oneself mad with it.

This hesitation lasted only a moment and then she resumed her downward run, feet easily remembering the wide curve of the stair, the heavy bag and visor jogging at her back and her gear squeaking and creaking. She didn't mind the dark. As a girl this vast ruin was her playground and none of it was strange to her. She kept her fingers on the wooden rail, counted its marks, joins, breaks, as she traced her way to one of the lower levels where an elevator waited for her, its small cabin glowing by the light of a single tiny lamp. The battery was going. She must remember to renew it, she thought, as she stepped inside.

The outer cage doors were missing but the car doors were well oiled on their tracks and slid shut with a click as she turned the key. This connected the power cores and suddenly the whole car lit up brightly, soft apricot beams from the roof panes illuminating its rotted velvets and water-stained panelling. Tralane put her fingers to the drive plate and felt the judder of old machinery coming to life. There was the alarming whine of a wheel whirring up to speed on a rusty axle, the grinding of bearings that were long since powdered, and her rattling descent began. She wondered if she would be the last person to use this part of the tower. Her daughters had so far shown almost no interest in it whatsoever, so she wasn't sure they even remembered it was there. She liked to imagine their faces, herself laughing with them, the delight they would feel in discovering an unimagined wealth in what was, to them, a huge and boring ruin. But another impulse also lit in her, one which clasped itself tightly around the higher tower, and everything it held. Later, it whispered, later, when they are older. And she didn't want to share it. So she wiped a brief tear out of her eye on the unyielding toughness of her leather jacket and spent the minute of her journey brushing through and restoring the braid of her hair. It was hard to manage in only one minute and the task kept her from thinking of the other reasons why she had not passed on her legacy.

'Axle grease,' she thought, considering where to obtain it and what to say that it was for. Plus there was no denying that she must do something about the influx of mercenaries flooding the Terraces and filling the girls' heads with speculations that must remain idle, unexplored and mysterious. She felt sad that the war had brought so many of them and glad at the same time. She approved of diversity and particularly an incursion of new men, but in spite of the city's trenchant propaganda she didn't expect many of them to be returning and the prospect of girlish broken hearts on top of what other horrors may come was enough to set her teeth grinding. Besides that, most of the recruits were from various misogynist regimes and tribal factions which would make them at best exhausting and at worst dangerous to inexperienced women who had spent their lives in the matriarchy of the Gleaming.

'Maybe there will be Sircenes?' Isabeau had already said several times, wistfully. No no, Tralane had assured her, the last of the Sircenes were all here, in the Gleaming, nodding their days away in the Academies. Of the remaining hundreds of named families most were mixed bloods, like themselves, who had yielded to the conquering triad of the Golden Empire in ages past. There were no Pureblood Sircenes on record, although there were possibly a few by accident or some who had deliberately forged their census documents. There would be no grand revival of the magi lines. But the notion, inspired by Huntingore's rich and extensive history and, she recalled with a roll of her eyes, all the stories she had drilled into them as children for the sake of heritage as much as adventure, was much more alluring than anything a suddenly prescient mother could say.

Minnabar had been contemptuous of both Tralane's and Isabeau's attitudes, but she was old enough not to have to care about the consequences of this, spending most of her time with a gaggle of late teen girls drifting from one house to another in a freefloating blur of study, application, conspiracy and partying which was a typical young Gleaming web at its most potent. Tralane knew they sneaked out of their Academics' care and down into the Terraces several nights a week and her nerves on the subject were almost frayed to splitting. One second she felt proud of Minnabar for her hellcat manners and her fire, the next she was terrified of what might happen if any of the Terrace lowlife took her remotely seriously or even noticed her. This was before one considered what the Gleaming lowlife had already contemplated.

The young men of Minnabar's group to whom she had free access gave Tralane no cause for concern. That was probably deeply unwise of her but Sircene bias must come out somewhere and she didn't reckon there was a handful of spit among them.

With their pleasant, bland manners and overeducated tempers they were perfect foils for the all female web itself, or had been, until stranger meat had arrived, reeking of unlimited testosterone. Now Tralane rather hoped the Sircene youths would find some backbones and rise to the challenge but also dreaded the prospect. Tending black eyes and broken noses was the last thing she fancied and she could imagine much worse results. Somehow she must think of a project to stall the web and keep it bound to the Sircene citadel.

The echoes of her own footfalls tapped her mind like impatient fingers trying to point out the obvious. She knew it would come to that eventually; only the treasures of a secret, ancient world might prove strong enough to lure the girls from disaster, or she'd got nothing. But not today. Then the car came to a slow, quaking halt. She heard the cables plinking their stress like a badly handled piano and stepped out, locking the doors behind her and secreting the key by jamming it backwards into the lock of the unused cage gate on the outside. The light went out as the cores were unhitched and a grim darkness returned. A faint pattering of what she thought must be rust falling down the shaft made a rainy sound.

The return to her present was as unwelcome as the detour into maternal guilt. She undressed and redressed in the freezing anteroom of the lower tower without the luxury of distracting thoughts as the cold was distraction enough. She packed her gear away carefully, drying it all and checking her air cylinder, the connections and the hose before placing them in their velvet-lined cases and closing the lids. One at a time she stowed them in their fitted positions in one of the many pilot's wardrobes that lined the walls. It was hard to imagine there had been a time when this room had buzzed with talk and the pungent smells of leather oil, engine grease and volatile ether as flyers came and went all day long. Before she had discovered the Flit plans no pilot had been here for forty years and the only craft abroad belonged to the Ministries' official weather service. When she was satisfied that nothing seemed out of place she summoned a witchlight to run before her and passed through the remaining levels, halls, workshops and corridors at a brisk pace.

The statues of the ancestors watched her from their plinths and recesses, their eyes coming alight as she passed in answering glow to the witchlight's temporary power. Each one of them represented a lifetime of study, thought, research and mastery into their particular magic and its technologies. Tralane knew only a few of their number in any detail, and not even all of their names. Most of what they had achieved was lost in time now, the library having been burned during the early years of the occupation when the Gleaming was a mage city of the Sircene and not simply the higher city of the academics floating above the vast, sprawling powerhouse of Glimshard, second city of the Golden Empire, Westernmost Outpost of Civilisation.

Since then, knowledge had been restricted to what had been saved by the Huntingores and other families of the lines and in recent decades that had been kept rigorously secret, both from the Academy and each other. The Golden Empire was being pressed upon by the unholy forces of the Bitter Circle, a loose alliance of hundreds of outland nations, and in its distress it had become fanatical about the claiming of any useful power for exclusive Imperial military use. Tralane was not alone in understanding what that meant for ancient magi and potentially difficult lines of engineering. Firstblood mages of the Empire, halfbloods and lessers all struggled with Sircene work and it was often considered more of a tolerable indulgence than a true science. It did not take well to written transference by any methods and routinely failed to submit to standardisation when Firstblood mages attempted its works using their methods. It would not take too much trouble or prompting to finish what they had started a century earlier and wipe all Sircene knowledge from the records.

Tralane had known all this for so long that most of a sense of urgency about it had passed until one of the Imperial scryers at the Ministry of Defence had discerned her skill with the crystallo-graph. Now she felt plenty of urgency, though she would not run. She descended until she reached the half-used rooms of the lower tower, on a height with the majority of the Arrays that made up the Gleaming. These had been the living quarters of the families of the Sircene sorceresses and their interiors provided modest rooms with excellent views whose furnishings were still reasonable, if thoroughly neglected in her case. In other, better populated Arrays, life went on at all levels, but Huntingore was threadbare and scanty. Tralane used her excess of space for stor-age now and tried not to notice that it was all falling apart.

Old furniture, broken children's toys, uninteresting tomes and crates of things that might have been alchemist's bottles or kit-chen equipment were stacked carelessly about. The dusty spokes of a spinning wheel mocked her efforts at serene domestication. She vowed to move it, as she had vowed to move it at least a hundred times, and darted past into the next hall.

The doors locked themselves automatically, their sturdy magic as solid as it had been since the tower was built a thousand years before. Nobody that the head of the house deemed unfitting would be able to enter any opening in Huntingore regardless of their skills in any craft. Those were the days, Tralane thought, and longed to know the methods and the powers they used then, but the door and window seals were only a fragment of the things she didn't know. At least they kept her family secure. She was grateful that they worked and that would have to be enough. Meanwhile she had returned via a roundabout route to a stair that bypassed their living areas close to the ground and would lead her into the gardens. From there she made her way unseen to the cab stand at the very edge of Marigold Park where puttering jalopies of various sizes were waiting.

By now it was nearly dark and the rain was pounding down.

16

Tralane's heavy oilskin mage cloak completely concealed her. Water dripped off the cowl past her face. It was hanging so far forward she would have been blind without a charm on it to let her see through the cloth as if it were only a veil. One of the smaller cars was lit inside, the driver smoking a long pipe in his portion of the cab and looking unconcerned. She opened the door and found the occupant waiting, his pinched face hard with his own sense of self-importance in his work as he reached for the bag. He didn't even attempt to look at her face.

'I hope they all break,' she said coldly.

'Let's hope for your sake they don't,' he replied, checking the contents with brusque efficiency and then stuffing bag and contents swiftly under his seat, sliding the panelling there back with practised speed. 'Wouldn't like your girls to find theyselves the wrong side of a draft, would we?'

To this there was nothing Tralane could say. The sham of any kind of conversation with this man was something that made her gorge rise. She came close to ill-wishing him and only the sense that they were in public stalled the coil of power, a thin whip in her chest, trying to slither up to her eyes and find its target. She stepped back and slammed the door shut on him, making it seem as though she was simply glad to be sending him on his way when she would rather have used all her strength to stop his journey, his purpose, his smug superiority. But there was no use in her anger. The Ministry would have its weapons, and for that they needed her. The war needed her. All her efforts, daring, the glorious flight, was in the service of death and destruction.

A black weight crept up her arms and into her shoulders, cold, its own kind of petrification spell. She stood on the rain-wet pavement, just another bystander lashed by the weather while around her the Gleaming went on with its complacent, luxury-ridden business, replete in the assurances of being a step away from trouble. The seat of true power sat on the High Terrace where the old palace had been part-converted to the offices of government. It was a time of administrators and the Empress presided over them without causing much turbulence.

Tralane turned and walked back through the streets, herself and her previous path all tainted by the fulfilment of business. She took the public elevator at Deciment and watched the thriving, shining night lights of the Terrace sink away until the car was surrounded entirely by purple magelight that blocked out all views.

She listened for conversation among the other passengers to distract herself from her miserable turn of mind and was strangely rewarded. A couple of older women, one in the crimson workaday robes of a Firstblood professor, the other gaily dressed in wet Array finery were talking about the influx of fighters to Lower Terrace where they had spent the afternoon selling for their guilds.

'A Karoo, can you imagine!' the Array woman said, shivering to add to the drama of her moment. 'Talking animals they are.'

'I don't know about that,' said her friend. 'I saw him and he looked quite humanoid. The rumours of beastmen are surely exaggerations. They are simply different.' Her voice suggested otherwise.

'Pff, a score of the Circle's vile spawn couldn't be any stranger. And looks are deceiving. There's no man that colour in a natural creation, nor that scale either.'

A pause ensued in which Tralane wished she could look at their faces but her hood and their relative position made it impossible.

When the Firstblood spoke again her voice was rich with speculation, 'He was huge.'

Tralane found herself smiling. Then she thought of Isabeau with sharp alarm like a jolt of electricity in her nerves, and especially of Minnabar, with a cold certainty plunging in her midriff. Neither of them was equipped to deal with the devastation that such an opportunity presented; its potential for disastrous romanticism was beyond endurance. She doubted most of the Gleaming would escape it. Prior to the exciting drama of the new war they had slumped headlong into a decadent decline and this combination of renewed energy, a resurgent interest in the values of heroism and a vague awareness of their own jaded appetites had already given rise to an abysmal tide of musical and novelised twittery extolling various religiously inclined ideologies of virtue, nobility, sacrifice and tragic love. Farce had yet to raise its head – this surge was in its primal state yet – and Tralane found herself braced as if for a long fight as the momentary silence in the rising car spoke volumes about the activity going on inside the fervent imaginations of the occupants, herself included.

Karoo. A race from so far away they were considered beyond civilisation, as elusive as the two-headed wolf of legend. Tales of them were as old and unlikely as the idea of a Sircene revival but in these days Tralane could only wish they'd had the sense to stay away from everything associated with the Golden Empire, which didn't exactly have a pure record on its assimilation of outland tribes let alone its reputation for sport with those considered to belong to subspecie groupings. The Sircene had survived only by hiding in plain sight and by virtue of the fact that they were visually identical to any of the wide variety of human types that considered themselves bloodline Empire natives. If anyone in a position of enquiry had known there was a significant difference or two it was long since forgotten. They were meted out the regular treatment for conquered people who had some uses to the major lifelines of the Empire, no more and no less, and even for historians they were of only marginal interest, counting the exception of Tralane herself and this crystal business which was secret and therefore didn't count, she fervently hoped. But a Karoo being alive in the city was enough to stir two dozen scholars from their rest. Corsets all over Glimshard were being hauled in extra inches all around her, she fancied, as it occurred to her that maybe she ought to be one of them.

CHAPTER TWO

BORZE

'And how is our friend from the north working out?' Fadurant Borze, seated on his horse for what felt like the fiftieth hour in a row, rested his hands on the pommel of his saddle and took some weight off his aching seat bones. He couldn't decide yet what to do about the Karoo and would have welcomed any news that would give him an excuse to make a decision to remove him, either to the front, or to some outpost, or into a grave – in fact anywhere other than keep him inside the city where his presence alone was sure to create trouble. But the Empress had granted the foreigner leave to stay under her own protective order and employing him where he was useful was at least good for keeping him under observation, not to mention favourable for Fadurant's reputation with the Empress. Fadurant was grateful that he was experienced enough not to be overly anxious about foreigners, even subspecie ones of surpassing rarity, but he still didn't like it. Thus, he cast this apparently lighthearted question out on to waters he was hoping would supply a nibble to feed either his hopes or his fears.

The reply didn't even bob the line. 'He is, as you suspected, taciturn to a fault. He fulfils his duties in training the men for combat. They respect him though I could not say they like him. He eats, he shits, he collects his money as the rest.'

To his left, his adviser and second, Parillus Gau Tam, was relaxed and at ease. His mount was fatter than Fadurant's, of more humble carting stock, and offered a broader seat and what looked like a much softer ride. Parillus steered it with a careless but steady yaw on the reins, taking them up the blessed final ramp towards the lower gates of the eastern wall. Over its high top they were able to see most of the capital's sprawling hillsides climbing steadily towards the clustered citadels of the Terrace. From the Terrace's heart a thick trunk of what appeared to be many fine crystal stems drew a straight line upward in shining facets of rose and turquoise. Ever-undulating internal lights seemed faint in this hot afternoon of glare and dust, the outer veils of this stem flickering and unreliable in auroras of changing hue. The Gleaming, its heavy flowerhead, was mostly lost in hazy cloud but occasional spires and towers of the Arrays far above them caught the light and glinted down. Where he had once felt awe at the sight of such power, majesty and scale, Fadurant now felt an uneasy apprehension and only a flicker of appreciation at being the child of such an important place. The world, he'd found, was full of important places.

He gritted his jaw so as not to actively grind his teeth and pushed his arse back in the saddle pan, trying another angle. His horse was, thankfully, too weary after the long trek around from the nearest staging post to do any more of its irritating capering. Fadurant tried again. 'You seem to be holding something back.'

'Do I?' Parillus was languid, savoring whatever it was.

Fadurant waited him out, watching the guards on the gate towers move in a sudden burst of activity as they recognised the colours on the horses and his shield. A black line appeared in the gate itself and the two halves began to inch their way open. He could just hear the creak and grind of the old chain gears and imagined the oxen huffing out of a doze, crossly smacked with sticks on the backside in the stinking darkness of the gate chambers while the stick boys hollered in hoarse, ammonia-worn tones. It had been his job, once. He could never understand why it hadn't been automated.

At last Parillus drawled, 'The University want to send a delegation.'

Fadurant felt the first breath of a potential reprieve stealing through his bones. 'Of course you said no.'

'Yes, of course I did.' Parillus ignored the stares of a small caravan of traders who had moved aside on the road so that he and the general were able to pass abreast of each other. What his horse lacked in appearances it made up in the finery that Parillus ensured it wore to mark his rank – all the paraphernalia of a jousting knight trailed from its harnesses, stained with sweat and road dust now, which made it look all the more extravagant. He knew the importance of impressing the population's lower orders with this cartoonish nonsense to distract the gossip mongers from more sensitive business. He paused and flipped a few copper coins and bronze stravetti for the caravan's children. Someone tsk-ed but he ignored that for the sake of enjoying General Fadurant's rigid jaw and hawkish intensity as it hung on his next revelation, paralysed by manners and station and their long friendship from demanding instant satisfaction. He relented, slightly.

'Soldiers heading for the front deserve the greatest privacy as they undergo the rigours of hard training. It is a matter of seriousness and dedication that cannot be thrown off course by such frivolities as an *audience*. It would be demeaning to the men's honour to be treated as experimental subjects. Conscripts may soon be required, and we must be seen to be treating both our homegrown troops and our mercenaries with the utmost respect. After all, they are about to put their lives on the line for our safety and prosperity.' He waved his hand idly as he mocked his own grave tones in repeating this propaganda. 'But I did mention the training hours.'

There was no hesitation in Fadurant's grabbing the implications of this nugget. The game of catch was what made even a dull conversation enjoyable between them. 'You will cram the yard gates with speculators, idiots, and gawpers then?'

'Possibly quite cram them entirely,' Parillus agreed and left a few seconds' pause so that they could both build up the image of journalists and commentators being frustrated in crowds of go-sees and the vast entourage of vendors and petty thievery that would follow this pilgrimage – eminent distractions all, and good for morale though neither man had to say so. 'Although some may be given special access privileges to spectate with the overseeing officers. May.'

'Upon what determination?'

'Whomever you see fit to entertain with the sight.'

Fadurant narrowed his eyes even though they were within the wall's shadow. 'Is there some advantage within the University?'

He had been so focused this last year on building up the front to resist the efforts of the Circle to repel Imperial presence from anywhere near their borders that he had ignored the city itself until his return a few weeks previously. He'd forgotten how annoying it could be when there were so many extramilitary factions to take into account. He left most of that to Parillus, whose well-bred upbringing and lengthy education had made him ever more the diplomat and less the soldier than Fadurant himself.

The initial reply was lost in a hastily arranged fart of horns, which announced their arrival, from the nearing towers so that Parillus had to repeat himself. 'The Sircene woman is among them.'

A circle that had been wide open in Fadurant's chest and mind closed neatly as he heard this – it was the same sensation he felt when he was able to see through the last few moves of a game or a battle plan to a clear victory position, even though he wasn't able to explain exactly yet how it would work. He knew that things could be dovetailed and all that was required was his will to follow the sign and continue his efforts; the details would appear in due course and reveal what they had to reveal to him in the future, each step following the last. He need do no more than trust his instincts. Of course it was slightly galling to realise that Parillus' facility with local intelligence had put him at the advantage and he, Fadurant, was merely being led by the nose at this stage, but he forgave it because he was sensible enough to know that one man's attention would never be enough to maintain his position. Even so, their accord was a glad enough thing that it let him almost enjoy his last stretch of ride as they took the direct route towards the barracks.

'Call her in,' he said as they arrived in the yard, fanfared slightly better this time in a barrelling trumpet roll, with several cohorts of men managing to make themselves into orderly lines before they had turned the corner. The flags of the twenty-eight army legions snapped pleasantly in the fresh wind. A stink of sweating bodies and a whiff from the latrines greeted them. Fadurant felt light as he dismounted and handed his horse over, even giving it a pat on the neck. However poorly they may think of him and his position, he was always gladder to receive a woman, even spar with one verbally, than a man. Then he glanced to his left where Parillus was also looking.

The Karoo was there. Head and shoulders taller than any Empire man with a muscular physique that was spare and clear-cut, he looked like a stone sculpture of some legendary fighter. That was where the extent of his resemblance to men of the Empire ended however. He was blue-grey and white, the colours marbled darkly on his back and the backs of his arms, light on his front and undersides. He was also as thickly maned as Parillus' horse, with silvery white hair that surged not only off his head in great hanks but from his neck and along the length of his spine too, disappearing under his belt in finger-length tufts. To either side of this, tiger stripes of intense sunburnt orange spread out around his ribs and waist, feathered the edges of his neck and emerged either side of his head in triangular ears, their richly furred points tipped with lynxlike purple feather hair that flicked whenever the ears turned – something they did independently of each other in a way Borze found disturbing. He wore nothing but tough trousers, panelled with leather reinforcements, and leather rolltop boots, all of these well-mended and old. His face, like the faces of the Empress' favoured horses, was pale grey, marked along the length of his strong, straight nose, nostrils and lips with indigo stains like ink dropped on soft paper. In deep pits of this unnatural shade his orange, slitted eyes with their yellow iris-rims showed no white at all except at the very ends. Black lashes completed the shocking effect of the indigo. Across the sheer bony impact of his overly masculine features with their hard right angles this peculiar natural enhancement looked to Fadurant's eyes like the makeup of a courtesan. He wondered if the Karoo knew that junior officers called him Tigerlady behind his back.

If he did it wasn't bothering him. The Karoo was completely at his ease where he leaned against a wooden column of the verandah that surrounded the yard on three sides, providing shade and access to the barrack houses. His relaxation was a stark contrast to the rigid attention of the soldiers in their rows in the sun. He made no sign of acknowledgement to Fadurant and Parillus except for the merest nod which managed not to lower the steady gaze of his offensive two-coloured eyes one bit. Fadurant envied such natural dominance even as he responded to it. It was an effort for him to do nothing but turn back and continue on his way. Beside him he felt Parillus brush his shoulder in an unconscious movement away from the alien man.

Fadurant felt he could weather such minor slights. He

accepted the fact that some people were just stronger than others, though he knew it might appear weak to some of his men. Parillus disliked nature's quirks far more – he believed in self-determination over all things and suitable displays of subservience to higher ranks.

'He ought to stand like the others,' Parillus said as they turned the corner and went under the arch where the long building of the headquarters ran the length of the Fields Wall.

'As I understand it, this has been suggested,' Fadurant said. 'But if the reporting corporal was correct then there is no way of making him do so, short of beating him to death, and at the moment he is a necessary device. Not to mention the fact that one does not wish to expose one's seniors and ministers to displays of that nature quite so close to home.'

'We should send him onward.' Parillus was determined.

'I don't want to lose him yet.' Fadurant scowled and speeded up his step on his way to his offices.

He and Parillus had their differences but it was where they were similar that they were weak and they were similar in that they could both see the sophisticated side of things too easily. The Empire at Glimshard was a place of long-term social games of subtlety; it was easy to forget that other peoples didn't pursue their lives this way.

The Karoo was a windfall in truth, a strange kind of queen piece handed to Fadurant in a game that had few such things that could be turned in many directions. But he was also a rank outsider, a loner and a thorn in the sides of the training sergeants who themselves must keep to military discipline and ensure it among the men. He was a goat (a wolf was the first image that came to mind but it didn't fit the metaphor any way that Fadurant liked) among what were essentially sheep, and they must not lose sight of that. As if that were not enough he was also a curio or living fossil that the University thought it might prise out of Fadurant's grasp. And this was before Gleaming's social hounds got wind of his presence and sniffed blood for the dancefloor. The only consolation was that the war itself was as yet unfelt except in the private pockets that paid the war tax and so Fadurant, as the only general in the province, need not do anything at great speed.

That made it all the more difficult.

He marched to his study, glanced over the day's intelligences and the chalkboards where the country was mapped, ordered drinks for them both and took a damp towel offered by one of his attendants to briskly rub his face and hands clear of dust and the horse grease that blacked his knuckles. Reluctantly, he voiced his intention. 'I think we should have a dinner,' he said and massaged his sword hand where it had suddenly developed a pain in the joints. 'Invite Tralane Huntingore and whoever her academic cronies are, and anyone you think ought to be indulged. The usual officers and staff to attend.'

'Spouses and partners?'

'Included. Everyone included that may be has some interest and sufficient standing. I leave the details to you. You're better at these things.' Fadurant was glad to. He had never enjoyed great events or the gathering of intelligence by other than straight-forward means.

Parillus grinned. 'Real news is short here. We should make it a large affair. Returning injured heroes, a celebration of our... Well, our holding of our positions.' He hesitated and the shift of subject came with a change of energy in the room from playful to cool. 'The Karoo may bolt.'

Fadurant unbuttoned his tunic and wrested open his shirt neck, turning to the ceiling fan and sighing as his attendant closed the door behind him. 'I thought you didn't like him.'

'I didn't plan to *invite* him. I think that so much attention near the yard may cause his departure. I'd no sooner summon him to a society event than I'd bring a hunting dog.'

'He might take the scholars with him. Trail after him into the countryside and get lost.'

'You won't be so easily off the hook.'

Fadurant snorted, knowing it was true. 'Then we should post some men at the yard gates each day with orders to act as discouragement. Let him see some resistance to the rabble. And ensure he remains in his own quarters when he is not employed. Does he go out into the city proper?'

'No.'

'Fucking, drinks, cards, smokes, enchantments?'

'Nothing.'

'And no more word on what his real reasons are for being here?'

'No more than what he originally claimed.'

'Hmm. Cash in exchange for services I quite understand. Mercenaries are ten for tuppence at the moment. But to be here, just now, after so long, when Karoo have never come south of Jiljarga in living memory ... There has to be something else, Parillus.'

'Maybe there is. But possibly it's personal. I mean, he is the only one. No scouts in Jiljarga or even Tocastine say otherwise. I sent a man up north to go as far as he could and look for others but he has not reported.' Parillus was already bored of this angle, his mind busy with the construction of the party. Fadurant could tell by the way he was staring out of the window.

'Forget it for now then. Let's see if we can worm something out of the Chancellors at this gathering. I would bet that crystallographs are not the only things that might be dusted out of the archives and made use of, given the right incentive.' Fadurant was thinking of the seemingly unending parade of dreadful creatures that prowled the limits of the Circle's lands; engineered beasts or found ones he knew not but they were often pressed into service by the Circle onslaught. Imperial cannon and gunshot, even their arcane artillery, failed to do more than stall their progress. The beasts in themselves terrified the soldiery facing them, a power no mechanical device could deflect. There was a primal horror about Circle warfare that he needed to find an antidote for, or at least an anaesthetic. Magic was truly the only recourse he could think of, though using it extensively for violence went against Imperial temperament, especially that of the scholars who bothered the Empress' ears.

'Yes,' Parillus said, lost in thought, his gaze moving steadily upwards to the Gleaming. He glanced at Fadurant and they shared the concern before he moved smoothly along. 'But don't worry about that. The Ministry has the relics and the Library all in hand.'

Fadurant gladly gave up responsibility at the mention. He joined Parillus in taking off his travelling uniform and exchanging it for more comfortable, clean versions. The drinks arrived and Parillus poured them both wine and cold water. He drank as he was handing Fadurant's cup over to him and the general remembered a time when they had been formal, distant, polite: an officer and his assigned subordinate, strangers. That path had a few more miles in it, he felt, with distaste. He turned to what he knew and summoned the officer in attendance.

'I will inspect the recruits on the training field.'

But before he was able to do so the door opened again without warning and admitted a slender teenage girl, bare of leg and arm, damp and panting with healthy exertion.

The Empress' colours of magenta and gold covered her athletic uniform of shorts and vest and shone in a halo of soft light from the diadem that held back her brassy hair. This charm would protect her from almost anything within the city, even the ire of interrupted officers who knew better than to try and harass one of the Empress' runners, however impudent.

The girl, flushed and bright eyed, sure of her position, announced with careless grace, 'Her Majesty the divinely magnanimous Yaphantine Shamuit Torada wishes to enjoy your

29

conversation at her gardens, Fadurant Borze.' She beamed a smile of white teeth at him, at Parillus and at the sergeant in attendance before turning on her slender shoe and speeding out. A flourish of air swirled in her wake that smelled of dust and rain, floral shampoo and the tantalising hint of girl sweat on warm, bronzed and freckled skin.

Fadurant noticed with amusement that none of them moved for a good two seconds after her departure.

'If I could bottle that I'd rule the world,' he murmured, not for the first time.

The other men, well used to the Empress' couriers, grinned wryly their old agreement and at a glance from Parillus the sergeant bit back whatever heartfelt crudery he had been going to share. Fadurant would rather he had said it to cut the air, but he'd learnt to live with manners.

'Parade cancelled then,' Parillus said. 'I think I will go across to the Ministry and see how their research fares. You need to find another dress uniform.'

'I shall locate one, and ready a fresh horse,' the sergeant said and departed with a click of his heels.

'Horse,' Fadurant repeated grimly, massaging his aching ass, and took a last look outside at the training yard. He knew what the Empress wanted to talk about. It was the same thing everyone wanted to talk about.

The Karoo was standing in the middle of the melee arena now, watching recruits grapple with one another as they attempted to disarm opponents of wooden weapons at close quarters. The Empress' runner ran right past him on her course to the gate in what was a clear detour of curiosity.

Several of the new soldiers stopped to watch her, though no Imperial boys lifted their heads. The jaw-droppers were the mercenaries from the less developed kingdoms, no doubt wondering that her whimsical flit through their ranks seemed to take precedence over their own importance. The position of women in the Empire was beyond them for the most part, as frequent disciplinary hearings and subsequent lashings made apparent.

The Karoo paid no attention at all to her, but moved forwards and tripped the two gogglers nearest him so they landed heavily in the sand. Fadurant couldn't hear him but he could tell they were being treated with fitting discipline for their failings. A second or two later the entire line up was on its face doing pushups and lizard runs from one end of the yard to the other. Lines of sweat marked the ground in brown strips.

'Bottled,' he said to himself, watching the tall grey and white figure with unhappiness that made him glad he wasn't given to brooding. He caught Parillus' eye, 'I'm going for the bath and to get properly dressed.'

'Aye,' said his friend, not taking his eyes off the yard. 'I'll see you later.'

CHAPTER THREE

TZABAN

Tzaban was seated beside the mess table's open end because he was too big for the benches and because it was the only place that marked him apart from the men he was training. The tables were set up on the verandah in the shade and there was a stone seat close enough for him to use so that he wasn't entirely out of the conversation. The blocks it was made of were cool and he felt calmed by them and connected pleasingly to the earth. For all its brutal daily guests that place was peaceful. Whoever had chosen it and laid out the big square had picked a good spot and intelligent shapes of stability and purpose. Real rage would be hard to sustain there.

'My father was a soldier in the war, a hero,' a young recruit was saying eagerly. He was seated on the far end of the trestle where the lunch was being laid waste by himself and his twenty-four troopmates.

Tzaban cradled his dish in one hand and held the spoon in his other, moving his soup about curiously as the boys told their tales. It was a clear broth made from boiling some kind of bird bones, with cut vegetables floating in it and at the bottom were thin noodles which dredged up suddenly into the light. There was a pleasant feeling to it, a wholesome, restful quality.

He liked to watch it move under the slow stroke of the spoon as he wondered what he could say in answer to their questions about heroes that would not start an uproar. He said nothing, but gave a nod to show that he was still listening. They were so used to him now that they forgot to ask anything about Karoo; used to him not answering.

'He means the last war,' supplied a lad further down the row with a graze on his cheek from when Tzaban had put him on the floor for staring at the girl. 'Not this one. The one against the Maldimanzians.'

'My dad was in that one too. He was a cavalryman.'

They soon forgot to address Tzaban directly at all with the much more rewarding sport of rivalling each other to distract them, and he was content to be forgotten. Their language was an effort for him to engage with because its patterns so seldom followed routes he found natural. As a result he spoke only if he must, and then with care. When he listened it took so much of his attention that he felt uncomfortable. So much focus was dangerous, drawing him to a point, forcing him out of the world and into himself. Unless it was truly necessary – and it almost never was – he ignored the words that came out of people's mouths and instead listened to the roll and flow of their voice and watched the signs they made. These things revealed a great deal, though it was not always the same thing that the people concerned were discussing with their words.

In his own home speaking aloud was rare. He longed for silence, but stoically, knowing he wasn't going to get it. Fanning around his back the disturbed veils of his energy still swirled and curled themselves around the turbulence of the running girl, mulling over the track she had carved through the yard and the shape of the trail she had left behind in him.

The shock of her transection of him, he knew now, was because of the taint in her energy pattern. It dragged at his sense of personal danger like a hook in flesh. The peace afforded by the lunch break finally let him witness the resulting changes in himself without distraction and he realised that it was not she personally whom he must be aware of, but one close to her, to whom the hook itself really belonged. An obvious deduction would have pointed at the Empress but Tzaban wasn't familiar enough with her that he knew it was not so. He did not recognise the hook's maker. Further investigation must wait until nightfall however, for until then he was occupied fully with the men. So for now he stirred his soup and watched the vegetables rolling in its golden depths and felt the drag of the noodles which he decided to save until last.

The soldiers had finished their own soups and the loaves of bread that had come with it and said they were still hungry. Talk of wars and the morning's exertion had changed to talk of chops and beer. They looked for a second course.

'Is this all there is?' the young man who had spoken first asked him.

'Yes,' Tzaban said. 'If you live long as a soldier you will often be hungry. Better get used to it.'

They began to complain. He knew that their own commanders would order silence but he didn't bother them with it. He had only one lesson to teach them but he knew it was futile to express it aloud, in the words, because this would have no effect. He would simply repeat it over and over in as many ways as he had to until they understood: it was not what the world was which mattered, it was what you believed about it that determined what happened. A meal was not enough if you expected more. It was the stuff of miracles if you expected nothing. It amazed him that in a city of mages and universities nobody had ever bothered to give them the most basic instruction in how to live well, or at all.

He finished his own soup and put the bowl on the table and glanced out at the sun. It was noon. They had left him his piece of bread. He took this and kept it in his hand. 'This afternoon we run to Pyaska and back. Those ten coming in last will clean the clothing and boots of the rest as well as their own.'

'But Pyaska is eighteen miles away!'

'Fifteen across country,' Tzaban said, 'though there'll be no penalty for taking the roads.' He looked at their dismayed faces and smiled and leaned back on the barrack wall, closing his eyes and easing his shoulders where they were tight until he was quite relaxed. Twenty years of spying on the Imperial lands had given him a confident memory of where everything was and how best to cross it. He would not cheat and change his form. 'I will give you a half hour start on me. Begin whenever you are ready.'

The sun was lulling, the shade steady. He slept.

TRALANE

Tralane Huntingore put her range-vision goggles down and thought about what she'd just witnessed, her mouth hanging partly open. That Karoo must have been there quite a while for those half mercenary and half city lads to look at him as one of their own. Soldiering and male bonding in general were strong however, stronger perhaps than the Empire liked to give credit for. It seemed to temporarily overrule the species issue entirely.

She remembered the Karoo's mouth moving and felt a soft, liquid glow in her lower belly. She ignored it. He was half naked, powerfully built and spoke to every primal bit of reproductive flesh she had left, and she had quite a lot left, so that was allowable noise, not of interest. He spoke Imperial. That was of interest. The goggles had been able to pick up and interpret his words perfectly well, although they dubbed him with the standard issue male voice synthesis and she was sure he didn't sound like a twenty-five-year-old city lothario with a high class accent. She would have given a lot to hear what he did sound like.

35

She put the goggles up and looked again, the window seat that she was perched in chilly even though the sun was hot. Through the thin silk of her blouse she felt her body tauten, nipples hardening.

He had claws instead of fingernails, she could see them on his hands as he rested them on his legs. Their dark lozenges were retracted to a fingernail length, the tips deliberately square blunted, but the hands themselves were quite narrow and fine. For all this artistic nicety however they also looked strong, calloused and capable as if they had started out as a delicate watchmaker's instruments and been adapted by hammering and hard labour into tools for many other purposes, most of them violent.

She wished that Carlyn was here with her. Carlyn Loitrasta was her best friend and Professor of Natural Science, which meant that most of the time she was holed up in the University or else travelling around grubbing up dirt and loitering about incognito in tiny hides peering at wildlife. The Karoo certainly counted as wildlife. Carlyn would have loved this. And she would have known what to say about it from a scientific viewpoint, whereas Tralane was ignorant of what she was looking at except to note that all the muscle under the fur and the way that he moved probably meant he was a very fine specimen.

The goggles hummed, taking readings and measurements for her, directed by the minute shifts of her focal point as she peered through them. They were a wonderful find, from a year ago when she'd had a brief two-day dedication to cleaning out one of the attics. Discovering them had put a joyful end to the tiresome notion of ordering two hundred years of family clutter and begun twelve months of painstaking effort researching and fixing the goggles instead. Their technology was partly revealed in manuals and blueprints she had in her library but most of the effort had been trial and error. Even now they were only partly functional to judge by the inactivity of many of the icons in her display, but the farseeing aspect of them worked just fine.

Later she'd invite Carlyn to dinner and tell her the good news but for now it was all hers. The delight of the reward made her toes curl with glee.

'What are you looking at?'

The sound and proximity of her daughter's knowing, languid voice made her start guiltily. Isabeau was standing there, hands composed before her, the very picture of bookish innocence. The contrast between appearance and vocal delivery was Isabeau's deadly weapon and Tralane was disappointed to find herself as disarmed by it as anyone.

'The lower city levels,' Tralane replied, not dishonestly but with the dissembling of long practice. She let the goggles fall into her lap as if it was no matter and patted them. 'I still can't activate half their uses. Don't even know what some are.'

'Can I see?' Isabeau sounded as if this might be the most boring thing in the world but also something that must be tried out and confirmed by imperial edict.

Tralane quietly thumbed the key for defocusing. 'Of course. Help yourself.'

She held the goggles out now and watched as Isabeau eagerly picked them up. Isabeau was the image of her father, a lanky girl with mousy straight hair that went blond in the sun and skin that easily darkened though relentless indoor pursuits had left it pale. Freckles and a pair of spectacles covered her nose, giving her a tawny owl look. Or so Tralane liked to see her. In truth she was aware that Isabeau, despite being only seventeen, deliberately cultivated the appearance of a middle-aged librarian who probably gardened lettuces as an exciting hobby. Isabeau's extremely academic school was very keen on both achievement in the exams and formal rectitude in the face of their quasi-religious authority and Isabeau demurely ticked every box. The better to pass unseen, Tralane thought.

Tralane sometimes wondered whether any of her had made it into Isabeau at all, or if she was going to replicate her father,

Desmatras, in every degree. At least she had not turned religious, or if she had, Tralane didn't know about it. For Isabeau it was, like most everything, just one more interesting human foible for study.

This was as expected. At thirteen, girls merged into peer group webs of their own within which they socialised and went about most of their daily existence, so Tralane's influence on her was now even slighter than it had been during her childhood. Isabeau's web was centred on another maternal house in the Diaspa, the Sorority of the Star, and it was rare to see her at home these days.

Now that she had a moment to observe her daughter it seemed to Tralane that she ought perhaps to investigate a little more about this web. Only preoccupation and an ugly suspicion that the Diaspan household were Reformists had prevented her. Well, that and a streak of laziness. She trusted Isabeau to have good sense and she didn't want to have to get up to struggle with idealists. Although probably ...

And then she watched as Isabeau's mouth fell open at the incredible power of the goggles – so much more than expected – and she wondered if she had been entirely wise to think Isabeau so grown up.

Isabeau tapped the controls on the rims with the tips of her fingers. Her tone was devoid of calculation, rapt. 'I had no idea anyone could see so far. How does it work?' She held the goggles away from her to examine them but there was little to see.

'You need the bridge to work with it,' Tralane said, indicating the junction on the side of the right eyepiece where a bridge's jacks ought to go.

'Oh that thing. Does that even work?' Isabeau dismissed any mechanical interest readily now she had found something to look at. Tralane betted she knew what it was.

'I'm getting better at it obviously, otherwise this would still be junk. But half of it seems to be dead, like so much else. I just

38

happened to get lucky the other day and triggered the focusing mechanism.'

For some reason, Tralane didn't mention the lipreading function. She wasn't happy with her own understanding of it yet and she was surprised to discover that she was afraid of humiliating herself in front of Isabeau. Their entire life as Huntingores had been punctuated by discoveries of one device or another in the jumble of crap known as 'the Archives', followed by a long list of questions from both children to which Tralane almost inevitably had to answer, 'I don't know.' That in turn was followed by a traditional roll of the eyes and then their departure from the conversation and usually the scene. Now she didn't want to say that again. She wanted Isabeau to coo over the marvellous, mother-fixed-it goggles.

'What in the hells of the ells is that?' Isabeau fiddled the focus dial.

'What?' Tralane waited, smug with knowledge and only vaguely surprised by the swearing, fudged as it was into something almost unobjectionable for public consumption.

'I don't believe it. Castira Amegzu is walking out with Daraon. That bitch.' This last was spoken with a kind of cold pleasure rather than rancour.

'Don't you mean "that dreadful girl"?' Tralane teased, rather pleased that Isabeau was finally giving in to some genuine womanly feeling rather than kowtowing to the stricture of her schooling.

'I mean "that bitch".'

Halfway into a frown at the fact that Isabeau was watching the social whirl of youth on the streets instead of anything worth seeing, Tralane paused. Daraon was a young man who was a part of her household thanks to his tinkery leanings and the willingness of his parents to supply funds for his upkeep and tutelage under Tralane, and he was also apparently devoted to Minnabar. What Isabeau reported did not bode well. Minnabar had no patience for part-timers. Tralane changed her snort of derision to, 'Why aren't we saying "that bastard"? And maybe they just met up.'

'Yes, his face looks *exactly* like that, the bastard.' Isabeau's sarcastic drawl was so cool it almost froze the air around her. She sniggered, a suddenly much more childish expression, and Tralane sighed. The sisters were ferocious rivals. Isabeau now had some rare and valuable ammunition. On top of everything else, now she could look forward to domestic upheaval. She made a mental note to rake Daraon over the coals.

'Right, that's enough of that. Give those here, I need to work on them.'

Isabeau reluctantly handed them over. 'Can I borrow them later?' She looked back over the view.

Tralane followed her gaze and saw, as usual, the misty blur of the lower city far beneath them, barely even able to make out people, let alone their expressions.

'If you're good,' Tralane said. 'What are you doing today anyway?'

'I'm going to the Library,' Isabeau said with exactly the right amount of bored ennui to make Tralane suspect she wasn't. But the Library would certainly be in the list of destinations even if studying was not the point of going and it was futile to prod and poke; she knew how far that tactic had got her own mother.

'Do I expect you for dinner?'

Isabeau shrugged. 'Yes all right.' Her pale face was already faraway, focused on other plans. She left, turning towards her own room.

Tralane took another look down. The soldiers had gone. In the shade of the colonnade the strange man slept, in repose looking more human and less like a beast. The mane she had supposed was made of fur turned out to be silky hair that had been waxed or clayed into near motionless submission. Astonished by the details she zoomed even further in. What she had taken to be paint or tattoos was the real colour of his skin. Lilac and burnt orange. Only on flowers had she ever seen such intense hues in nature, or on the wings of birds.

There was a blur. He had got up, she realised, as she was focused close-in. She quickly reoriented just in time to see him turn the corner of the yard and vanish into the dark streets beyond. She picked him up again at the gate, clad in an over-sized shirt that covered him enough to make him pass for a big man, and a farmer's field hat that hid his ears. He loped with an impossibly long, relaxed stride, and took off across the scrubby ground towards the farms. A few calculations and she figured he was going about twenty kay an hour. Faster than any Imperial citizen could run, for sure.

Those long, powerful legs, the foot lifting into an interestingly long lever, striding on the toes, the whole bouncy, taut power of the limb springing almost effortlessly as each step launched him forward and then recoiled ... She must look up the kinesiology of that ... But then other and more pressing questions pushed this aside.

What was he doing here? Why was he there, unannounced but nearly visible? If she had seen him then others would too. The army must know or they'd have shot him. They seemed to have employed him instead. So he was clearly here at the general's and the Empress's command. But why was such a valu-able and interesting, not to say paradigm-shattering specimen, not with the Magisterium, as an honoured guest, a miraculous visitor, instead of being used like a common soldier? She didn't understand it. What was going on? Some play of the military against the Magisterium? It made no sense.

She determined to get to the bottom of it as soon as possible and that meant only one thing. It was time to pay a visit to Shrazade. Tralane folded up the goggles and looked at them with sadness. Shrazade would talk for a suitable payment. Tralane didn't need to search house or bank to know that the only item worth the information was already in her hands. But she badly didn't want to lose the goggles. They were one of the few things, the few keys, to the whole lost artefacture of her line. If she gave them away who knew if she would ever get another? There must be something else.

As soon as she thought this to herself she saw it. A crystal, one of the perfectly cut lozenges from the array, filled with the cacophony of the storms. She had kept one, claiming it broke.

She'd kept it for research because damned if she'd be a part of something she didn't understand, especially under duress, especially in the war. It lay in an upper attic inside one of the abandoned research benches, the relic of yet one more fruitless project she couldn't give up and couldn't progress. Regardless of whether or not Shrazade had the knowledge to understand what it was the fact that it was a military-grade weapon component would be more than enough to make it attractive to her magpie intelligence. And Tralane betted that for every thing in existence Shrazade would always know a woman-who-knew. It was because of Shrazade's unique connections, her personal and interpersonal web, that Tralane knew her.

It was always a dodgy business though, netting up with unknowns, even via a trusted proxy. Shrazade's reputation was that of the absolutely confidential proxy. Her wealth and power rested on that. Tralane would have to trust her

Without a second's hesitation she collected the crystal and her satchel and exited the house at a run, shoving her worn leather hat down over her hair as she closed the door after her.

ISABEAU

Isabeau watched her mother leave and wondered where she was off to that could be so important. From her bedroom windows the upper city was easy to see but the lower city was shrouded and she finally felt the surprise stab of envy at the viewing goggles she hadn't felt before as she looked down now and saw nothing but the cloudy blur. One up to Tralane, she'd finally made something work that was actually useful. Isabeau considered this as she bathed and set her hair in elaborate braids.

She dressed in her scholar's robes that marked her out as a first-class student of a restrictive, monastic college; fine, pale grey fitted even around her face, and dark slate blue on the top in a heavy but graceful habit. A starched wimple and hood completed the outfit, rendering her absolutely covered. A thin lawn veil draped across her nose, weighted to hang straight so that she could breathe but her nose and mouth were concealed. Only her large grey eyes were visible and the hood shadow hid them from most angles.

Since she was fourteen Isabeau had taken to wearing the full adornment with great satisfaction in its anonymity and absolute, immaculate charter. She was treated with respect and deference, even by older women, and permitted to pass unnoticed socially, which was the real benefit. Nobody paid attention to scholars' wanderings or pursuits. Eccentricity or devotion to knowledge were presumed as standard and thousands of girls preceding Isabeau had guaranteed her status by their unswerving adherence to their vows. You could say anything to a scholar without fear of it getting around. You could safely ignore them. You would be beaten senseless by the College Guard if you tried to interfere with them and could be executed for impeding them by the Empress' standing edict.

At school, in her adoptive home and on official business Isabeau also maintained her Sorority's particular devotion to serenity and purity of all kinds but she had a few hours free of all that, as always on a Setday at this time, and after gathering her scroll satchel and her writing kit she headed out on foot, as she had promised, for the Library.

On the broad street between the family mansions rising up

in terraced strata to the heights of the palace at the peak there was the usual daily traffic of servants, tradesmen and freewomen flowing steadily upspiral and downspiral in the late afternoon warmth. A narrow passage opened up for Isabeau, thanks to her robes, allowing her an easy way downspiral to the large open squares where the mansions gave way to institutes, clubs, galleries and meeting houses.

Isabeau left the main spiral and crossed the Sun Plaza, enjoying the light between the stalls selling drinks and cakes, the tables of gamesplayers and the quiet buzz of conversations under the awnings where the more openly social Sororities gathered in fine weather. She hurried across into the dark shadow cast by the huge, temple-like structure of the Library itself but turned at the last moment into the colonnades along its flanks, walking quickly in near darkness and shade that was so deep it was almost cold.

A lone drunken soldier, resting after a night out in the unfamiliar heights of the upper city, was the only witness to her passing down from the Library's rear gates, across the Sainted Yards and into the alleys that serviced the twin streets of Rose and Gathering. Cleaners, cooks and wait staff rested under white shades, warming themselves at small braziers as they ate, chewed cola and smoked or talked between shifts. Isabeau passed along to the frontages and entered the end shop – a fabric emporium. Inside she made no pretence of browsing but walked straight through, between vast arcades of towering, vivid bolts of all colours, shot with gold, silver and copper. She paid a silent tip to the owner and passed through the curtain at the back, along the narrow passage and into the storage room – a path she would never have come across were it not for a happy bookish accident in which the route and the manner were written down in the code of a Sorority she wasn't supposed to know about but had discovered shortly after donning the habits and inspecting the darker recesses of the Library proper.

The storage room had several doors leading to the alley and one behind five never-to-be-sold bolts of unfashionable flowered calico: quite invisible to any who did not know it was there.

Isabeu slid carefully, silently, demurely under the flowery, pink and white angle of the calico bolts and undid the door latch with the prescribed code. She stepped through into darkness and closed it behind her. In the confines of the tiny room her breath and movements became loud, massive. The pitch dark and closeness was absolute – nobody knew who or where she was at this moment. She lingered, absorbing the feeling along with the cedar smell of the wood. This was hers, all hers. She was hers, all hers.

Then she undid the exit door and walked through into a slender and dim corridor, unused save for those who came and went as she did. The wood here that lined everything was smooth, dry and delicious with varnish. Thick carpet rendered her slippers absolutely noiseless. A dim, single light gleamed from a crimson nook at the end, revealing that the way was clear beyond it. Just before the sliding door that would lead out a recess provided a bench, a chair and a wardrobe, all empty. There was a small table with a central well containing dry biscuits and fortified wine. Towels were racked on the wall in neat rows. A basket stood at the side, empty and waiting for laundry. A few damp footprints on the cotton floor rug were the only evidence that anyone had been here lately. Isabeau measured her own bare foot against them as she removed her shoes and stockings – someone taller and larger than she. It pleased her to see the prints. She sent a blessing of fortune in prayer to whoever had left them.

With the same precision she had used to dress she shed her outer robe and hung it up. It was cool in the hidden room but as she removed the headdress and placed it on the bench she felt only how delicious it was to have walked and been warm and then to remove the heavy clothing and be cool. She didn't think overly much about what she was about to do. There was no need to.

The tightly fitted facemask – silvery grey – she left in place beneath the veil, attached to the braids of her hair. Since she carried nothing worthwhile except her scroll cases and it was inconceivable anyone who came here would interfere with those she placed her underthings neatly on the bench. Just before she left she selected a white ribbon from a hanging rack and tied it about her waist loosely, then keyed the sequence into the brass panel beside the sliding door.

CHAPTER FOUR

BORZE

Fadurant Borze found reclining difficult to master. It was all wrong. Not relaxed enough for lying down and not alert enough for sitting, it left him at a loss as to know whether he ought to be ready to get up or too uncomfortable to go to sleep. However, the steam room had nothing but recliners and so he was forced to perch edgily there, up on one elbow, pretending to be at his ease enough to chat with other men. Fortunately, several other high-ranking officers were there all struggling equally with the trials of being off duty and in the bath house, a civilised and civilian pastime if ever there was one. Without appearing to cluster they leaned around together and discussed the ever-important war, the state of the army and the difficulties of managing mercenaries in the rank and file. After about twenty minutes of this each of them was sufficiently soothed to retreat into their own contemplation, oiling and scraping. Fadurant, as always at this moment, was reminded inescapably of baboons.

The room saw a steady passage of naked men of every kind making their way on the slow pilgrimage. It began with tea and the washing of feet, then progressed through the tiled scrub room with its steady scent of herbal soap and the low grunts of those being washed by professional hands; salt and sponges, brushes and lots of elbow grease, the splatter of vast mounds of white suds on to the tile in regular gouts, the swish of the sweeper, the spray of water in jets across the floor a rushing cascade, gutters swilling over with the excess of cleanliness, the walls dripping with lengths of flowering vines that shimmered in the mist, their leaves bursting with freshening airs. After this pummelling came the steam rooms, immaculate white tile. Here the men lay about pinkened, glowing, breathing the thick vapours heavy with healthgiving essential oils. Beyond that the lesser steam vaults offered places to pause and linger, talk business, catch up on the news and enjoy the womanless peace. Here they oiled their smoothed hides, had their nails attended to and took the spa waters in long iced sips or slept wrapped like mummies in acres of towelling until attendants woke them and ushered them onwards to the cold plunge, yet more towels and then the upper floors for dining or onward to the labyrinthine interior for sex, or further grooming, plucking, sugaring, haircuts.

It was a tradition to attend the baths at least once a week and Fadurant kept to this minimum on principle. More would signal a taste for luxury and less would render him socially unapproachable, not to say a poor role model for the men. As the hour for steam slowly passed, he played the usual game of pretending that this time he would simply have a haircut and go, knowing all the while that he was instead going to walk the circle.

Meanwhile, he noted the comings and goings in an idle way until he saw a tall, dark-skinned figure step out of the soap room and almost instantly fix upon him with a knowing, amused glance.

Zharazin Mazhd wore the red wristband of the bath house's highest cadre of clientele and his hair in a bound queue of black cloth to protect it as it soaked in some fancy liquor. Fadurant, with the receding hairline and close-cropped grizzle he preferred, thought it looked like way too much effort but then Mazhd worked all of his erotic capital and Fadurant needed none. Judging by the colour of him and the run of water he had just been waxed from the neck down, but his face went unshaven. The stubble on his jaw was finely trimmed, its semblance of carelessness only improving the overall look. Mazhd had eyes that appeared as blue-black as his hair unless seen in direct light for the dark chocolate they really were. Calculating eyes made for scanning vast horizons in brilliant sunlight but just as good at scanning ballrooms and midnight alleys. He was a civilian but to Fadurant nonetheless both ally and liability as part of the Infomancy – their loyalties lay with the Empire, rather than Glimshard in particular, and right now that was a conflicted loyalty, Fadurant guessed. For Fadurant it was city first, everything else second. Whoever Mazhd rubbed along with he would first rub along with the Empress Torada and her interests or Borze would have his head.

They greeted each other with the careless familiarity of deadly enemies and Mazhd took the recliner opposite Fadurant which had just been vacated. Mazhd was fitter and leaner looking than any of Fadurant's men, his out-Empire Plains ancestry obvious in his girlishly small waist and surprisingly broad shoulders. His muscles were defined, cut and wrapped around his bones like taut ropes – they made Fadurant weary and impatient; he would never look like that again, even if he did have the daily hours to spare on flinging himself through the necessary training. As if all that were not enough, few in the city were as well-favoured of face as Mazhd either, thanks to some happy accident of crossbreeding plains business. All that high cheek, prominent forehead, square-jawed bone and then that sculpted mouth that would make a woman look hard but made a man look powerful. A charming camouflage for a mind he knew to be quite peculiar.

Fadurant didn't care about these things – had learned not to as it would never pay – but he knew how much it was all worth in the world, and in the palace, and he was used to accounting for everything and knowing who stood where. He and Mazhd took in each other's relative values, decided upon their equal merits and nodded graciously to each other.

'Strange times,' Mazhd offered, swinging his long legs up on to the bench and leaning back. He was shorter than Fadurant and his feet didn't hang off the edge, the bastard.

Fadurant grunted assent, knowing he wasn't going to get a free tip but detecting the suggestion that there may be things worth knowing which his official channels did not provide. What else was Mazhd for?

He glanced around the room, more a signal than a real check – he knew there were no reformists around at this hour of the day. Their knees were on their prayerstools at home or in the temple as twilight descended. This was why he chose to bathe now.

'You must have some knowledge of the north,' Fadurant said, knowing many ears were turned their way. 'Is it worth my engaging your archivists?'

'On any subject, of course,' Mazhd said easily, leaning back on the rest and closing his eyes. Steam collected in a sheen of perfect droplets all over him as it ran in hairy, irregular rivulets over Fadurant's unkempt limbs.

Fadurant brushed a trickle from his nose and sniffed. 'Send me a boy with the details. My office will arrange payments at the usual rates.'

Mazhd turned his head, dark eyes, dark lashes – that combination the ticket to so many secrets, so many beds. Fadurant felt that he was looking at an exotic creature at the zoo but this time not a baboon; he wasn't sure what Mazhd reminded him of. If it weren't for the fact that Mazhd was well known as a swordsman and a barehand fighter the gulf between them would have been impassable. The bath house was full of ladies' men

50

that Borze couldn't and didn't want to understand. They were like overgrown boys with soft figures, studied manners and lots of talk. Women liked them for some reason and that was that.

'Someone is making forbidden things. Someone is hiding in the city.'

The words were so unexpected Borze took a moment to process them. Mazhd had spoken so softly he might as well have been whispering in Borze's ear. At the same instant the floor boy came through and flung a bucket of cleaner beneath the benches with a watery rush that drowned most of the line out. Perfect timing.

'Here?'

Mazhd made an almost undetectable shaking motion of his head. No. He mouthed a word then in silence, drowned again by the cleaner's second sluicing. 'Protection.'

Fadurant put his head back on the recliner and stared into the swirling steam. If Mazhd would not speak without guarantees of safety then it was something he had to know, but he had no power to save Mazhd from anybody capable of threatening him. Sufficient money usually did the trick, but Mazhd did not play cat and mouse so he was not holding out for a better deal by asking for the impossible. Mazhd's information must include people in high places. Probably higher than Borze. But also within reach, or else the suggestion would have been pointless. He thought of the mercenaries so swiftly employed, without references beyond basic tests.

They did not speak again. Borze would have to plan on how he could repay this service. He could not end up on the wrong end of a kindness from the Infomancy.

With any last shred of hope for rest extinguished Fadurant got off the cursed recliner, gathered his towel up and left. He turned into the circle's dim corridor without a hesitation or a second thought.

The tiles and the angles of the turn combined with the rush

of the fountains to effectively drown out individual voices or words. Sound washed the air in a continual stream that was not loud but still deafening. Mazhd would have had to embrace Fadurant and speak directly to his ear in here. Fadurant, imagining it as he walked, found the idea repellent at a visceral level – he had never felt any doubt or ambiguity about his own preferences. He always turned left off the circle, towards the only place in the house there would be women, never right into rooms where men sported with one another.

Today an impulse he did not want to examine too closely made him choose the room where the women kept their anonymity and offered themselves cordially to anyone. There was something egalitarian and kind in the gesture that touched him much more than being chosen from a crowd would have done. An honest appeal for sex from both sides and nothing to lose or gain but some moments of pleasure.

There were no recliners here, but many padded benches upon which the men sat and waited or engaged with their partner in full view of the others. It was courtesy not to pay attention to anyone's identity here, for any reason, though all were free to look as they pleased. Many simply watched and took care of themselves as there were not usually enough women to go around. Women, Fadurant and every other man in Empire knew well, were spoiled for choice when it came to sex so that the bath house was only one of many possible sources of indulgence, whereas men had to know their place and compete successfully. This room, he supposed, had the gratification of virtue added to it in that the women were apparently offering a selfless service, although the anonymity meant there would never be public recognition of such a thing. In the spirit of the place, he knew most men attempted to repay the generous favours with competence, even reverence. What kind of man would do otherwise?

The girl at the fountain, turning as she bathed herself in warm water falling from above her, was a surprise even to him, and he'd seen every kind of woman in here. Not least because he'd seen her the week before. Then she had been quickly seized upon, but at this moment as he walked into the room she had just stepped into the flow through the central arch that led to the women's exit. Her grey mask and golden braids stood out against her pale skin as rich colours. The white ribbon on her waist marking her was barely visible. Against the blue of the tile and the mosaic she was milk white, only her nipples standing out in dark coral on the new fullness of her unfinished breasts.

Purely by chance his pace and motion brought him to her first, before she had even turned once. He took her by her upper arm in a gesture so firm it surprised him. They both paused. The grip and the speed of it were unseemly. He was prepared to let her go if she gave him the signal, although a surge of ferocious possessiveness was already on him and a readiness to fight. In his hand she was smaller than he had thought and her flesh was soft, almost without muscle, it yielded around her bones so easily. For a moment he was worried that he had hurt her. He felt the eyes of the room on him, the rise in tension as she lifted her face to meet his eyes through the mask. One gesture from her would cast him in a shame that might bar him from here for ever. He felt desperate, foolish...

But she bowed her head demurely and put her hand on his chest instead, over his heart. Acceptance.

He swelled with pride and desire, rescued, a thousand miles high, a stupid lad with his heart beating, a blush on his face and a standing cock that raised a wry laugh of recognition from the benches. Friendly, that laugh, even when it was envious.

But now all his attention belonged to her as he escorted her to a vacant alcove. Through the eyeslots of the mask he fancied her eyes were dark blue as she watched him for the formal sign language which would let him tell her what he pleased without either of them having to betray themselves through their voices. His hands on her delicate, new skin looked huge, rough

53

and powerful. The sight excited him beyond explanation. He was glad for the oil he'd bothered to use. It hid the callouses, softened them into things fit to feel with.

She looked down at them too, as he touched her waist's slender, slight curve and cupped her breast. Her neck flushed a soft pink and a murmur of appreciation from behind them deepened the colour. Her nipple hardened and rose under his thumb and she placed her hands involuntarily on his shoulders for balance. Her responses aroused him painfully. He wanted to keep her. He wanted to show her off. She was rare. He wanted to give her and take her.

They sat on the bench, him astride it and she with her soft round bottom tucked against his cockstand, her back cradled against his hard body, inside the embrace of his arms as she leaned back, turning her face to his neck. He spread open her legs, feet drawn high, knees up and wide, so that she was completely exposed as his fingers slipped down – the skilled swordhand caressing her smooth, naked mons and brushing her lips there, sliding between them, moving them softly apart whilst his shield arm braced her against him, claiming her breast, pinching that delicate, hardening flesh between finger and thumb so she gasped and moaned. He was so strong he could pin her effortlessly if she had not been completely submissive.

The girl wound sensually against him, reactive to his every touch, her skin sliding against him in the mix of oil and water with an effortless ease that threatened to undo his control. He held her harder to him, warning her not to, and lifted his swordhand once to flash a sign where she could see it. She turned her masked face fully into his neck where his head bent next to her, as if wanting to hide and held fast to his raised arm with one hand while her other joined his between her legs. She opened herself with her fingers to the gaze of the men before her and Fadurant slid his own slippery middle finger softly over her taut, swelling flesh teasingly until she arched her back and then he let the tip slide inside her.

Unbelievably he felt a soft, wet rush meet him. His first thought was that she was bleeding and lifted his hand but it was clear. She whimpered, a pleading noise. He understood that and put his hand back where it had been. One by one he slid his fingers inside her until they were coated. With each withdrawal she moaned and cried, her head free of him now, looking down at herself, her hand digging into his arm with a grip much stronger than he would have given her credit for. He watched with her his own thick fingers pushing effortlessly into her, sliding up and over the shocking red rose of her swollen lips, being enveloped by the thick petals of them as he teased her. She tried to wriggle, crying protest noises that were lost in the wash of the noise as he slid his first and second fingers into her with slow authority, much slower than she would have liked so that he could feel the steady swell of her inside, experience telling him it wouldn't be much longer.

Beside them he heard a woman's voice say something in a warm tone and a sharp sound of a man's climaxing grunt. Vague movements, suggestive ones, were all around but he could see only her, only himself.

He pushed his fingers deep, all the way, careful because she was so delicate and he felt he could hurt her, eager because her body wanted it and he was intoxicated with what he could do to her and the fact that this girl wanted him to. He thought of the Empress's runner crossing the baking square, trailing a wake of gleeful distraction, the Karoo ignoring her as if he were a stone. This girl was the same age. She wouldn't be a runner, too slight. But she ought to be somewhere. He wondered why she was here but then she cried out as his hand moved and he felt a tremor around his fingers. She got up at the same instant he withdrew his hand, placed her hands on the bench before her and presented herself to him on all fours, legs as wide as she could make them, standing on her tiptoes. Her back arched, begging for it and as if he wasn't going fast enough for her her left hand abruptly flashed out to sign at him; she asked, didn't demand, even on the edge of her orgasm, and that was more than enough for Fadurant.

He took her by the hip, seated his cock firmly in her open rose and penetrated her with a thick slide, afraid he was going to be too much or too slow. She backed to meet him until he was all in and felt the end of her. It gave her pain, he knew by a moment of wincing, but then she pressed back again and made a soft sound of despair as he made her wait, holding her there. He knew that if only he could time it right he could extend the moment on the brink, bring it to a rise and fall. No man wanted to be witnessed as incompetent. He couldn't afford to be, even here, where the conspiracy of anonymity was so intense only a political play of real significance would ever threaten it, and even then such a gesture would have serious repercussions. The Empress would dislike it and her displeasure could be fatal. Even so.

This thought allowed him to keep control even as the tight press of the girl's body was almost unendurable. She did not sign again. Another man walked close to her, stroked her under her chin gently, signed to ask if she would be staying. When she signalled yes he gave her his ribbon and she wrapped it around her fingers before he walked easily away to a seat beyond Fadurant's sightline. The etiquette was precise, commonplace. Fadurant was surprised by the severity of the possessive urge that swept him suddenly. He was no boy. He knew the ropes. Why then this?

He withdrew almost all the way and then with idle pace pressed himself back into her, knowing as he did it how much this gave away his feelings, their incorrect, incontinent power. The sensation was exquisite. She was delicious – hot, sweet – the best he had ever tasted. He could not fathom it. She was not even his type.

The girl made near inaudible noises of surrender, of pleading, though he heard them well enough. She pushed herself at him. To his right an older man snorted with amusement at her eagerness, surprised too, enchanted no doubt, Fadurant thought, because he was. Abruptly becoming aware that he was the target of too much interest he moved with speed, certainty and strength, doing hard to her what he would rather have done gently. It had the desired effect. She came near immediately with a series of sharp exclamations which she tried to bite back. He did not stop until his own climax came a few seconds later. Her knees gave way then but he was strong and let her down on to the bench gently, withdrawing in a gracious kind of ease that wasn't his style at all, but was the style of the Circle. He would have kept her with him all day if she were a girl in his room and not left her body at all.

He had to make himself leave her there and go shower in the falling water around the central column. He didn't look back at her – what was the point? He had no idea who she was nor was he meant to. His abandonment now marked the end to a perfect encounter.

His body burned with a feeling like trapped light low in his abdomen. It pulled towards where he knew she was behind him. Annoyed with this foolishness he stepped out, took a fresh towel and busied himself with drying. He looked up once, at the doorway just before he was ready to leave.

Zharazin Mazhd leaned there in the curved aperture. His field of vision held Fadurant within it certainly but the pits of his eyes were directed behind, at the girl and whatever was happening to her now. Fadurant passed him as he left. Neither of them made any effort to acknowledge the other.

Isabeau, spread-eagled face down on one man while another braced himself over her from behind, doubly penetrated, fastened her hands on the unyielding stone of the bench legs as she rested her head on her supporter's shoulder and closed her eyes. The pleasure she felt was enough to make her delirious but one fact stayed in her mind with uncomfortable resilience. She had some strange attraction to the man who had first claimed her.

This had surprised her enough to almost shake off his grip, because she felt these things for no men. If she had she supposed she would be part of some web like her sister's crew, forever and exhaustingly embroiled in one pointless and gigantic drama tangle. Supposing it an accident of circumstance, but nonetheless interesting for that, she had decided to allow him to continue, with a scientist's attitude to the results. She had expected a courteous, responsible kind of effort and had been prepared to act her part to speed his pleasure – her own pleasure being very much determined by exactly how grateful or how needy the man of the moment appeared to be. She was open to anything, so long as she felt that she was in the controlling position of the bestower; goddess of plenty.

Instead, what had happened? She didn't know. It had been out of her control. She didn't even know if it was him or the fact he had taken immediate command of her, or the fact that he had instructed her to open herself to the gazes of the others as if she was his and her body was something he could give or withhold from other men at will. That was a barbaric thing. In Empire it was out of the question. Why then had she felt impelled to watch him touch her and found the sight so exciting she could not stop herself? Only considering it from the cool distance of a rational perspective erased the alarm that it had made her feel. Only accepting these other men, feeling herself well and appreciatively used, restored the world to its even keel.

The man inside her ass came first and the strong thrum of it passing through the soft wall of her body caused his friend to trigger as well. The two of them spent strongly in her and she rewarded them with a bitten shoulder and muffled but genuine cries of her climax. In her mind's eye she saw his rough fingers slip inside her, claiming her for the other men.

She felt that somehow his face was familiar although she'd glanced at it only for a second. Her train of thought was disturbed as her present lovers withdrew themselves, one or both of them setting her gently and alone upon the padded bench. As soon as they had gone she felt bereft and curled up. Another woman in a red headdress came up and put a hand on her shoulder to see if she was well.

Isabeau nodded, signed that she was only resting, but then got up and removed her ribbon. She showered and permitted a tall and dark-skinned man to oil her body. He was very muscular and agile looking. His hands were slender, long fingered, graceful as silk. He looked at her with large dark eyes, liquid blackness ringed by dense lashes. Plains eyes, emphasised by the pulled back hair, the shadow of stubble on his jaw. His touch was as caring as any Isabeau had ever felt. He made no effort to be sexual although he was erect and his mouth was full with the telltale swelling of desire. He was the most beautiful man Isabeau had ever seen. He anointed her and smiled at her and held her hand so she did not slip as she passed through the exit door and out of his existence.

What did that mean? What was it for?

The confidence she had come with and had come to reinforce was gone. She understood nothing.

After she had dressed she went out and tossed her notebook into the first trash bin she passed on the way to the Library.

CHAPTER FIVE

MINNABAR

Minnabar Huntingore pushed her way to the front of the crowds at the barracks' yard using smiles and elbows and a natural otter-like grace to reach the heavy black iron bars of the gate. She was vaguely aware of the others in the web moving with less verve behind her but they didn't matter. She closed her hands around the cold iron – why was it cold even on a sweltering evening like this one? But mercifully it was. Cool smoothness flowed into her blood as she was pressed up against the rods. The crosspiece cut into her waist as she put her foot on a low horizontal and stepped up to gain a vital extra ten centimetres of height. As she flexed her legs she felt her strength and beauty completed with victory over all the other poor fools gathered there to catch a glimpse of this rare, this fabled exotic creature. She didn't care whose feet she'd trodden on to get here nor what anyone thought of it. She would be first. She would be centre. If there was something to be had here, she would have it.

The bars were deliciously cold against her face. She felt Marina arrive beside her, knew her by the smell of expensive old perfume and the sudden rustle of taffeta silk from Marina's dress. To the other side and behind them the odours of hot flesh, soaps and fabrics briefly rose over the hot dry dust smell and the rich stink of horse dung, freshly dropped by the cavalry passing out of the yard on their evening tour of the city periphery.

'Oh, nobody there yet?' Marina sighed. She was permanently anguished by the shortfalls of life in Glimshard.

'Wrong, caballero. They're staggering in right now...' Minnabar pointed to the corner of the yard which led via a long staircase to the Soldier's Gate in the city's wall. There several young men in sweat-stained and dusty cloth armour were resting in the shadow of the wooden gate, sides heaving as they caught their breath. But in spite of this nobody was waiting for them. The rumours that had flown from wall to gate to street to Minnabar's ear said quite clearly without mistake that there was a tiger man in the army, a creature, a beast, and that he was running around in the countryside with a group of recruits, back and forth through the fields like a shepherding dog, *sometimes on all fours*, while men of reasonable fitness threw up their guts in their efforts to beat one another into his good graces. He was handsome, he was vile, he was monstrous, he was incredible – Minnabar longed for it all to be true. She wanted badly to be thrilled by being scared out of her wits, shocked by the improbability, the daring, the sheer unexpurgated and delicious outrage of such a being entering Glimshard at all. They were fables. They were not real. She would have preferred a unicorn but if this were true then it would seem that their small, ordinary lives were about to be lifted into the miraculous realm of magic and not the shambolic engineering or piddling alchemy of the high city and all its boring drone of war.

Around her, the press of people increased all the time so that when finally the last grey-faced recruit staggered through the gateway and collapsed at the feet of his squadmates in a heap of Steppe-brown rag she was almost crushed to the bars. Marina was nearly in tears although she kept her position. Minnabar felt a quick hand pick her pockets, but it hardly mattered. Across the vast, empty dust of the training yard the last recruit was being inexplicably pelted with boots. Meantime, the officers, notable by the red and gold trims and their tabards bearing the golden web, were shaking heads and knocking their knuckles together, handing over bets in pay scrip. One, she fancied the highest rank present, his cowl tasselled, was laughing, collecting the most and then he raised his arm in a half-salute half-huzzah as the object of his successful gamble came loping through the shadows and into the last light of the dying sun.

For a second the hubbub dimmed as everyone gawped. Minnabar stared with her eyes as wide as they could be. In the first moment she was so rapt and so ready that she couldn't make sense of what she was seeing; the colours, the shapes, they didn't link up into anything she knew. There was a background of sandstone walls, a foreground of yellow dust. The long shadows of brown-clad men formed a dim pool between. From this emerged a white and blue figure. It stood in the light, rippling, until perception snapped into place within her mind's eye. As the crowd went silent the creature, the Karoo, finished his long top-to-toe doglike shake and looked with surprise in their direction.

Minnabar felt Marina's fingers close tightly over the top of her own, a clammy, strange crab. His basic shape, massive shoulders, tiny girlish waist, long, powerful legs, the low tilt of his head with its forehead-first weight, all said man. The breath that moved his entire body, his poise, the lash-twitch of his long tail and the energy all directed towards her said animal. His eyes were human and intelligent, bright as those of a picturebook devil. In the split second that his attention went that way she felt their gazes lock together and across the silent wire of that gap a question and answer pass instantly. Then he was turning away, snorting and tossing his heavy mane of white as he laughed at the state of the soldiers lying about on the ground spent, still throwing their boots about like boys while Minnabar was frozen in place; liquid bronze cooling down into the statue that single

62

question and answer had made. She'd felt lust a hundred times before, knew all its angles, but this was a new thing to her. She didn't understand it at all. In that single, nearly unseeing look, she knew he had seen her, acknowledged her and gracefully passed on her. Until then she didn't know that she had been on offer. She was a tourist. She was a voyeur, not a participant. There had never been any question of a deal. She'd come to see a monster.

By the sounds of the conversation suddenly bursting around her in explosions of verbal colour she wasn't the only one who'd had an odd moment.

'Minna, did you *see* that?' Marina demanded, looking up to her for an explanation.

Minna, who knew it was not a see but a feeling, that it was more than a look – was a contract, understood and could not say because to put it into words made it ridiculous and her with it. She looked down and returned the clasp of Marina's fingers. Marina's green eyes reflected absolutely the surprise and near alarm of her own. The blush on her cheeks was hot, intensified by the reddening sun. Minna felt it on her face too. Then as one they all craned for another peek, safe now that his back was to them. There was as much outrage and jeering as there was anything in the rising noise. Minna could understand that.

'Veterans,' Marina hissed to her, shrinking closer as a man near her bawled for the Karoo's head on a stick. Then Minna realised it was his death they wanted.

It was the first time Minnabar had given a thought to the war as an actual thing that affected people near her. She looked at the man who'd shouted and read such a hatred in his face that she had to look away before it was turned on her. But before anything more could happen a fanfare of horns at close range stalled everything once more. There was a scramble, a mutter and mumble and shove as everyone turned and attempted to get enough room to bow to the white entourage of the Empress.

The worst thing about the passage of the Empress was that you wanted to see her, Minnabar thought, but because you had to bow and look presentable, you didn't. You saw a glimpse of the white-robed men carrying the banners to either side of the magnificent black stallion she rode, the ones picking up its skirts and her train, the backs of them as they went on their way... You saw, if you were lucky, the naked torso of her bodyguard Hakka the Steppe Hunter who had been slave-stolen from the uttermost barbarism of the east and broken like a horse to her hand, or the fabulous swish of the tassels on his glinting polearm. You might see the girl runners around her, handing out sweets to the children from their flat baskets of glittering papered gifts, tiny vials of scent to the men and tickets to the women for opera, science or dancing. But you never saw her. Now Minna caught glimpses as the cortege passed slowly between the spectators and passed within inches of her nose as they moved between the gates.

Her face was covered in the scholarly veil and the rest of her was coated in gold and white. They said her battle armour was less of a fancy get-up but Minnabar had never seen this outfit. Now she looked after the Empress's small, upright back as it sat the fiery horse with ease and wondered again if she really was plain, like they said. She had to shuffle, squeeze and complain as soldiers rushed up to push back the iron bars in the wake of the snowy cavalcade.

Finally, the gates closed but the retinue effectively blocked everything that Minnabar was able to see, even when she climbed. She stuck it out until the white reorganised itself. The massing clouds of banners and the drifting veils of shining witchmist, set up to screen the Empress from the common gaze or unknown assassins, moved like smooth oil. There was a pause as the yard was filled with white fog that curled in on itself, and left cold droplets to trickle on the gate bars. She could see the edges of it evaporating away into the hot air and hear the far side gate that led on to the palace high road opening up. By the time the mist had dispersed the yard itself was empty except for a series of soldiers standing at attention looking baffled.

The remaining officers bowed to the crowds as the last vapours drifted to the ground and sparkled out of existence. Some of the tiny lights became silver coins which lay there until a sergeant picked them up. He gave them to the boot-cleaners who had run in last but Minnabar was looking everywhere for the tiger. However, the Karoo had vanished. Of course, the Empress had taken him.

'You know what that was,' Marina said as the crowd began to scatter and they were able to gather themselves.

'No,' Minnabar replied, still wondering over what that glance had meant. If the Empress had taken him personally, she had done so as a public sport. Why had the army not sent him if she were interested? She scented trouble and it made her smile.

'Well I think it was a rebuke. Like she hasn't had her turn.'

Minnabar nodded, seizing Marina's hand and taking the path upspiral as fast as she could. It was nearly dark now and she hadn't been so far downtown in a long time, certainly never this late. Suddenly her adventure seemed more foolhardy than it had before but she wasn't about to let that slip to Marina. 'You're right. It will be the talk of tomorrow. And we saw it all! Let's get back up to the Sun in Stone before everyone else does!'

The Sun in Stone was a tea house in the midst of Starred Circle, the heart of the high city and its gossip hub. Many webs used it as a base of operations in good weather, loitering for hours between classes and appointments under its red and yellow awnings. Minna's web, the Scarlets, usually took a table in the middle. Thanks to the speedy footwork of Yenie, small, mousy, sweet tempered and malleable enough to be persuaded that reserving the space was a more important job than going with Minna to the barracks, it was ready and waiting for them.

Yenie sat beside the favoured spot, her reward. Minna sat in it, brimming with importance and the sensation that something was about to happen – she didn't know what or to whom, but something. All talk centred on the Karoo.

'They are part of the Circle,' Daraon said with conviction from his position at Minna's feet, a place he had taken lately to lounging in with apparent careless and natural submission.

This statement caused all the less serious jabber to stop, and not only at their table. Faces turned from other webs, both female and male.

'But that would make him an enemy,' Yenie said, so quietly she was almost inaudible.

'Top marks for voicing the obvious again,' Marina said. But nobody seemed to want to join her and another moment of silence passed.

'I don't know that he is really related to *the* Karoo.' This from Sarine, a rival web's vital axis. The Ivory Circle specialised in occult historical knowledge as the chief marker of their exclusivity so her remark carried a great deal of weight. Daraon by contrast was known only for his intentions to join the army as soon as he was legitimately able.

'Do go on,' Minna invited, even though this was a hijack of a private discussion. Her generosity was never dispensed without reason however, and she was gratified to see members of both webs brace minutely in preparation for defence.

'They are from the extreme north, the Resolute Forests. Records of contact between them and the Empire or them and the Steppelanders all suggest they are extremely reclusive and highly intolerant of trespassers. There haven't been any noted meetings between Karoo and Imperial peoples in over four hundred years.'

'And now one just happens to turn up and join the army,' Daraon said sarcastically. 'For no reason at all. Certainly not because this is also the first time in history that an Imperial war has brought us into conflict with Karoos.'

'That explains nothing, because he's from the north, nowhere near the battles,' Sarine countered, undaunted. 'But there is something odd about it because the Karoo have always been shamanistic, dedicated to nature, and to peaceful existence. The reason they shun humans and magi is because they've always judged us to be wantonly destructive and careless. They have never had any kind of warriors even though there have been rumours of violent put-downs when the Steppelanders got too close. And that Karoo there was nothing like any reports or images we have of them either.' She got out her tablet and swept her hand across its blank grey face, a trail of blue fire showily revealing her considerable magical powers as she summoned up the document she wanted, causing an image to emboss itself into the semi-malleable clay before hardening it. She showed this around.

'That looks like a tree,' Marina said scathingly. 'It's hardly even humanoid.'

'Well they all look like that,' Sarine said. 'And this was an image capture, not a drawing.'

'They don't, clearly,' Daraon replied, leaning on Minna's leg. 'That one down there looked like a beast.'

'Half a beast,' Minna said, eager to have her part in things. 'He looked like a man with fur and a tail and a mane.'

' A really big man,' Marina added.

'The colours were amazing...' And they were off again.

Nobody had captured an image of him, at least not on the public mage net. After searching for and failing to summon down any of these they had to satisfy themselves with the hastily drawn and coloured sketches done by the few artists who had managed to catch a glimpse – one of whom must have been in the army for his picture was extremely detailed and, to Minna's mind at least, accurate.

'Who did this one?' she drew up the signature marks but it was unfamiliar. Parillus Gau Tam.

'He's the general's second,' Daraon said, glancing at it once. 'Some say lover but they're just jealous of his position. Gau Tam oversees the welfare of the men while Borze directs their actions.' He drew up an image of the man himself from the public array.

It showed a man in dress uniform purples, his face clearly of Glimshard aristocratic stock – sculpted and rather refined with the careful pose of one who is making the most of themselves. His dark hair was pulled back although the pins on it demonstrated that it was cut in a fashionable flop, the sides razored with patterns that matched the Empress' formal livery. Minna considered him with more interest then than she might have. A dandy soldier, as opposed to the ones Daraon seemed to idolise. Now she looked down at Daraon with a thought,

'Where were you this afternoon? You were supposed to be looking out for us.'

'I was on the battlements watching the training,' he said, flicking his hair back over his shoulders with what she had always felt was devilish abandon and now suddenly saw as coquetry. 'Who do you think sent in the first report that the Karoo was here? Anyway, I don't know what all the fuss is about. He doesn't look so much like any beast I know. More like a girl's toy. All orange and purple – where in the world would *that* be a camouflage?'

Minna had to admit he had a point. She hadn't thought of this. 'Then it mustn't be for camouflage.'

'Unless he can change colour,' Yenie said and when they looked at her with a gaze they had mastered over the years which said, 'Oh, not your childish imagination overdoing it again! *When* will you grow up?' she frowned and muttered, 'I'm just saying. There were things in the news about Karoos changing colour and other things. They are . . .' She hesitated and they all felt her anxiety about what she was about to say, damnation or acceptance hanging on a single word. She whispered it in the

68

end, after such a long delay, so unconvinced that nobody heard her or cared to pay attention, 'Bioplastic.'

'Perhaps it's for female Karoos.' Marina suggested over the top of Yenie's statement. 'They might like that.'

Then the conversation went predictably and Minna floated in it, witty, charming, alluding to an apparently vast knowledge of sexual mores and conduct as they laughed in speculation about Karoo mating principles but all the while that moment, that look through the bars across the yard, burned away like acid in her stomach. Seen and passed over. She persuaded herself she'd imagined it. In Glimshard there was no greater power than being an attractive, well bred young woman. Well, there were two but both were irrelevant.

One such power was being a mature and titled, moneyed, educated or otherwise endowed woman; this was all for Minna's future as the automatic inheritor of her mother's titles to the Huntingore estate and assets, a private stock of gold to be spent as time revealed it. She couldn't now compete with such women nor did she attempt it as it would have been quite stupid but then again, they were not in the same market. All Minna had to do was continue on her way until time bestowed position in those ranks.

The other greater power was to be Empress. There was but one of these in Glimshard and Minna was not she.

However, those things aside, she was the hub of her web, the daughter of an impoverished but respected house, and she had enough support from her mother to do whatever she wished and little enough interference. Unlike bookish, hopelessly naïve Isabeau whose awareness seemed suited to imaginary worlds and clockworks she was well used to being an object of desire with all its possible pleasures. She had never in her life come to the attention of a male and been concluded irrelevant. It was galling. But at the same time as she wanted to take insult she found it difficult. There had been something polite about the gesture, a sort of 'Thanks, but no thanks'. To offer herself up and be turned down by any man was... It was... unimaginable. Her entire life was spent blissfully turning aside the overtures of others, especially men. Even older men who were not of interest had to politely offer her their admiration and she was always careful to flirt, but not too much. Enough to make him feel appreciated. Little enough to be sure there would be no further pursuit. When the admiration was embarrassingly sincere or exceeded a polite deference to beauty, she displayed heartless ingratitude as the only reliable method of discouraging such awful behaviour. Anything but sincerity in old guys! Deploring the shameful situation of men being allowed to reach desperate straits like that was always a good topic of conversation though whose responsibility it was they were never sure.

And now she had apparently offered herself up to this creature which was not even a man – doing him the most outrageous favour, unthinkable really. And he said no. Just like that.

Thanks, but no thanks.

'Minna!' She was being poked hard by Daraon in the side of the leg.

'What is it!?' she snapped, furious.

'Would you or wouldn't you do the funky monkey with the purple tiger guy?'

She realised she had drifted off and now was stuck for a moment. He said no. But Minna, although hurt, was not stupid. She took a quick inventory of faces, read the likely signs. 'Not unless it was for a very large bet.'

'But so furry,' said Yenie wistfully.

Minna looked at her. If Yenie thought it was a worthwhile idea she could safely discard it. 'Gross,' she said, ending the matter although everyone was grumpy with her because she was supposed to be the wild one.

She didn't know why she had said it then. She didn't know how she could get things this wrong. She was always right about

70

what to say and when to keep things running smoothly and everyone on her side. The feeling of being foolish now was unbearable. As if operating on some fiendish schedule Astor Banch chose that moment to appear.

Languid and tall, intelligent and a favoured scholar at the University, Astor was exactly the devil Minna would wish on her sister. They would have made a perfect pair. Unfortunately, he had no detectable interest in anything other than astronomy, physics and claiming superiority for his vocational net over social webs such as the Scarlets.

'Don't you ever talk about anything but sex and fashion?' he said as he passed her on his way to the group of mostly silent, studious men waiting for him at the edge of the café.

'No, Astor,' she said, so out of joint that she couldn't even sit up and flash her corseted cleavage at him. Her only consolation was that she knew she sulked prettily. 'Only the important things merit attention. Go back to your books, there's a good boy.'

'I would have thought you'd be boning up on your biology about now,' he replied smoothly, adjusting the large case of crystal he was carrying. 'Won't you be needing that to figure out how to seduce the Karoo? I hear they have surprising anatomical differences. It would be a shame to fall flat on your face in the middle of a seduction, now wouldn't it?'

His delivery could almost lead a person to believe he was sincere, Minna thought. Almost. If you didn't know exactly how smart he was. But she suddenly wondered if he were right, if he knew so much more, if he had seen a truth in her that was too hard to stand: she was shallow, she was fickle, she was out of her depth and was about to be revealed as strictly small-time business, just one more young woman who played all her cards on her sexual attraction and used it to manipulate men... Oh this spiel was well known to her. There were more than a few all-male nets who held fiercely antagonistic views on the subject. Astor however was not among them. He just wanted to prove himself a superior being and the general superiority of intellect over everything else in life, especially sex. Astor longed for the world to run on rational rails, greased with information, rewarding only those who were proven correct. He was simply baiting Minna, and to her chagrin she was biting.

'Well luckily that won't happen,' she retorted. 'The Empress has him now. Maybe you should take your biology theses to her? I'm sure she'd be very grateful.'

'That particular front has already been covered by the Professors of Exobiology,' Astor informed her, deadpan. 'If he had fallen out of the sky I might have something to say about how hard he hit the ground and how many pieces he would have been in, but that's about it.' And so Minna's ignorance was proven. She had not even insulted him.

'You're mean,' Yenie said to him suddenly in her little girl voice. It was surprisingly cutting.

'And you're stupid,' he replied after a moment's due surprise and recovery. 'You hang out with people who use you and don't care.' And with that he walked on to his waiting tea cups and pale companions.

Yenie sat, rigid and silent, a study in the effort not to cry.

Minna looked after Astor with loathing.

'He's an asshole,' Daraon said, waving one hand to order more tea, more cake, more everything on Minna's tab although he ignored Yenie. He patted Minna's foot, as if she was the one who needed consolation.

Her back was to Yenie, but she betted the little fool was still blinking back tears. She thought that she ought to defend Yenie and kick Daraon for his thoughtless misdirection, but she didn't want to. Instead, she felt angry that Yenie was such a weakling. She glanced around the web and saw expectant faces, waiting for the cue of what to feel, who to talk about, what to say next... She used to love that feeling of command it gave her but for some reason that was absent today. She picked up the largest piece of cake.

'I think we should have a party.'

They dissolved into excited planning almost immediately. Minnabar felt the awful moments slipping away from her into the past. Soon she had nearly forgotten them and when full dark came on and the moons rose she led the way home as if nothing had happened.

TRALANE

Tralane was in the kitchen talking to Carlyn when she heard the commotion of the web's return. Both women stopped their conversation and turned an ear to the half-open door that led on to the halls. Tralane's senior student, Jardant, continued his methodic rolling and slamming of bread dough on the stone slab at one of the workbenches. Beyond him two of the lesser house retainers, a mother and son, chopped and stirred at soup and some kind of fruit pastry preparations without looking up from their quiet organisation. As in most of the larger houses in Glimshard, early evenings were a time of congregation in this room and its size and organisation reflected the expectation of large and hungry crowds. Tralane's had the majesty for five times the five actually present but unless the Scarlets were in for feeding it rarely saw even that many at once.

She met Carlyn's gaze. Both women mouthed the overheard word, 'party' and grimaced. At once they began to gather their plates, bits and pieces of cigarette fixings and the wine and made noises about moving up to the workrooms for Jardant's benefit.

He wasn't fooled by their apologetic mumbles and lifted his head, straightening as he gave the dough a really good slam into the marble, resting his hand on it so that his palm and fingers sank slowly through the shiny mass and it oozed out all around in huge, elastic bulges. His white linen shirt hung off him like a workman's tunic. Between it, the black marble and the white dough he was a showground curiosity, a blond, tanned, worked-out labourer absorbed in his task. His every move was as apparently studied as an expert model under the constant and constructive eye of the photographer but at the same time he'd always seemed to be absolutely oblivious to all the reasons that Carlyn had nicknamed him Best in Show. Tralane thought the entire thing was a masterful performance to begin with but in the four years he had been her student and among her household she'd never been able to get proof – if it was an act it was one without any intervals.

'I see what you're doing,' he said, looking at the guilty pair of them through hanging golden curls.

'Bring some more wine when you come up,' Tralane said. 'I'm going to have another crack at the goggles. You can show Carlyn your new equipment.'

He shook his head. 'Fine. But I am not cooking for all of them. I'm not even making tea.'

'Jard, I've told you a billion times, you live here. Do what you like.' Tralane tucked the wax-wrapped cheese under her arm and grabbed her glass.

'She treats me like a servant,' he grumbled, going back to the bread.

'You let her,' Tralane said – another mystery there. Jardant showed no inclination to do anything about Minnabar's suggestive commands other than tolerate them as though he really were a servant. Technically, his position as student included household duties as part payment of his education and board but there was no question that Minnabar pushed her luck with him, although she usually reserved it for when there were some Scarlets around to observe. He was only six years older than Minnabar, which left him fourteen short of Tralane but always chose older adult company over any younger. The other obvious possible reason for his disinterest was not in doubt – Jardant dated men and women but had never done so with any serious intent. He was married to engineering.

Tralane and Carlyn left him to his fate without a backward glance. Carlyn led the way through the halls and over the worn carpets with ease, taking the first elevator up to the level of the array and then walking to the workshop via the stairs. The high-array elevator car was officially broken and Tralane wasn't even going to tell Carlyn she had fixed it. She looked at its dark doorway as they passed it and felt a flicker of pleasure at her secret, the roof deck, the hidden flyer. It was followed by a slew of cold disquiet as she was forced to also remember the purpose of those things, what they'd been reduced to. Her mind filled with the image of Alide's smug face and the over-scented smell of his carriage.

Carlyn pushed the workroom door open and Tralane took a deep breath of the chemical odour there – polish, oil, degreaser, burnt metal. Better. She was able to deposit her half dinner on the bench without slamming anything. Carlyn walked her bottom on to one of the wooden stools opposite Tralane and set out her picnic items with precision, pushing Tralane's instruments and debris aside with careful moves of her small hand. Carlyn's home was neat and everything she owned was organised and clean. She never made any remarks about Tralane's surroundings for which Tralane was grateful.

'So,' Carlyn said, looking up at the glass roof overhead as it began to rain. 'You've got some big news?'

'I can lipread at five hundred metres,' Tralane said, sitting down in her old armchair and resting her plate over the worn blurt of stuffing that was flattened from many similar crushings. She was about to say more when there was a knock on the door.

'Yes?' she called, wearily, seeing Carlyn already drawing breath to reply.

Jardant opened it and leant half into the room, arms still

dredged to the elbow in flour. 'Runner here for you.' He retreated and there was a brief murmur and scuffle of the odd dance of people trying to dodge one another and both going the same way. A moment later a girl with a brown ponytail and immensely long legs dressed in the Empress' tabard and shorts paced into the room and looked around with an 'oh my' glance at the paraphernalia until she caught Tralane's eye. Then she gave a small start, as though instantly reprogrammed with manners.

'Pardon the interruption Professor Huntingore. I've been asked to convey an invitation to you on behalf of the Empress and General Borze. There will be a banquet and dancing with entertainments at the palace tomorrow night. Please attend by the seventh hour. Shall I take your reply now?' She handed a silver envelope to Tralane, addressed by an expert scribe's hand. Tralane knew from experience that all details would be inside, together with a written invitation.

As she took it, the runner looked at Carlyn and gave a small bow. 'And Professor Loitrasta. I also have one for you.' She pulled a satchel around from where it had been hanging behind her hip and riffled through a large number of silver envelopes, at last finding the correct one and handing it over.

'Thanks,' Carlyn said, leaning forward to take it and being careful not to dislodge her dinner plate. She added as she returned Tralane's glance, 'Of course we'll both be going.'

'Marvellous!' said the runner with practised joy. 'I will convey the good news to her Highness forthwith.' She was about to leave when she paused, hand on the door, and turned back. 'That man who showed me in . . .'

'Jardant,' Tralane supplied with clear pronunciation. She saw Carlyn smile out of the corner of her eye.

The runner did not notice. 'Is he your . . . um . . .'

Tralane fought the urge to roll her eyes. 'Student. He is my senior student. But not my Um . . . so feel free.'

The girl twitched with genuine pleasure, hands briefly

clenched, eyes alight, smile brilliant. She almost squeaked. 'Thank you.' And was gone, her soft and rapid tread vanishing almost instantly along the hall.

'Good old Bestie,' Carlyn murmured, biting into her apple. 'Now, about this lip-reading thing. What are you talking about? Some piece of equipment I assume.'

'Well, I was going to tell you all about this Karoo creature but you know about him now,' Tralane began. She picked the goggles off the bench and skipped back to the recordings she'd made earlier, handing them over to Carlyn with casual grace, as if they were a commonplace item.

Carlyn took the goggles and looked down into the eyepieces which were already playing back the juddering, badly focused images from that afternoon. She looked up at Tralane, put her dinner plate on the floor and then with a quick look at the straps, put the goggles on her head. 'Holy fuck.'

Tralane paused to enjoy the moment. It was sweet, being able to share something she'd made, done, found. Inside her mouth news of the crystallograph and the storm recordings waited, longed, begged to be said. She knew that if they came out then Carlyn would be endangered. But without her Tralane didn't know what to do. She'd spent a lifetime being casually contemptuous of politics from her convenient position in the back end of a forgotten subject. Now that her research was known to the Minister of War, was required, was conscripted, secret, she couldn't think straight. The sense of personal danger and of threat to her family was so intense it made her thoughts scatter. Her tongue was twisted with the need to talk and the imperative not to. Now was the time to be clever and cold. She needed reassurance so badly.

'Empress took the Karoo to the palace,' Carlyn said with disgust. 'Probably showing him off.'

'She'll give him back.' Tralane said thoughtlessly.

Carlyn pushed the goggles up on to her forehead. 'Well,

treasure, you certainly found a damn good gadget here. Don't suppose you've got more than one pair?'

Tralane shook her head. 'There may be more but...'

'Yes, trawling through the Archives required. I see.' Her gaze was unusually sharp and made oddly more so by the jaunty angle of the goggles and her mass of blond curls. 'You look like death, Hunt. What's the matter?'

Tralane, unable to stop because the thought had just occurred to her and she was in such familiar company, said. 'Someone in my house must have told them.'

'Told who what?'

Tralane realised what she was doing. 'Sorry, thinking aloud.'

Carlyn pulled the goggles back down again for a minute and then took them off and handed them back. 'Do you want to talk or am I going to have to beat it out of you?' She sipped her wine and frowned. 'I'll set Isabeau on you.'

Tralane pulled the obligatory face of mock horror. 'I can't tell you. It's under the war act.' That at least was true.

Carlyn stuck her jaw out and then hesitated, watching Tralane's face. 'You're not kidding. Are you in trouble?'

'Yes. And that's why I can't tell you about it,' Tralane adjusted the goggles.

'But... is it about the pamphlet?'

Tralane glanced at a box under one of the benches where several hundred undistributed copies of the damned thing gathered dust. 'I don't think so.'

'Because you're not the only one who thinks the war is a complete mistake. We've been trying to get permission to send an investigative team to the front because of the involvement of the Karoos, but all the Ministry say is that they can't spare the men to protect an expedition. They seem to be expecting an opportunist attack from the plains, which I have to say does seem likely but it's all because we're stretched out to buggery

78

and beyond with the effort of reaching so far south. It's insane. Even for a significant find. There'll be other finds.'

Tralane nodded. The pamphlet and its arguments for abandoning the southern front seemed like ancient history now. She wished she'd never written the thing. 'It's possible someone took that more seriously than I thought.'

'You'll have to stop being cryptic and implausible if you want help. It was persuasive but it wasn't that good.'

Tralane looked at Carlyn and sighed. 'Maybe it will all go away.'

'They've started poking around looking for weapons,' Carlyn suggested, sketching in the air with movements of her wine glass. 'They're flat out of ideas with current technology and they remembered they had a Sircene stockpile up here in the old town and maybe there'd be something in it worth having if only they knew what it was.'

'You're partly right,' Tralane said.

'You haven't been taking the war seriously have you?' Carlyn sat and gave her a long, accusing stare. 'Ah, don't look so annoyed. Nobody has here. We're all encouraged to think of it as the Empress' project, and her problem, a feature of the larger Empire that's nothing to do with us and never likely to touch us. Not generals are we? But now we're sending our men and soon there won't be that many left.'

Tralane sat with this for a moment. Her objection to the war had only really stirred recently once she'd begun getting letters from the Ministry asking for reports on her research. Until then she had only been aware of it as a thing that cropped up in the news. She looked at Carlyn, smiling faintly. 'I've been a fool. Why didn't you tell me?'

Carlyn shrugged. 'It was never a good time. You looked happy for once. Didn't wanna spoil it.'

'I did?'

'You did.'

'Because I had my head in the sand again.'

'Not in the sand. In the guts of the mystery machineries. It's what you're meant for, Lane, so don't take it as some kind of accusation. We all have our things. After Sundesi you deserved a little me-time.'

Tralane barely winced at the mention of her ex. 'Doesn't seem like such a good thing when it means I take my eye off the ball everywhere else and by the time I look up everything's shot to hell.'

'Yeah, well. Like I say, we all have our things. I just see yours easily from over here.'

Tralane noticed the shift of tone. 'So what have you been missing?'

'Minor inconveniences of departmental funding. But I'm on it now. Anyway, tell me more about what you've been working on.'

Tralane took a deep breath, held it for a split second, then, 'I've been trying to understand how the crystallograph works.'

Carlyn looked at her flatly. Crystallographs were few but they were hardly legendary. They recorded sound into crystal which another crystallograph could play back when attached to the correct speaker apparatus. They did suffer, however, from the fact that although their operators knew how to use and repair them they did not understand what exactly was going on. Only engineers ever used them, employed for the purpose as Recorders and Relayers, and sometimes they tinkered and attempted to record images or thoughts, but they had no theory as to the exact nature of the workings. They knew what things did. They did not know why. As with most Imperial technology it was a trade secret bound in the blood of the lines. It wasn't just that machines were difficult to use or required special skills; non-bloodline engineers could not and never would be able to understand them. This was also true of other physicomagics, such as alchemy and metallurgy.

Lately there had been attempts to advance abilities using

music and art, but these only enhanced latent abilities, they did not open gateways where the blood kept them closed. Tralane's crystallograph was hers naturally, doubly so as a Sircene-line device. If anyone was going to come up with the theory of how it worked, she would, and if she didn't, then nobody would. It was her duty and her joy to attempt to fulfil this destiny. But for Carlyn there was that moment of pause where she must think and adjust over her natural reaction to say, 'What's to understand? They work just fine.' Much as Tralane would say to Carlyn if offered a shot at decoding the useful information from a rock. They had to struggle to even want to know anything about non-line expertise.

Pursuing the knowledge for its own sake was also a specialist inclination, one rarely mentioned except in the exclusive company of other academics. A scholar's purpose was to serve, not to gain unexplained and mysterious powers which might threaten the natural order that went, Empress: Ministers: Sciences and Arts: Everybody Else. Theoretical work was threatening in and of itself because it offered understanding that could not be explained to non-liners. Not even the Empress. It was for peacetimes, for lazy times, when practical affairs were ebbing. For Tralane to admit to theorising now ought to lead Carlyn to suspecting correctly that this was work connected to the war.

Carlyn had her moment of time out, thinking. Then she said, 'Did you get anywhere?'

Tralane nodded. There was no point explaining the details. 'Can record images.' She did not mention the thoughts, the memories she had put into the crystal without meaning to. She wasn't ready for that herself. 'And I can process the recordings through the Bridge into other devices. I think it's all about natural patterns, even apparently chaotic events have patterns of a kind within them you see if you—' She broke off, already aware she'd gone too far and was about to head into the dead zone where Carlyn couldn't follow. 'The input of the recording can be used to make other things, I mean not sounds.'

She got up and opened one of the cabinets, leaning over a tottering pile of odds-and-ends boxes. It tipped and then gave way. Amid a shower of old circuit boards, wires and screws she grabbed for the thing she wanted and came away with it victorious.

'What's that?' Carlyn asked obediently as Tralane brandished the object in her hand.

'That,' Tralane said, straightening her arm and taking aim at an empty degreaser canister on her primary desk, 'is a gun.' She caressed the trigger point with her index finger. There was a strange distortion of the air between the gun muzzle and the canister, like heat waves, or a jagged break in reality that was over as soon as begun. With a strange cracking, tearing sound the canister flew apart into several pieces. Powder, splinters and larger bits scattered over a wide area, some of them flaring with heat and smouldering before they went dark.

Tralane bent her elbow and put the gun up, pointed at the roof, careful to remove her finger from the trigger. She thumbed the safety on with a caress to the grip and then looked at Carlyn's shocked, open-mouthed face with a grin of triumph that she just couldn't help. The smell of melted plastic and burning degreaser overrode the delicious smell of dinner but to her it was no less attractive.

Carlyn regained her poise after a moment. 'Who else knows about this?'

'Just me,' Tralane said.

'Jardant?'

'Nope. But this is not pure Sircene tech. This is from the Conclave Distribution. So, my bet is that there are other things like this out there somewhere.' Tralane popped the pack of the gun and took the knuckle-sized crystal shard out, holding it up to the light between thumb and forefinger. 'This is the magazine – the thing that determines the nature of the shot.'

She looked at it as Carlyn squinted. So small. The recording inside it was simply the background burr and hubbub of a few moments at one of the Scarlets' parties; people talking, a little music, some laughter. She could only imagine the scale and purpose of what her storm crystals were going to do.

They heard footsteps outside in the corridor at the same moment. Tralane slipped the crystal into her trouser pocket and lobbed the now-useless gun up into the same jumble of crap it had been in before in the top section of the cupboard. A few cables fell down but they landed amid the general mess on the floor just as Tralane got back on to her seat. There was a perfunctory knock and nearly at the same instant the door opened and Minnabar leaned in, both hands on the frame. She kept her feet at the threshold as though crossing actually into the lab would burn her toes.

'Mom, can you give me the keys to the solar?'

'No,' Tralane said, picking up her wine glass. She knew that Minnabar wanted to take her party up there so they could lie around under the sky feeling like miniature queens of the universe and that was fine except the last time they did it they left a stinking mess which she only discovered a week later when she went in to do maintenance on the house energy system. She'd spent an hour hoofing trash and wiping surfaces. Minna had been turned to dishwash duty for a week in response and had succeeded only in aggravating everyone by cracking, chipping or breaking almost every whole dish in the house. Plus all the protesting 'Laters!' that had to be endured every time the allotted hour came around.

'Aww. I promise to clean up.' Minna had adopted the whining tone of a three-year-old, slightly modified by a knowing attempt at cuteness and an evil-eyed promise of sulky retaliation.

Tralane felt herself weaken and Carlyn's attention on her. 'No.'

'But Mom!'

There was apparently no back-up behind the but. But was self-evidently righteous. But.

Tralane looked over her glass at her younger daughter. 'Go away.'

Minna hung even more, like a torture victim, like a saint about to be dragged away and martyred. 'Awww ... but I'll clean up after. I promise. And the others. We'll be good.'

'I said no drinking. You covered my sofa in beer puke. No.' The sofa had had to be burnt.

'Moooo-ooommm! I'll take care of it I swear. The others promise too. We know we were bad that one time. One time. Come on. Pleeeaaassseee.'

Tralane picked up the nearest soft object – a worn piece of foam padding that had once housed a medium-sized power converter – and threw it at Minna's head. 'No. And don't hassle Bestie.'

'Who?' Minna batted the foam away irritably, but confusion briefly overrode it.

'Jardant,' Carlyn said with an indulgent aunt's tone. 'And I can't believe you really need the solar when you have such lovely rooms of your own plus the Karoo to talk about all night. Did you see him?'

Minna pulled a face of knowing, catlike pleasure as she gave Carlyn all her attention. 'Well Jard is fending off that runner in the kitchen although I don't give him more than two rounds before he goes down. And I did, I did see!'

Tralane snorted with amused irritation as Carlyn leant forwards, all agog.

'I knew you'd find a way! How did you do that? I heard it was a crush.'

Minna tossed her head. 'That's for me to know but ...' She

hesitated, then realised it was Carlyn she was talking to and rushed on. 'He was sooo tall, and so big, and so furry and lilac and orange and white ... I swear I've never seen anything so freakin' odd in all my life!' She shuddered. 'Eew.'

Carlyn nodded, disappointed. 'I guess you didn't get close enough to make any real observations.'

'I saw the Empress arrive and leave. She went right past me, this close!' Minna held up finger and thumb millimetres apart.

'Mmn,' Carlyn wasn't interested in Empresses except as the best examples of blood telepaths.

'Better get back to your party,' Tralane said in a commanding tone. 'There're jugs of new wine in the pantry. I daresay we won't miss it if just one goes astray.'

Minna rolled her eyes, 'Thanks, Mom.' She lounged away, mollified, sighing heavily at the hard state of her life.

Tralane turned to Carlyn and shrugged. 'Bribery with alcohol. Never fails. I wish our family weren't so predictable.'

Carlyn glanced up at the cupboard where the gun had rattled its last. 'I wouldn't call you predictable, Lane. That's the last bloody word I'd use for you.'

Tralane grinned, 'Yes well. Let's turn our minds to something useful shall we?' She picked up the goggles and recued her recording of the Karoo. 'My turn I think ...'

CHAPTER SIX

ZHARAZIN

Zharazin Mazhd followed Isabeau Huntingore from the end of the street where the secret exit of the Rose let her out into the yards. Wrapped up in her scholar's robes and hood she didn't make any effort to notice her surroundings. She walked silently and quickly with the tread of a missionary, focused on immaterial things. He could have walked directly behind her and she would not have been wiser. It was remarkable, considering. But then she probably had faith in the secrets she'd learned so far. He shouldn't be surprised. She was so young.

She hesitated on the corner and he saw her throw a book into one of the open trashcans although she barely broke stride to do it. Within moments she had gone and he was there. He reached inside and retrieved it, slipped it into an inside pocket of his overcoat – one of many for just such moments. His action was nearly as smooth as hers. He followed her at twenty paces as she marched back to the Sun Plaza along the dark colonnades of the Library. She had a real stalk, the kind of movement he associated with women twice her age. It combined with the sensual, beautiful feel of her skin under his hands and the extraordinary performance he'd witnessed in the Rose to make her one of the most unusual people it had ever been his pleasure to spy upon.

He had no reason to do so – no official reason such as a paid scrip – but the same instinct that had propelled him to pursue the mystery of the dark speck in the skies for its own curious sake now made him sure that there were rewarding things to be had from this pastime. Not to mention, she was Tralane's daughter. He had schooled himself to have an eidetic memory for faces. One quick perusal of the Who's Who every year was enough to keep him current on any notable person, right down to the least short-term lecturer in the University's least popular subject. Isabeau Huntingore was in there high up, like all the rare blood families. And you didn't get more rare than a Sircene maternal line crossed with an Arost paternal input. He would have suspected a child of intellectual conjecture, an experiment of lines, had he not known Tralane Huntingore well enough to see that Isabeau was purely an accident of youthful infatuation and a careless disregard for consequences.

Of course the one thing he hadn't seen was her face. But there were few Arost children of the right age in the city, and none with the freedom Isabeau had to roam at will. Touching her was all the confirmation he had needed. She shared Tralane's genes and Zharazin knew those. His particular blood talent was the ability to identify lines from the touch of a single cell, the composition of a face or an individual's scent. He was also able to predict correctly the likely outcomes of any combination of hybrids or pedigrees, any combination of individuals, purely on spec. If he'd been born female then he would have taken his place among the echelons of the Legacy as one of the invaluable Mediatrices whose wombs were capable of genetically recombining zygotes into necessary, viable or important forms, drawing on their vast Memories and the Morphatic Libraries of the Blood. A lifetime as the highest and most valued being would have been guaranteed, personality no object.

As a male he was strictly limited to recognition and no more – a talent scout or matchmaker at best, a shoddy snooper of personal tragedy at worst. He'd been both, still was, when the money was necessary or the job essential for the furtherance of his career although he scorned the ability. It was effortless, like breathing, no challenge, no skill involved. Spying on the other hand, real spying, real information dealing, that was all about skill and instinct working together, patience, endurance, insight, timing; things worthy of respect.

He was interested not so much by Isabeau's perfectly ordinary reaction to Borze – they had great genetic potential which their bodies recognised with a rush of exchanges even when their minds weren't up to the task – but by her later indifference to her own enjoyment of the athletic intervention of the two younger men.

As he'd watched them he realised she was only half present. Most of her mind was already absorbed with something more immediately interesting. He would have given a lot to know what that was. He would have given a lot for her kind of detachment. Even watching them had made him want to bite his fingers in frustration. She on the other hand – flew like an eagle.

The men had not cared to notice as they'd been primarily infatuated with their good luck in finding such a nubile, young girl through whom to bond with each other. Zharazin had envied them. He'd no such passion for any man. Ordinarily he didn't wish for one. Only when he saw it and understood he had missed a facet of worthwhile experience did it occur to him to think of it. Meanwhile, in the midst of a semi-sacred spiritual act of potential transcendence, riding the fierce train of her body's pleasures like the captain of a peerless warship, Isabeau Huntingore had remained ineffably cool and untouched, queen of everything.

He had trouble even now as he followed her relentless tread in trying to figure out how such a girl could ever be anything other than immaculate. You could fuck her twenty ways and not puncture her, hammer like a machine and not break her. She was curious steel.

And just fifteen minutes before that she'd been so unutterably the willing carnal property of Fadurant Borze that men were talking about it in tones of bitter envy before Borze had even left the building. They stared at him with new respect, grudging but nonetheless real. What could you do in the face of a man like that but stand in baffled acceptance?

Now Isabeau sliced a path through Sun Plaza. Zharazin took an oblique way, only keeping her in sight, his movements languid, carefree, the antithesis of hers in a dance he had to be careful of – too skilled and it looked deliberate. Oh the difficulty of appearing accidental while being as calculated as the most rigorous horoscope. But he was spared the exultation of his best skills. For some reason she changed tack abruptly as she neared one of the better tea-tents, giving it a wide berth, then resumed her course. He realised where she was going: the palace. He almost missed the reason for her detour.

Minnabar Huntingore, brazen bronzed girl of society, was holding court. Thank the gods for Isabeau, Zharazin thought as he saw this. Without her he would have gone unreminded of the youthful underclass, obsessed as his mistress was with the higher, harder workings of the adult minds in Glimshard. She missed a lot because of that. One day he knew it would be important and in this entirely unexpected coincidence of finding Isabeau Huntingore and following her – somewhere in there lay the key to undoing his service from Shrazade. Of course, protecting Tralane had nothing to do with it. He hesitated as this thought came unwelcome into his speeding mind, a ghost on an adjacent track – a feeling which always presaged a significant vision His bones hollowed, ready for flight. He was not up to the task of saving Huntingore from the Infomancy and the Minister of Defence. It was an iron mantle, too heavy for a mink like him.

He was forced to pause, to mine this moment of vision.

They came without warning and left the same way and must be hunted in their time and not his. He felt around in the far dark recesses of himself, in his hands and in his guts. He felt a trap on him, cold metal pressures on the backs of his hands, against his elbows and the tops of his feet even as he continued walking in the dusky, seductive sunset light. Calculating people with power were arranged against Tralane Huntingore, although they were not in position yet. That was a way off.

He crossed a black bar of shadows where the palace banners cast flicker-edged pitfalls on to the immaculate paving. Ahead of him Isabeau Huntingore proved an untouchable course and finally he stepped back into its groove and felt the warmth of its security ease the cold of his insights a little. He became the page to her queen. He followed her under the arches and through the tented way, lined with guards who turned a blind eye to her and a weather one to him. He had a billion reasons he might go inside the palace on his own account. He was well known.

The guards gave him disliking, slant looks that cut to the quick of who he was. No finery you can wear, they said, that can disguise your true form, your filthy foreign blood. They hated him very well for all he could have, for the secrets he must know and the places he could go and all the more because the law and the way of things prevented them laying a finger on him when up on the high Steppes they'd have been on him like a pack of dogs, ripping and tearing until nothing was left but a bloody stain.

Mind, on the Steppe he'd have cut their throats himself long before that and left them empty shades to wander the windswept hills forlorn, forgotten by their women.

He smiled at them, their red, bubbling deaths in his eyes, and they turned away one at a time. The fuck-you contest pleased him.

Ahead of him, Isabeau's knightly stride took her to the outer yards and following became difficult. There were many others around now, passing back and forth on minor businesses with the lesser offices of the city courts and other bits of formal mundanity that required signatures, papers, meetings and handshakings. Fortunately, his past as a delivery boy and his subsequent elevation to diplomatic status within the Infomancy meant most of them simply assumed Zharazin was on official duties with someone else. He was able to reinforce this with smiles and the touching of the air that showed willing for a handshake without the time or effort needed to actually touch another, pointing generally where Isabeau had gone as if his meeting lay coincidentally ahead of him. He swam along this river of recognition, seen by everyone, noticed but not noted.

His body shimmered with sensual delight in this liquid deception. He recorded it as another notch in the post he'd set up for Isabeau – part of an inner forest of record wherein he kept all his tallies – hers a slender white stripped branch stabbed into the earth with emphatic force among the varied uprights. And then she took her significant turn and he walked past, light with amazement and quite unable to pursue since there was no possible reason for him to do so.

The door with its heavy hanging bead curtain yanked aside and tied with an old scarf, a steady, opulent darkness within, red lit if you could get your eyes to find the light, more of a nest or a den than anything else for the woman who kept it and possibly lived in it, without any kind of title; it was marked on his inner map in letters of black, red and gold. The Empress' silent favour posted her there. Halfway between commercial Glimshard and the Court at a distance that was locally known as Safe or Summons – too far away to hit or be hit by directly, close enough to see.

He knew very well whose offices it was, if you could give that kind of name to a hovel full of shite. He knew who Isabeau was speaking to with such careless, vigorous disgust when he overheard her say,

'I've had second thoughts. I accept your offer of an internship or whatever it was you were offering.' And then, a fraction of a second later, just before his walk carried him out of earshot, she added with uncertainty, 'If it's still open, that is.'

He felt astonishment write itself across his face, opening his eyes, parting his lips, charming them into a curl of wonder. Isabeau Huntingore the student of Parlumi Night?

In the quiet forest the pale branch put down roots.

Zharazin moved on. It was getting late. The Empress would be closing her final court session and moving into the early evening's relaxation. But of course now she had the Karoo. He moved with authority through the corridors, all the time planning an excuse to gain entrance but the place was thick with other busybodies all hoping for a similar opportunity. Against his will he slowed down and made small talk with a number of lawyers gathering in preparation for a mass exodus to their company halls; they liked to keep infomancers on their good side. Among them he saw Granth Tabror, Minister Alide's closest personal friend. He was arguing quietly but intently with a young woman wearing senior prosecutor's robes although Zharazin was too far away to hear the words. They broke it off as they neared the pack, both looking as if they were well displeased with grim business and each other.

Zharazin made his goodbyes and caught the prosecutor eyeing him. He recognised the momentary stillness of someone putting a name to a face in a place and stood still cooperatively until acuity replaced the brief emptiness in her eyes.

'Infomancer,' she said, beckoning to him with one hand, the other supporting her large stack of files. 'Attend me, please.'

He moved towards her and she led off without a backward glance, confident that he would obey. He did, of course. Regardless of what she wanted her air of command was deeply attractive and there was always the lure of the unknown to add to that – a lure he had never successfully resisted.

Their walk took them into one of the annexes, an ordered, near silent place of whispering clerks and rustling papers overlaid with the smell of tea and spiced biscuits. The prosecutor headed directly for a private carrel where she must routinely consult with her opposite numbers on cases whilst searching for common grounds. She indicated he could take the client seat opposite her own, then dumped the papers unceremoniously on the edge of the massive desk – a block of wood that would have burned for weeks in an emergency. She dumped herself into the consultant's chair. She was small and light so the leather only creaked and then left her like a slouched pixie in the scoop made by years of much fatter legal arses. It somewhat spoiled her air of power and made her look girlish and vulnerable. He suspected this was intentional. It worked. He had to exert an effort to maintain his louche detachment and charm while uneducable parts of him struggled to rush forward and act protective. Luckily he had a lot of practice in not reacting to basic feminine control strategies. Parlumi Night had taught him very well.

'My name is Dresilan Shon,' she said, quiet enough so they wouldn't be overheard. 'I make sure guilty people get what they deserve.' Her accent was so high town he could picture her in elocution lessons training the Glimshard slum vowels to round out, though traces of them lingered here and there; the promise of a shiv hidden in a silk stocking. She smiled prettily.

He smiled back, slow, charmed, waiting for the other shoe to drop.

'One of my deserving cases has recently attempted to plea bargain by offering the Empress the names of several people whom he alleges are conspirators in a plot of some importance involving one of our sister cities. I have no means at present of determining whether or not the names he dropped are of value and I need someone to find out for me . . .' She stopped, her dark brown eyes radiating steady concentration, willing him to get the picture without her having to state it. He knew this type of hesitation. He'd just used it on Borze.

'Without going through the usual channels?' he suggested, relaxing now that he understood this was simply work for hire.

'Exactly. If you wish to take the job I expect total confidentiality. Absolute. The payment would reflect this of course. And there would be a sum for your expenses and bonds to cover injury and death in service. Standard measures.' Her face betrayed no particular interest as she relayed this laundry list although suddenly every hair on his body reported trouble. It might have been the bonds. They were only offered for Special Service Agents, which would ordinarily have been recruited officially via Shrazade herself as head of the Infomancy. Excluding the system meant the system was under suspicion.

Zharazin saw his field of vision flatten as he considered it, even though he knew he was considering it purely for show, just so that it looked as though he had a grain of sense and cared for his own hide, possibly his reputation, maybe that he was assessing whether or not he had the skills and the balls for the job. In fact he was simply savouring the moment, a delicious, open slit of opportunity, all difficulty to come, all ripe and ready.

'Why would you ask me in a public place?'

'I am seizing an opportunity presented by chance. I know you sufficiently well by reputation that I am sure you won't say no, so let's not pretend you will.'

He felt slightly daunted but he shrugged and grinned to show she had nailed him.

She had not finished however. 'I expect you have not considered the outcome if the names prove to be sufficiently suspicious to demand action.'

'That... would depend on the nature of said suspicions.' He was listening now, listening hard.

She nodded, 'Much would then be asked of you, Mazhd. The

Empress would not have time or means perhaps to dispense justice in the formal manner.'

Killing. And then afterwards, if he lived, he could expect a new identity if all went well and a fresh grave if not. And if all went well and Shrazade found out she might choose to impress her new recruits by making an example of a traitor: she'd make him into Living Memory, the fate of all disloyal infomancers: he would feel nothing, just eat, live, shit and speak when spoken to until old age or dementia ruined his storage capacity. Yes, much indeed. And it was already too late to say no.

'It sounds dreadfully expensive,' he said, smoothing the perfect line of his tailored coat.

'Even more than you think,' she said, closed her eyes for a second and sighed out through her nose, a short and dismissive sound. When she opened them again she gave him a smile and stood up. 'I am done for the day and I could use some relaxation. How about dinner and dancing? Are you free?'

Now they exchanged frank and fair looks, conclusion foregone. It was the fact that she didn't care if he said no that made him say yes and mean it. Yes to all that. Yes.

CHAPTER SEVEN

TZABAN

Tzaban was surprised to be hijacked directly off the parade grounds, and by the Empress in person and not some gang of lackeys. Her retinue ignored the hastily self-arranging soldiers, attempting a lineup while her horse paced between them like a galleon moving under silent sail, its massive quivering nostrils the only sign of agitation. Tzaban adopted a submissive, gentle posture, three-quarters on and relaxed while a stream of barked orders and scraping boots passed around him in a flood of nervous tension. His brief island existence ended as the horse arrived, and then its partner, an altogether more massive animal whose gaze and curved neck held generations of haughty power like a drawn bow. He didn't even need to look at the rider to understand who it was: her bodyguard, the Steppe nomad. Their horse-talking skills were legendary. The animal's every inch spoke for him and promised Tzaban death if he made a false move.

A shimmering white veil surrounded them. He was aware of mages moving within shifting folds of light, planeshifting as they cast the glamour that enclosed him with the Empress, the guard and one of her running girls. To his left, the crowd faded out into a soft, rushing quiet and brilliance. To his right, General Borze alone remained standing on the stone flags at attention, saluting. Tzaban watched him for a cue and saw absolute dedication and respect in the general's eyes. He bowed his head and waited.

The runner, a tall and gawky girl with short black hair who barely came up to his shoulder, moved forwards as if underwater. Her movements appeared confident but he could smell her fear of him. It combined with the other odours of her fertility, the stallions' barely restrained energies, the Steppe horselord's dominant tone and a soft, mesmerising scent like opium, Imperial female and roses that he knew to be the Empress – a unique smell. Once, when he first came across it, snooping around the palace towers in his winged form, he had thought it was a perfume. Only after a while did he understand it was actually her and although his body identified it with those plants that was only because it had never before had a template with which to identify an Empress. Even on him it had a pacifying effect, although not as powerful as that which it exerted on other Imperials, he was sure. This was why the runner was treading so carefully towards him.

He bowed his head as low as he could without seeming ridiculous and let his body drop into a smaller shape. He thought it better not to look up, even though Borze did. Borze was one of them. He was not. The girl's fearful energy washed at him like a clammy wave. He saw her holding something out, heard her start talking in a whisper which she quickly cleared with a small cough and made into a proper voice,

'We do not wish to imprison you but please accompany us back to the palace.'

He reached out and took the silvery paper she was trying to give him, studied it for a moment and then said truthfully, 'I cannot read this.'

She looked at him for a moment and then nodded and took it back, turning it the right way up to read it for him but she was interrupted by the Empress's quiet, soft voice.

'Be at ease, General. Tzaban, it is an invitation to be my

guest. Will you come and stay a few days? I would be glad to get to know you better.'

Tzaban felt the subtle power of her persuasion like a soft hand on the back of his neck. It was a caress. Force would have made him shy but he expected compulsion of some kind, not this. For a second he was undone. He was sad when his sense of self returned and felt the looming presence of the bodyguard's intent held in check only by the near-imperceptible chains of rose and opium.

'I will come.'

'Run with our girl.' Again, that touch: velvet smoke on his nose, on his skin.

'In her footsteps,' he agreed, still staring at the pavement, the horses' legs, the girl's hands fumbling with her useless note.

'And you, General,' she said, a smile shaping her voice. 'Be also invited.'

The white company moved forwards and he fell into place as promised, his eyes on the girl's back as it moved with the strong, regular stride of her paces. His feet had twenty miles in them already but he didn't feel that at all, didn't see the streets or the people, the veil or anything but the moving back in front of him as he focused on his discovery: the Empress was dangerous in a way he'd never suspected. This kind of rule and mastery was familiar to him, but he hadn't seen much of it among the human population. Mastery of energy and intent combined with biochemical pressure – that was all a Karoo thing. Ordinary humans, even the Imperials, had never had much of a hold on him. This on the other hand – this he had to find out about. And where Karoos would use force most of the time that way, she used ... What was that? Affection?

He would have liked to say it hadn't worked, that he had to go, that this was part of his mission anyway but he wasn't sure and that was enough to scatter him about. It took the whole road up to the palace to pick up the pieces. The only upside was that, apart from the Steppe man, there was nobody there who noticed his confusion.

Tzaban attuned to him as they arrived, realising that he was the best barometer for judging the Empress. Always beside her, chosen for deep instinctive reactions to her every mood, he was a book Tzaban could read: one without words. The man's back showed only devotion, there was no danger.

They arrived at the doors and the white, dazzling veil fell away. He looked up from the narrow waist and tabard he'd been watching and saw Borze getting off a horse, fussing his armour as he attempted to look prepared. The runner looked back at Tzaban and beckoned. He followed her and the retinue indoors, suddenly feeling huge as the building closed in around him, shutting away the sky and the space.

It took all his composure to work himself into the tiny enclos-ures and not panic. He was grateful then for the girl and her eager steps that tried to be away from him and slow enough not to seem like running at the same time. He mapped himself on the four bare inches of skin above her belt, made himself small, becoming domesticated, mannered, quiet, contained.

They came to a large room, mercifully high and round, full of banners and flickering lights but even so, better. There was a circulation of people – servants, courtiers, guards – and then he was left alone. The Empress was in her throne, at the centre, higher. The guard stood lower, at her side, very still and relaxed, hand on his polearm. Tzaban recognised someone who knew he could win any fight he wanted to and although it spurred him to challenge he didn't rise.

'Be at your ease,' the Empress said, her voice lighter in here as if it had to diffuse across a wider area.

Tension left Tzaban's shoulders. He straightened and looked up, suddenly fundamentally uncertain that all his submission had been his choice. He would have hated to meet anyone this way, with that doubt in his gaze, but when he saw her he found himself staring with all expectations lost.

The girl standing before her chair was small and aside from some decoration on her white robes, undecorated. Her brown hair fell softly around her shoulders and framed a square face with a long, strong nose and large, intelligent eyes that looked at him with vivid interest. A gentle kind of artless sweetness and genuine amazement shone out of them. Freckles splashed her nose and cheeks and her lips were chapped pink with anxious biting and what he thought was a degree of arousal, possibly for him or about him. She was about sixteen, maybe not even that.

He glanced at the bodyguard and was met by a familiar wall of male conviction that resolved only a moment or two later into wiry power, muscle, a dark skin, long braids tied back in a gold tail, heavy brows, eyes like liquid death. There was nothing about Hakka that didn't belong to her. He might as well have been an additional limb, so much he was part of her person.

Tzaban looked back at the Empress and then searched for Borze, found him kneeling on the carpet, head bowed.

This time there was no velvet weight on his own neck. Tzaban knelt anyway, on one knee, feeling the run suddenly as an aching pull in his legs. The Empress was the focus of his attention, drawing it out of him as surely as if she'd sliced him up and pulled out his guts. Her energy was phenomenal. He couldn't reconcile it with that slight, unimportant form. It seemed to belong to something much bigger and more impressive than a simple human woman. When he closed his eyes he saw something he didn't understand. Eight. She was one but to the power of eight. He opened his eyes and looked up.

The girl spoke in a soft voice; she sounded like a dutiful daughter. 'Please be at ease, gentlemen. No ceremony now. We have had enough of that today. This is an informal meeting.' Even her voice was ordinary. There was a croak in it from a great deal of talking that had gone before. Tzaban vaguely recalled that she held courts all day.

He got up to his feet and stood at his full height. Her throne lifted her high but he was nearly at eye level with her. He did not look at her directly, although Borze did, as though they knew each other well and he was in trust. Tzaban was surprised, even more so by her faint but sincere smile as the general spoke.

'Your descent has spared me a difficult journey.'

The Empress waved a hand, dismissing his thanks. 'I saw no other course of action that left any of us with good face. This way I look commanding and you look honoured, our party will be extended across the city and everyone in the ensuing celebrations gabbles about our guest here without actually seeing him any more.'

Borze nodded, looking quite boyish under her approval suddenly. The Empress turned her oddly serene regard to Tzaban. He assumed from her statement she intended to incarcerate him. Her words remained directed at Borze.

'What report do you have of him now that you have had a chance to observe?'

Borze looked straight ahead. 'He is as he claimed, a survivor, a fighter, capable of training others.'

The Empress wrinkled her nose. 'No, but really.'

Borze relaxed abruptly as if he'd had his strings cut. 'I can't find any sign of misdoing in him. He goes where he's told and does his duties. If he has a vice I don't see it. Doesn't spend money on anything but food and not much of that.'

'How disarmingly dull,' the Empress tapped her fingers on the arm of the throne and looked at Hakka who had not moved in all the time they had been speaking. 'What say you, Hakka?'

The guard shifted his weight slightly, looking at Tzaban with a flat, immovable gaze. Tzaban made himself look down at the floor though it cut him half through to do it.

Hakka's voice was so low it had a resonance Tzaban could

feel in his gut. 'Highly dominant. Full of secrets. Waiting for something. Not immediately dangerous but potentially so. A master of energy. Jai Karoo, a shapeshifter, by his smell. He has been here before, I recognise his presence, though I didn't know it at the time.'

Tzaban's eyes flicked back up to Hakka almost against his will. He had no idea how this man knew so much.

'Well, Tzaban, your posture fools nobody here, stand tall and be yourself,' the Empress said in her soft voice.

He straightened but he didn't square off with Hakka, he kept that man and Borze at oblique angles. To his surprise the Steppelander relaxed, and that sudden permission allowed him to do the same. Borze seemed unaware of the exchange. Tzaban decided to speak his mind and dare the consequences.

'Why is it so many of your people are blind to their instincts?'

The Empress put her head on one side, considering. 'Are you referring to the natural order of power between individuals?'

Borze stared at him, rightly looking as if he felt insulted by the charge but Tzaban had no time for such things and ignored this. 'Yes.'

'I am not sure they are blind, it is simply not the focus of their attention, as it is yours.'

'It affects them, but they act as if it also affronts them,' Tzaban said, pursuing slowly, stalking. 'As if it is theirs to change, but make no effort to change.' The language was hard; words bad enough but worse in the foreign tongue. He hoped that his tone and the attitude of his body correctly filled in the missing gaps and showed his patience, puzzlement, distrust and respect.

'I am sure it does affront them very much,' the Empress said, sitting back and drawing her legs up under the white dress until she sat inside the throne's seat completely, arms wrapped around her knees like a little girl. 'It is our fancy to imagine we have outgrown our primal natures and educated ourselves away from their grip upon our actions. I doubt there is a mage or a vaut in the Empire who doesn't consider themselves superior to those we term animals and lesser. And they include most of the less magical population in those categories.'

He hadn't expected her to be so candid.

There was a small commotion and the guards on the door opened it suddenly, causing them all to turn and look, led by Hakka. His continued calm informed Tzaban this was someone he knew who posed no kind of danger though Tzaban's nose suddenly told him he should lie flat and try nothing. His skin crawled with the need to do that as he remained standing at the Empress' command; he didn't understand and froze solid, fight in his limbs so intense that they started to twitch.

The Empress craned her neck without otherwise moving and then sat up as she saw who it was and clapped her hands once in pleasure,

'Master Night! Thank you for coming at such short notice.'

Tzaban turned and Borze made an awkward salute – one of many they seemed to drag out for various occasions and which Tzaban had learned indicated an acknowledgement of a social equality but a spiritual deference to the receiver. The second part of the gesture, indicated by the depth of the head dip and retreat, was significant. He longed to escape. Night smelled strange but the Empress overpowered that and he was now only a polite toy, able to move and talk by her will alone.

'Honoured Guest Tzaban, this is our most valued Master of the Call, Parlumi Night,' the Empress said, her tone glowing with affection and a tinge of mischief.

The woman – no, the man, Tzaban thought, correcting himself and then suddenly being plunged into profound doubt. He stalled into a mental and physical silence on that point of identification, awed by his own inability to decipher the gender or the identity of the person as they flowed towards him. He was forced to assess them point by point instead of as a whole.

Parlumi Night moved in soft, liquid curves, a ballooning,

complicated gown emphasising and following every gesture in vast trails of ribbons ranging from white to dark charcoal grey. The curves and the sensuality spoke of women to Tzaban, but the authoritative power of the stride and the juggernaut energy of the progress, as relentless as it was graceful, said that this was a male in command of a territory. A smell of mineral elements, warm animal musk and flowers washed up his nostrils in a tide of further confusions. His nose, never faltering, informed him this was a female in oestrus. It was also male and considered itself unassailable and on home ground.

As a final desperate act, one he never normally resorted to, he looked into the face.

It was no help. Handsome, delicate, made-up and strong, it looked back at him and enjoyed his astonishment with the kind of expression that suggested this was a very great pleasure indeed. The smile was, if anything, more disarming than the rest put together. The smile would be happy to eat him alive.

There was only one word really to describe such a biological mixup with that kind of mind in residence and that power of spirit animating it. Parlumi Night may have looked human but her resemblance to most of them ended right there. Tzaban knew Karoo when he smelt it.

'I thought you'd like to meet up,' the Empress said.

Tzaban looked at her directly. 'Who else knows?'

'Nobody outside this room, I can assure you,' the Empress said. 'What ARE you doing here, Tzaban? Why now?'

At her tone, Hakka relaxed and leaned on his polearm, fixing Tzaban with a heavy, interested gaze. Tzaban felt, bizarrely, that he was among friends. Borze also turned. Parlumi Night stood, politely attentive.

He gathered his words carefully, turning them over in his mind before he spoke, to be sure. 'You are fighting a war you cannot win. All of you will die. I have come to persuade you to stop.'

The Empress frowned and the sense of her presence increased

dramatically. He felt the other seven focus their entire attention on him and knew then they were truly different people, not some odd eight-spirited person. They saw through her. He knew of shamans like this in the high north, but this felt different and he didn't have the ability to see how.

Tzaban waited.

'What makes you so sure?' the Empress asked.

'You're fighting the Karoo now,' he said. 'All Karoo. Not just in the south. Karoo are one, like you and the others in your mind. Step back into the plains, mountains, deserts – all the places the humans live – and it will be over. Continue to the forest and it will also be over. Karoo need the forest. We already let you roam everywhere else you are able. But you will not have the forest. Retreat or push on. Live, or die.' The speech exhausted him.

Borze was scowling, thinking hard but he wasn't going to speak. Parlumi Night's eyes glittered with feeling but even she would not interrupt the Empress' gentle silence.

'If this was your purpose, Tzaban, why didn't you talk to me first? Instead you come to the gate, ask for the general and seek employment like any hired mercenary.'

'I was studying you close by. Karoo ignore humans, mostly. Only where we are forced into the same region, then we look, listen. We see your activity in the land and water, in the air. But don't know you. I came to learn.'

'Alone? Into the middle of the enemy? Just like that? They send just one man?'

'Not all Karoo could come here. Maybe only I would come.' He glanced at Parlumi Night, shimmering in her dark robes, unsettled. 'But some others must have been before.'

The Empress was on the edge of her throne. 'Who were you to report to?'

Tzaban stared at her, blinking through the question. 'No one.'

'Who is your commander? Who is in charge?'

Tzaban met her soft, grey gaze. He wanted to please her very much but he had only the truth to offer. 'No one.'

'If you know so little about us how is it that you know I am joined to the other seven Empresses?' Her manner remained girlish but the pressure she was exerting now, chemically, was so seductive and compelling he felt entranced almost to make up answers in order to satisfy her. He recognised this but had no defence.

'They are here,' he sketched his hand in front of his face, to show her that he saw them in hers.

She sat back. 'Are all Karoo like you?'

He glanced at Parlumi Night, not understanding why she would say something like that, as part Karoo herself, when the answer must be obvious. 'No.'

'How many are like you?' the Empress asked. 'Like ... cat people.'

Tzaban looked at her, the soft scent pressing at him. 'I don't know. Some. Maybe.'

She scowled, impatience arrowing at him. 'What do you mean? Where are you from? Borze says the north. Your kind live in the north?'

'Some Karoo live in the north. But only I am like me. Among those in that camp most are shamans, but not like others. They want to be alone.' A massive gulf opened before him. He must explain things and bridge it, but he stalled, unable even to start. 'I had to leave them. Was not like them.'

Parlumi Night stepped forwards, breaking the rigid framework that held him in place. 'Don't worry so. Our ignorance of Karoo is legendary stuff. Come, why don't we eat and drink and you can explain a little more?'

Tzaban stared at her, unable to believe she had broken the Empress' rapture at all, and was not being rebuked. Instead, the Empress clapped her hand to her mouth before removing it to say, 'You're right! Borze, go summon the girls. Food and drinks.

106

We'll go into the Lounge. Too too focused in here. What was I thinking?' She hesitated then and turned back to him. 'Tzaban, are you for men or women? Or ... no ... well ... are ... Do you, would you ... Parlumi, help me!'

Parlumi Night smiled and the room darkened to Tzaban, as if a new, particular night was falling; the soft and seductive dusk of spring evenings. He realised belatedly that this was the reason for her name.

'I do not require a mate,' he said, feeling defensive hackles rise.

Parlumi Night looked him in the eye and her gaze seemed to lengthen as her eyes narrowed, drawing thoughts to a close. 'You are mistaken,' she said. Tzaban did not falter but she shrugged softly as if he had. 'It is females for him in any case, but he's not like these lollygagging Steppelords, all macho honour and command and fake restraint.' Here she shot Hakka a wry glance but he pointedly ignored her. 'He is slightly unnerved by us as too alien, as well he might be. Hence he declines. I wonder ... Perhaps you wouldn't mind my student joining us?'

'Hey!'

Tzaban was startled by a shove and the voice. He looked to his side as he staggered and saw Hakka, who had jolted him, looking at him with knowing and amusement, also warning. The urge to fight subsided. Too late he realised his hands were flexing and stalled them. He bowed to the Empress but she was looking at Night. He inclined his head one degree in thanks for being prevented from issuing Night an open challenge, which would have been disastrous.

'*You* took a student?' the Empress was saying.

Night shrugged, 'One does as one sees fit, no?'

'Yes but ... You never take students.' The Empress was both amused and somehow disheartened by a surprise. 'I distinctly recall you saying you would never take another student after Zharazin Mazhd as long as you lived, though you were always close-mouthed as to why.'

'Well, things change, don't they?' Night said and the two of them shared a glance that promised there would be some form of explanation or reckoning later on.

'In that case, by all means, we would be most interested to see said changes in action,' the Empress agreed. She stood up and beckoned them all, looking at Hakka until he left Tzaban and came to her side. 'To the Lounge.'

Tzaban was seated on his own rug as part of a circle that placed him opposite the Empress. She put Hakka next to him, Night on the other side between them. Borze she placed between herself and her guard. Runner girls were sent out for supplies and to fetch Night's student. He didn't miss Night's gaze close on him as the girl in question was escorted into their midst. If Night wanted some special information by viewing his reaction he could hardly conceal it.

She was small, young and pale, wearing what he came to know as scholar's robes – a huge swathing affair of greys. Its cowl was back, revealing her face, wan, tired, nervous. She had pale hair of the kind Tzaban associated with inherited weakness but her expression defied that. He saw a relentless kind of intelligence in her eyes. She was at a cycle point that made her interesting, but not compelling. When she saw Borze nothing flickered in her facial composure but her hands shook. Tzaban sniffed the air compulsively and concluded they had mated recently. The entire city reeked of sex, it was not surprising in itself. But she and he both seemed to think it was and that puzzled him. He looked at Hakka, his touchstone.

Hakka was looking at Night's student with recognition of some kind, but his interest was other than sexual. Tzaban wondered if it was because she was so young, could not be more than sixteen, he thought, or because of some other feature that marked her out. He looked at the Empress and saw the similarities between the two as the Empress herself rose to make formal introductions. A glance passed between them that was purely two young girls acknowledging each other as simple peers, looking to see if each was friend or rival.

Tzaban knew of no other place ruled by women than the Empire. He knew this young Empress was an anomaly – most of the commanding powers were offices held by mature if not old matrons, but these two together suddenly hit him like a bolt between the eyes. He saw hope, life, fertility, power... He blinked and the moment passed. He heard the others speaking as his mind tried to grasp something alien and profoundly important. Alien, familiar, it danced just out of reach. He unfocused, sitting still, barely conscious of his surroundings so that when the student turned to him he could only blink his eyelids low and let his chin drop to mark greeting her.

Her name circled with the insight in his mind. Isabeau Huntingore. They became tangled, irretrievably. He did not know why the Empire pursued its war with the Karoo, but he did understand now that there was some hope of his mission succeeding. He felt that these humans might survive an introduction. Blinking, he found Parlumi Night observing him.

'To return to our most interesting subject,' she said, clearly meaning him. 'What exactly do you mean that the northern Karoo are not like you? How?'

'I was outcast,' he admitted and felt the bite of that humiliation and rage all anew. He had to rake a hand through his hair to smooth it down, stall his aggression. 'I was, am, throwback. They were peaceful. I am not. They are joined... like you...' He looked at the Empress. 'But I am not. Not with them. I ruined their unity. And,' he waved a hand down the length of himself to indicate he meant physically, 'I do not resemble them. I am for fighting. They are for peace. They are part of the Karoo inner creation. Dreamers. I outside that. I into the world. No place with them more. No place anywhere.'

Now they were all staring at him. He sat like stone.

'But I thought you said you had a mission. Who sent you?'
'I did.'

The Empress looked at him. 'You're alone?' she asked finally, all her thoughts dropping to that. He saw disappointment, disturbance.

'Yes. No. No Karoo is alone. All Karoo are one. I am not with them. Not same as alone.' But he wondered if it was.

Hakka spoke, 'No two Karoo are physically alike. All of them seem to have a mental connection – hm, not like Imperial telepaths – there are no words involved as I understand it. They just know what's going on when they choose to link up.'

Tzaban burned to know how the Steppe man knew this but he did not speak.

Hakka looked at him, 'Are you locked out of that speech? Is that what you mean by not with them?'

'Yes,' Tzaban said, continually surprised by Hakka's very un-Steppe behaviour and manner of talking, his very Steppe posturing, intended to demonstrate clearly that there was one Lord of the lands and everyone could fuck off if they didn't like it. To the Empress, Hakka showed almost no deference but Tzaban had no doubt if she had ordered it he would have cut his own head off without a second thought. This un-tallying between thought and action, body and mind, bothered him like flies.

'Why?' Night asked. Her voice was honeyed, a coat on its intrusive curiosity.

Tzaban fumbled about in their too many words. 'The tribe in the north, all tranquil. I am not. Told me to get out, head south, to places you are fighting. Or just go. I ruin their dream. Ruin their peace. Not welcome any more.'

He did not mention when this had happened, how many years had passed and how slow his progress south had been, that instead of passing through many foreign territories he had lingered here to watch and study creatures that seemed more like

110

him than his own kind. Those illusions had died by now. Living on the Steppe had done that: Steppe humans led harsh lives which he would not have minded but for the frequent brutality. He had been thrown out for aggression, but their daily petty cruelties, their culture, depressed him. He'd lived apart from them too, paying visits, and being visited by those who thought he had shaman powers to invest in them. When he didn't they let him alone.

Living here seemed, even after a few days, impossibly hard in a completely different way. A year of spying had brought only a superficial notion of the reality and to understand it was beyond him. Only despair would have brought him here. He hadn't recognised it until now.

Night's student opened her mouth, glanced at the Empress, at Night, and then said, 'Do you speak for the Karoo?'

He attempted the truth again, sliding off its precipitous faces. 'They do not know my words or deeds, but I speak as if for them, what they would say. Your trespass is not allowed. You will be consumed if you do not retreat. Please retreat.'

'But you're here talking for yourself, they didn't ask you to come,' she said, unnecessarily he felt. So many repeats.

'They did not ask me to come. I speak for myself. I speak for them.'

The Empress turned to the general. 'Borze, what exactly has he done here?'

Tzaban waited, grateful to be out of central attention.

'Trained mercenary recruits in survival, fitness.'

'Did you ever see him fight?'

'No.'

'Tzaban. You were outcast for breaking the peace. Why? What exactly did you do?'

They were masterful in not staring at him.

'I broke their dream.' He knew that would not be enough. 'Not did something. Am predator. Not fitting. Bad dreams.' He

111

felt hopeless in his stuttering and looked at Night, wondering why she did nothing to help when she must know how to say these things. In that glance he saw she didn't. She was not *enough* Karoo. 'How did you get made?' he asked her, searching for anything.

'No idea,' she said in her purple voice. 'They found me at the city gate in a sack.' Her near-black eyes bored at him as if she'd drill out the answers she wanted but she didn't speak. At least in that moment she was Karoo.

Tzaban nodded. The scent of the Empress, soothing and heavy, filled his nostrils. He almost dozed and the words of his only significant question fell from his mouth like dislodged stones tumbling down a hill. 'Why did you attack us?'

'We didn't.' The Empress said. 'You attacked us.'

Tzaban lifted his head against the pressure of her, looked at her plain girlish face with its eightfold gaze on him. Paused.

'You seem baffled,' the Empress said.

He had no answer. But if she was lying he could not detect it.

Borze spoke, his voice gravelled with disuse, 'Is it so impossible?'

Tzaban nodded. 'Only attack for trespass, or killing. Stealing maybe.'

Borze looked at him, grim-faced. 'Could you be mistaken?'

'No.'

The Empress nodded. 'I have reason to believe you are right.'

Borze shot a look of pure surprise at her. Only Hakka seemed unmoved by the news.

The Empress waved her hands, a grey look about her. 'Enough for today.'

Borze began to protest but a flick of her finger cut him off mid breath. 'I know, I know. Just go. We will meet again tomorrow.' They left without a word.

Once they had all gone she turned to one of her runners. 'Give me half an hour and then bring Alide.'

CHAPTER EIGHT

TRALANE

Tralane lay awake into the night, staring at the dusty bed drapes overhead, thinking that one day soon she ought to get up there and unhook them for a good cleaning. The dust was actually collecting into balls in the glamorous dips of the red voile, balls that were even visible as spheres of shadow in the piercing light of Annasmoon.

Ann was close today, on her third swingby of the year. Across the city, astrologers' lights burned late into the night as they cast auspices for the followers of Anngwyn, laughing and dancing goddess of the moons. Annasmoon was the largest of the five Lilypads of Anngwyn and subject to the most intense prayers. Tralane could see the lights from her window and just hear music from somewhere between her house and the palace wall but the wind was in the wrong direction to bring any more stray news, be it melodies or cooking smells. Tralane kept an ear out for sounds of shattering that might signal the party in the Solar breaking important things, but so far only shrieking had pierced the calm of the house. She heard the cats walking around on the loose boards, making their nightly mousecapade runs. She listened for, but did not hear, the rattle and whirr of the elevator car from the street to the first floor which would have brought Isabeau home. But it wasn't only this that kept her awake.

She kept thinking about the crystals.

If Alide was making weapons with them, he had to be getting the rest of the tech from somewhere, and why was she the one having to supply the key component? Anyone able to use, modify or access that kind of device had to be able to make recordings, didn't they? The Empire was short on airships and small planes but not so short they couldn't have used one to make the trips. Until now she'd mostly been so panicked about her situation as his little minion that she hadn't done anything other than scamper to obey and pray he took no further interest in her daughters. But now she had the luxury of another sleepless night staring at drape dust it started to occur to her that this miserable little fiasco was more troubling than it looked.

She battered her mind against it for half an hour, then as the bell towers softly chimed the night tones for midnight she gave up. Do her bit and get out or snoop, think and find more trouble? That seemed straightforward...

She heard a tread that was heavier than a cat outside. One, two, the top of the staircase, three and creak... Up to her door. The knock very quiet in case she was sleeping.

For a second she fought it out: lie awake following mental thought trains steaming in and out of hopeless, empty stations or derail everything until the morning and get at least some sleep? Oh, no contest. Especially since Jard could help her find Isabeau later.

'Come in,' she called out softly.

Jardant let himself in and closed the door. 'You should be asleep.'

'So should you.' Tralane flipped the bedcovers back and watched him as he undressed.

'I had to wait until the bread was done.' He posed

unconsciously, making all the angles that showed off his muscular body, proud of himself as well he might be.

'I see you got rid of those tan lines,' she said. The curve of his buttocks was perfectly hemispherical and no longer clearly two-toned. Even in the violet shadows of the moonlight she could see it was a single colour and pictured the dark bronze with a sigh.

'I went up on the secondary decks,' he said. 'Clearing out those sheds up there like you suggested. Not too overlooked, seemed a shame not to lie out there.' He left his clothes at the end of the bed and climbed in, a familiar ease she so loved to see moving his limbs effortlessly into position over her, his knees knocking hers apart with friendly insistence. He was already hard and risen.

She pouted at him and he grinned, relenting, 'Oh all right.'

His pretend reticence amused her. She never knew if he was kidding or not but he moved up the bed easily and looked down, making pleased nonsense noises as she let his warm, heavy cock batter her lips a few times in play before licking all of its deliciousness into her mouth. She missed the heady thrill of having a lover she was in love with but Jard's easy affection was butter and sugar, caramel-good and the delight of this pleasure and his generosity was enough to be grateful for.

When she had satisfied herself on him he settled down on his elbows and they shared a smile as he penetrated her. Jard and she had an expert ease about it now; he made it effortlessly to full embrace in one move. She wrapped her legs around his waist. With him all there, so hard and real and loving, she couldn't think about anything but how good it felt; she forgot everything, exactly as planned. They shared kisses of fondness, moving together, until it grew too intense and then she luxuriated in gazing at his handsome face and body as he worked and she laid back in the pillows, lazily bringing herself up to orgasm with her fingers as she watched him. He timed it so that he hit his peak a few moments after her, drawing hers out with his. She wondered briefly about the runner, but didn't ask him. As he rolled his heavy weight to the side and withdrew to lie on his back and catch his breath she stroked him gently on his chest and arm.

'Thank you.' She was always polite.

He smiled, eyes closed. 'Most of the stuff in those sheds was salvaged for raw materials. What's left isn't much more than slag. I've separated it out by whatever it seems to be made of and later I'll go through and pull out any rare metal or crystal. What about the rest?'

She couldn't care less at that point in time, wondering how he always managed to get back to work so fast. 'Sell it for meltdown. You can keep forty per cent, for your labour.'

He reached over and took her hand in his. 'I guess it isn't the market values of scrap keeping you awake.'

'Isabeau isn't back yet.' She rubbed his thumb with hers gently. 'And I got a letter inviting me to a meeting with Borze.'

'Oh, the army must have got wind of your research.' Jard squeezed her hand briefly. 'Or they want to take your Flit.'

Tralane actually hadn't thought of that. Now that she did she frowned. 'Because of the Karoo, surely?'

'How many Sircenes do you know still actually getting their hands dirty on salvage?' he said.

Now she thought of it, not too many. 'You're supposed to take my mind off things, not put more on it.'

'Want me to go look for Isabeau?'

Tralane stared up at her dust balls. No, she wasn't going to be one of those precious magi mothers keeping tabs on her grown daughters' every move. 'Yes, please.'

'Sure she didn't go back to her old web?'

'No. But she didn't send a message.'

'Any clues?'

116

'Am I being a fool? She could easily have gone back to the Sorority of the Star and forgotten to write.'

He didn't reply immediately, then said, 'I'll walk over there and see. If not, what should I do?'

She felt stupid. 'No, don't. I don't want them thinking I don't know where she is.'

Jard sighed and rolled over. 'Where else would she have gone?'

'The Library.'

'Shut hours ago.'

'Then I've no idea.' There. She'd admitted it. Every piece of foolery was exposed. She both cared too much and didn't know enough. Crossly she got up and pulled on her clothing, realising only as she was zipping it up that she'd put on her flight silks.

'You're flying at night?'

'Easy with those goggles. Now, where are they?'

'Think you'll find them in the observatory with whatever's left alive of Minna's party,' Jard said, yawning.

'Oh, what idiot gave them to her?'

'You did.'

'Stay here and keep things warm. I'll be back.'

Jard yawned and nodded, rolling his eyes at the same time as he snuggled into the pillows.

Tralane left the door ajar in case Isa came back and needed to find someone in, then marched towards the observatory, taking the staircases two at a time in an effort to wake herself up when her body was grumbling that it would much rather be asleep. She let herself into the observatory as quietly as she could, some part of her wanting to sneak up and find out what was going on even though it would annoy Minna. Because it would. She paused in the doorway when she found the lights out. There in the dark as she expected the rugs and corners were lumped up with various pairings from the web, quietly into each other or

117

playing card games, drinking, their hands alone lit by the glowfly magelights of their minor powers.

She was caught by the sight of Minnabar, seated in the command chair beside the astroscope. She was lolling there, kicking one foot, the goggles strapped to her face. Her head was thrown back, staring out into the night sky through the long slit of the observatory's gaping roof hatch. A long, smoking cigarillo dangled in her fingertips, sweet fumes giving away its relative innocence – hard drugs were for master alchemists or those of sterner constitutions than a Sircene adolescent's. Her other hand was slowly adjusting some of the dials on the side of the goggles. Her mouth was partly open, lower lip bitten in concentration. A pang went through Tralane at seeing her alone there, but it was the alone of choice, not exile and the pang felt like pride. She stepped quietly forwards and made some noise as she got closer.

'Minna, I need my goggles back.'

Minnabar jumped, sat up suddenly and cracked her forehead on the low overhang of the astroscope's eyepieces. She cursed and pulled the goggles off her head. 'Mom! What the frack?'

Tralane held out her hand and Minna dumped the heavy item into it, getting up, rubbing her forehead, scowling. 'Where are you going anyway? What's with the...' She paused, realising the eyes of the web were upon her, at least those able to look her way. Tralane saw her hitch up her poise and smoothly correct herself. 'Take them. Your beast man is very beast-laaaay.' She drew out the last syllable a long way, mocking him and Tralane both with it, withdrawing herself entirely from any group that might have an interest in such a boring creature.

'Glad you won't be wanting them again, then,' Tralane retorted without a second's hesitation and walked out. Outside the room she leaned on the closed door, eyes shut. One day she'd realise she wasn't supposed to compete with her own daughters. One day. Then her self-pity annoyed her and she stood up, snapped on witchlight with her fingers and followed the halls and turns to the elevator and on up into the heights of the Array.

It was colder higher up and she was glad to get into the leather flight suit's outer casings and stuff her hair into the heavy helmet. She set the goggles over the top, firmly, and it was only when the Flit was out of the shed and sitting quietly in the storm's aftermath of light winds that she reached up and wondered what it was that Minna had been looking at.

Without adjusting the controls she set the eyepieces in place and lifted her head to look at the sky. There was a lot of light from the city's glowing werelit spires and all the high antennae that winked in reds and greens, but this was cut back to a glow at the edges of vision. Beyond that, where her naked eyes would have seen the familiar constellations, she saw a vast blackness, but judging by the tracking speed and run numbers she was looking very far out – the distance finder when she located it at last, after an age of squinty prodding, revealed it was focusing light from over twenty klicks out. She would have expected that for stargazing. Then her finger slipped and there was a pop and whirr from the goggles and a sudden rising high-pitched whine that was the sort of noise that never sounded good. The viewfinder gibbered visually, flashing and sparking.

'Oh come on!' Tralane muttered in desperation searching to press any key, any place, that would restore them. She feared with horrible, impending dread that she'd broken the damn things. Then there was a low clunk, which she felt, as if something had clicked over inside them. Something the size and colour of a silver coin whizzed across the viewfinder and was gone. She tried to track back and it whizzed past the other way at high speed. After a few moments of neck-aching effort she managed to make her moves so small she was sure that it was an object very far away she was looking at and finally, by leaving the Flit and bracing her head at a painful angle against

119

the wall in the lee of the old flight tower, she was able to gape up at the thing hanging there against the ink black of the night.

It was roughly spherical, silvery grey. It had angular designs on its surface. It had a receiver dish. It had antennae, short and stubby. There was an odd glowing field around it, a larger sphere, that flickered occasionally in the same way as a bad electrical connection. It was absolutely and unmistakably a piece of engineering. She fumbled, trying to find the record controls, but then, a smarter and more self-preserving bit of her mind made her take the goggles off slowly without moving her head. She held them at her side and found herself looking up at Makto, Saint's Star, which had for lifetimes upon lifetimes been a minor part of the small constellation Agvan, Priestess of Memory. It was a small star, almost invisible to her from here, in the city.

She looked a few more times. To be sure. To know, for certain, what nobody else knew or had ever suspected. Then, because she already had planned it, she pushed the Flit out, braced the wings and pushed it to the runway. She reset the goggles to see in reduced light, taking out the diffusions of the city's blur, until they tracked her pupils and focused with her, on the streets of the Gleaming below or even the landbound parts of Glimshard far beneath.

It bothered her, as she circled slowly, that Makto was only apparently forty thousand klicks out. She knew that no stars could be so close. It was ridiculous. But then, so was being able to see that far away. In fact, she was minded to think it was impossible. These two things alone were fascinating. But to have a star become a small, created piece of technology – THAT was beyond her ability to comprehend right now. So, instead of trying to, she let it alone and took a route that avoided the palace air flight patrols to scan the streets below and pretend that she was not looking for Isabeau, was not about to fly over the barracks and see if the Karoo was out under the moon, howling, or whatever he did on a night. Probably sleep, said her wiser self. Probably fast asleep.

But as she soared, finding the thermals coming out of the alchemical works, she was able to look over the side and take her time to enjoy the view. Her control of the basic instruments was second nature to her hands and feet, and the goggles, connected to her aetheric bridge, tracked her intent with precision.

Thus it was that she watched the late night raking of the parade yards and the slow, steady return of the general to his lit apartments overlooking the same. He passed alone in his heavy formalwear, with the ease of a man far from war and in no way worried about whatever infomancers might be trailing him. She wondered what kind of a headworld he lived in to feel so secure and for a moment envied him ferociously. Then she turned towards the white curlicues of the Sou'Western end, where Isa would be if she had gone back to her web full of those icy, frigid bitches... Tralane caught herself. No, they were not. They were nice, pleasant and slightly overacademic women who had decided to channel everything into their hunt for knowledge and the recovery of lost skills. It was noble and nearly saintly. She was almost one of them, and still she wanted to puke every time she saw Isabeau in those pretentious grey robes... Her hand on the control rod juddered and the Flit, always unforgiving, went into a port slew that she irritably corrected, lining herself up with other towers to be sure not to hit anything while she ogled away.

There were no people in the streets of that district. They were all abed, she thought, of course, or else taking light snacks and educational conversations before retiring. Belatedly she recognised the grumping of her stomach as envy. Why should she be envious? Because her house rotted while theirs prospered on? She was her own mistress. But so were they. And their magic and their skills were evident across the city written in hard light and the smooth function of every civil piece of infrastructure from the stem to the elevators and even the drains, while she grubbed her attics and came up with, well, with goggles and a gun, and some weapons of mass destruction.

Anyway, there was no sign of Isabeau. She had to admit she had never really believed there would be. If she was in the Sorority house she would be asleep in her cloister well out of sight. At least, Tralane felt, she had managed to prove there were no people out lying dead or assaulted. But even this effort was a weak failure at covering her embarrassment at her own anxiety. The cause of that was not the sisterhood of course. It was Alide.

Her turn towards the Ministry was automatic. She glided smoothly across the quads of the colleges, the rising pomposity of the administrative architecture that had been cut off by the previous Empress and rendered into large gardens instead of a bulky fortress. There she saw a black group marching purposefully and amid them the small, hustling form of the man she detested. They were moving towards the palace road and runners were with them. An official summons then. Rather late. She wondered why.

Her route then forced her to spiral a little around the busier parts of the city, using the lift of cookhouses, bakeries and the smouldering luxury of forges, to gain some height back again. She thought fondly of her partying days in those narrow alleys, drunk on cheap fizzy grog, kissing whoever had looked good in the bath house a few minutes before – and of course they all looked good seen through drunken eyes... Oh, the hangovers! She was smiling as she turned over the Rose, not least because of her clear head, and then realised that she could, if she wanted to, slip over the dark and uninviting draperies that shrouded the infomancer's Domicile with such exotic glooms. They were old and tattered, fallen away. Shrazade had no intent of spending money on frippery like that when she could be using it elsewhere. Romance be damned. She was known for her hard head and harder heart.

It was dangerous however. They had anti-aircraft defences although none allowed to be used against the palace air corps.

Tralane took a guessed vector and slipped along the edge of their walls. She peered intently.

Between the ragged edges of the drapes she saw into glass-roofed rooms, pristine and white. She saw unknown machines. She saw the infomancers in their grey and black uniform dress at work steadily, lying in slings or splayed on the floor, bodies abandoned as their minds flew far and wide into unknown worlds that they created or which created them; she wasn't sure how it worked. Their magic was beyond her ability to comprehend. She knew only what was written in stories about them, or in their known records. Down there all the messages of the Empire were passed and sorted, known, fixed, interfered with... The infomancers could build structures from thin air, and speak to each other across infinite distances. And some of them, yes, were more ordinary spies of course. Everything has its darker edges.

Without warning, a shot arrowed up from between the angles of the silk banners. Tralane saw it as a flare of vivid purple streaking into her field of vision, impossibly brilliant like an emergency flare. She tried to avoid it automatically but the Flit was much too slow. The dark bolt clipped the Flit's wing and sent her into a slew so that she had to fight and think hard to find corrective manouevres. She managed to get into clear air away from the Domicile but she had lost so much height that she'd crash into a building before she made the next thermal source. With a sinking heart she realised two key points. One was that her wing was now on fire. A black and purple flame crept slowly across it in a smokeless menace that looked worse than an ordinary fire somehow. The other was that the only way to gain enough altitude to go home was to employ sorcery.

In a city of mages that was hardly news but Tralane's Sircene sorcery was something that could not go unnoticed. She wouldn't care under ordinary circumstances. One matter transmutation was minor, if technically illegal outside a controlled laboratory within the city limits, but now Shrazade would surely know who had been idly looking and, worse yet, Alide would eventually discover her moment of idiocy. What he would do about it...

She was about to lose control, her speed so low. Without a second thought she reached inside for her ability. A powerful draught of hot air bloomed under her wings and shot her skywards in a terrifying piston of speed so fierce the burning wingtip cracked and, with a groan and a sputter, then a thrum and a scream, the Flit's tiny engine yowled protest as it was simultaneously revved by massively multiplied explosive force within its cylinders. She found herself just north of her own house in a helter-skelter spiral. She heard the engine head crack with a horrible, bone-rattling bang just after. Real, orange fire waved at her from the prop end, black smoke streaking with it. And then she was in a second by second battle to keep her position, using heated blasts of air to stall her, change direction and adjust her angles.

After what seemed a painful age of waiting to die and fighting not to the Flit landed on the deck like the plummeting heap of junk it now was. The undercarriage at least held. It bounced, rolled and skidded to a halt. She had just time to prise herself out of the harness and jump free. A second later and she'd iced the engine and the wing but her pride and joy was a smoking wreck. After so little practice she ought to have been relieved she hadn't blown herself up. Energy from alchemic conversions was hard enough to manage at the best of times. Reversing was ten times worse. She'd been superlative. She deserved a commendation.

She put her face into her gauntlets and yelled at the top of her lungs.

When she'd exhausted every swear word she knew and felt that tears threatened instead she made herself fold up the Flit and put it away properly. She had begun to shake and weaken with the ominous onset of aetheric fatigue by the time she was done, but she put up her small werelight and studied her burned wing by its glow. The goggles confirmed the worst. The magical bolt was Lucent technology, a spell of finding and searching, of marking indelibly. Standard shot for spies, she thought. Tracing you this way was easy. If she left it the spell could easily reactivate from the dormant stains in the canvas and wood and slowly creep down through her house transmitting a steady stream of information back into the Domicile. She'd half a mind to let it. Maybe her junk would fill their heads up and constipate them fatally. But no. With a bitter feeling of defeat she extended her hand over the purple marks and dismantled the spell's structure, taking most of the wing tip with it. A better mage would have been more delicate. Tralane's efforts were more butchery than finesse. She watched the objects gleam and disperse, felt the hot, buzzing flow of the siphons shift the mass to energy and information, easing them into temporary vaultspace. Her aptitude separated the bolt virals from the originals easily. She let the bolt's potentials back in as heat, to warm herself, and then she remade the wing without the hex, as it had been when she'd left and it was still antique-but-working. Even if the cost of such massive conversion was going to be hell to pay she'd at least protected her home.

Makto shone down at her through the slats of the shed, flickering not with its own fusion but the dysfunctional fields around its puny body. She had the sense to lie down and put her head on her hands before the fatigue and the dreamstorm of transmutational psychosis hit and she blacked out.

Her final coherent thought was petty and recriminating: why the hell couldn't she have just stayed in bed with her damn student?

CHAPTER NINE

ZHARAZIN

Zharazin Mazhd sat outside on the lawyer's balcony wrapped in a bedsheet, smoking. She sat next to him in her half of the sheet doing the same only with much deeper satisfaction. He'd never seen a woman smoke with such focused, intensive pleasure. If he'd had more of an ego it would be bruised by now watching that after what they'd just concluded in the bed behind them. He asked her why she liked it so and she said,

'Tastes of everything I'm not,' she grinned at him, knowing he'd appreciate her remark for the pretend tough it was; that it was and was not the truth, simultaneously. We must rebel, we are the law.

He forgave her instantly. 'Uh huh.'

She slid her cool ankle against his. 'So what were you really doing there tonight?'

'Following someone,' he replied. She had a spectacular view, all over the Glimmering's best angle, whiskery lights above and blazing buildings beneath: the palace, shining as if it was made of diamond, and behind all that the inky night with the Steppe-fires too small to see. Above, only stars and the cool regard of Annasmoon, so subtle it was only felt like whispers on the skin.

She had the sense not to ask who. 'Did you lose them?'

He thought about it. 'No, I don't think so.'

'You don't sound certain.'

He smiled and was surprised when she leaned over and gave him a smoky kiss. 'It's an art, not a science. I found the unexpected. Always good.'

'Even when the quarry gets away?'

'Not the quarry. The lead.'

She nodded thoughtfully, eyes slitted against the smoke as she dragged on the expensive stick. 'Prosecuting is like that. The case, in this case.'

'Not the defendants, the law, the truth?'

'Don't tease me, you bad man.' She blew out, looking through the smoke haze briefly as the wind bore it away. 'I defend ideas against other ideas,' she said after a time. 'I know it ought to be people against other people, but it never is. An army of evidence is assembled, one locates the key pieces, it is a form of game. If one is lucky one may say convincingly "This Happened" but that is not important compared to how much one wants to believe the ideas of what happened and how much the jury wants to believe.'

'That's very cynical.' He finished his cigarette. He didn't enjoy smoking enough to go more than halfway down a stick. The first gulp of the herbal smoke was the best, the hit of the deep calm that followed it like a dive into a dark and silent personal lake. After a minute the mind got used to it, the body exhaled, it was only fooling around. He took the rest to show politely that he appreciated the gift. 'Or it's very calculated. Are you trying to impress me?'

'Pah,' she said quietly. 'What for?'

He waited, sensing she wanted to ask something – something that she could have only reached by the path from picking him up for a job, the dinner, the dance, the bed, the view and the cigarette.

'What is it like in the Domicile?'

He hadn't expected that one. He studied the night view, avoiding looking in the direction of the building itself. 'Quiet,' he said. 'Like a Library.'

'No, I mean, the Infomancy, the feeling of it. You must know so much. How do you keep it organised? How do you prevent yourself confessing?'

'I wouldn't be much of a spy if I told you that,' he said.

'It's not as if I could use the knowledge. Your aptitudes are beyond me. My interrogation techniques are purely verbal and voluntary. Only infomancers may inquire without permission.'

'I'm not doing that.'

'You'd say that obviously.'

'Obviously. But how can I prove it?'

'You were Night's student, I assumed Infomancy was not your primary talent.'

Here we go, he thought. Now we are getting there. Why is it always Night?

'I'm not her student any more.'

'Why, what happened?'

He considered answering. Sharper and more agile minds than hers, with claws and teeth, had asked this of him. His refusal had sent him to Shrazade's personal inquisition. He had resisted her. On nothing else. She knew him inside out and back to front, all except the meaning, the point, the significance and the experience of being Parlumi Night's student. Weeks of darkness, weeks of pain and silence. Threats, made not with words but nightmares. He had never spoken or shared a single moment of it. Sometimes he wondered why it was so important to him. The details, wearingly prosaic after such a massive build-up, could satisfy nobody. They'd certainly never satisfied him.

'I'd rather not say,' he replied finally.

'They do say confession is good for the soul.'

He was glad she had decided not to pursue it. In gratitude he said, 'They're wrong.'

She put out her cigarette beside his in the sand tray by her foot. 'Come back inside.' It was a suggestion, not an order, so he followed it obediently. As he turned to close the shutters he saw a streak of purple fire against the blackness of the stars.

A picture built in his mind, behind his eyes, a composite layered and provided for him by the Relay. He excused himself with some bullshit about having an early start, about not crowding her as he collected his clothing from the floor and the chair. He dressed swiftly and she responded with amused grace, not fooled for a second, before seeing him out barefoot at the door.

'Don't be too long.' She swung around the doorframe by one hand, like a kid, smiling at him. He felt he had made a friend, surprised himself.

'I won't.'

He waited until the pad of her feet had taken her back and then walked to the fire escape slipway. The doors were alarm bolted but his lockpicks opened them with a flutter of sorcerous binary platitudes. Inside the cool tubular chamber he left the racked heatproof pods alone in their netting and tucked in his stray shirttails before sitting on the low friction polycrete and allowing himself to slip away feet-first around the helter-skelter pipe. Around and down he floated, braked at intervals by the automating adjustment of the polycrete's surface to the speed of his descent so that he seemed alternately to rush with silent grace and freedom, then be plucked at by sticky hands, the world turned to glue. He arrived in the featureless dark of the safety bay at ground level – as much as there was such a thing as ground in the Glimmering. At surface level anyway. Getting out required only that he push the door. The clockticker whirred and he heard the quiet clunk as it satisfactorily concluded counting one in and one out of the escape.

The door led out into the rear yards, filled with waste bins and at this time of night the carts and busy dark figures of the Gleaners. Zarazin slipped past them in the shadows and they let him go without comment. The infomancers had them on a significant retainer. He heard their cheerful hummed songs pass between them in a susurrus of question and answer, call and response as their rapid fingers passed over every bit of rubbish, identifying it faultlessly and tossing it into the long rows of baskets on the 'osscart. At the cart head the two tug horses chewed steadily from their nosebags, turning one ear only as he passed them by and emerged into the grand sweep of the halfmoon gardens and their meandering road.

He made quick progress through the deserted high town streets, his route more or less direct to the grand upspiral passage from which the Huntingore mansion rose in steady antique bulwarks towards the sky. As he climbed the outer walls, following the path he'd used before, he signalled back to the Relay that he'd take care of this mission. He felt Shrazade's amusement loitering like a sulky kid in the back of his brain but she had no objections. The Relay's connections faded out gently, like water running down a clear drain, and he was then alone on the increasingly sheer and derelict walls of the towered rise. Before another half hour passed he was glad he'd left the pitons in position. The slender fibre rope uncoiled readily from the pocket in his overcoat. A gift from the Spiderworks, it came with freerunning grips fitted to it or he'd never have been able use its narrow braid without tearing his hands to pieces.

The coat sagged heavily as he climbed on, weighed down at one side by the book he'd saved from the trashcan. His progress up the wall in this place, with this book, tracking that woman made a pleasant spell in his mind. A brimming anticipation filled him like Twogas, lifting him on. At least this time he did not have to wait for hours at the top of the Array. He wriggled over the creaking safety lines of the tower flight deck and paused there only to gather up his rope.

The deck was empty. He'd expected that. She would have had time to land and secure the Flit by now. The Relay had informed him that their cast had been dispelled or at least spoiled, so it was likely the machine was back inside its shed. Thanks to his earlier suffering he knew which dilapidated hovel that was and made his way directly to it across the weed-strewn paving. The Sircene spellwork protected their doors, windows and apertures, he had determined previously, but they did not invest in rooftop surveillance these days. Why would they? He felt like he'd been the first person to come here in decades. Tralane Huntingore's foolishness in leaving matters like this worried him. At the hangar's rotten door he stopped, finding it closed but the locks open. An oversight as she hurried back into the house? He looked over at the stairwell's iron gate. It was slightly ajar.

He curled his gloved fingers around the slippery wood and lifted the door open, trying to support the hinge in case it failed or gave him away with rusted complaints. Before him, the oddly folded shape of the Flit was just detectable in the near-total darkness offered by the gleam of a dying werelight on the floor near his feet. As he glanced down at it he saw a shining tress of coiled black hair.

He was on his knees, stripping his gloves before he had a thought about what he was doing. As his fingers checked the pulse at her throat he conjured his own light, careless of being seen, and set it above them. She lived, but the slow beat and the vanishing werelight that signalled the end of her natural magical energy supply confirmed that she was in hibersleep. The only remedy for it was rest. Zharazin studied her closely for any other signs of injury or infection but he found nothing. Satisfied for now he had to fight a surprisingly strong desire not to leave her side in order to move around and take a tour of the Flit and its condition. It wasn't the desire itself that surprised him – he knew he'd feel that because he'd been around Tralane enough to know that they were a good match for each other; a strong physical response was only to be expected given his talents and her present total vulnerability.

Meanwhile he studied the aircraft for the Infomancy. It showed fire damage and there was a strong smell of kerosene and burning oil that all confirmed the extinction of a significant fire in the engine. He didn't know anything about such objects but even he doubted it would fly again any time soon. Of the tracer spell there was no sign. He checked the ground and the walls but the building was clear. The only conclusion he could draw was that Tralane must have burned it out or undone it. He betted the latter. Combined with controlling the fire, landing and picking out the sorcery no wonder she was comatose. But although this deduction satisfied him enough to transmit his conclusions to the Relay it left a much greater question Shrazade at least would want answered: why was Tralane Huntingore overflying the Domicile?

Her lack of care in security inclined him to believe it was an accident. He hoped it was. She wasn't cut out for covert ops. But it was cold and getting colder, even though the storms had passed. He made his way back around the Flit and bent down again to pick her up, planning to take her into the house and hope that it was uninhabited there and also warm enough to leave her safely. He was just beginning to lift when he heard the scrape of a shoe on wet stone. If he'd just dropped her he would have been fast enough to spin around or duck and roll but as it was he hesitated instead and then felt something blunt, metal and cold shoved against the side of his neck. He didn't know what it was but it didn't feel friendly and the voice that went with it had his death in its future, shaky and breaking as it was,

'What the hell are you doing to my mom?'

'Take it easy,' his practised drawl was steady although he didn't move at all, even though the position, leant over and half lifting was quickly becoming agonising. 'I'm going to take her into the house. That's all.'

There was no lessening of the pressure on his neck. He felt the tremor from the girl's arm coming through the object, the frequency of her panic rising. That he didn't know what it was played entirely to her advantage and he knew he had to control both of them quickly so he started talking.

'In a moment I'm going to count to three. When I get to three I'll stand up and turn around and you can check and see that your mom's all right. Okay?' His own muscles were starting to judder and burn with effort.

The thing withdrew from his neck, although he could feel it brushing his hair.

'Yeah,' the voice was a whisper, all that the owner could choke out.

'One, two, three.' Zharazin straightened up, praying, and slowly turned in little increments until he was facing the girl in the werelight of his own making. Tralane's daughter, he saw, the one that looked just like her. Minnabar. Good thing it wasn't Isabeau or he'd probably be dead by now. He looked at the object in her hand, automatically opening a wideband to the Relayers so they could search their databases and identify it for him. Sircene technology, he thought and they confirmed it a split second later. Yes. It was a gun.

Tralane's head lay against his shoulder, a feat he managed by adopting a hell of a posture part bent backwards. Her dead weight was hard work. He stood very still as the girl peered, unwilling to get any closer to him.

'What are you doing here anyway? Why are you here? You're trespassing. I'm arresting you.'

'All right,' he agreed, thinking this was by far the easiest path for all of them. 'Can we go inside though? It's cold and your mom needs a warm safe place to sleep it off.'

'Sleep what off? What have you done to her?!' The gun shook. The knuckles on the hand holding the gun paled.

Zharazin remained calm and smiled. 'She's in hibersleep. She had to use a lot of magic to land safely.' He met Minnabar's eye steadily, all his facial nuances tuning themselves to the friendly shapes that a lifetime of pleasing others had taught him.

'That explains how she got here. How did you get here?'

Zharazin gave her credit for not wavering. His arms, tired from the climb, hurt in fresh and inexplicable ways. His back hurt. 'I climbed up the side. Can we go in? I can't keep holding her too much longer like this. I need to move.'

She nodded. 'You go first.' Then she backed outside. Her own werelight appeared then, a bright orange sphere that indicated plenty of reserve power. Up on the tips of the aerials the signal lights in red and green surged in brightness as though bolstered. He wondered if this was part of her talent as he followed her in careful steps. As she led them across the flight deck to the house door, watching her footing, keeping the gun level, he let his head bend close to the sweet head on his shoulder and let himself be intoxicated for one moment by the odours of leather and smoke and the repeated reports of her beauty like tiny fireworks in his blood.

But if he thought he got away with it he was mistaken. Minnabar stood aside for him to go first into the house. As he passed her she snorted at him and in the exhalation of her breath, her contempt for whatever she thought he'd done or meant, he smelled her father and mother in her and understood something fleeting and odd about her, himself, the world. He saw her standing on the palm of his hand. He saw Isabeau; white wood stuck in the ground in the tall forest of grey upright trunks. He saw a clockwork object being repaired, unmatched cogwheels meshing together and spinning for the first time in harmony.

Behind his back she closed the door. He heard it clunk shut with a heavy, final sound and the gun nozzle pushed against his back through the coat. 'You're going to go where I say, just because I need you to. After that, you're my prisoner. You do what I say. Understand?' Her voice juddered, squeaked. He smiled although she couldn't see it and walked forward into the staircase, leaning against the wall and its bar for reference and balance as he carried Tralane, sleeping, down into her house. Although Minna had been able to lock him in he doubted she knew who he was or that he was still perfectly able to remain in contact with the Relay. He confirmed that he was entering the house and then cut the connection himself, indicating that he required silent time. He needed all his attention. The stairs were covered in small stacked items that seemed to have been misplaced or were in transit somewhere. Below it was worse. He almost fell over a packing crate. Around him he saw huge rooms filled with bric-a-brac, walls covered in vast portraits, packed with paintings as if no centron of space must go uncovered. Finally, he saw before them at the end of the hall the weak light and wire cage of an elevator. The gun poked him.

He could have done any number of easy escapes. He walked into the shaky car, feeling the floor tremble unnervingly. His arms were nearly numb. He leant on the wall and the entire thing jolted that way as Minna got in and shakily closed the door. The journey down was noisy and terrifying in its own claustrophobic way. He memorised the operational sequence and felt himself falling in love, slowly, surely, like being hit by that unexpected wall all over again. Night always said it was voluntary. Everything. You chose. You fell, or not. You made the world, or not. The lift's descent and his own fate were the same. He felt them smooth into one action and knew she was wrong. Sometimes there was no choice. Things beyond volition spoke with greater power.

By the time they reached the lived-in sections of the house he was in so much pain he noticed nothing of his surroundings beyond whether or not the way was barred or free of obstructions. Minnabar hissed whispery instructions, 'Left here! Right now. Second right.' Who could live in a labyrinth like this? He felt others awake in the building, entire apartments passed by, their closed doors sheltering the minor families that came under Tralane's ancestral web. They were hers to provide for. They worked for her in turn, although judging by the state of their joint fortunes he understood this didn't amount to much in the grand scheme of the Empire.

'Now put her down.'

He turned to the side where a long sofa banged his knee and placed his burden on it. He reached out with the intent of placing a cushion under Tralane's head but was jerked backwards suddenly. He couldn't keep his balance and staggered into a low, heavy table, sitting down on it involuntarily. Minnabar leapt back, both of her hands training her weapon on him. She looked grey and shaky but he didn't know what the gun could do, so even though he doubted her willingness to use it enough that he felt no real danger he sat where he was and rested in gratitude, easing each burning muscle in turn. He was proud of her willingness to defend her mother, however foolish her moves.

'And now?' he said after a few seconds of silence had passed.

'Now,' the girl said, clearly inventing on the run. 'Get up.' She indicated with the gun in case he didn't understand her.

He stood up, beginning to see the room they were in. Weak lighting revealed vast, cumbersome furniture from earlier ages, worn to the last weft in places, stuffing oozing out here and there. It was untidy. Books and tablets were roughly stacked. Plates and cups were scattered about. The damasked walls glowered at him with their crimson and gold, daring him to disobey a lady of the house. He smiled at them, having no intention of doing that.

'Back the way you came.'

He looked down at Minnabar and said gently, 'Don't let her sleep it off alone. If she doesn't wake up by dawn you must call a doctor. Prolonged hibersleep can become coma if it goes on too long. It's not harmful but it can become extremely difficult to wake out of it without the proper assistance.'

'Just move!'

The speed with which anger rushed her amused him but he didn't show it. He turned and walked, alert this time, as they left the lounge and passed along several corridors and down a stair.

'Here. Open the door at your right.'

He did so and found himself in a bedroom, the air and everything in it tired with neglect. Before he could turn around the door slammed shut – he was sure she had not touched it – and he heard the locks turn.

'You can't get out.' Her voice came through the heavy door weakly, the statement sounding much more like a question than it should have. There was a pause in which he could almost hear her thinking of what else to say to him. 'We'll be back in the morning with the officers.'

Well that was plausible at least. He smiled now that she couldn't see him and finding himself tired now pulled back the dusty coverlet and examined the bedding. It was a little musty but clean and there were no signs of insects or mice. He turned the pillow, removed his coat and boots and lay down in it. By his witchlight he took out Isabeau's discarded book and began to read.

TORADA

The half hour that the Empress had requested between Tzaban's departure and the arrival of Alide left her alone with Hakka, although this was not truly alone any more than most of her waking hours were. Everywhere she went, and all the time, the presence of the seven was with her, sometimes vivid and fully alive, racing with words, feelings and images, sometimes quiescent – a background hum like the purr of a cat that let her know they were alive and available, closer to her than her own skin. She didn't know what thoughts of hers they prowled among. She wasn't sure if they padded silently around when she was asleep, plucking apart her plans with their claws. She knew that they could.

Since she could remember they had always been there, although it had not always been the same seven people. By the age of four she had learned a few ways to shut them out of her waking thoughts. By fourteen she was adept at closing off pieces of herself, from them, and from her own awareness. This took its toll however. A long period of blockades was exhausting and there must ultimately come a reckoning to settle matters. Sleep was one method, if she removed her restrictions, though then she didn't know what the other Empresses did. Another was meditation, which she preferred. At least awake she had her bodily sensations to alert her to the activities of the seven. They were not, as she had been brought up to assume, always on her side.

By this moment of the day she was long overdue for a break, but she did not want to be disadvantaged when Alide arrived. She knew he had his own scouts and agendas, his missions. She was reasonably sure that her welfare didn't feature highly in any of them, at least only as an accessory to his greater plans. For the time being their goals coincided: maintain the safety of the city, the integrity of the Empire. She wondered if he knew that she had her eye on him, that certain of the others also followed his progress and said nothing, not yet, no. For now let him do as he pleases and meet his fellows here and there, accept his consignments from Spire and from Dirt that passed no duty warehouse on their way.

Suppose she needed his great ability to construct and mastermind devastation? He was one of few who had such ruthless, imaginative resources and all resources were valuable. Even the despicable ones that wish you dead, she thought

Torada herself, left to herself, just for now, in silence, beckons Hakka to her and he comes eagerly. He is all strength and animal comfort as he folds her in his arms. She knows nobody understands the story of how she came by him. They say she tamed him, like a horse, like a wild animal. This is not true but it's a much better and easier story than the truth, so she's let it become that. He understands her, at this animal level, as he and that Karoo, Tzaban, have an understanding too. Only the animal can keep you alive.

She rests in his arms, a ragdoll, and he hums to her some Steppeish tune, a bit mournful as if the wind got into it. The vibration of his voice is soothing. For reasons that are deeply ground into her she never lets anyone see this, save Hakka's lovers, her other guards. They don't count. They belong to him as he belongs to her and will say nothing.

'What did you think of Night's new student?' she asks.

'Temperamental,' Hakka replies softly, continuing his song after, rocking her, kissing her hair.

'And the General?'

'Out of his depth.'

'And Tzaban?'

'Karoo.'

Even to the Steppelanders Karoo means unknowable, it's a synonym for it.

'Truthful?'

'Ayah, of course. Tiger has no reason to lie, hm? Tiger does as he likes, says what he likes, fears nothing.'

'Do you think we will all die?'

The humming stops. 'He didn't lie,' Hakka says finally and squeezes her tightly, so tightly that she can feel herself made of tiny bird bones under her thin skin and all of them ready to break like twigs. To be hugged by him is a beautiful thing.

Torada closes her eyes in the crush, safe, hidden, secret, silent. He smells of sweat and the tanner's leather mixture and the soap they wash the cotton with and home. She is stealing time, stepping out of it. This relationship she has with him is only possible because of her talent – Torada is the Beast Empress, the pheromone queen; through her the city and this fragment of Empire swirls in a biochemical harmony of subtle persuasions, silent communications, and with the exception of Night who is gifted enough in her own way to see it, nobody understands or even realises it except herself. And the seven. Of course the seven. They study her as if she were an experiment, the city her testbed.

In the scented constriction of Hakka's arms Torada feels the pressure of the outer world and all of the reactions in the population that she is keeping at bay: their jealousy, their aggression. Empress Nyalin, envious for reasons Torada doesn't understand, says she runs a sex-rich economy in the kind of voice reserved for condemning criminals and calls her the Pacifier, or in her most resentful moments, Slut. Torada knows because she sneaks around in Tekara's head at night and eavesdrops on her careless conversations with Haruzh and Tiskla. Dirt, Spire and Wit, she calls them. She wonders if they know. They must know. Dirt with her agricultural garden wonders, Wit charming with words that do such clever work they might have a life of their own, Spire planting ideas as Dirt plants seeds, inspiring and pushing. The other three – Jagoda, Haru Ri and Meixia are far more pleasant, to her at least. She thinks of them as Sister Chimera, Sister River and Sister Cloud. They all have variants of the same basic talent as she does. It isn't so hard to understand each other. What Torada doesn't understand is why her version alone causes hesitation, as if it is a second-rate charm. Low, say the three of differing powers. The Sister Empresses – she doesn't know what they think, they aren't the sort to comment. She would ask but if she found them all against her the endless subtle pressure would be too much. Even Hakka's arms couldn't counteract it.

Torada makes her people put kindness first. Generosity in mind, body, soul. She doesn't know where she got this belief from but it's the one at the centre of her. It is one of the only things she likes about being her.

All too soon her time is up.

Hakka lets go and retreats. She sits alone the final minutes and uses a serape to cover the marks on her skin where his armour has bitten and left red lines. Her runners return and freshen the room: new flowers for the evening. From the distance she hears the guards calling. Alide has arrived.

CHAPTER TEN

ALIDE

The Empress looked like a child waiting for a dreaded lesson as Horad Alide approached, his pace suitably firm but respectful. The glassy distance of her pale gaze revealed the intensity with which the seven others rode her. He was glad of that. Dealing with her on her own filled him with distaste and anger; she was no more than she appeared, a slip of a girl unsuited to managing what she must manage by youth and inexperience. Add to that her pallid and uninspiring form and he felt insulted. Of such stuff leaders were not made. Birth and its accidents, he supposed. Nature throws up some oddities we must find charming or strangle. At least now the urge to strangle is finding slow satiation and he fancies he can see it in the glimmer of her wandering gaze as her eyes track thoughts and words not her own, from those who inhabit her and in whose confidences he rides smooth and sleek towards the throne.

The horseman, Hakka, looks as if he'd like to fight. The man's no more than a trained creature, lower than a horse but slightly better than a dog. At least he fit his purpose. Physically past his prime and ever lacking the raw power of a physical adept, Alide finds to his disgust that he still reacts with respect to the brute. Alide has never been bullied, but he has always felt as if he was, by dint of being unable to join in with the strongest at their own games. As a natural defence he developed his internal resources but it irked him as dishonest even though surely it's better to be the owner of fine horses than be a horse in a stable? His own failure to rise above such pettiness was an abhorrent weakness. His mouth tasted it as he passed Hakka's leaning spear. To push one's rage into constructive issues, that was the mark of the man he had made of himself. And not a day went by he didn't have to think again on it in this loathsome place, fat-fed on sensuality and rotten with contentment. Without him they would have fallen to the primitives long ago.

He bent his knee formally at the dais as he always did and went about the calming business of removing and handing his outer coat to his assistant, who was yet too insignificant to warrant the use of a name.

The Empress addressed him in the cold, ghostly tone of the Eight – a sound that never failed to make him shiver with irrepressible dread, coming from her ordinary throat. It carried the harmonics and resonances of multiple speakers in a way unnatural to any human vocal cords, and that would have been alarming enough, but in addition it boomed, like the ocean in a huge seacave, and it broke at the edges into distortions that were surely sounds unproducible by flesh. It was unlike any other voice and its effect on him, as on others, was absolute. It spoke and what it said became the truth by which life would continue. He was so used to it now that he could witness his own craven response and laugh at it, though he couldn't alter it.

'We are disturbed to hear of imminent war with the Karoo. What say you?'

He was prepared for this in advance, had been working on his response since the Karoo itself arrived in the city proclaiming honest soldiery. 'The incursion of the relic digsite on to the Overgrowth is very minor. We have no intention of staying there beyond the necessary length of time it takes to conclude the expedition. It is at the behest of the University and the Magisterium that we are there at all. Our defences and military operations are solely acting to protect the civil engineers at the sites. We have seen no emissaries and our only encounters have been with the wildlife.'

'That is a pretty way to describe a massacre.'

Alide ground his teeth, silently. His jaw ached. 'It is the expedition that is the aggressive action. That is your business, Highness. To facilitate the expedition we must have soldiers, munitions, weapons, activity within the Overgrowth.' He may, he realised a moment before the hammer fell, have overstepped the mark in telling her what her business was.

The voice pressed him to the back of his skull as if he were a strip of wet paper. 'There is almost nothing left of the expedition. Your business.'

This rebuking crush had also happened before. He waited, the silence returned him to himself. 'In terms of the Empire as a whole its interests are best served by completing the Expedition in the hopes of retrieving artefacts that will be sufficiently useful to overpower those who seek to destroy us. The portal at Breakneck Pass is complete and the Southern Aspect portal functional as of last week. This will end the need to cross hostile territory between us, ending the skirmishes with the Steppe clans. We may withdraw from the campaigns there immediately by your command. Any residual ill feeling from the Circle will then become border issues and given their behaviour one may anticipate a lengthy guerrilla situation so I suggest strengthening the outposts, maybe sending some fortresses down there and then infiltrating the population with sleeper agents.'

He paused, his gaze around her sandalled feet, seeing almost nothing. Checks and balances tipped in his head on the elegant fulcrum of the ever-changing moment. He knew she was experiencing her own version of this, wondered briefly what that was like: eight clockworks attempting to mesh. What gears she must have. What complexity. He spoke again as she paused. Her expectation was tangible.

'I recommend you use the Karoo infiltrator as an expert to prove his good intentions. If he is promising war we will show faith at least to hear their part by sending him south to the front. He will ensure the safe conduct and conclusion of the mission there, explain to the Karoo that we have no intention of lingering. If our safe exit is managed we might consider some longer attempt to establish communication. Who knows what lies underneath the Overgrowth, after all?'

And, he thought, if he is a spy, and he is, and if he complicates matters here too much, which he does, then he can be got rid of there very easily. After all, hundreds have already vanished without trace there. How difficult would it be to lose a few more? But then he closed down those thoughts. He knew she could not read them but it felt dangerous to even think of them in her presence. They led inexorably towards his treachery, hidden in the centre of his brain. The Karoo were the perfect gift. He could destroy Glimshard and remake it, corrected, with such an instrument. But that was a delicate thought, fragile as crystal. Then he knew who else was trouble. Huntingore. Who knew what was in that rotting cache of hers? But her daughters would be easy to manipulate if she was out of the way. They were little more than children and their heads full of social nonsense.

'You would need more specialists there too, of course,' he added, as if generously thinking of this to aid the situation, and then wondered if he went too fast, too far. He had to fight not to look up at her and then her voice hammered him flat within himself.

'I will take your advice under consideration. Leave me.'

He bowed and took his leave. He was unable to consider his own mind until he was clear of the courts but when he did that low, grinding anger rose up first from the wreckage she made of him. It dulled on his walk back to the Ministry. Although it was too late to do anything but sleep now he still went about the movements of returning, sifting his papers, closing up, pausing to eat at the late night rice stand. Snuffling through peas and chopped meat with hot sauce, he was able to consider it at last from the happy distance of an hour.

He liked to pretend for most of his life that it was the Empress' power of control over her subjects that he was opposed to, in principle. It made her a tyrant, potentially absolute, and her ministers and courtiers only tools. As a male and one of a specific family, he could never rise higher than he had already. He was made to serve, but he baulked at it, not because he didn't want to, but because it was not voluntary. He felt, as it galled him, that this position was inherently ridiculous: he was suited to his post, his life was reasonably good, his health adequate, his wealth generous. He was free, outside his duties, to do as he liked. But when it came to the duties, particularly those he must serve the Empress direct, he resisted. He knew that if it were not for this perversity he could have been content and his life a rounded, wholesome thing instead of this twisted, dry meander it had become. He saw that his – spite, was it? Very well, his spite was unfounded. The Empress was not a lone operator. She absorbed the will of the population in as many ways as she exerted her controlling guidance on it. Nobody here could be said to be exempt from the sum total of the will of the whole. But he blamed her. He disliked her position, so powerful and unbalanced. He disliked bitterly the physical vessel of her present avatar in this city. So young, and he was not. So inexperienced, and he was not. It was more than that ... more.

He had to stop eating. Food was lodged in his gullet over a spasm that sent a curl of hot acid up into his throat and burned him. Even thinking of her made him ill. He stretched up to his tallest, sitting in the conservatory of his house, alone, in the dark, with his food on his lap. He knew it was craven folly to envy her and hate her. It was pointless. She was no more the author of her situation than he was of his. But he could not stop and as he sat, listening to water drip from the long leaves of his bromeliads into the moist dirt and waiting for his stomach to stop its contradictory revolution against his taste for spices, he knew that it was because he enjoyed hating her. It added a dimension without which he would suffocate in greyness; his own of course, for he had so little of any note to do, until lately. He'd created malice from boredom, because he liked conflict, and the hidden drama of it fed the hungry, vicious beast he fancied lay inside him, perhaps inside all men, mad with civilisation's curfews and desperate to rend, tear and destroy with the sweet taste of justice. For a defence there must be an attack. To look like the defender when you were not required only the right bait and the right timing. The Karoo were, to a fault, mindlessly vicious and provoking them was child's play compared to provoking the Empress. But you had to practise with what you'd got.

He fooled himself he'd accept a stronger woman on the throne of Glimshard. He smiled, knowing he could find another reason to dislike her, or someone else to make war on. Contentment. He began to eat again, more carefully, his guts calmed by this sense of endless purpose. He went alone to bed in his quiet house and set his water clock to wake him at dawn. He would ride to the portal and see it working. When he was satisfied his agents were in place he could return and tidy matters in the city. Borze would have enough to deal with in counteracting news from the expedition front and by next week the interest in Tzaban would have worn off a little.

Before he put his light out he wrote and sent a few letters. One was to Shrazade, asking her for an inventory of the Huntingore house. She must have a way. He didn't care what it was, or what it cost. He wanted to know what else was in there. He enclosed the Ministry Seal with instructions as to how she might present her bill upon success and dispatched the letter with a runner from his own house who was well versed in handovers: by the time it arrived at its destination there would be nobody in the city who could have said where it had originated.

He put out his light and slept soundly.

TORADA

Torada closed herself off from the others and they also retired to think on matters, agreeing to regroup in a few hours' time. She waited for the strange off-balance shift to settle as they departed from her consciousness. In the first instant, as ever, she missed them, even Spire, who wanted her dead. For a few minutes she lost control of her body and when she returned to it she found herself on her bed, the cool sheets under her, Hakka leaning over her, watching and waiting, his expression hard and dark with concern.

'I'm all right,' she said, crossly, as usual, so glad he was there as she pushed him away. Under her fingers the incredible hardness of his arms was like marble. She always marvelled at it, so different to her own even though she did train and thought of herself as strong. That idea too made her want to laugh and finally, rid of the seven, she did. She felt so exhausted she could have been transparent, worn to nothing.

Hakka obediently played his part in the old ritual and got up from the bed, stretching and yawning. He brought her a lightly alcoholic fruit drink and she sat up on her pillows to sip it. Runners came, saw, dashed off to set evening lighting and dispose of loitering courtiers.

The doors closed with a soft thud of padded joints meeting. She heard the bolts slide home. From their adjoining suites Jago and Eth padded quietly in; beasts from freshly opened cages. Both men were as efficient and deadly as Hakka, albeit very different in personality and style. Both wore their ceremonial white and red livery to mark them as her property, her personal guard. Jago was the taller and heavier of the two, dark as a mahogany table, his hair, eyes and skin all the same colour, his serious nature evident in every deliberate, exacting move. Torada, herself now alone and not the Empress, feared Jago a little.

Eth, approaching from the far end of the room, was so light and springy as he ran he seemed half the size he really was. Instead of Jago's full formal robes he wore only the kilt section and darted barefoot, not booted, to catch up so both of them met Hakka in the middle of the circular carpet. Tawny and narrow-limbed Eth's pale gold hair streamed unbound, at Torada's request, the fringes tamed in two bound ropes by silver rings. He joined Jago immediately and in silence to divest Hakka of his heavy plate chest and greaves, harness and cloak.

Torada loved Eth, sweetly, fiercely. She loved to watch his long fingers tangle and caress Jago's fingers as they unbuckled their lover from his trappings, loved to see Hakka emerge like a horse from under the saddle now that he was off duty at last. They could never leave her unattended, but the routines for shifting responsibilities were well worn-in. By his dress code she knew it was Jago who was in charge of her security now although none of them were permitted to leave her or separate while Hakka slept and rested. For this reason, and because Hakka was her greatest, dearest friend she had employed Night's unique skills to hunt down Eth and Jago, to be sure he was well cared for – to be certain that he would be loved as she felt he deserved. It was recompense for her theft of his life. She knew it was not enough. She wished it were. She would have given him anything. Herself the least of it if he had wanted that. Probably it was better he didn't. She told herself that daily. Probably it was better.

Now she hugged her pillow to herself, hid in the pile of them, nerveless and wan, and devoured with her eyes what she would never have for herself. She watched as Eth impishly stood on his toes to kiss Jago as if he were stealing apples from a tree. Jago always made like it was nothing, Eth always smiled, eating up Jago's single downward glance of pleasure and dancing off with it. He was happy by nature. Jago and Hakka both lightened in his presence. She did too. He flashed a grin at her as he turned, seeing her where she always was, alone in the middle of her huge bed. Then his attention was all given over to Hakka, who sat and accepted the rubbing of his shoulders, neck and back by Eth's sensitive hands. Jago watched them for a moment, dark and smouldering, then turned to take up his post across the room, between the doors, his swords rustling quietly against the cloth panels of his tunic. His impassive face reflected his inner control. In response, Torada relinquished the last of hers, sinking deeper into the bedding. With the three of them present she could sleep. But instead she watched with her sore eyes.

Eth, who slept the mornings out, was full of energy. He worked on Hakka's body where the armour had marked it, where he knew all the knots built up from carrying the weapon and standing about all day long. Hakka drank water as he was treated, murmuring to Eth so Torada couldn't hear the words. She liked their gruff, low voices. Eth's was softer and lighter. Hakka's in relaxation was more gentle than usual. The tones and vibrations altered as they spoke; once they had cross referenced information the cadence became playful. Hakka caught Eth's hands, oil rubbed and slippery, and slid them on himself, fingers in the same caressing dance as Eth and Jago's had been, before he stood up and with a sweeping turn picked Eth up in his arms and carried him over to the bed.

Jago shifted his weight, his spear shaft clanking softly against one of his swords. Torada scooted over to the side, a girl in an enormous cotton wasteland, behind boulders, as Eth was flung down beside her in a gasping, laughing heap. She hid her grin in a bite of pillow as Eth's outflung arm reached further and tickled her at the waist. He turned his pretty head for a second and said,

'You're not even dressed for bed. Dayclothes? Bath?'

She poked him in the ribs, too tired to move, and they both paused to watch Hakka shed his undergarments and crawl on hands and knees, naked, over Eth. He smiled slowly into Eth's face, a knowing, carnal grin, and at the same time picked up a loose cushion and batted it over the top of Torada's head.

'Go get your bath.'

'I can't,' she said and he batted her again, the blow as soft as a cat's paw and modified by the cushion's overstuffed down. Under her pillow-wall Eth's hand found hers for a second and gripped tightly. She closed her eyes and concentrated. When Hakka kissed him, the hand loosened, thumb caressing her thumb gently. When Hakka entered Eth, the hand gripped hard for a moment and then relaxed and opened. She stroked the oil-softened skin with her fingertips and imagined their pleasure. The bed bounced her lightly as they moved and their growls, moans and sighs filled her ears.

She thought of Spire, maliciously, and held Eth's hand, longing to be touched. She knew she could do what Spire did, and move into Eth herself, feel what he felt as Hakka made love to him. But she didn't want it stolen and, as she was, she had nobody but the seven. She had nothing but herself and her intent not to harm. Spire was right. Pathetic indeed. And now maybe not enough to hold against Alide, who felt like he meant her ill. His presence made her scalp prickle.

She pushed the cushion off her head and watched Hakka and Eth kiss. When Eth begged and Hakka teased him she lay still, heart pounding. Watching them transported her to the same state, all wanton longing and nobody to salve it. She closed her eyes again and thought of Isabeau Huntingore, how pretty, how cool, how aloof she'd been. Eth's hand was so strong, so calloused, so *him* there was no imagining that to be Isabeau's hand. She and Isabeau would not growl and grunt deep like men. Isabeau was light and cool and rounded, soft as the pillows on her, delicious as the feel of the fine sheet and the passionate, intense heat of her beautiful bodyguards. In that, yes, she could be the same. Maybe…

Then Hakka found Eth's errant hand, searching for it to pin it down with his own. He crushed her hand under it.

'Hold him.' Hakka's guttural command was for her. She gripped as hard as she could and felt Eth's palm mashed flat between hers and Hakka's. Between her knuckles Hakka's fingers bit in painfully. Eth cried out as Hakka changed his stroke, voice assenting wordlessly as Hakka told him, 'Wait for her.'

Torada rolled to her side and pushed all the intervening pillows away. She looked at Hakka's body, saw Eth's pleasure as the initial softer tones of romantic lovemaking gave way to him getting the long, hard fucking he was begging for. She watched Hakka's fascinatingly hard and thick member slide and slide again into Eth's body and her own body shivered, tingled and shocked her with the build of heat as it pretended this was her, for her. She was Eth and she was Hakka, giving each other this burning, fierce, needful thing. She was muscle and sweat, she was taker and taken. Her small, weak self, reached out, stretching towards believing it so much it filled her senses and became true, inside. The power, the smells – always so contradictory; sweet, corrupted, clean, dirty, reckless, careless, rich and living conspired to help her. She felt Hakka's hand holding her into them. His permission, Eth's agreement, Eth's begging… Eth's *face*— Her other hand was between her legs, feeling her clit as a cock, like Hakka's, being him, taking Eth.

'Come,' Hakka commanded and Eth cried out. The sight of his ecstasy brought her own on her.

Torada looked into Hakka's eyes, seeing him still in control, waiting, as she obeyed him too, shaking, helpless. Only when he was certain she and Eth were done did he look down at his lover and thrust himself hard and fast until he froze and then bent down slowly in a long shudder, face pushed into Eth's thick, silky hair. His hand on hers released and she let them go, pulling the hand back to her and cradling its sore, agonised joints against herself. Eth smiled at her, turning his head and she put the fingers of her other hand against his lips, wet, and he licked them, eyes glazing briefly with the intensity of the reward. Her body was not like other women's. She felt rather than heard Hakka grunt with amused recognition as he realised what Eth was doing. Eth would be hard all night now, and Hakka wouldn't get much sleep.

Soft and peaceful in the afterglow she looked on her men with love, and wished such love on everyone in her care. Pleasure and love together, only that, and afterwards gentleness and peace and more of the same, on and on...

She began to fall asleep, building up walls against the seven to keep them out of this, her space. She didn't care what they thought of her here, or about it. This was hers.

Torada waited alone with Jago as Eth and Hakka took themselves off to the bath. Runners came and set the lamps low, cleared and prepared the light evening food, the chilled carafes of fruited water and wine, tea and heated water on the night burner. They opened the garden wall and set the hanging veils and the darklight vigil torches so that the cool high breeze floated into the room over the hot stones and warmed earth, the plants and their heavy freight of blossoms before gliding into the room and over the bed. Insects, attracted and redirected by the darklight torches, remained unharmed outside.

Jago moved closer. He had a mistrust of the garden's open roof, though it was watched by clockwork gargoyles of Sircene making who were more than capable of raising an alarm or capturing intruders. Like the Illathil and the rest of the human races outside the Empire, he had a deep mistrust of all things mechanical. His dislike was even greater than for all things magical. Combine the two and it made him serious and grim, permanently bad-tempered. She'd always hoped this was why she felt such dislike from him; because she forced him to accommodate these things in his life, rather than for the necessity that he exist under her permanent observation and have his natural affections directed by her. She wasn't even sure how much he understood of that. She had taken such pains not to push anything that was not already underway, like rolling a rock downhill.

She missed Night abruptly. Night always knew how much of anything it would be wise to tell. Her advice was invaluable. She had told Torada in no uncertain terms that revealing the truth of his situation to Jago would be a disaster. So when she watched him now, adjusting his position to cover the open wall, she suspected that it was not his dislike but her own guilt that created the uncomfortable wedge between them. She wanted, as every night, to somehow make up to him the things she'd stolen away.

'Jago', she whispered.

'Empress,' he said, watching for the return of Hakka and Eth. Across the winding glitter of the stream the lights of the bath house were visible. Lanterns glowed with colour along the winding path between.

'What do your people do when they discover traitors but have no evidence?'

'Strangle them in their sleep,' he replied without hesitation.

'But what if it turns out later that they were innocent?'

'A week of mourning is appropriate. Payments are made.' His voice growled softly.

'Do you investigate the mistake?'

Jago shrugged indifferently. 'That's Lords' business.'

'You are a Lord's son.'

'I was a Lord's bastard, Highness. I am elevated further now as your creature than I would ever have been there.' His tone remained factual though she tried hard to detect gratitude in it.

She listened to his armour creak as he moved. She hoped Eth would take a long time bathing Hakka. It was rare she spoke to Jago alone. Her daring and the moment overcame her sleepy exhaustion. She felt an opportunity, but to gain what, to go where, she didn't know. She felt she could easily make a silly mistake.

'If you could have the life you wished, Jago, what would you have?' Thinking maybe one day she would give it to him, if it was within her power.

'I don't dream, Highness. That's the business of Angels.'

She wondered if it was humility made him say it, or simply lack of imagination and a desire to go unnoticed and unpunished.

She said, 'Is everything someone else's business, Jago?' but before he could answer she heard Eth's laugh and then saw a shadow bound across, blocking the lanterns out in sequence. He ran through the veils, trailing them over both shoulders, and leapt on to the bed beside her in an effortless bounce, landing lightly and flopping down on his belly on the sheet. Torada imagined, briefly, because it was painful, that he was her man come to play. She wondered what that was like. But even the notion of having someone... She turned it aside. It was useless and, worse, it was weak. Empresses were alone. To want otherwise was to be unfit for the position. She was unto herself sufficient. She must be.

Dirt had told her it was common for her age to feel such indulgent whims – but in time it would pass. She understood implicitly, without any of them mentioning it, that there was even among the Eight, a hierarchy. Dirt was stronger than Spire. Wit was stronger than Beckons. She felt certain she was the weakest so far, along with Murmur, but in the same way she knew that she felt that there was a potential in her to become the strongest. She looked at Eth and saw he was utterly in her

155

power. He grinned at her, flushed with the warm results of Hakka's lovemaking and his anticipation of more of it and she closed her hand hidden under the pillow.

It would be so much easier to crush than preserve. What she spread from this room – all these bonding, soothing, calming plans – was subtle and uncertain compared to Jago's solutions: crush, command, destroy, intimidate. Could she really convince herself that this was the path to follow when all seven said it was simple romantic stupidity, her youth and inexperience, her unwillingness to accept the truth of human nature spread all around them?

She smiled at Eth as he returned and looked at her, questioning her silence. She opened her hand, slipping it out towards him to tickle him on his flank and make him laugh. Jago relaxed at the sound, polearm clinking. She ate up Eth's happiness, his sexy, self-contented daze, and spread it out, through the veils, into the garden, beyond the gargoyles and over the city, down and down in scentless clouds; one night-blooming flower.

She fell asleep to the sound of Eth and Hakka's quiet talking.

CHAPTER ELEVEN

TRALANE

Tralane Huntingore woke up with a headache to end all headaches, body sore and stomach growling. She stared for a few moments at her own worn carpet before understanding there had been a dislocation. She recalled falling unconscious on the cold paving of the Flit shed and expecting to wake up there. After that, blank. She closed her eyes but nothing improved except the fact that she didn't have to think about taking the carpets out for a good beating one of these fine days because, really, they were beyond that.

She decided to leave the issues that were biting her until a little later on, when she felt less like volunteering for an early grave. Unfortunately her appalled inner self would rather play back the horrific descent to the flight deck, complete with telltale magical interference in a nonstop loop as it tried to inspire bleating panic. Tralane had never been one for bleating or panic however, so she let it carry on in the background whilst she dealt with the more pressing task of how to get off the couch and to the medicine cabinet. Her effort to get up seemed to go well at first. She swung her legs off the sofa and felt her boots hit the floor. Something fell over. As she sat, resting on her elbows, she saw it was the cup of water someone had thoughtfully placed beside her, alongside a plate holding honey biscuits and pain tablets. She swallowed the caps dry, forced a biscuit after them and lay down again to wait for them to have an effect.

When she was able to get up she stumbled back up to the flight deck to check the Flit. She saw the marks of several boots in the dust on the stairs and someone had swept off the banisters that curved under the disapproving family portraits. The doors were all closed, but not locked. The lift had been left with the door half open. She sensed the hand of carelessness at work and automatically thought of Minna, but Minna couldn't carry her. The Flit was scarred in the colours of the infomancers' curse but whole. The fuel tanks were empty. She bent down to the earth floor where she had laid, studied. A man's boots.

Who the hell had been here with Minnabar in the middle of the night? She wanted to think it was Best, but she knew Best had left the house to look for Isabeau. One of Minna's friends? She couldn't imagine those youths doing it, not without supervision or the gift of a hernia. Still, she didn't have any other idea and she was, aside from the hangover, unharmed.

She closed up carefully and traced the route, looking for clues. She thought, only then, about the goggles, and stopped, but a patting found them heavily lodged just over her forehead, which explained the tight feeling. The gun, an image of it, passed through her mind. She recalled the thonk and clunk of it landing in the cupboard where she'd tossed it. Pausing only long enough to shed her flight suit and stuff it roughly into place, she descended into the workshop and went to find it and reassure herself of its concealment.

Twenty minutes later the workshop floor was filled knee deep with clutter and she was still gunless. She looked at her clock – six. Dawn was here. No gun. She stepped over a low wave of half-melted smartblox and took a final glance at the worktop in the hopes of seeing the crystal core left there by some ignorant thieving hand but the worktop was bare. A sick and horrible feeling rose in her throat. She considered, then hopped to the door and went down, thinking maybe Best had come back and already taken it to safety, not really considering that she hadn't told Best about it in the first place.

The first door she checked was her own. Her bed was as she left it, cold and empty. A twist and a few doors further on she opened Isa's door and saw a blonde head on the pillow, immaculate grey robes puddled on the floor... But there was time to consider this small anomaly later. Closing that door she snuck onward to Minna's room and came up with an empty. The signs of tempestuous haircare and dressing littered the made bed. *Party*, she thought, and went back to the solar observatory. There she found most of Minna's web slumbering in piles, but no daughter.

Trying not to feel that options were running short she took the fastest route down to the kitchen. On the way she passed the guest rooms and had gone beyond them several metres before backtracking and looking down that hall again.

There, sitting with her back against the wall, knees propped up against each other and head hanging to one side, was Minnabar. Her hands were balanced on her knees, arms stretched, and in between them, dangling from her loosely curled fingers, was the gun. The barrel was pointing down towards her feet now, but obviously it had once pointed at the door in front of her. This was shut. Tralane took this all in slowly, and then walked up, her attention on the door, and on the gun. Minna's mouth was half open and she was deeply under. Tralane prised the gun gently off her, thinking that it wouldn't wake her but at the movement Minna started suddenly, muttering. She blinked up at Tralane and glared at the door, then back up. Seeing Tralane's finger against her lips she stayed silent and jabbed her finger repeatedly at the door. Tralane signalled with a nod that she got it.

Minna got to her feet stiffly and whispered quickly in Tralane's ear, 'It's Zharazin Mazhd.'

Tralane took this in for a minute and felt the cogs slowly chunking around in her head, each chunk accompanied by a steady beat of pain in her temples. She couldn't think why she knew the name, but she did. Infomancers. Oh, no ... She stalled out at that point. How the hell could he have got here so fast? It wasn't possible. Nothing added up. She erased everything and went back to the facts. Her daughter was holding a gun on a locked door. The door wasn't going anywhere, and neither was whoever was inside the room, unless Sircene blood ran in their veins and she doubted that. She beckoned Minna to go with her and led the way to the kitchen. On the way there it occurred to her that the reason Minna would be there doing that must be fear. Why?

In the kitchen, she closed the door and looked at her daughter's bleary, exhausted face. Minna was about half the girl who had sat staring at the sky through the goggles. She looked twelve years old again and Tralane felt a stab of fear go through her, wondering. 'What happened?'

Minnabar had the face on that said she wanted to lie but wasn't. 'I was using the farscope. I didn't know you were out until ... You know that the flight deck is linked into the scope systems, right? Well, I saw it tracking something. I was trying to see out to those weird things in the sky, but when the activation clicked on I thought I'd just look and see what was going on.' She looked down and squirmed, holding on to the edge of the table as she sat herself down, leg tucked under her, and then lay flat over the tabletop, head on her arm, looking at Tralane with big eyes.

Tralane just nodded. She knew soft soap when she saw it but the time to pursue the details was later. 'Go on.'

Minna bit her lips together, chewing slightly, then said, 'It was you. In the Flit. I saw you, guessed you were looking for stupid

Bo-girl as well, as if she'd be caught dead with you finding her.' A snort here and then, carefully. 'And I saw the shot... Was it a shot?' Her eyes flicked up to Tralane's and there was that scared little girl again, waiting.

Tralane located the hard liquor from the bottom cabinet, took out a bottle, uncorked it and poured two shots. 'Yep.'

Minna swallowed hard and looked at the glasses. 'Who's shooting at you, Mom?'

'I made a stupid mistake,' Tralane said, slamming the cork back in with a blow of the side of her fist. She shrugged and sipped. It tasted like burning embers. 'Crossed infomancer air.'

'What was that flare?'

'Tracer fire. I got rid of it but... Obviously too slowly.' Tralane rubbed her head. She looked around for sugary things and located stale buns that the web had made the day before. They probably didn't want them any more. She started to eat one, tossed one to Minna. 'So, you saw the shot and then?'

Minna swerved her gaze by turning her attention to the bun. She began to pick it apart with her fingers. 'I thought you were going to crash.' Emotion made her lip tremble but another, more pragmatic, determined urge, made her bite it still. 'I thought maybe they'd come after but probably that you'd make it and maybe crash and I didn't want to see it so... I had to go up there but I was too scared to go without something... So I went to the workshop first and it was just there, on the workbench.'

'Are you sure?'

'What? Of course. It was right there. And those power crystals were scattered around it like... Most of them didn't fit it so I guess you were looking for the right one. Anyway, I could see which one would work and I figured obviously it needed a focus, so I put in the one lying next to it, took off the safety and hoped it had enough juice to blow the shit out of... I mean... Well, it's a gun right?'

Tralane realised she was halfway to grinning even though her mind circled firmly down on the point about the bench. *The gun was on the bench.* Not in the cabinet. 'Go on.'

'Yeah so,' Minna cleared her throat and sneaked her glass to herself, sipped it, made a face, 'I went up on to the roof... that lift is a bloody deathtrap by the way, but yeah, you know that so... I went up on to the roof and I saw a light inside the shed. I thought it was you but then... When I got closer I realised it wasn't the right colour. So I sneaked up and that's when I saw him bending over you. Mazhd. I thought he was gonna – I didn't know what he was doing so I...' She stretched out her hands, fingers the gun now, pointing it, 'At his head and made him take you inside instead.'

Well that answered the carrying question, Tralane supposed, taking another swig from her glass. She eyed Minnabar and the gun, then slid the gun along the table towards her. 'Take it apart.'

Minna frowned but her hands left the remains of the bun and moved to the weapon almost automatically. Without hesitation she turned it around, opened the seals, popped the clasps and released the magazine crystal, then the power splinter. She laid these neatly aside and undid the catches that held the barrel to the stock before looking along the barrel and checking it for damage.

Tralane watched her in silence, pleased and slightly alarmed. 'Why stay outside the door?'

Minna looked up at her and then back down at the barrel. 'I couldn't remember if that door locked only to us or... I thought maybe he'd make a fuss and someone would let him out. Or... he...' She staggered to a halt in the sentence, flustered. 'He's very tricky. I didn't trust him.'

Tralane finished her drink and looked longingly at the bottle but she left it alone. 'You're probably right about that but I don't think blowing him to bits is going to solve any problems.

162

Clean that and put it back together and then take it back to the workshop and lock it up, would you?'

'Sure.' Minna cleared her throat a little, hesitating.

'And then get to bed. It's four in the morning.'

'It's six.'

'Do you know what time Bo got in?'

'Ten minutes before Bestie. About two.' Minna absently recalibrated the stock, flicking through its various attunement options and barrel fittings. 'You have more barrels for this?'

'Only found that one so far,' Tralane said, now certain she had missed a trick in not employing Minna sooner. Weaponry – who knew? She frowned but that hurt so she had to stop it. 'I can't face interrogating that man now. Let's leave him until later.'

Minna nodded, her attention absorbed with her new toy. Tralane left her there and heaved her tired bones back upstairs, wondering whose great idea it was to live inside a tower. She stopped at the prisoner's room and opened the access panel in the door. She could see in, but he would have no idea about it. She saw, dimly, that he was stretched out on the bed, no, in the bed. He was snoring lightly, at about 2000 rpm, she thought, smiling because it sounded like a very powerful but extremely distant engine passing behind a row of short but significant hills. There was a book open on his chest. Well, he wasn't trying to sneak out. He was sleeping. That was good. She could too.

She sealed the panel and went to her room. Best had appeared in the middle of the bed, sprawled like a starfish, mouth open, managing to occupy the entire thing. Dawn light was seeping through the curtains. She undressed and then looked around, found an old journal, rolled it up tightly and smacked Best firmly about the butt and shoulders until he grumbled and kicked around to make a cave for her under the covers. His eyes were still closed as he held up the quilt.

'Where've you been?'

'Out,' she said. 'Where've you been?'

'Looking for you.'

She felt a pang of guilt and wormed her way in next to him. He let his arm fall heavily over her with a sigh of resignation and muttered, 'There you are. If I'd known, I would have stayed here.' He sniffed, thought. 'You smell of engine oil. What have you been doing?'

'I flew out to look for you and Bo.'

'That was a long time ago,' he sounded accusing and hurt.

'I fell asleep upstairs,' she said. 'Someone left the workshop door open. Were you in there?'

'What would I go in there for?' He grunted crossly and warmed her feet with his.

'Must have been Minna,' she said, nothing exactly untrue there. She sighed then, as if she wanted to unburden herself, and told him the night's story.

He thought it over. 'You think I went into the workshop for the gun?'

'No,' she said. 'But whoever did that must have been disturbed when Minna went up. Clearly they didn't know what they were doing. The pieces were all over the place. Any engineer would have known a power splinter from a focus core.'

'Did you check the whole house?'

'No I…'

He groaned and got out of bed. 'They could still be here. I'll go. You just, stay out of trouble.'

She was too tired to argue. She lay down in his warm patch and curled up in the quilts. The door closed after him. No, she didn't think he was up to anything. But somebody had found that gun and tried to mess about with it. How? She fell asleep thinking about it.

The morning brought uncomfortable answers. Since everyone had been up so late the night before there was a sluggish family convention for brunch at noon. Carlyn was first on the scene, having come with big news of her own, but had to wait as nobody was up. She busied herself making pancakes. By the time Minna's web had started to crawl out of the solar in search of food she'd gone through pancakes shaped like clouds, like trees, like vegetables, and was leaning over the skillet dripping batter off a fork trying to make a springbuck with antlers that was robust enough to survive being tossed.

A few minutes later Tralane found her holding the iron spatula and staring at the springbuck's severed head hanging from the edge of it.

Carlyn looked up, smiled, hesitated, peered at Tralane's face and said, 'Long night, darling?'

Tralane took in the rest of the room, which was nearly emptied. At her glance the last of the web picked up their plates and slid obediently out of contact, snatching bottles of juice and packs of bread to take back to their lair. When they'd gone she collapsed into the worn armchair at the head of the table and put her head down on her arms.

'There's a man locked up in my guest room.'

Carlyn switched off the burners under the skillet and sat down on the bench next to Tralane, pulling a plate of pancakes towards herself. 'Was he trying to escape?'

'Ha ha. Maybe. What're you doing here so early anyway?'

'I have to pack for an expedition. We leave in a week's time. I need to talk to you about it but it can wait. What're you doing up so late with male prisoners?'

'Getting shot at,' Tralane said, unable to resist before explaining the story.

'You idiot,' Carlyn said several times, and at the conclusion. She had finished her pancakes by then and was sitting with tea, blowing at the steam coming off it. 'Are you going to leave him there for ever? I hope he had a toilet available or you'll be scrubbing something shortly.'

Tralane groaned and picked up her cup. 'Fine, I guess it's

time to let him out anyway. He hasn't actually done anything except trespass, really.'

Carlyn stared at her. 'Did you lose your marbles? He was obviously sent to check you out more thoroughly. I'm surprised no one's come for him by now.'

Tralane shrugged. 'Well they haven't.' She hadn't mentioned the part about the gun, why it was on the bench. She wanted to, but she kept it to herself. It felt like the information was loaded, exactly like another sort of weapon. She drank coffee, ate pancake coated in butter and sugar, waited for energy to come back to her and listened to Carlyn talk now about her expedition, a hasty summons from the Empress, an urgent mission. It was only when Carlyn nervously let slip that she was headed to the front that Tralane started out of her half trance and the prospect of having to meet Zharazin Mazhd evaporated for a minute.

'I'm sure you'll be going too,' Carlyn said. 'I don't know why you haven't been called already. You're the best engineer in the city.'

'It's a dig, what do they need me for? Civil workers do the heavy stuff. You futz about with brushes. How hard is that?'

'Lane, what's got into you?'

Someone was messing with my gun. And only you knew where it was. 'Just a hangover and a foul temper. Nothing new. Let's go see what the infomancers have to say.' She rolled a pancake up, stuffed it in her mouth, picked up coffee and started to move but found her way blocked by a yawning Isabeau in the doorway. 'Gracing us with your presence?' She tried to say this but it was muffled by pancake and came out as a hummed line of sarcasm which Isabeau rolled her eyes at. She passed Tralane and sat at the table, studied the pancakes, and took the nearest after a moment.

For a while Tralane couldn't understand what was new, then realised it had been a year since she saw Isabeau up in the morning in her pyjamas and not in the grey scholar gown. She swallowed pancake and took the rest out of her mouth. 'What happened?'

Isabeau shrugged and got up to look for cutlery and to find a drink.

'I was out looking for you.' This emerged a lot more shrewishly than Tralane had intended and she had to stop herself. An eternity of disappointed mothers in the Huntingore line bore down through her and made her sound like a vengeful harpy.

Isabeau poured a calculated amount of coffee into a mug and measured out sugar, one grain at a time, almost.

Tralane felt herself growing old, grey and irritated.

Isabeau stirred methodically, tapped her spoon and picked up her mug. She looked up over the rim. 'Hello Carly, Mom. Sorry I was late.'

Tralane reached for the patience of the gods and didn't find it. Instead a thought occurred to her. 'Did you leave your web?'

'Yep.' Isabeau picked up her pancake and turned it around, frowning. 'Is this meant to look like a horse?'

'It's a camel,' Carlyn said.

'Ohh ... Oh yeah.'

'So,' Tralane said, attempting measured and calm. 'Two years of study and apprenticeship after six months of begging and pleading to be admitted, plus a thousand dinari on special tuition and you've just walked out on the most advanced and prolific and respected scholars in the Empire because ... ?' She ended on a rising note, waiting, wondering when she'd learned to get so pompous and feeling it nearly physically hurt.

'They're wrong,' Isabeau said. Her voice was cool and flat, as if the subject was boring and the question uninteresting. She sliced off the camel's head and then segmented its body into neat pieces, more or less as if following the chart of butchering cuts on display in the meat shops.

'Wrong,' Tralane said, wishing so very hard she could step

out of this awkward thing she was becoming and into something more useful, or at least warm and caring. But those parts of her hadn't woken up yet.

Isabeau looked at her as if she were hopelessly slow. 'Yes,' she said. 'Wrong.'

'About what?'

'I don't want to discuss it.'

Tralane felt a flash in her head, both pain and light. She felt Carlyn touch her arm and looked at her. Carlyn's blue eyes and golden curly hair. Carlyn's knowing look of sympathy.

'Bigger fish first,' Carlyn said. 'Let's get one thing done at a time. She's not going anywhere for now.' She took Tralane by her sleeve and pulled her.

Tralane followed, feeling distinctly that she was about to overload and blow some kind of permanent fuse in her head. Following Carlyn seemed all she was good for. She toyed with the idea of going for the gun but that wouldn't do much good. She wasn't going to shoot Mazhd. She wasn't sure she could speak in the same room with him, so pulling a weapon and killing him was beyond the wildest realms of possibility. Why did it have to be him? Wasn't there some other gossip-sucking, sneaking, untrustworthy sonofabitch they could have found to do the job?

She ground her teeth when she saw Minnabar coming towards them as they walked to the room. Minna ran forward to hug Carlyn hello and then trailed them.

'Go back now,' Tralane said to her. She didn't think they were really in danger but she badly wanted not to be witnessed in front of this man. It wasn't as if she had anything to hide about him – he had never been her lover. They'd met once, at a large social event, some Academy prizegiving, and she'd asked for an introduction because she was drunk and feeling frivolous and full of herself. He was notorious; illustrious because of being the incomparably mysterious Night's student, and just then

168

remarkable for their separation. The rumours had run riot from esoteric to erotic and usually a confabulation of both. Tralane despised the situation intellectually as fatuous but she'd seen him across the room – why was it the distant glance, unobserved, that mattered so much? Anyway, she had been unable to prevent herself fantasising about him. Later that had made her ashamed, to be so like everyone else. Then it had been exciting. Carlyn had made the arrangements. He had been polite and attentive, she remembered, or thought she did. They'd talked of everything but what she wanted to know. He'd been alone but she doubted there was a bed in Glimshard he couldn't have been in that night. It was the night she'd been called home suddenly in panic, to find Minnabar with a virus, vomiting on everything in sight, including her one evening gown when she had gone to commiserate and offer weak tea and dry biscuits. For all these reasons now she felt justified in sending Minna away.

She was ignored, naturally, and as she reached the door she realised the truth of her shame. In front of Mazhd she had no power. She'd given it all to him when they met, even before his lips had touched her flux-burned knuckles and before his fingers had gripped hers and hidden the black grease lines that would never never wash out beneath her nails. This made her girlish and foolish and beneath respect. It was an idiotic thing to have done and even now the perverse joy she felt about it was breathtakingly stupid. She inhaled and attempted to suck the gift of it back again with the air, but a sullen weight in her chest said the magic had not worked. Her palm on the wood undid the locks. It was resignation, not authority, that let her open the door and step into the room with the calm, steady stride, and resignation that prevented her from acting with surprise when she found him lying atop the neatly made coverlet, reading a book.

My, she thought, this room is damp and needs airing out. She saw his boots lined up neatly at the bed's foot, tucked under it as if they belonged. He got up in a fluid, single movement, book cast behind him, and made a half bow which looked apologetic.

'I'm glad to see you looking so well,' he said. His expression was sincere.

Tralane blinked speechlessly for a moment, then laughed. He laughed too, but kindly, with her. 'I suppose Shrazade sent you to find out why I crossed your border.'

'Of course,' he said. 'But given the weather we are prepared to assume a mistake.'

'How generous,' she said, disliking the sensation of being on the hook in her own domain. 'You assume correctly however. I lost too much height and it was cross you or crash.'

His smile stayed in his eyes, a sparkle that would not diminish even when the rest of his face became more serious now that they had dismissed the first bit of business. The second, the matter of her disposal of the spying spell, was much more significant and she didn't want him to seize the initiative, nor speak of it before the others. 'I suppose I should thank you, but I'm not going to. I want you out of my house and I never asked you into it.'

His glance, a half bow of recognition accompanied by the merest lowering of his chin displayed his understanding of her although he looked hurt. 'Of course, I will be going immediately now that you have kindly let me out.' He turned, put on his coat and collected his book and then paused in the act of slipping it into the coat pocket. 'I understand congratulations are in order.'

Tralane searched her mind frenetically – congratulations?

He segued effortlessly in to save her. 'On your daughter Isabeau's acceptance as the student of Parlumi Night.'

She searched his face avidly but there was no sign of mockery or anything besides genuine approval and a search for her own reaction.

'Oh that,' she said, as if it was old news, mentally preparing to stake Isabeau out to dry. 'Yes, we were all so surprised.'

Behind her she heard Carlyn clearing her throat with a magnificent cough. Minnabar's voice rose over it in an indignant, 'Wha-at?!'

Tralane levelled her gaze at Mazhd. 'I'd be most grateful for any advice you might have on that score. Isabeau is much younger than you were when you held the same post and her background is far different.'

Mazhd's hand, elegant, poised, lingered and touched the book in his pocket. His dark eyes filled with soft invitations. 'I'm afraid I would have to know you personally much better than I do before I would be comfortable revealing information about my relationship to Night.'

Tralane studied him. It wasn't him – he was delightful – it was what he represented that made her hesitate and her head spin. She told herself that at least. Yes. It was not easy to deal with the massive disruption such a person could make to her life. But it seemed that there were more reasons to agree and move on than say no and refuse. If only he would put into words all the things he seemed so eager to say with his expressive body. She was flattered and she didn't trust that. But she saw too that Mazhd could be a barrier against Alide, a conduit into circuits of power that until lately had held no interest but which now felt like they strangled her all the time.

'You can come over for *ikasen* then,' she said. 'Be here by eight.'

'Thank you, I will.' A subtle glow of deep satisfaction rippled over him and she wondered again what she was walking into.

A surprised silence behind her met her statement and she took the moment – rare and precious – to step back and gesture for him to precede her out of the room. She saw Carlyn mouthing 'What?' to her as he passed by. *Ikasen* was dinner for two, an invitation offered when one wished to explore the possibility of a relationship of note with another. Everyone else was automatically excluded. Minna's eyes were also wide.

Tralane returned a glance of 'so what?' to her daughter and winked at Carlyn with a confidence she didn't feel. She followed Mazhd to the outer door – noting he never took a wrong turn – and showed him out. Once he'd gone she closed the door and leaned against it looking back to the kitchen turn where the others stood watching her.

'What have I got myself into now?' she asked them, only partly rhetorically. She groaned and hit her head against the solid wood gently.

Carlyn was smiling at her. 'I wish you could see your face.'

Tralane thought about the gun, the crystals. 'Keep that image because there's more to come.' She pushed off the door and strode back to the kitchen, turning with purpose and authority – but Isabeau was already gone. 'Dammit!'

'I can find her for you,' Minna offered, a promise of cold blood in her voice that Tralane took to mean she hadn't been in on Isabeau's doings either.

'No, let her go, I can deal with her later,' Tralane said, exasperated beyond measure. 'Right now I have to ... clear up here and ...'

'You should get some sleep before your big night,' Carlyn said, beginning to collect up the dishes.

'Oh it's not a big night, I just said that so we'll have time to talk.' Tralane was taken aback by her own glibness.

'Right.' Carlyn ran water and soap into the sink. 'Well, I have to go finish packing for my expedition shortly so right now your priority is handing me dishes and talking to me.'

'I can't believe you asked him for *ikasen*,' Minnabar said, although she was attempting to slide out the door before some domestic duty was pushed her way at the same time so Tralane merely awarded her a suitably haughty withering glance of dismissal of the opinion of someone young and ignorant in the face of a better. It kind of hurt the cheeks and she was glad when Minna twisted out of sight and padded off towards her room.

'He is NOT the daddy type!' Minna shouted with warning tones from the hall.

Tralane ferried the ex-pancake plates to the sink and watched Carlyn scrub them with unbridled enthusiasm. She put her hand on her friend's shoulder and rubbed it. 'Duck and Diver are going with you?' She used the pet names for Carlyn's colleague-lovers to try and inject a bit of comfort into the conversation. She didn't feel there was all that much comfort to grab on to realistically. Carlyn's emergency dispatch was so unusual that it set all kinds of alarm bells ringing in her head, connected up inevitably to the war and the quiet daily statistics of those lost in the south. Selfishly she longed for the dull days when there was nothing to do but climb the stairs to the lab. But she massaged Carlyn's shoulder and watched the dishes emerge, steaming, on to the drainer.

'No,' Carlyn said. 'As I understand it from the requisitions it's a skeleton science team. Or ... it occurred to me that maybe they're sending one at a time in case ... Well, so you only lose one at a time and not all of them at once.'

That had also occurred to Tralane. She couldn't say something flippant to try and soak off the implications. She stared into the soapy water flowing around Carlyn's reddened hands. 'Carly, that gun I showed you ...'

Carlyn's hands stopped, submerged to the wrist. Tralane felt a sickly rush over her skin, as if relief and fear made a slippery cloak together.

After a minute Carlyn said, 'I don't have any way to defend myself, Lane. I thought I'd just try to see if I could make it work like you did and then— No. I thought I'd take it if I could use it because I got this sample back from the site. And it's old. It's so unusual, Kamatek, but it answers so many questions, or it could, if there was only more. And the other expedition didn't come back with it. And I have to go. But anyway, I couldn't figure out how to work the damned thing and then Best came and found

173

me with it. I asked him not to tell you because— Lane, I know it was wrong. I was wrong. I'm so so sorry.'

Tralane thought it over. She felt betrayed but in a way Carlyn had done her a favour. There was a thing in the sky made of metal where a star should be and she had a daughter who was a natural teksmith, so adept that she could do in a minute what took Tralane a day to figure out. She wouldn't have known all this, perhaps, without all that. And she could feel Carlyn's mortal dread in her shoulders, even though it was the word 'Kamatek' which lodged inside her own gut. If a Kamatek depository had been located then that explained a lot about the war and the silences, the deceptions, the lack of public knowledge. She tried and failed to suppress a thrilled jolt of anticipation because it was disloyal when Carlyn was so afraid.

'I understand,' she said, and she did. She patted Carlyn and nudged her out of the way of the sink. 'Let me finish that. You make some tea.' She couldn't directly forgive her because that would have dragged up too much there was no point in dragging up, but there was no need to. They both knew what it meant and that it was over.

Tralane washed the plates, grateful to be able to do a job well and easily, then dried her hands. 'I can't give you the gun,' she said. 'It's dangerous if used incorrectly and—'

'You don't need to explain,' Carlyn said. 'I've proved I can't use it.'

Tralane bit her lip, thinking, but all her solutions only led others into danger. 'You could play it sick. I'm sure there's something you could take that would fake a good illness.'

'No. I'm going.' As Carlyn looked up, her eyes were full of the same excitement that Tralane felt at the prospect of a discovery. 'But if I don't come back I've left my affairs in Duck's hands.'

'Don't be stupid,' Lane said. 'Of course you'll come back.'

'Yeah,' Carlyn said. 'Well at least there's no trouble with the journey now they got the portgate up and running. In and out like the proverbial Lothario.' Her voice trailed off at the end of the sentence. 'Did you know they took the tiger man to the palace?'

'Probably a good idea.'

'Nobody's allowed to see him. Only the Empress, Alide and Professor Utaska.' A note of professional jealousy had crept into her voice. 'Because they want me to go south I can't be in her group even though I'm going right into his territory, well nearly... Can you believe it?'

Tralane nodded. 'They don't trust him.'

'Oh? I thought it was that they didn't trust me.'

Tralane didn't know what to say now. She put her hand out over Carlyn's hand. 'It'll be okay. They're probably just being very cautious.'

Carlyn nodded, but Tralane saw she wasn't believed. She wasn't convinced herself.

CHAPTER TWELVE

TZABAN

Tzaban lay in his panelled room and listened to the Empress and her guards making love. He had a comfortable bed he could have been in but he lay on the stone floor under the opened window, trying not to notice the smell of its metal bars. He had expected to be imprisoned and this was much better than the cells at the barracks, but he was surprised to find how hard it was to endure even knowing that if he had really wanted to he could escape.

He felt a dull kind of defeat. After the audience he was convinced they would not listen. No, that they *could not* listen. Their words were poor at conveying what he meant. They didn't seem to grasp the truth of Karoo: that you were one, but also, you were all. He felt despair, because of all the Karoo he was among the most individuated, the most able to see how the humans all lived in close-confined isolation. But even he didn't really understand them, nor they him. He had seen they didn't believe him when he told them that Karoo would be the end of them. The wars they fought amongst each other did not hold any precedent for them. Violent and barbaric, they hacked, smashed and exploded one another with varying degrees of ferocity. It amazed him. Even more so because. as human, once they were dead they would not return in any meaningful way. Their flesh rotted into the earth or burned to greasy ashes.

Karoo on the other hand ate each other and were reformed, becoming other, becoming new. This is why his genesis had been such a bitter surprise to them. He was made to hunt and eat, both Karoo and not-Karoo things, and they had had such high hopes for him of an entirely different kind. He ought to have been the pinnacle of their Dreaming line, a flower. But he was all pelt and teeth and none of his forms were remotely peaceable. They'd tried for years, thinking he'd change but, in the respect of his nature, he could not.

He rolled on to his back and looked up at the stars. Plains stars, he knew them all, the true stars and the glittering motes of the compass pointers which sometimes whispered to him about things in distant places. He scratched his belly and smelled the odd perfume of the Empress descend afresh from the terraces and gardens above him. It bathed him, invaded him. Avoiding it was impossible. He felt his energy subtly shift as his body responded to the commands it carried. Peace and contentment eased into his bones. He lolled in a haze of pericoital satisfaction, surprised by its pleasantness. He wondered how much the races of the plains were subject to her controls if even he was affected. It perhaps explained the relative peacefulness of those tribes whose territories bordered on the city's own.

He found himself rolling on his back on the sculpted carpet a moment or two later and blinked in surprise. She was more potent than he'd thought. He didn't get up. Rubbing his shoulders against the bulky wool was oddly satisfying. He fell asleep there, sprawled at the foot of the bed and woke in the middle of the night as he sensed an approach through the dark.

He rose to his feet, noticed the lamps had been put out without his noticing. Then the guard's halberd knocked the door to announce a visitor and the bolts slid back.

Parlumi Night passed silently across the carpets, he and she greeting one another without voices. He attuned his energy to hers as was only correct with her as the dominant presence and they established an immediate rapport before they got too close to each other, he half turning aside to her approach. Her examination of him was brief and unintrusive.

'So, here you are, the infamous Beast of the North. I have seen you in dreams of my own but you never saw me. Is it true you have no Dreaming skill at all?'

Tzaban felt himself in danger and forced himself to breathe easy although his instinct made him want to freeze. He would not let her know how much he was intimidated. Any female Karoo was potentially a threat in her ability to subjugate him to her will, but this one, halfbreed as she may be, was exceptionally charmed. Her energy was held in check but he felt it over him as wide as the sky and heavy as a storm. He had no intent of becoming hers, so he must be careful.

'It is untrue. I stalk there most successfully.' He wondered that he had never felt her presence. Perhaps she was lying. He would not put it past her.

'It must be embarrassment at their failure that makes them claim it, that or they don't know.' This was question more than statement. Her attention closed around him.

'I am exiled far for a reason.'

'What exactly is so very upsetting? The hunting?'

'I was made to unite the Dreamers. They envisaged peaceful waters and pretty meadows, an end to slaughter, an end to suffering. I am Red Death. My nature is profoundly offensive to them regardless of what I do.'

'I wonder,' she said thoughtfully and he heard her nail tap against her teeth. 'Well, we'll see what you're really for, won't we? My Mistress the Empress wishes you to accompany a mission south to the forest line. You are to be her agent, the shield over her diligent hands. You are to parlay for peace. Do you think you can manage such a task?'

Tzaban felt blood drain out of his face and hands. No. Of course not. She knew it as well as he did. It was impossible. Why would she ask? He waited.

'The difficulty,' she said after a moment, 'is that there's no telling a human about Karoo. They simply never get it. You will fail and they will fall. Who you side with really doesn't matter. But *what* they are so bothered about does matter. To me. I don't want it buried under a Karoo overgrowth or stuffed and abandoned with human dead like some reliquary. Not until I've seen it.'

He felt her uncertainty harden to a point and determine that she wanted to be sure of him. He knew he could not escape.

'Lie on your back,' she commanded.

He made no effort to comply. It may as well be this way as another and further pretence would serve nothing. Instead he tilted his head and growled lightly, a warning.

Night exerted the full pressure of her will immediately, perhaps sensing that no weaker action would get a result.

Tzaban remained standing and turned to face her, forehead lowered. The experience of her was overwhelming. She was a wave waiting to break on his head. The desire to kill her became nearly unbearable.

Abruptly she released her thrall. His eyes widened. It was as if he suddenly exploded back into the world.

'Oh, I see.' She watched him. She was the still one now. Their roles in this moment had reversed now that the essential heresy of his existence was revealed. 'That is why.' She thought for a moment and he could almost smell the trail of her passing across the logical hunting places: he had been exiled because he was uncontrollable. He was a predator. He was a failed chosen son of the sacred Dream. Therefore she must ask, what had become of those who had rejected him. 'Did you kill them?'

'A few,' he said. His teeth hurt with the need to bite. 'They wouldn't stop.'

'If I hadn't stopped, would you kill me?'

'Yes.' He noticed she hadn't suggested he couldn't. He had no knowledge of what she was able to do, but it didn't matter. He would have killed her or died trying.

'Then you are an interesting anomaly,' she said, adding with a tone of rich amusement, 'and they made you for peace.'

'Yes.' He hesitated and then felt himself smile. 'Maybe the mistake was in not specifying how peace was to be attained.'

'Maybe,' she said.

The question of whether they ought to test one another lay between them in the air. She could smell the truth of his statements, but she didn't know herself whom he had ended and who spared, nor why, nor how. He in turn suspected already that she relied entirely on intimidation to do her work for her in these cases. Without meaning to he felt his right hand flex and the claws try to spring out, blunt or not, itching for the feel of flesh under them. He very deliberately turned his back to her.

'Tzaban. What do you hope to achieve? You must have known you would end here. Even if you are let out you won't be unwatched. Every moment you are here plans about you are being cast elsewhere. You could have run wild and nobody would have found you.'

'I had to come.' He felt no change in her. 'Why do you let them carry on, when you know how it must end?'

'The end is not certain.' But she said this without conviction. He felt the pressure of her ease, an opening hand.

Because she didn't believe it, he ignored the statement. 'I can see why you have stayed here. They think you are special. You are revered. Powerful. You don't miss Karoo.'

'I never had Karoo!' She spat, suddenly. His fur rippled with reaction to her anger, but it wasn't directed at him, it merely circled and passed him, bounced off the walls and objects in long ricochets, slashing the air into bits. His hair bristled but he was trying to listen without moving and betraying his thoughts.

To live so long and not be connected – the idea was nearly impossible to conceive. He at least was still joined, albeit in a self-imposed silence on both sides, but he still felt the truth of Karoo. He wondered if hers was choice, or unhappy accident of birth. If the second, how had she discovered so much of what it was to be Karoo by herself? A fleeting sense of kindred swept him from the back of his head to his tail. His hostility began to unbend itself.

Her voice was cool when she spoke. 'Most of the people here have no idea what I am and I like it that way. The Empress, her advisers, but no more. You, on the other hand, stick out like a sore thumb.'

'The only difference is that they are blind to your differences,' he said, but thoughtful, sensing they were not trading insults here but instead attempting to stagger somewhere new. She did not want to be revealed.

He wasn't sure how he felt about allegiance. She'd been in human lands and worlds more intensively and intimately than he ever wished to be. Their pathetic senses of loyalty to ideas – always confusing thoughts with reality – that might infect her too deeply and leave him exposed to threats she had yet to brew. He distended his nostrils but all he smelled was the transforming perfume of the Empress with its determination to turn everything it touched to sensual love. His body reacted helplessly – another reason not to turn.

Behind him Night's voice wound its own spell of seduction. 'You can never belong here. They will use you, and when that runs out they will cut you in pieces to discover how you work, what you are.'

'Then you are useful,' he said. For the Empress he might have agreed. She alone so far had shown him courtesy and a sweet heart. Night was too afraid to do so and that made him turn against her.

'I have learned to be.' Another half statement, protective,

pretending what it wouldn't deliver. She wasn't going to be the one to take the first step. She would push him until he did what she wanted. But Tzaban could never take those terms.

'I am useful,' he said, though he'd have liked to see anyone try to cut him in pieces. He would have welcomed the opportunity to return the favour. Everyone here was prey and them thinking that they were otherwise irked him like an unreachable itch.

'See you stay that way.' He heard her acceptance of their bargain in those words that said she was watching his back. Her step forward was made. There were no details, but that was typical Karoo. One is allied or not allied; the details are unimportant and there is no limit to it.

Tzaban turned around. Night was looking at him hungrily.

'I want to see this place,' he said, nodding his head in the direction of the barred window through which the starred night and glittering city were visible. 'I want to see it all.'

'Then you'll have to behave,' she said, moving closer.

He felt the subtlety at the last moment. That prompt, that tug at his sense of desire. She wanted him to obey.

'No.' He glanced at the bars. They felt threatening now and running filled his legs and made them shake.

Already this humanoid form and all the attendant things it brought was making him so like them, so unlike what he had been before. He looked at the room and the city and saw ideas made real in a way that Karoo would never attempt and it fascinated him. Karoo would not build it. They would become it. As the humans had weapons so the Karoo had him, their peacemaker.

He took a step towards her, unthinkable in Karoo terms where any female or demi-fem determined the approach and survival of a male. He knew immediately by her mild reaction of surprise that she had no idea how unthinkable it was, knew her connections and understanding were intuitive only, not experienced, not knowing. They would change each other and there was no way to predict how.

'No,' he said, head down. 'You don't know what you're asking.'

Even as he said it he recognised that he hadn't come here by accident. Of all the human places this was the one that most closely resembled what he knew. The females were dominant and he was comforted by that even though he could not submit to it except in the way of civilised creatures, through necessity's simple freedoms of choice that were no choice at all.

'That's exactly why I'm asking,' she said and dropped the glamour of her energy like casting off a cloak. The nakedness of her ambition and intent hit him like a blow to his face. She would dare anything to satisfy her curiosity and desire. 'Isn't the problem between us the same as the one between you and the humans anyway? And here I am. Halfway. Dare to bridge that gap.'

Tzaban was afraid of what she was but he knew it for a root fear of male to female across the ages because they were always lesser, and could be taken or eaten without mercy.

A Karoo female when faced with a Karoo male of interesting speciation could assimilate all he was by a variety of methods; copulation, symbiosis or ingestion. It was the role of males to travel and glean. High intelligence, self-awareness and self-preservation were not features they often possessed. They were created unequal, even amongst themselves. The currency and beauty of life's variety, as collected and prepared, was the only value they had. They were more rare lately, as Karoo had spread and its diversity had reached a plateau. They were risky business.

He was so curious. He pounced on her in a fluid leap that knocked her back on to the rug she had been standing on. Midway through the act, as his hand made contact with her face to turn it, he was caught in what felt like a soft cloud that slowed them both down. Dark energy billowed around him, scented with violets and the sweetness of her heat. They collapsed slowly, limp and feathery where he was braced for hard impact but his palm ended up on her cheek, fingers gripping her skull and turning it away from him to the side, his body over hers, arm on arm, legs on legs, pinning her down. Everything that was hidden in her fine clothing became apparent. She was strong, but untried. Her face dropped with dismay as she attempted to heave him off and only lifted his clamped hand and ruthless knee an imaginary amount before falling back. Outrage and pleasure briefly warred in the half of her face he could see. He would have liked to look in her eyes but he knew that danger too well.

The fact he was alive now was a good sign. He coiled his tail carefully and bent his head down, nostrils distended to take in every scent of her, skin and breath, whiskers tasting the air around her to see how much of a threat she was.

A moment of sensory shock numbed him. Whatever Karoo was, it had so little human in it, and she had so very much human in her. Greed, intoxication, his nose filled with it until it was all he knew. She was talking but he didn't hear. He felt the skin on his hands burst where he gripped her naked arm, the sting and flicker of needle tendrils plunging deep – his mind's eye suddenly filled not with Night but a terrified Steppe girl squealing and running from him, her wrist red, ripping shreds off him in a bloody bracelet. Feels cold air on his bare teeth, icy, hurting. Pumping up his arm the knowledge comes rushing, explaining everything about those first humans he found, their camp, their lives, their weakness, their death. He licked his sore palm and left that place, running over rocks. When he came back later in the year he had significantly changed. He looked, spoke, almost like a man.

CHAPTER THIRTEEN

ZHARAZIN

Diary, Entries 166-8

I decided to ask what considerations the Sorority recommended for locating a mate, if we were to do away with the pronouns. Sister Auchie said it must be first the good health, then the Talent combination and its possible outcomes, after that the looks of the male (she assumed breeding-mate you see as I did not use the correct pronoun to indicate a loving partner of any suited gender), for beauty generally indicates a strong and robust constitution, after that his friends, since he may be judged well by those whose company he seeks and maintains: after that his character and after that his charisma and latent 'appeal'. *His* gender only has bearing insofar as it may or may not impede said breeding. I said, fine, that covers Empire men. What about the rest? She looked blank. Finally she said, 'One does not breed outside the Empire. What would be the point?'

It occurs to me that the Sorority has entirely missed the point sociologically. Surely the point is desire, which is the only impulse one does anything for? A walk behind my sister (a block behind, but she's easy to follow as she never pays any attention to anyone except herself) puts a spanner in the cogs of the very notion that the desire for sex has its point anywhere near the Sorority rulebook. There are enough foreigners from the barracks creeping back in the early hours after midnight to prove that. I don't think everyone is filling out forms and pursuing a rigorous algorithm of selection – unless they are doing that unconsciously, of course. If so, it is not an algorithm that the Sorority has heard of. An algorithm for desire would be so very useful! Although I might have to expand on the notation re the genders issue. I will ask Sister Auchie why it is that the inbuilt process for selection of mates is insufficient and they have attempted to impose another.

Cross. Idea of Algorithm of Desire met with derision. Auchie mentioned Night's student, called him a halfbreed bloodmancing animal and made the sign of Annasward though there were no trace presences about. She said he would know it if noses could talk. I don't know what she means by that but her expression indicated she was having some kind of intestinal problem so I didn't ask.

Zharazin closed the diary and rested it on his stomach. He pondered what they were teaching girls these days. He'd always wanted to know. It was disappointing to find that it was as dull as this. He didn't see how you got from this diary to sauntering full of confidence, naked, at the Rose. He longed to know what it was that went on in that pretty little head. He considered the Sorority of the Star: superficially they were a group of aesthetes and philosophers who had come to be considered valuable as a relic of older times and socially acceptable only because their scientific education in certain areas was unrivalled. Politically they were a negligible force. However, they originated in Spire's city, Zenithpoint, and had migrated to Glimshard towards the end of the last Empress' rule as part of a cultural exchange which the Infomancy had largely ignored. As far as he knew

186

they didn't have any involvement with spies, but he spoke aloud the notion it was time to review this assumption.

'You've been a very busy man,' Shrazade said to him from her lounging spot in the hammock a few metres away. Her perusal of what he had read and his own reactions to it were nearly simultaneous, even though it had also passed through the entire collected net of Infomancy minds in relay. 'I should commend you if it weren't for your deplorable lack of faith.'

He said nothing. He knew by now she only wanted answers to direct questions from her servers. Anything else was merely an irritation to her own trains of thought and you derailed her at your expense. The lack of faith was her perennial accusation, fairly levelled; he really had no faith at all in the infomancers as the active force for Glimshard's good that she felt them to be. He, and they, simply knew much too much. Sometimes it felt that the infomancers were more like herdsmen, whose cattle were violent brutes that must be kept far from civilisation; the people are better off in ignorance rather than be aware of this vast galaxy of bitter brewing spites.

She plucked the image from his mind and examined it. He knew it pleased her because she said nothing, only stretched. The hammock's silk knots creaked. He looked across at her and she smiled at him; an ordinary woman long past her prime, a little overweight, and very lazy, but with an expression that was as sharp and glittering as the edges of a secret stash of diamonds. She wore plain, easy clothing, tied her hair back without thought; since he'd known her it had silvered to white with only a few streaks of black left in it.

'It is convenient that Huntingore finds you worthy of attention. We would be glad if you accompanied her to the ball. At her side you will find yourself drawn to conversations we will find most interesting. Particularly if she receives a call to the digsite by that time.'

Minister Alide, Huntingore's bane, was the key supplier of

news about the dig. Zharazin had assumed the precious crystals he was blackmailing out of Tralane were for the portal project, but it seemed not. A mole in the engineers said he hadn't seen anything like that in the works. Shrazade was annoyed that she did not know what they were for either. She knew that Huntingore must know and now she was pleased to push Zharazin's personal feelings. He was surprised to find that for the first time since he'd been admitted to her service he felt this an unwanted invasion. He wasn't sure, had never been sure, exactly how much he would be able to conceal from her. He had simply thought it easier to assume the answer was nothing and until now it hadn't mattered. He hadn't mattered to himself.

Shrazade leapt on that without hesitation. 'Night abandoned you, Mazhd, and I took you in. Don't forget that when you feel so sorry. You kept your place in the world, thanks to me. Now read the book. There must be something in it worth the knowing.'

He'd become so adept at surrender, he realised, as he lifted the book and opened it again to the next page. Years of practice had left him with an empty place inside into which he poured the days to later unpack and see what he thought of them. Like this diary, but far larger they were vast memory palaces for private consumption. As he read and processed the diary for Shrazade, he saved it for himself, knowing he would give it a different interpretation on his own, knowing it would write itself into him in ways that would emerge recognisably only now and again, through channels that Shrazade and all her mindpicks had no way to touch. It was only because he lived his memories in his body, in words and actions coming from within, that he knew he was still worthwhile after Night and he parted ways. It had been dark that day, and bitterly chilled, and his skull hurt with the aches of it even now. It had been so foolish and so unnecessary.

Now his eyes fell onto hasty writing in Isabeau's scrawling, awkward hand and gradually he felt the same chill pass into him.

Entry 169

The Sorority claims that the Rose, the bath house, is a late addition to Glimshard society set in place by the Empress' predecessor, Divit, as a result of her taking the philosophy of amoral love to heart in the wake of a tragic bereavement. The Sorority are prepared to accept the subjugation of men to women for the purposes of female entertainment as a matter of natural courses and in any case men are free to refuse the advances of women, although they would be sorry and stupid to refuse women of any power, as the scandal sheets can weekly testify. Powerful men are are another matter. And it was, the Sorority claim, as a gesture to pacify *them*, that Divit founded the Rose bath house and within it the sacred coils of desire.

I am still not sure what 'sacred coils of desire' means. I think it is a euphemism but a cross-reference to Parlumi Night's seminal text on the Call, indicates it is both mystic and literal. Men walk a genuine spiral within the building to the place of their desire – this is representative of the journey of the spirit to carnal birth in the world and the sexual acts engaged therein are literal and spiritual in nature, sacred to all who participate in the spirit of the Rose. As they say, 'Compassion's born when two souls meet.'

The Sorority take a loftier and more intellectual view of this: they see it as a place where men of means may go to rut at their leisure without having to involve themselves in any form of intimacy whatsoever, with a woman or a man. They have nothing to say about what a woman might gain by taking the position of first lover other than that it is a charmless folly. Women of the Sorority have no need of such self-debasement as offering themselves anonymously to random strangers.

The one thing I can't fail to agree with in all this is that one should not talk about what one does not know. I find it intolerable that there are things I ought to be held back from knowing. I am old enough to leave home and do as I please. I know very little about love but unlike my stupid sister I always know exactly what I feel about everything. I suspect that this is the 'Royal Knowledge of the Self' that Night goes on about. If so, I don't understand why people find it all so difficult, but patently they do. Therefore there is something going on that I do not understand yet.

This must be remedied immediately.

Following the neat flourish of determination after this entry the pages of the book were blank.

Zharazin closed his eyes and rubbed them gently with his thumb and forefinger. Behind him the hammock creaked.

'My my,' Shrazade said dryly after a moment or two had passed. 'I seem to be so old I can barely remember being that ruthlessly idealistic. Or is foolhardy the word I am looking for?'

Zharazin fought and struggled to remain silent in his mind, not to connect everything that resonated with the fearsome tolling of the bell because he didn't want her to see it in its awful entirety; not just himself but Isabeau laid bare. He and Isabeau were different of course, but on the points where they crossed you could get enough data to start making maps. It took every bit of ability he had to wall off what else he knew that made Isabeau's final statement so much more than a girlish, petulant demand. Yes, she was ruthless and she had a steel mind. But it was so much more so than Shrazade presently imagined and he felt he had to protect Isabeau from that.

His silence was noted.

'And so she becomes Night's student. Impressed by something. And Night must be so impressed with her. But you, of course – you know nothing about the details of that.'

In fact he didn't, he only guessed, so it was no lie to say, 'I don't. I do know there is suspicion about a plot to dispose of

190

the Empress and now I see a possible merit to investigating the Sorority But these things have no link that I can see.'

'Alide's plans or others beyond that?'

'I have no idea. I would guess that with so many newcomers and mercenaries making their way into the city hoping for a longer war that this would be a good time to send assassins.'

'The Warbeasts are massing to the east,' Shrazade said, 'Warbeasts' being a code for all the minor enemies of the city and its environs who bore grudges against the Empire of one kind and another. 'And tomorrow there is this ball, the grand spectacle of how well things are, the showing off of the outsider, the statement Alide will make about the war in order to get more money to fill his chests while he lies about the losses. Find out if Borze is making preparations for a defence of the city. And who from first. The Warbeasts or something closer to home.'

Information sifted out of her mind like dust and into his, pollen to stamen, burrowing tendrils here and there, searching for connections, for what he thought likely, for what his senses knew before they reported to his conscious mind. Yes, he was picking up signals all the time for her even if he didn't know what they all meant. The process was something he couldn't do anything about. Being in her employment demanded it. He saw himself mined and holed like a mountainside, gold dust in the streams prospected, veins searched for.

'You know,' Shrazade said thoughtfully as dusk finished falling. 'If you want to impress Huntingore you should bring her a gift she will not expect. I have the very thing, as it happens. I'd like you to take it, as a goodwill gesture.'

Zharazin doubted it was that. But he took it at face value. 'Of course. How thoughtful. Thank you.' And let's say nothing about picking my brains too far – it's all about give and take.

'Good. I'll have it wrapped. If she asks say you bought it at the Antiquarian Palazzo from Asmik.'

Asmik was an infomancer operative, he'd confirm any story.

Maybe he'd even sourced the object himself, though Zharazin didn't credit Asmik with anything more than a natural scavenger's eye for the main chance. Asking to see it beforehand was, however, pointless. He wouldn't have known an adze from a zarapt.

The distraction was welcome. He felt Shrazade move out of his mind like a departing ghost. She may have left things behind. He'd find out. Meanwhile he checked his memory palace – nothing had moved. The white bark tree in the grey ground stood out stark and lonely. Sometimes it was hard to know what these things meant. He knew Isabeau was one of a kind. That at least was easy to see.

He left the book behind now that it was of no more use to him. Shrazade would archive it. He exited the room by the back way, hidden from most users, even her finest. It allowed him to leave the Ministry directly via a tunnel of passages that took him down near the barracks and let him free via the back of a hack dentist's store.

A strong smell of alcohol and Fashspark's Powders almost made him sneeze as he emerged into the operating room. In the chair someone groaned. It was the dentist, Morater, half passed out on his own cheap medicines. Zharazin stood on something hard where his path crossed the open doorway and in the light flickering through the grass strip fly-screening he saw it was a molar, black at the centre. Because there was money in teeth – for alchemical powders – he kicked it back into the shop before hurrying along.

Glimshard smouldered in the new night. The Barrack End Road was smug with horse droppings and witchlights, the print of so many strange boots in its mud that it was bloated with information. Westmen had come, he saw, and more Steppe-sons, and others from further afield whose cobbling he didn't know at first sight. He kept to the edges, the parcel from Shrazade in his hand because it was too heavy and wore his cloak down at one side in a distorting fashion. A glance up at the high windows where Borze kept his offices showed lights gleaming, men standing, talking, gesticulating, but idly, importantly. There was still time for speeches, then, and anecdotes and postures. Zharazin passed on.

As he reached the Upspiral he trod on the first paving slabs of Deyaut Place, one way that led to the Rose. It was the slab which in his mental copy of the city, opened the path to the last day he spent with Parlumi Night. As he moved rapidly through the light pedestrian traffic towards the stem and the social world of the artists at Monparauk Square, he simultaneously followed Deyaut Place's hidden route into the past.

Parlumi Night's office of business opened into the Courts. It was rare that anyone except a messenger of the Empress came through it, running and in tabard, but it was closed between midday and sundown when Night preferred to sleep. She didn't like sleep very much, but she wasn't able to avoid it entirely and being nocturnal meant this time was the best. Zharazin was only nocturnal by necessity and slept twice, once in the mid-afternoon and once in the early hours of the morning.

On the day in question they were both in the deep recesses of her twilit apartments behind the offices, where black and purple blinds screened out nearly all light from the generous windows overlooking the palace gardens. They lay on the bed, everything in the room made of blue and pale blue shadows, including themselves. A little music played, a recording of temple flute and chimes from Zharazin's mountain home. The strange bulky box of the Repeater Coil hummed a little underneath the tones, off key, but not enough to spoil anything. It needed repair. They burned incense they both liked, sage and lavender. It kept out bugs.

He had been her student for two years. The Call, which had been to him and many a total mystery, was now familiar. To begin with because he was foreign and not an adept she

193

had taught him as a philosopher. They discussed the nature of attraction, and how things became bound to one another: people, animals, plants, societies, chemicals. His talent complemented hers. He understood the combination of one being and another, their potential for reproduction. This did not always go along with personal attraction. She understood everything else, it seemed – every signal, every symmetry, every desirable and repellent feature of each thing to another in the world. This was the Call, of liking to liking, the glue of the daily business of life. She had ways to encourage it and ways to sever it. People supposed her a matchmaker but she despised the notion. He understood their assumption more forgivingly, being much more human than she was.

Her halfbreed status was like his, mixed parentage, mysterious circumstances – she suggested he could even be the result of a pollination between his human mother and the plant life of the far Northern Steppe in an effort to explain his slender Karoo leanings.

She on the other hand was more like a Karoo who had happened on a human form and wore it in order to pass as one, but carelessly, features always slipping through. The exact details of their inheritances were unknown to them: Night never knew her parents, if she had had any, and Zharazin's mother had never spoken a word about his father, or much of anything. The Steppe people led simple, harsh lives utterly unlike Empire humans, and their virtue was stoic silence about most things. What was unknown could not be held against you, even if the evidence was staring you in the face and talking to you. He'd always been different and it hadn't mattered. It was his own need for exploring that had led him away slowly but surely to Glimshard, the city on the plain, and to Night, with whom he had fallen in love.

They were discussing the unspeakable issue of enmity between Empresses. Night was concerned about protecting their own Empress, but gloomy too. 'She is too different. Her ways and why she has them. I can't feel a path to harmony between them. There is a path of repulsion active between her and the Dirt Empress.' She turned on the bed restlessly, arm flung over her face. He let the sheet slide with her, away from him, and knew that soon she'd be dancing if she did not conclude her thoughts. She processed things with her body. Her mind didn't work without it. And she saw in terms of connections and roads, ways in, ways out, infiltration and assimilation. In that he knew her very Karoo.

Zharazin saw it differently and tried to express that in ways she understood. 'That woman, Dirt, took another kind of path. Her life is nearly done, she has no children and she thinks only about profit and labour, how to manage the land and cull the seasons. She favours the company of Parchers and eats only once a day. Her devotion to her own spirit is very great, the more so because she believes that she paves the way to another life with deeds of sacrifice. Our Empress is everything she isn't. It is like an insult in one way, rejecting all her advice and experience. Glimshard nullifies her. And because we survive she fears she might be wrong, in case Glimshard's path proves better and the afterlife doesn't exist after all. Or it does and all that effort wasn't needed in order to get there. She would have spent herself for nothing.'

'You think she wants to prove her way by force?' Night sighed, thrashed restlessly, fighting with his notions as if they were pests on her skin. He knew better than to try touching her at a moment like this.

'She doesn't want to be or look like a fool. Her pride won't allow it. Reason can swing in the wind with that kind of person.'

'I cannot understand those who desire these cool, dry, dead things,' Night said after a while in which her violence grew less and finally left him naked in the air, sheets tangled around her like a shroud. It was warm so he didn't mind it. 'Production, methods, systems of thought as if thoughts needed a system. It grinds my soul to dust. This is how minds are trapped and evil brought into the world. And you make excuses for her, as if she is innocent.'

'I'm only pointing out why she is as she is, as far as I can guess. It's not an excuse.'

'It is! You think it is all right to lead thousands with that kind of banner?'

'It is how things are. Humans like putting things together and organising them. They fall in love with their ideas as much ...'

'Blasphemy!' Night hissed and Zharazin shut up. The room had sunk into an ominous gloom. 'Heresy,' she said, tasting the word, trying it out, her tone uncertain. She hummed and her mouth shaped syllables meaninglessly until finally she said with conviction, 'Abomination!'

He felt he had to defend the race, the position, somehow. 'You would rather what?'

'I would rather they navigate by the true ways: loyalty, jealousy, passion, desire, love and loss and heart and body. Not these paper idols, these analyses and methods. Zhara, you, why are you standing for them?'

'I'm not. I am trying to hold another point of view so that yours isn't the only one. I tend to agree with you – the intellect is only a servant of the masters – but you can see why it's attractive to want to regulate life, to make it easier and less painful ... Not everyone experiences this passion and love the way you do.'

Parlumi Night rolled suddenly and immediately into his view with a rustle of silk. Her body pressed over him like soft, ripe fruit. Her breath smelled of mint and liquorice. 'Listen,' she said. He felt her tendrils puncture his skin, almost like a tickle, they were so fine, so subtle. 'This fairness you are clinging to. What is it for? There is no fairness in nature, only the rule of fitness, competition and a little luck. The strong can be bested by the weak if they are cunning, and that is strength, but here you have weak people making castles of ideas and forcing everyone to live in their weak little worlds. Because they lack heart and conviction. They have too much power for their puny vessels but they remain uneaten'

Zharazin felt her various venoms entering his blood and lymph. He felt slower, milder, and knew he had moments before the edge of his awareness became fuzzy and his body's humours began to merge with hers. She'd win an argument any way she could and consider it fair. He pushed her off him, snapping the injectors even though it would leave a painful rash in his skin. 'No. Maybe. Only within the domain of your vision. There are other visions. Just because you are as you are does not make you right.' His words lost their way. He sat up and rubbed his arm, leg and chest where they were sore.

She looked at him with a sullen, spoiled expression. 'How can you say this when you know very well that we understand them better than they themselves can ever do?'

'That's your conceit,' he said, finding himself more at odds with her than he wanted but unable to stop. 'It's not for you to judge them any more than they can judge you.'

She laughed at that. 'Idiot,' she said, fondly. 'It is for everyone. The fact is they don't know how they are ruled, even within themselves. Karoo know. They always know.'

'Yes,' he said. 'But Karoo are not free of it. They vie and fight and eat each other all the time. It's not better, only different in its appearances. At least the humans don't always end up killing each other.'

Her long tail lashed the bed silently. 'Desire is the path, the only path.'

'What about altruism? Parents protecting children, or their interests?'

She had nothing to say about that. Karoo had no altruism, did not breed in human ways and parented or not as their genotype

197

demanded of them. Their unity bound them but nothing else tied one to another, across or between generations. Friendship, loyalties, mate bonds – these things existed sometimes, to greater or lesser degrees. They were all kin and so none had particular kin loyalty to another. They had no particular enmity either. It wasn't that she had no regard for what he said, it was that she could not grasp it at all.

Reluctantly, after a while, she admitted as much. She asked him one of her favourite questions, as an apology of sorts, and approached him gently to lick his arm where it was leaking tiny dots of blood, to fix it with her saliva. 'Tell me what it was like, growing up with a mother.'

He relented as her nursing took the sting away. He told her the familiar tale, dwelling on the parts that fascinated her; these were all concerned with connection, loyalty, moments of care and sacrifice, ordinary things as far as humans knew. He was sure his childhood was not exceptional in any way, other than for his fatherless status which had left him and his mother at the whims of the married women until she was taken up as a wife by an older herdsman who had enough money to buy her out of her animals. He left by the time he was ten.

'Did it hurt, leaving?' Night asked, rapt as a child herself.

'No,' he said. 'I was old enough, it was expected. Being different, it was the right thing to do, take myself away. It was approved of. She knew it as well as I did. I went with the spice traders on their spring pass and came to the Empire as fast as I could.'

It had hurt of course, but he was used to swallowing that kind of thing by then, had grown used to it over the years and now still tended to believe what he said about it. It hurt unbearably, like many things that everyone smiled and put a brave face on and said were good deeds. It made most of the Empire think the Steppefolk were hard and unfeeling brutes. But they had only chosen a different way to deal with things. It wasn't that they didn't understand. They understood very well but it would take a better storyteller than he was to explain how they showed their kindness and sympathy in actions, gestures, little deeds, glances, the touch of hand on an arm, a nod, a moment of silence. It was nothing like Empire life. It was so far from it as to be nearly unrecognisable.

Night waited, clinging to him like a lost person in a desert, waiting for a drink of water.

'Do you think that everyone is capable of understanding each other?' he asked her then. 'If they had enough time and patience, if they wanted to enough?'

'No,' she said. 'History is particular to the individual. Every moment turns a new pattern. Why do you lie about your childhood, Zhara?'

'Because it's mine,' he said. 'Do you understand that?'

She looked hurt and nodded, withdrew and lay down beside him again. A hot breeze moved the curtains. 'You and I are done here,' she said. 'That hurts and is sad. I have nothing else and you don't want me more.'

How to explain a thing like that to someone else? People assumed they had argued and broken up over a critical analysis of the Call – the theory of desire. It was why Imperial people broke their friendships and alliances, over ideas and principles, over hypotheses and the right thing to do. He couldn't say into that expectation that they had simply run to the end of their road and had come upon it surprised and dismayed, so attuned to their commitment to pursue their callings that they couldn't lie about that even for a moment to one another. It was the Imperial way to find a compromise, to soften a blow. But a Steppelander simply took the blow and Karoo accepted what came without trying to turn it, they sank or swam.

She took his hand and their fingers interlaced. 'Where will you go?'

'To the middle of things,' he said. 'I have to find out for

myself if you are right. I have to prove it until I don't have hope in mutual understanding any more.'

'I wish it wasn't so,' she said, ending on a rising tone, trying to comfort him with what sounded like a small girl offering up a statement to be disagreed with, to show she knew her place.

'So do I.' He didn't know what she referred to exactly with that wish: did she want her statement or their parting to be undone? He decided he didn't want to know. It could be both. It was both for him.

They slept together until the next afternoon and then he rose and left without another word.

Until the afternoon he followed Isabeau Huntingore to her offices Zharazin did not see her again.

CHAPTER FOURTEEN

SHRAZADE

'Mazhd's greatest fault is that he doesn't understand hate,' Shrazade said to Alide as they met in the gloomy confines of the infomancer's sanctum. They sat in a room she had chosen to emphasise claustrophobic responses as she knew he hated confinement. 'He can witness all kinds of acts and not see simple loathing in them, always looking at other motives.'

'It's not your business to speculate on motive,' Alide replied, apparently relaxed in his chair although she could smell the faint scent of sweat. 'Only to report the facts. Motivations are for inquisitions to bother with. Neither you nor I have time for them.'

Shrazade inclined her head politely in a gesture of agreement, feeling a deal of satisfaction at this, although she couldn't disagree more. If you were sure of them, motives were more valuable than any facts. Motives were a person's soul in action, rules of behaviour which could be used in any number of interesting ways. She was not so naive as to assume he spoke the truth of his views here, but Alide had always been a straightforward person, unafraid to hide his opinions, even when they opposed the Empress. Until now she had wondered if this was a ploy to develop his public face as an honourable man. Lately, however, she had come to suspect that he did not realise the depth of his betrayals. For some reason he was convinced of his own correctness so much it did not occur to him that others may feel differently about where the right of things lay. She surmised from this in turn that he must have a backer, a confidant, who held a position of some prestige. She could not under any circumstances see Alide as the kind of person who could stand alone this way, but he certainly could be lulled into security by a sponsor. Now she wondered who it was and as he began speaking again her mind began to plan out who she would use to find this out, and how.

'Have your spies in the Plains States discovered more?'

'War councils are gathering over the next few weeks,' she said. 'The reports have reached them that many of the mercenaries are not returning from the front. Nor is the portal trusted. There will be moves to attempt to destroy it, and there are spies in the city attempting to discover how extensive the defences are. I have let them move relatively freely so far. They are particularly interested in garrison numbers and the intentions of Borze considering war with the Karoo. They watch the passes to the other cities avidly. They have probed the palace arrangements, but I have fed them disinformation about the methods of communication between cities and within it. We are hampered somewhat by the other cities themselves however. We believe that the city of Grass has a portable portal device or caster which they are denying at present. But they have an equal number of engineers and technomancers to Glimshard. Plus my operative has witnessed portal usage by small numbers of people without anything like the structures we have built on the pass. I would say that if you are going to achieve anything in the southern digsite you will have to achieve it very soon.'

Alide nodded slowly. 'What of the Karoo at the palace?'

'An unlikely anomaly,' Shrazade said, pouring tea for herself. 'But not, we think, the first of more.' She knew that Alide had approved sending the Karoo south to the site, together with Huntingore and an elite troop of homebred guard. That meant he had got what he wanted from the engineer. She knew it was a weapon of some kind. With them gone the Empress and the city would have only the cut-down remnants of the army to protect them. No doubt Huntingore was typical of her type in having no clue of her place in the play of such things – that pamphlet she'd written proved that she had barely opened her eyes outside her laboratory in the last ten years. And now Alide was hoping to bury her in a distant plot of land because he would never leave a scorpion alive under a rock once he'd turned it.

Shrazade did not point this out as she was sure it was part of his plans. All that frustrated her so far was the lack of any hard evidence that he had insurrection on his mind. She fished, idly.

'You will not go south yourself?' she asked and with pleasure saw his chest puff up.

'Certainly not. To abandon the city to my inferiors at this time would be treacherous.'

'As you say,' she sipped the tea. Perhaps he would only wait for nature to take its course here and for the Empress to prove herself incompetent. If he were wise he would do that, she thought. No need to push when events already turn in your favour. She briefly considered the alternatives.

A new Empress would mean changes. There was no Empress in waiting, as far as she knew, although cities had a way of keeping these under wraps until the last moment, for their own protection. Before Torada, Glimshard had been ruled by Divit. Fierce and martial, Divit had not much time for men of any kind except as necessary adjuncts for the continued existence of the people. She had been the one who had built the army so successfully for Torada to inherit. Men were employed in it sacrificially, with honour but no pretence. Divit saw them as expendable units and, under her command, they agreed. The city had been full of grimly determined soldiers, noble and self-sacrificing. She and Torada were worlds apart and the Glimshard that Shrazade knew now was unrecognisable to the one of forty years ago. Shrazade preferred Torada's sweet generosity of spirit to Divit's driving ambition. She did not want to lose it already, especially when it was so unproven. The other cities had familiar demons at their heads. Torada was an unexplored avenue of being and as such, fascinating. But she knew most people did not like unfamiliar things. In that they were weak, and she despised them. Alide's failure to adapt left him well inside this bracket but though she had looked for connections that joined him to Dirt and her city of Grass, these remained elusive.

She maintained a silence and waited for the crushing smallness of the dark room to work on Alide, counting how many seconds it would take for him to bail out.

'I must be going,' he said, making a show of getting out his pocket watch and observing it.

More than a minute, she thought, not bad.

'Yes, allow me to show you out.'

When she returned to the room the tea was cold. Mazhd stepped out of the hidden alcove and began to clear the table.

'You,' she said to him. 'Must stay away from him for the time being. But at least he thinks you're less than competent now. He thinks you are my stooge in Huntingore's arena. Don't waste that, will you?'

Mazhd smiled. 'I don't think he's the one, do you?'

'Conspiring against the Empress? No. It threatens the city and he can't do that, he doesn't have it in him. But he knows the person who is. You must go do your duty by that lawyer now since her wishes coincide so neatly with our own.' She watched him as he prepared to leave. 'If your loyalties are tested, Mazhd, don't make me regret all I've given you.'

He looked at her carefully. 'Of course not.'

'The city before everything,' she said. 'Everything.'

He nodded, and left.

Tralane sat at the workbench and watched Minna disassemble and reassemble the gun. Her own piece of the Flit's engine hadn't changed in the last forty minutes. She was mesmerised by the speed and accuracy of her daughter's hands on the piece, as if she had worked on these objects for years. The expertise was in itself pleasing to watch, but the implications of it stretched into her worried mind.

'Is there more of this kind of stuff up in the attics?' Minna asked, so absorbed in her task that she didn't bother looking up. Her fingers picked up and put down tools automatically.

'I don't really know,' Tralane said. 'But you're welcome to go search. I only found this because ... It was an accident. I just tripped over it.' She waited nervously to see if Minna would catch her cover-up but Minna just kept on working.

'Uh huh, well where was it?'

'In the Long Gallery, among the older stuff. It's very dusty in there. You'll need a mask.' Tralane sighed at the state of the house. Her daughters would inherit a crumbling heap and be lucky not to end up in a pile of rubble if she wasn't careful. Maybe she should cultivate a builder ... And then she looked at the time and the blood all drained to her feet. She swore and then Minna looked up, fully attentive.

'Mom!'

'I invited Mazhd for *ikasen*. He'll be here in fifteen minutes. I haven't done ANYTHING.' Tralane pushed the cylinder head aside and looked at her hands – an oily, black disaster. She rushed to the sink and began to scrub at them with a brush and the hard, blue soap.

'That's today?'

She glanced over and felt a twinge of sweetness as she saw the same distracted surprise on Minnabar's face as she knew often covered hers. 'Today. Right now. Special dinner. Do we even have food in the house? Did Best bake?' She stared at the slick of grey foam on her fingers, wondering how she was going to get through this. Clothes. Baths. Table-laying. Cleaning the good dining room. What a farce.

She rinsed her hands. Black lines under her nails, grey on her palms. Ten minutes. It was hopeless. A wash of pre-shame flooded over her with the unpleasant warmth of unexpectedly wetting one's pants. She stood with her hands in the sink and looked through the grimy window across the spires and roofs to the palace.

The ball.

Tomorrow. Dresses. Grandeur. Talking up your work for money. Everyone to impress. She had nothing to wear. Literally. Nothing. Too late to order it. Possibly not to hire it.

'Minky,' she said, still staring out the window, feeling the precious seconds wash past her with effortless force. 'I need your help. I need a dress or a suit and shoes for tomorrow. You're good at that kind of thing.'

'Never mind tomorrow, what are you going to wear now? Not those rags? You look like you were just exhumed.'

Tralane found her vision refocusing on the glass panes in which she could just make out her own reflection. Exhumed was an understatement.

'I think the moment has come to redefine *ikasen* politically and reclaim it for the working classes,' she said. 'Its flamboyant efforts and outmoded expectations belong to a bygone age of gentility. Nowadays we should really be much more honest and less like a shop window.'

'Nice try. Go take a shower. I'll find you something to put on.' Minna hopped off her chair and yelled as she went, 'Issa can delay him. She's good at that.'

Tralane almost smiled and then thought about Isabeau – no, not a good idea. Mazhd was a tricky bastard and Issa said whatever was in her head. No. She ran after Minnabar as fast as she could.

Nine minutes later she made it to the kitchen. Isabeau was standing at the oddly immaculate stove, stirring a pot of stew, her finger in her mouth and a frown on her face.

She turned to Tralane and looked her over with a cool eye. The finger popped out of her mouth, 'Not enough thyme. Or savoury. That hair can't be deliberate?'

Tralane looked at her, at the stew. 'Who's that for?' She pulled the combs out of her hastily pulled back hair and shoved them into the pocket of her trousers.

'It's for you,' Isabeau said, adding minute pinches of herbs to the pot. 'I knew you'd forget. Bestie made bread – that's in the small oven so it looks like you made it. Dessert is in the pantry under the yellow cloth. If you eat it all I'll be cross. I want some later. I put wine in the cooler. The only bad news is that you'll have to eat in the kitchen. The dining room smells like mouse pee. I think they're in the seats. Oh, and you're wearing that shirt inside out.'

Tralane stared at her for a moment and then went to hug her. Isabeau was like a little rigid totem pole but she patted Tralane's back.

'I love you, thank you,' Tralane said.

'Yup,' Isabeau said, smiling as the door bells sounded. 'I'm going out now. See you later.'

'Later, smelligator,' Minna murmured, passing Isabeau in the doorway. Issa did not respond.

Minna grinned as Tralane wrestled the shirt around. 'I'll get that shall I? Oh no, wait. Issa has him.'

They both froze to listen, Tralane fumbling buttons, eyes wide, as if this helped her to hear better. From along the halls they heard Isabeau's cool cordial greeting and then Mazhd's black velvet voice replying. Issa said not to trip on the carpet hole. Mazhd assured her he wouldn't. Tralane snatched her hand out of her waistband at the last moment, hoping she had tucked all the way around.

Issa appeared, sliding sideways with an offhand gesture that suggested a hint of discomfort. It distracted Tralane so that as Isabeau said, 'Your guest.' Tralane was looking at her with some amazement and didn't alter her expression as she turned it automatically to the man following her through the door.

Mazhd as a guest looked different to Mazhd the spying invader, she thought. What she dismissed before as of no consequence – because all she had felt was fear and resentment of what he represented – now she saw with surprise was beauty. It wasn't simply some physical happenstance collection of features that fitted that word but a combination of natural looks that had been taken care of a little, not too much, clothing that was elegant and perfect, but not too much – everything about him from his hair to his shoes revealed an intelligence at work that had seen and understood her and kept her in mind as it created this image. He was less than the supremely groomed man who had been here before, full of his role. He was simply there, himself, slightly unshaven, loose haired, unadorned. She saw it only because Isabeau had thrown her out of her own awkward effort to become The Woman That Invited Mazhd with all the implications of that onerous task, and she was just looking at a man in her kitchen offering himself for her approval.

She found that her jaw was slightly open and there was an expression on her face she didn't recognise but it made him smile and behind his shoulder it made Minna stare at her with widening eyes. Mazhd was holding a gift-wrapped box out to her. She found herself walking forward, smiling. She took the box – surprisingly heavy – and leaned forward to kiss him on the cheek, 'Thank you so much.' She glanced at her daughters, 'You know my girls, I think – Minnabar, and Isabeau?'

'We have met,' he said, smiling but he turned and greeted them again, hesitating in order to offer them the opportunity to decide what meeting it would be. Minnabar smiled, grabbed his forearm and kissed his cheek. Isabeau did the same but with far greater detachment. Her eyes slid their gaze away at the last moment and Tralane's heart hitched with that same momentary pause of curiosity. Something...

The sisters left on their cue, silently, and then she was alone with Mazhd. She gestured at the table and chairs. 'Please do sit down.'

The table was bare wood. The chairs were hard, plain. The kitchen was warm though, and thanks to Issa's presence, tidy. Mazhd did not seem to look at any of it, only at her. He sat as indicated and put his arms on the table, leaning there comfortably.

Tralane looked down at the gift in its sash of formal coloured papers, 'May I?'

'Please,' he said.

His gaze followed her hands. She tried to prise the glued edges carefully but shredded the hand-dyed softness of the weave nearly instantly and then ripped it off as if she'd meant to do that all along. A simple box opened to reveal a satin padded lining with a bulky, brass and silver metal object cushioned inside it. It had been polished up to shine. She picked it out and turned it about, spirits rising as she recognised bits, pieces, then realised its nature. 'A solar collector. How... *where* did you get this?' She'd seen them in books, heard of them, never seen one for real. They were extremely rare and, as with all the others that had been painstakingly illustrated in the scrolls, always found broken.

'From a curiosities trader,' he said, still watching her handle it as her fingers prised and turned various small protruding clockworks.

She chewed on her lower lip as she had a quick peek at the casing. When recovery crews who had no aptitude took salvage they often dismantled objects incorrectly. All the workings were inside the egg-shaped casing that lay beneath the folded silver petals, of which two were whole though the rest were made lacework with holes and tears. Parts of whatever it had been attached to crusted this, making it impossible to open on the spot and she looked around quickly for her small screwdriver set before realising she was being rude. Her heart was racing with the thrill of it and she made herself put it back in the opened box, making it their centrepiece. 'Do you know what it is?'

He shook his head. 'I assumed by the pricetag it must have some value.'

'It's a device for taking the energy from sunlight and making it into aetheric charge that can be used or stored... the storage part is missing but I think I have one that could fit it.' She lost her thoughts, looking at the connectors and imagining how she would wire things together.

'Does it have a name?'

'Sunflower,' she said, snapping out of it and smiling. She opened up one petal, draping the flimsy foil over her hand to show it off. 'They also say they had ones that could work from moonslight. They're extremely rare. Kamatek – the technology of the first makers,' she said, too used to talking to Bestie and downgrading her explanations as fast as she could on the fly.

'So... not Sircene?'

'No, not particularly, all the aetheric power devices are universally appreciated by any engineering line mage.'

'I thought the power all came by... well, I... magic,' he said, frowning so that she smiled, seeing that expression that she wore when forced to think of something she had no clue about.

'Glimshard power is all Kamatek, but not this kind. We don't actually understand how it works to be honest. Only how the devices that manage it operate. So, yes. Magic.' She sighed. 'One of the things we are always hoping to find is a text or a technicum that would explain these things. I understand from reports that there may be some of this at that dig. The one that caused the war.' She looked at him, wondering if she had said too much.

'It's a very lovely gift. Thank you.' It was significant and when she met his gaze she saw they both knew it and were calculating how significant it might be. 'Why did you ask me here tonight?' he said. 'I know for the dinner but... Was there another reason?'

'I thought spies were meant to be subtle,' she said, feeling the sudden rise of all her problems towards the surface. She'd been an idiot to think that she had the skill to socially charm anyone. He hadn't even been here five minutes.

'I'm not here to spy on you,' he said, smiling softly. He had perfect teeth. Abruptly she realised how many far better woman had surely been here before her. This had been a terrible idea.

'But you thought I must be wanting information from you.' She turned and went to check the stew, copying Issa's tasting test in order to buy time.

'Everyone does, so don't feel badly about it.'

'I don't. I mean feel bad. Or... I suppose the information thing is inevitable. Why did you say yes?' She turned with her finger in her mouth still from tasting the gravy, wondering if she should add salt or not.

He stared at her and she knew why they said Steppe people had inscrutable eyes. His expression was unreadable, like a cat intent on something. Then he gave that ready smile again, warmer now. 'I wanted to. For myself. In case it really was dinner and not fishing.'

'What if it's both fishing and dinner?' She took her finger out slowly, wondering what the hell she was playing at, but his playfulness invited the same in return and suddenly she found she was a sucker for it.

'At least I get dinner,' he said, shrugging lightly, smile in place.

Tralane thought she detected a hint of weariness in his look, as if he was preparing for a minor blow. She picked up the salt pot and put it on the table instead, before opening the drawer and locating sufficiently clean utensils to set out. 'Yes. You will get that.'

211

'That olive colour really suits you. With the amber necklace. It's very lovely,' he said.

Compliments. She fumbled around in her social reticule. One said thank you and acted normally. She glanced up, trying to place the cutlery properly, 'Thank you. You ...' Damn, now she had moved to repay it with another compliment and had no idea what was appropriate. She looked at him. 'You have very nice teeth.' He chuckled at her awkwardness as she froze for a moment, mortified. 'Thank you.'

She leant on the table, glanced down at her blouse, realised how low it was, sighed gently and looked at him. 'I'm not good at this. My daughter made the dinner. My student made the bread. Oh gods the bread!' She turned and grabbed for a cloth, went to open the small oven and discovered she was in time. It had not burned or dried to a rock, mercifully. She yanked the tin out, pleased her fingers were toughened from years of metalwork so the heat didn't really burn her. It was agonisingly hot even so. With a curse she dropped it on the hob and then with a few prods and shakes managed to get it out and on to a rack with minimal loss of crust. She put the cloth down, sighed. Wondered if he was already heading for the door.

He looked at her with a gentle smile.

'So, like I said. Not good.'

'I'll be the judge of that,' Mazhd said and grinned.

Shit, she thought. He actually likes me. For some reason this hadn't figured in her plans. She'd felt at the time that it would be a good idea to cultivate him but that was a fantasy in which she possessed all the acumen he actually had instead. 'I guess we can't help our employers,' she said, finally realising that she was missing wine at this point. 'Do you have a preference for wine?'

'Expensive wine,' he said. 'Soldiers' beer. Cognac only if the Empress drinks it.'

'She doesn't drink it here,' Tralane informed him and went

into the pantry to the cold cupboard to find one she liked. White, sour, with a sharp mineral bite, yes, probably anathema to the stew, she really had no idea. At least the speed of her uncorking and serving it was suitably impressive. 'To an interesting evening.' She offered a toast to him.

'It's already that.' He raised his glass and took a mouthful.

She was pleased. His hair hung across his face for a moment in curved blades as he put the glass down, hand on the stem and contemplated something. She wondered if she was foolish, if he would tell anyone anything for any money. She had no idea how infomancy worked, only what she had heard from others; they knew each other's minds, could rifle them like looking through drawers in someone else's house. Even against his will he could betray her. But how, to whom? Why?

'Did you see the Karoo?'

He looked up, tilting his head so the blades slid easily aside, became a waterfall. 'Not close up. But I hear he's really very much like one of us, just looks superficially like an animal. I'd not bet on that being true though.'

Tralane nodded, her mind's eye filled for a second by orange and blue tiger stripes. 'You were Night's student. Was she... very different? I only met her twice, in passing.'

'She's different, but not so much in form to look at if that's what you mean. It's all inside, with her.' He rubbed his forearm with the other hand in a quick brushing gesture that could have been a stroke or wiping something off and then smiled and composed his hands again.

'Karoo are such a mystery,' Tralane said, to cover for him, and turned to dish out the food and cut the bread. Who said things like that anyway? Her own self-consciousness and the sensation of stepping on eggshells was driving her crazy. She longed to be reboring the old engine cylinder and glanced at the Sunflower with envy. You knew where you were with objects. She arranged the food and sat down.

'Not as much as people like to think, but they are better left alone,' he said, waiting for her to begin eating.

Tralane tore up her bread. 'I'm in the shit, Mazhd, but you know that. You probably know more about it than I do. As you can see, the house is falling to bits. I don't have anything to offer you but difficulties. But my friend has already been sent to this digsite and that leaves nobody in the city with any power to look after my girls and my household when they send me. I need someone to watch my back but I've got nothing to offer in return right now except goodwill. That's why you're here.' She looked up, any effort at pleasant formal socialising gone. Guilt bit her but this was better. For reasons she didn't understand she trusted him. All it came down to in the end was that.

'You want me to act as your surrogate?' He had paused with his spoon halfway to his mouth, looking over it at her.

'I want you to keep my girls out of trouble. I don't care how you do it. I have no knowledge of the water you swim in and it wouldn't do me any good if I had it. You can find anything here that helps you, then use that. I need an ally.' She dipped her bread in oil and started to eat. Suddenly she was starving. 'If I find anything at that pit that might interest you, I'll let you know. It's not like anyone else there will see what I see, right? I'll pay you back, no matter how long it takes.'

Mazhd put his spoon down and sat up. 'That's an easily paid bill, Huntingore. I want only one thing. It's the reason I came here.'

'Oh yes?' She paused, braced for the worst, whatever it was, thinking she'd give him anything, even the gun, if that's what he was after.

'I want you.'

She stared at him and wondered if he was joking. No, he didn't have the right expression for that and anyway, it was a bad joke, without premise. She tried to see how she and all she had could fit into the bigger schemes of Glimshard, of which he was a part: the blackmail, the gun, the crystals, the dig – but she didn't connect that to him. He was an exchanger, not a prime mover. She tried to figure out who knew what and what it was worth but the effort was soon evidently futile. She had no idea. Suppose he were Alide's agent? It was possible but unnecessary. Alide had her in the corner he wanted already. She saw nothing immediately obvious that he had to gain, so she said the first thing that came into her head.

'Don't be ridiculous.'

His eyebrows came together in a frown that also tried on one side to lift into quizzicality. 'No, I mean it.'

Tralane picked up more bread in her grey fingertips. 'What for?'

'Love,' he said. 'I walked into you on a street corner, years ago, and since then you've never been out of my mind.'

Tralane leaned back in her chair, ripping the bread into tinier and tinier pieces on the plate, now at arm's length. She considered the possibility he was telling the truth. It was such a bizarre statement to try to pull on a woman of her age that she was forced to think of it. She could not in all honesty say the same thing. Mazhd wasn't unknown to her, but he was like the fine architecture or beauty of a finely planed wing – a theoretical aesthetic pleasure; one of those men appreciated rather universally, as if he was public property. Daydream material. Inconsequential. Until a couple of days ago he had been, well, part of the city wallpaper. She didn't remember the street corner, but she tried. She tried to imagine loving someone you had only seen.

'But you don't really know me,' she said, going for kindness and reality. 'It's flattering but – you could only love a fantasy of me. You have no idea what the real thing is like.'

He leaned forward over his dish. 'Try me.'

'What?' She stopped shredding, looked at his dark eyes – what was that colour even called? It was brown, or maybe it was purple. Like the eyes of those huge, malignant black cattle that roved the lower Steppe. She'd seen some once on a touring trip long ago. They had huge, curving horns and shaggy bodies and were known as the most ill-tempered and dangerous beasts.

'Test me, ask me anything.'

'About me?'

'Yes.'

She felt stumped, and that they were bordering on stalking territory. She raked her mind for some intimately acute and telling fact but nothing came to her.

'Then I'll tell you one,' he said after a minute had passed. 'You are bored, Tralane Huntingore. You have your work, your family, your house, your collection to work with, your lecturing at the University, and it is all you have known for years. The University is no challenge, the objects you find have only random relevance. Until the war you had nothing to struggle against. Now you are squeezed tight on all sides, you don't even know what your daughters are up to, and still you are not sufficiently interested to step forward. You are a beautiful woman, wasted.' He hesitated at the end and glanced down, as if he'd said too much.

Tralane looked at him, very carefully now. '*What* are my daughters up to?'

'I can't tell you that without betraying a confidence. Ask them yourself.'

Tralane leant forward suddenly, pushing her plate and dish aside. 'No, you explain what you mean or this interview is over.'

'I told you all I am able to tell. But it's nothing to fear.'

'Well that right there is one reason you won't get what you want. Playing games and holding information is not my idea of a relationship I want to be in.'

He sighed out through his nose and looked at his hands. 'You don't understand. I can't tell you things that are sensitive material to the Infomancy because they will know and after that I may as well jump off your roof right now. I can tell you that I know things but that's as good as it gets. What's going on is not illegal or dangerous. It's just interesting. I promise you.'

Tralane sat back and thought it over. It was plausible. The Infomancy claimed absolute knowledge and absolute security. The first part was clearly a boast but she could not remember any time that a leak or a scandal had come from that direction. It was one reason that people distrusted and loathed them so much. Their dedication to the city and its cause had a cool, inhuman perfection to it.

'I'm never bored in my lab,' she said. 'The rest of life – is more of a struggle. All its boundaries so unclear. But you're in so deep to everything going on. How can I trust you? It seems more likely to me that you'd be here for the Infomancy running background on me than it does that you... that you... Well, the other thing is just ridiculous.'

Mazhd looked up, hands curled around his plate, lax and helpless. 'The other thing is all I've got that isn't somehow connected up to the rest of what I do, or what I know. The other thing is the only way I can help you that doesn't come with loaded dice attached to it. It's true. It's mine. Not theirs. Mine. Nobody can touch it but me.' He looked at her with a fierce intensity and she felt his will trying to press understanding into her where she didn't have any; knew it was the gap between one skill and another, one ability and another, that he was trying to shove her across.

Tralane applied her engineering paradigms. 'It is not connected. So it can't transmit. It can't – be accessed? By others?'

'Yes,' he said. 'They cannot know it or what attaches to it. It is in isolation.' Relief and anxiety replaced the force in his gaze, but she saw traces of longing too, and loneliness of a kind she knew too – when you wanted so badly to share something you knew with someone else, and you couldn't because the importance of it escaped them. You were forever making settlements with them just knowing it was a big deal and you the same, for their big deals. You accepted it but you couldn't see it directly.

'I am your secret?' she hazarded.

'You are my castle,' he said quietly, sitting now relaxed, just looking at her over her ruined bread with a gentle kind of hopelessness. She knew that look too. When you just wanted to be understood and knew it was impossible. He gestured vaguely up and around with his hands, indicating the building they were in, her castle.

'Why would you wait until now?' she asked, still discomforted by the notion he was talking over. Loving her, for all that time. Whatever that meant to him. 'I haven't exactly been busy for the last few years, as you seem to have noticed.'

'My business kept me occupied with a lot of other things. And people,' he said, significantly.

'So what changed?'

'I worked my way clear of my indentured status to Shrazade. A promotion, if you like. It means I get to have some life that doesn't belong to the Infomancy.'

'What if I'd got married to someone else?'

'I'd still have made my bid. I would take second place.'

Tralane sipped her wine, all interest in food lost. 'If you've done your homework you know I haven't dealt in husbands so far. Why would I start now?'

'It doesn't have to be legal and formal.'

'What does it have to be?'

He sighed and looked deflated, so much so she felt almost embarrassed. 'It doesn't have to be anything. You're right. It's ridiculous. I don't know you. All I have is a fantasy. But it was a fantasy that kept me focused and purposeful through hard times. You never cared for convention. And nothing surprised me more than finding out you had a flying machine. Secret things you had. Such interesting secrets. And who can say why some people are more attractive than others? Many are suitable, but few are wanted. Well, Night always had her theories, but I've never figured it out.' He dipped bread in the stew and ate it. 'This is good.'

It was wrong for someone like him to look like that. It was his looks working against him in her eyes. If he'd been ugly, she'd have believed it then, she thought, vain as she was. But he outranked her in this and that made her suspicious. 'I asked you here because you're clever, and pretty, and interesting, and you snuck into my house and you didn't take anything or abuse my daughter. You easily could have. I know you weren't here on a social call then.'

'*Ikasen* isn't dinner.'

'No, it isn't.' She raked a hand through her hair, snagging it on a leftover pin. 'I don't know what I'm doing. I thought that was painfully obvious.'

He smiled, lopsidedly – a far cry somehow from his usual smile, as if this was his natural one. 'I was enjoying it.'

'I've never lived by my head. That was for work. I lived by my feelings. And that's what I'm still doing. You were a feeling. Everything after that is just what I say to make it look like reason.'

'It is reason. Karoo would say the only reason.'

'My daughter Issa thinks I'm quite mad.'

His smile continued, wry on one side, happy on the other. 'Does she have an alternative to offer?'

'Logically thinking it through, as if I were building an engine,' Tralane said, with a frown. 'But life's nothing like an engine. Not the kind I know anyway. I like my friends, I like my household, I'm happy as I am.'

'And men?'

'Come and go. I never found one I liked enough to keep around. My student notwithstanding, but he stays for the workshop and the knowledge and I wouldn't think otherwise for a minute.'

'But you share the same skill. You wouldn't marry him?'

'Oh, hell no. Too young, too...' She hesitated. 'Just no. He wouldn't want to anyway.'

'So you'd still be sleeping with him if I was in the picture?'

She paused. 'Are you going to be in the picture?'

'Is that an offer?'

'It's the kind of woolly suggestion that will place half the responsibility or more on you in case of system failure,' Tralane said. That damned lopsided grin. It took his handsome symmetrical face and all the calculated grooming and redeemed it. She wondered if he knew. He must know. But if she was going to be sucker-punched this way it wasn't like she wouldn't soon find out.

'I will be in the picture.'

His definite tone caught her by surprise, that and the look of quiet conviction. Her skin prickled with anticipation of something good.

'Are you hungry?' she asked him.

'Not so much,' he said.

'Thank goodness I didn't bother to cook it myself then or I'd be annoyed.' She took her glass and the bottle and stood up. 'Come with me.'

He stood immediately and waited for her to pass him on the way to the door. His hand closed on the wine bottle. 'Let me carry that.'

She smiled and tugged at it, taken aback slightly by how close and tall he was, her forehead at his shoulder height. 'Really I can manage.'

He didn't let go. 'No, I want to.'

She knew perfectly well it wasn't about wine or carrying things. She looked into his eyes. They had a wicked glint that made her skin shiver from neck to ankles. She let go of the bottle. 'Suit yourself.'

CHAPTER FIFTEEN

TZABAN

Tzaban was staring at the moon when he heard and felt the approach of several people at the door. He had been contemplating leaving.

All afternoon he'd sat patiently at the Empress' feet to witness the court she held – part of an effort she was making to show him Glimshard society, and her own position, he felt, though he was not sure why he warranted such an effort. Petitioners had come and gone in a steady stream and she had dealt with their business – usually matters that lesser courts had referred to her. She also held an audience with Borze again, to consider his views on the situations beyond Tzaban's immediate interest with other humans who skirmished on the city borders and around the region. Tzaban was not consulted. Borze seemed to think matters were getting out of hand, but was reluctant to reveal the truth to the Empress. Tzaban wondered why but as it was not his place, said nothing.

He guessed from Borze's looks and energy that the man considered his Empress too young, and that he was attempting to shelter her from matters he thought he would be able to manage alone. Tzaban well knew this was more a hope than a cold calculation. The city's garrison could hold off one foe, or march out and strike one or two, but it would never hold a concerted, organised attack off if the motley of local antagonists ever organised themselves. Borze gambled that such an attack was impossible, thanks to the mutual enmity of Glimshard's harassers, but it was not odds Tzaban would have wanted to play. Any canny observer would have seen the endless parade of southbound labour and soldiery and realised what that meant in terms of the city's security.

After this long afternoon with its circles and half truths, he understood only that the Empress was in a dreadful position that he would not have wanted for the entire world at his feet, not that this interested him much either. There had been only brief talk of the expedition to the dig and no hint given that his words of warning were of any use. He concluded that his mission had failed. Given that, there really was no reason to stay. Even if they wanted him to take their people south they still believed he could protect them or swing things in their favour, and he knew that wasn't true. He felt torn between attempting the impossible and abandoning them to whatever fell. He had no desire to see it happen either way.

Now it was dark and a cloudless night, the stars shone through the magelight glow of the high city, and he felt tempted to leap out of the window and into that endless, welcoming sky. His skin was already beginning to itch for the process of metamorphosis when the voices sounded through the door and the unlocking of the bars that kept it solid distracted him. Thin tendrils of scent preceded their entry: the Empress, Hakka, Night and some person who was new to him, a female and a very nervous one at that. A curious conjunx of their energies confused him; he felt urgency and doubt, determination riding over anxiety. Someone was carrying incense and before he even thought about it it made him sneeze three times in quick succession. He got up from the floor where he'd been lying and stood tall, adjusting his clothing.

Hakka came in first after a moment of grace, though he did not hold his weapon ready and his forehead and chin were low – he was like a ship's prow breaking the way and although Tzaban would not step back before him he did relax to show no opposition. The tall man glanced at him directly with a fraction of a nod: Tzaban returned the greeting. Then Hakka stepped left and the Empress herself came forwards, Night and the strange woman fanning out to either side of her in silence. The Empress was the determined one, then, he saw, Night was self-contained, subtle, the other a mass of nervous anxiety that made his ears turn back with dislike. He remembered his training in manners and bowed appropriately in silence. It was only as he straightened that he also recalled to check their clothing, knowing how much store and communication they placed in it though it was all hard work to read for him.

The amount of heavy beadwork and ceremonial decoration on the Empress made him feel a sudden strange conviction. He glanced at Night – she wore her usual inky coloured, floating attire that concealed so much. Then the one who was upset: also heavily robed and this one carried the censer which was hanging on a chain from her hand, waving slightly and filling the air with the heavy smell of oranges, cinnamon and rose. The words being spoken by the Empress filtered through all this to him very slowly, unwinding their sense in his mind almost as an afterthought. He looked at Hakka meanwhile, just one glance, and read all the grim intent and conviction there that he needed to see. A drop of sweat ran down the censer chain and he noticed it from the corner of his eye. He turned his gaze to the Empress, determined to see the full impact of her proposal written there – his future in those grey eyes, her lips pale under their glistening skim of wax.

He saw a human girl, hands trembling as she stood as tall as she could, barely up to his chest, looking up steadily without raising her head. He felt an oddness about her, as if the sheen on her face, made of burnished powders, was the only thing holding back a wave. It was so delicate, finer than the dust of a mothwing, but still it held against the tide of contradiction backed up against it. He tasted earth, blood and war. The incense faded as he distended his nostrils and found that she would not use the axe of her chemical command on him. She perspired from the weight of her ceremonial clothes, but this was only a hot, tired, underfed girl declaring wedding vows.

He bought a little time just looking from face to face to see if this was right, and it was. He searched his body for an answer, remaining still even after her mouth stopped moving to listen for any sign.

His own voice grated through the air when he finally used it. 'This will likely carry no weight with the Karoo.' He couldn't say none. It might have some. But it could go either way. 'It cannot of its own force end your conflict.' Now he thought it over he was not sure that the Karoo would understand the politics of humans, nor care. Marriage was a concept they could only have grasped as mating, and that held no long-term promise for them, nor any lasting interest. They might understand desire and the unfolding of new life and possibility. That was a kind of flower they could see and smell for something valuable.

The Empress' face went taut and pale, so much so he thought she might faint and moved forwards in anticipation of preventing any fall but she twitched upright and he realised it had never occurred to her he might say no. Perhaps he was not allowed to say it. Hakka's body had tensed. He waited.

'I am given to understand that there is a slender possibility it may ... that we ... if there was a child ...' She never let her eyes move from his face. 'Or even if we simply knew one another in that way, then you would have more to offer them than our words and treaties.'

Tzaban looked at Night and saw her work in this; she had explained Karoo matters more extensively to the Empress and been heard. He saw that the woman with a censer was a priest of a sort, an official in any case. His skin prickled. 'You intend to do this now, in secret? What will I be, then?'

Hakka made to speak but the Empress' hand flashed up, preventing him. He had to be satisfied with glowering. Tzaban smelled defiance and possession in his sweat.

'If I make it public there will have to be an enormous fuss, not to mention many objectors who will attempt to foil me and perhaps worse. Regardless of such considerations there is no time for that. You are to leave for the dig the day after tomorrow.'

He read in her face, in the shimmer of that concealing dust, that the resistance was more than any disinclination of the people. There were others trying to stop her and in spite of her position they had mandates to do so. Her gaze at him was pleading, if anything, begging him to end the fighting before her strength ended and they overran her from the inside. He knew it was not his war, not this one he saw in her and not the other one at the forest edge either.

'You don't threaten and force me,' he said, making it a question.

She shook her head, the heavy headdress of white wood and pearls like a coral forest clacking with her movement. 'You're free to say no. Do not worry. No harm will be done to you.'

He looked at the window. He breathed the air, scenting the open night far below them, full of wood and grass, damp leaves. He felt they would soon kill him here, if not her then others. He looked at her face. The bronzed dust shimmered over her skin. His wandering spirit returned through the window, sat with him, sank into him. He found it would not please him now to go and leave her with nothing.

He bowed his head to her, eyes closed. 'As you wish.' Although they were the correct words he found they came to his mouth of their own accord instead of being pushed and shoved there. He felt mild surprise that his own volition could make such a profound change in him so quickly, and then he endured the rest of the meaningless hour, following Night's instructions to him until all that must be said was said and done done. All he remembered of it was the stink of the priestess' fear, wondering what it was that made her so terrified when nothing of note was happening and nobody was there but the five of them.

When they had finished, the Empress herself had a grey-green tinge around her lips and her eyes were rolling in her head. Parlumi Night was holding to her left arm, holding her up by this time, murmuring to her reassuringly. Hakka, his face tight and ashen under its natural dark coloration, watched from only a half metre, ready to leap in. His anguish again seemed out of proportion to Tzaban which must mean something was happening he didn't understand. The priestess gathered her bits and pieces into a ceremonial bag with an unseemly speed and made some garbled goodnights and an exit without anyone paying her more mind.

'What is the matter?' Tzaban asked, looking at Night for his explanation with a direct gaze.

'The other Empresses,' Night said, staggering as the girl finally lost her fight to stay conscious and passed out then and there, Hakka already holding her other elbow and then taking her up into his arms where she slumped against his chest like a small sackful of grain dressed up in a ludicrous costume. 'They tried to stop her.'

Tzaban followed Hakka at Night's side since nobody seemed like they wanted to stop him. He was not of a Karoo blood that possessed mental linkage. It would have given him a vulnerability and he had been made as a lone and silent wanderer. Those that were able to hear thought were beings he felt repelled by, particularly since they often formed groups of set hierarchy and he couldn't bear subordination when it was not a voluntary thing. Even to see it made him feel mistrust and the brooding beginnings of aggression. He considered what it might be like to be a grouped entity and to stand alone against an opposition of seven equals, and when he and Night shared a look he knew that she also felt the same disturbed shiver in her spine. Whatever else the Empress was she had a personal strength in excess of anything most would dream of. It cast all her previous patience and thoughtful judgements in a different light. He became aware of himself becoming suddenly willing to bend perhaps, just in deference to that power. But still, a gestalt being was anathema to him. He didn't trust them. There were too many hidden hands and eyes far from wherever he was able to sense their intent or feel their presence directly. There were too many throats he could not tear.

She had not asked him to rule however, nor to share any of that burden. The marriage seemed so far only to permit him to accompany her and to validate his seizure of her *geha* – the knowledge of her making and body. He followed the others. They might mistake it for obedience but it was simply a matter of ownership.

In her quarters the other two guards were awake and serious. The one called Eth went immediately to Hakka and his mistress, hair a blond cascade always surprising to Tzaban in its incredible straight abundance. The other, dark and braided, stood silently and watched Tzaban with narrowed eyes but Tzaban did not deign to notice his hostility; he was no threat.

There was some fussing as they set her up in her own bed, Night circling until she settled beside her in a chair, doing something he assumed was medicinal with smoke and tinctures she dropped into the girl's mouth from a crystal wand. Recognising there was no use for him immediately Tzaban lay down at the bed's foot until sleep overtook him.

Torada woke to a gloomy midday. She heard rain pounding the garden, splashing on leaves and drumming the crystal glass panes of the dome overhead. Something was different... but she had a hard time for a while discovering what it was. Her mind and her *atman* were quiet, woolly, as if they had been stuffed with rainclouds and could hold nothing else. Gradually she became aware of Meixia and Haru, the Empresses Murmur and Beckons, at their normal positions on the public edge of her *atman*, the totality of her awareness. All the other places were empty. She searched discreetly, not wanting but still wondering about the others, but even a brief effort revealed the truth of their previous evening's declaration. They had gone. The Eight were in union no longer, the rest forming a seven, and only two of those were with her now, a secret triad.

She felt the distant awareness of Haru, keeping space from her until requested to move closer, as she always had. Meixia was sleeping – it being night where she was. She was not sure if their loyalty was genuine or spying for the rest. She knew her action had effectively exiled her. Only Meixia was close enough to be of any practical help, but even she might be forbidden to act. Torada, and Glimshard, was now on her own. Before she had to drown in the implications of that she lay and looked up at the glass dome and the rain washing it. She felt no victory, only exhaustion and a kind of relief that Dirt and Spire were gone at least, if not the rest. Dirt and Spire – she hadn't realised how much their disapproval had painted every moment of her life until now, when it was absent. She listened to the weather and lay still, relishing every beautiful moment.

A sigh from nearby interrupted her some time later. She looked around without moving her head, thinking first Eth, but then knowing it wasn't. Her room appeared quite empty and peaceful, as she liked it. But it was not empty. Her gaze moved to the end of the bed, then to the side, and she saw the white end of the Karoo's tail there, a plume like Hakka's polearm tassel, only shorter and nearly icy in colour instead of blond.

Tonight – tomorrow. She had only hours. He had to prepare to leave so he was out of the city soon. Mazhd had sent word he was sure something would happen over the next day or two but Alide had told her to hold back from action because seizing a few conspirators now would send the rest to hide. She must not have Tzaban dead. He had to be her emissary. Without him she had no chance in the south. And for the ball they must both be ready. She would have to convince the entire city of her wisdom when she was not sure it was wisdom at all. The Karoo, as she understood it, might simply kill him and then all this would be for nothing.

But first she had to face him alone, her husband, a creature she could not pretend to understand and upon whom so much hope was pinned. For a moment the yawning gulf of probabilities stretched out inside her, between the best and worst case scenarios. She knew herself hurtling into its black gap and for a moment froze before she reminded herself it had never been different. Just sometimes she forgot the gap when she had a great deal to do. She wished her choice had been more positive. She wished it had not been because she could not stand another minute of Dirt and Spire stalking her, knowing they had people within her walls who did not wish her to retain the Gleaming throne. She could not trust them.

She had married a Karoo. He was beneath any social level, outside any known group. She might as well have married the monster from the river bottom who steals small children from the shallows and walks in the night as a traveller, moving islands, moving always to fresh waters until dawn comes and finds it buried in the silt again, water overhead and shade and the ever-moving current.

229

She wondered what it meant to him. Nothing perhaps. He had seemed as unmoved as a stone by the entire process once he'd agreed and she'd no idea why he had changed his mind. The strangeness of that mind intrigued her; the world it came from fascinated her and had since childhood though nearly all Karoo stories were like the river monster, full of death and oddity. There were none with happy endings, unless the Karoo went away or were killed. Only her intuition and instinct had insisted that this one was important, against all evidence and lore to the contrary. She wondered if she felt up to what must come next, and thought that she would have to be.

'Tzaban, are you there?'

The tail lifted and withdrew. She saw his head and shoulders appear, facing away from her as he sat up and realised he had not changed his clothing, must have been there since the night before.

'Yes. I am awake.' He got up smoothly and stretched, surprising her with how relaxed he must feel.

She sat up too and pointed to the bed beside her. 'Please sit down.' It was nearly big enough for four, the edge did not bring him so very close.

He looked at the spot indicated and then after a moment walked around the curved side and sat there, one leg up with his ankle on the other knee, the shin resting like a kind of fence between them. His foot was bare. She looked at it, seeing how long it was, coloured deep blue, the tigerish markings on it nearly black all the way to his black toes with their filed black claws, and then up at him.

'Night has told me that you collect knowledge. I mean that males do that, where Karoo have them. And then they trade it to females for certain kinds of favour.'

His eyes were the most disturbing orange amber colour but it was less the colour than the quality of the look that made her almost lower her gaze, though she didn't. Years of training

230

distanced her from the primal domination she recognised in his face. It had been one of the first things she learned, although this was one of the only times she had felt a sense of actual danger in the act of not submitting. He looked as if he wanted to go for her throat. It was rather thrilling but she repaid him with an expression of calm enquiry. Finally he spoke.

'Yes. The only knowledge they care for is of the body, of the making and the growing, the shape and the spirit. All else is worthless. Mmn, except perhaps knowledge of rich land good for growing. But I would not bet my life on that.'

His seriousness on the final point rang an alarm in her. 'Is that a bet you must make?'

He nodded solemnly. 'Female Karoo are absolute and merciless. They are like Empresses, only all of them are Empress... hnn... something like this. To give false information, too little, worth too little... that is a fatal decision for any male.'

Torada found her hands clinging to her sheet and blanket. 'I do not kill people who make poor decisions.'

'Perhaps you should rethink that,' he said, apparently serious.

She was speechless for a moment, at the notion. 'How? Why do they kill? Wouldn't it be more sensible to let the male go and find something out?'

Now it was his turn to look confused and struggle with an idea. 'Gendered Karoo are rare, at least fixed ones. Females have no time for useless males. They are uh... waste of resources... empty hands always eating.' The eyes looked at her, knowing very well the talk was mostly a delay, but he let her have it. She wondered...

'Do you see me like them?'

'No,' he said immediately. 'You would have eaten me by now.'

'Eaten?' she repeated, faintly. His eyes blinked, slowly, for the first time.

'They do not like waste.'

'But—' She felt moved and put her hand out towards him,

231

suddenly not knowing what she expected him to do with it. His chiselled, angular features invited no sympathy. 'And if they eat you, then? Do they gain all that you know?'

He nodded once.

'So um, supposing they enjoy what you have brought and find it good. Then what?'

'Then I would survive.'

She decided to speak what was uppermost on her mind, and had been since Night first mentioned it. 'How do you pass the knowledge? Is it like human mating?'

Tzaban's eyes glowed briefly – a disconcerting sight even to someone as used to mages as she was. 'Not necessarily,' he said. 'It can be done many ways.'

'So when I must give this to you you don't have to...' She left it hanging for him to fill.

'No,' he said. 'I am human-like. Not human. That is not necessary.'

She felt abruptly disappointed and wanted to laugh at herself for her assumptions. 'Do Karoo have sex?'

He seemed to struggle with this. 'Anything could be that, or not that. Sometimes it is as you do it, but not... hm.' He lapsed into silence then said, 'You do it for many reasons, not only exchange. Our connections are different.' He shrugged at her, helpless to express it, and gave up.

'Will you take it now then?' she asked, trying not to let her fear show because she knew that it was dangerous to feel that around him. Night had told her his nature. But she was afraid that it would hurt.

He nodded. She marvelled at how simple everything seemed to be for him, and she envied him. 'Give me your hand,' he said and held out his own.

'Will it hurt?' She carefully extended the same hand as before.

'If you try to pull away and resist me, yes. But mostly me.' He took her offered hand and she felt small and puny, seeing

232

her fingers in the huge palm and grip of his. 'Now do not move. It will feel strange, prickly.'

She secured herself far from the Empresses, feeling a slight, odd burning where her skin and his met, then a sharp prickle as he had promised, but because she was expecting it there was no real shock and it was not very bad, like touching a sparkwire with a mild charge in it. She giggled, nervously, and heard footsteps as the sound attracted the guard.

Tzaban tensed and the sensation of pins and needles intensified too. She waved Jago away quickly as she could with her free hand, signalling she did not wish to be disturbed. His black frown was so familiar she saw no extra disappointment in it as he retreated again. Her commands were absolute and he would not return until she called.

'Is this...' she began uncertainly, staring at their joined hands, feeling as if they held nettles between them.

'This is all,' Tzaban said, his free hand reaching out to clamp her wrist and make it still almost as if he thought she would try to tear it away. His grip was much stronger than she expected, blood flow and bones nearly crushed as his hand engulfed her. She felt the roughness of his skin, sandy and tough as the pads of a hunting dog's paw. Although it was painful and made her heart leap with a moment of fear she said nothing and kept her face in its schooled expression of mild interest.

His orange eyes narrowed and his throat pulsed once as if he were drinking. She looked closer and saw fine threads at the edge of his palm and hers, joining them together, but so gossamer delicate they were nothing more than spidersilks, almost as thick, a little more green in colour where they massed together. With a shock she realised he had grown into her, like a tree putting down roots. She focused all her mind on it but it was not a mental thing and remained closed to her most powerful sense. She felt no robbery, but intuitively guessed he was drawing all knowledge of the how of her making out of her, harmlessly and without pain. It seemed wrong that he could take everything but the essence of her being and she not feel anything for it but this slight discomfort which was already abating to a simple blur of tiny pulses.

'This is how Karoo mate?' She heard the disappointed surprise in her own voice.

'Mmn, partly,' he said. 'Though the details of the contact are not important.'

Torada watched the filaments slowly withdrawing, at the very limit of her ability to focus her eyesight. They left her skin apparently undamaged and his the same. After a minute it was done and he let her go. She drew her palm to herself and felt it sensitised and sore. Then she examined his face. He looked pensive.

'Do you understand it? Do you ...'

'No,' he cut in on her, flexing and folding his own hand, exercising it back into its older useful form. 'No I can see nothing about you in it. That's not a skill I have. Only a female would be able to, but not always then. She could use it, but to really understand it in a way that can talk of it and calculate requires a blood-seer. Few of those.' His face had a faraway troubled look, or so she would have said if he were human. It was hard to know what it meant for him.

'We must seem very odd to you,' she said quietly, still unsure about exactly what had taken place. She had no idea what Karoo might want with knowing her physical makeup – she was not certain if her unique abilities were held in that. Most importantly she did not know if it would be worth enough. Empresses did not pass their powers through a maternal lineage. She didn't have insight into how she had become one. Instead of surrendering to her worries now when everything was so precarious and she felt desperately uncertain she pursued her curiosity instead. 'If you hand this over, how will you do that?'

'However is possible,' he said. His thoughts seemed far away.

She studied him in his moment of silence. For all his oddity he was compelling and attractive – the oddness only made him more so to her in a way she liked to think was the same as his Karoo curiosity for non-Karoo lifeforms. Technically, now that they had wed, he was hers but she had no illusions about the reality of that. He had been an obediently lifeless automaton through the ceremony, agreeing to what was required and showing understanding but nothing else. She herself, alone in her brief hours of freedom from the Eight, freedom from the city, the duty, felt a piercing loneliness and bereavement she could not articulate. *Eth's hand in hers, jerking with every movement of Hakka's much wanted, loved intrusion. Their ecstasy, the look on their faces, her grip on his palm. Hand in hand.*

She let her hand holding up her blankets drop them. Her nightgown was so sheer it may as well have been a fading illusion. She was tiny in the huge, empty bed and knew herself more adequate than beautiful. Her eyes were so large, so fixated, they seem to hold her whole soul in them. 'Please can you?' She didn't even know if he would comprehend it, but reading the real intent in people was something he never faltered at. She didn't need the words, not any of them, even though there was a floodtide the size of an ocean of all she wanted to say.

His reply was a slow blink and a dip of his chin, yes. The orange eyes reappeared, appraising her, and he began to slowly unbutton the front of his shirt.

CHAPTER SIXTEEN

BORZE

Borze disliked portal travel almost as much as he disliked the sense of cogs turning behind the scenes where he was not allowed to go. But plotting and Imperial machinations were at least known quantities in their way. The portal was a thin sheet of nothing suspended between a delicate framework of wires held and protected within a massive stone and lead shield and he knew nothing about those things. He didn't mind trusting engineers or other mages most of the time, but this felt much worse than guns and bombs and illusion machines. This was a warp effect on matter, on him, and he had no protection from whatever it did but he had no choice but to use it to pay his visit in person to the dig and return in time to attend the ball.

His horse, picking up his discomfort, pranced and champed. Behind him he felt the nervy shifting of men and animals who liked it less still and he kept his seat, pressing forward at the operator's beckon and hearing the thudthump of hooves going up the wooden ramp, rustling in the remains of straw kicked so many times it was grey and filthy. Through the veil he saw a mirage of a place that he knew only through scouts; men who had run themselves thin rushing to Glimshard across dangerous lands, alone. A year of that, and men lost and men dying and imprisoned, men sent south on a long journey that was better than its destination though they faced warring bands, thieves, ferocious Steppelords bent on snarling their power to the Empire. So few returning and those that did silent or mad. Glimshard's shame and his personal failing, he felt. Crossing this veil shimmer, crossing the river of his fear and responsibility – these were deserved trials by now, but he must hold his mind still and calm whatever he found there. Shrazade said there was fate waiting for him there, and she being not a seer but a dealer of fact, he knew it would be in the form of men, their voices, their doings.

His horse reared suddenly, trying to wheel to the side and turn from the strange watery shiver in the world that he urged it to go through. He sat it and let it have its moment, turning around to see the remains of the world behind him, looking down as he did so to the solid muscle and shoulder of his white mount, seeing suddenly in its place the shift and slide of the girl's limbs under his in the steam of the bath house. Gau Tam's voice sounded in his ears but he didn't hear what it said. He put his hand on the horse's shoulder, damp with sweat, and let his hand on the rein be loose so that it seemed he set it free. With this it calmed and stepped on, one hoof, another, the boards and the sandbags of the ramp noisy but solid and clearly present on the other side. Borze felt his heart lurch – a girl, a horse, moving into worlds that frightened them.

They passed through. There was a moment of silence and peace, no sensation, then a slow caress of humid air, the clank of a different ramp and the flap of flags and tent sides, desultory as they greeted him. Heat was like an everywhere coat, inescapable, claustrophobic after the clear plains breeze and the stallion shook its head and snorted, pawed the wood and voiced a loud call of displeasure.

Of the men there to meet him he recognises faces sent months ago, leaner and darker with battle hardness.

'Quieter if you please,' were the first words from the garrison commander, Barsan, his salute the greeting. 'Undue noises upset the forest.'

He wasn't mounted, none of them were. They were a cavalry unit once. Borze didn't ask, he knew it would be clear soon enough why. Behind him, Gau Tam began the complaint he held back – no horse, where is the ceremony, the regiment, the proper greeting? Borze ignored it all, rode down the ramp and dismounted as soon as he was able, handing the reins of the snorting, discomforted stallion to the nearest competent-looking soldier and removing his helm.

The sound was a sudden shock. He knew it of old but was not prepared for it. That background hum and whine and grate of insects, billions of them and none readily seen. The helm's leather pads had blocked it or blurred it with the rush of his own blood beating. Together with the heat it lent everything a sweltering, occupied feel as if there was no space here for new creatures, not an inch. All was claimed and consumed already.

Borze signalled for Barsan to attend him, leaving the cohort he had come with – poor offering to this garrison – under Gau Tam's charge. As the general and his commander here drew to the end of the tented shielding around the portal he spoke quietly.

'How goes it, Barsan? The truth, not some crap you'll tell Alide or the Ministries or the Empress.'

'I think you should see for yourself,' the commander said. If he reproached Borze for not coming in person sooner he didn't say it but Borze suspected it in the tightness of his voice.

The tenting opened on to a muddy track through sparse forest. The ground was livid green with moss and grasses, trees of kinds Borze had seen rarely, tall and draped with grey lichens and evergreen vines. Among this, the main camp was built up and fortified with spiked logs driven into the wet ground, pointing outwards. Gaps were filled with thorn branches. The portal station was at the centre, guards patrolling around it as well as at the periphery. The red of the science tents, traditional, had been muddied and rained out to a flat brown. The green army shelters were pale khaki. A strong and relentless sun beat through thin clouds that were building up in the mid-morning, promising downpours by afternoon.

Barsan showed him around the officers' tent, the mess hall, the barracks and the hospital tent, which was full to capacity and overflowing into a lean-to. Borze walked on rushes between the low cots holding men and women whose bodies were often unmarked. Their faces said shock to him, some inward and haunted, some quivering with repressed flight. Many were tied to their beds. They all breathed as if they dare not breathe, like children in the middle of the night in the dark, listening for monsters. The most unnerving thing about them was their silence. Once they were beyond earshot and outside again he noted it and Barsan said, 'They daren't make a sound. It's always some sound or other that triggers the attacks.'

'Why haven't you sent them back yet?' Borze disliked the notion of them being there, reminding the others, dropping morale.

'Alide refused to use the portal for them. Said it was a waste of energy and they would have to wait until the camp was closed.' Barsan paused. They had reached a gateway where several guards were standing, fully armed. He signalled for it to open, muttering, 'Dig's this way.' The track led on. They walked to the edges where the mud was less deep, slowly moving into denser forest until branches crowded overhead and blocked almost half the sky. On the way, Barsan's voice was quiet and Borze saw him watching every shadow.

'Alide doesn't want them back in Glimshard where people will start asking questions,' he murmured as he trod with catlike quiet over tussocks, Borze following his tracks as they moved over thick, half-crushed vegetation in near silence. 'He's paid the medics extra to keep them here and say nothing. He said his orders were from the Empress. Nothing must interfere with the recovery.'

The stench, Borze thought: mud and sappy greenness, odd plant scents and a thick fuggy ground humidity mingled with rot and a hint of putrefying flesh – the stench was like a living thing in its own right. He felt clogged with it already, contaminated, as he finally saw a glade ahead, and within it some kind of pit. Barsan led the way, agile and lightfooted through the mire, Borze trying to copy his practised gait over the awkward land.

There were soldiers aplenty here, pale under their visors, sweat running down and making their light jungle clothing cling to them. Flies buzzed everywhere in the light and larger insects, dazzlingly coloured, zoomed and droned just above head height, crossing and recrossing the opened pit and its broad, muddy border. Borze found himself watching them in blunt fascination, a kind of horror in their sheer size and audacity but a delicate wonder in their precise construction. Barsan ignored them, batting at a dragonfly that came too close to him with weary habit.

'I don't like it when they land on me,' he said. 'I feel like someone's watching.'

Borze said nothing but the thought had already occurred to him. His attention was sucked away however by the other features of the dig. 'Do you need so many men on duty?'

Barsan nodded. He spoke just loud enough to be heard over the saw and hum of the insects and the occasional whine and grind of machinery in the pit. 'Experience dictates it. We can go for many days and no trouble. Then without a sign – they're everywhere.' The man swallowed and shuddered, unable to contain his revulsion. He swiped his forehead with one wrist covered in a thick swatch of cloth to mop the sweat and Borze took note of that too. His own cropped hair was already trickling with moisture under his helm.

Barsan gave him the tour – the various tents, the huts, the fortifications, the drill for attack, the all-clear signal, the hours of operation. Borze's confidence in him grew as they progressed. Barsan was a tough vet and he had it in hand here, as much as that could be a description of a single, desperate outpost in a hostile land under constant pressure of siege. What startled him most was how small it was. He had sent troops here and got bodies back, or what was left of them. He had sent *so many* troops. The Empress had lost twenty-four scientists, engineers and magi.

Barsan took him down to the pit, following a broad path built up and reinforced with felled timber in long steps that ringed the sides. Wood chips and sawdust had been ground into the thick, dark mud and lower down in the heavy dark red clay that held the precious artefact in its sucking grip. Borze realised then why the fuss was so great. The thing was huge, a dark blue and shining cone of metal that stuck out of the ground at a vaguely obscene angle; blowfly iridescent but with a soulless, manufactured authority that could not be denied even as the earth attempted to swallow it whole. Everything about it was unnatural and out of place. Scarring and blast marks covered its surface and it was obvious that some of the scoring was where things that had projected from it had been ripped off. The mud stepped ramp that led around it stopped about fifty metres down at a hole in the side which was so symmetrical and well formed he could see that it was a hatch. A dim glow and cables leading to a crystal-operated generator rack showed where the expedition had gone inside. He felt as all those without any useful gift felt at witnessing the mighty feats of others' talents: humbled, fearful and resentful.

'It's big,' he said, for want of something else to say, forced to state the obvious and to understand the Empress' determination and the scientists' passion, the engineers' obsession. Artefacts like this usually came in much smaller sizes, from tiny fragments you could gather in your palm to oddities on exhibit at the Museum – things the size of carts at their largest. Things on a scale that he did not feel intimidated by. He was caught short by Barsan's bleak grin.

'This is just the tip,' Barsan said, transferring his gaze to the buried machine with visceral repulsion. 'Inside it's huge.'

'Like a house?' Borze said, hoping.

'Like a city,' Barsan said, killing his hopes with a kind of grim pleasure. 'Don't think even this phase of the expedition has got to the end of it yet.'

Borze stared at the cone. It was large but it wasn't a city. He realised why nobody was trying to unearth it now, why it could not be simply extracted. The sun was high, it burned him where it fell on his skin through the leaf shadows or seemed to, the shade icy in comparison. Colours seemed vivid. He smelled an unmistakable thick, animal musk and then something hit his face, hard and sharp at the same time. He blinked and saw that Barsan had slapped him. The sound of feet running through sucking mud struck his ears with incredible clarity and he saw, in slowed motion, the shapes of soldiers in jungle fatigues go rushing, leaping past him like bulky deer, bows and spears in hand. They wore scarves over their mouths and noses. Someone was tying something around his face too, and it smelled astonishing, the fibres, cotton, hot and dry, a damped splurge on it cutting through the scent of the sun with violent cold streaks of acrid mineral that made his sinuses flare icy hot. Mint and eucalyptus, he knew these, but not the buried power of magespelled camphor that sliced through to his brain directly and finally allowed him to move at a normal speed, his body restored to its rightful place at the centre of this miraculous wonderland of the senses.

'We're under attack!' Barsan was dragging at his arm, propelling him forcefully back along the trail and stumbling up over the wooden earth supports. 'We have to get to the shelter...'

Borze recalled the briefing. He hadn't questioned it then but he'd wondered at the cowardice of hiding in holes and behind so many barricades, not because he didn't understand the value of that in its place but the Empire had sent such massive forces, why didn't they have better than this by now? He ran with

Barsan, following the more experienced man only because he had kept so fit and able as a matter of pride, otherwise he would have been left for dead and the way that everyone was fleeing to their assigned positions he wasn't at all sure anyone would have stopped to help him. The running forced more of the strange odour up his nose, and more of the camphor's counterspell. He had his will and control back from that initial intoxicating paralysis but everything still moved as though time was stalling. They ran over the same ground twice, he could have sworn, before he saw Barsan's lithe body slide down through a barely visible hole in the ground, grass blades bending and parting before him as if he was swallowed into a strangely reversed earthen womb. Then he was following and falling, scrabbling, running again through a wood-walled tunnel half his height. Mage lights glimmered in the planking alongside trickling water. More dripped on his head as he scraped his back and his legs screamed at the pain of the crouching run.

They came into a torchlit cave, already full with the four men who'd reached it before them, eyes wide and wild above their green scarves, bodies hunched and shaking, sweating, the air filled with the stink of camphor so badly he moved to rip his scarf off and once again found Barsan's calloused hand saving him from himself. The man had a grip like iron. 'Keep it on, General, whatever you do.' Behind him one of the soldiers had brushed past to close the opening with a close fitted wooden door. It was so heavily carved with runemagics there was barely a strip of bare grain left. Iron bars battened it into place.

As his eyes acclimatised to the dimmer conditions Borze saw the stutter-gleam of a glowslate coming to life. It was propped on a shelf which was otherwise stacked high above and below with emergency crystal power packs, water canisters and dried food ration. A throaty, soft hum and the sudden wash of moving air across his sweating face told of air recyclers coming on, or at least one. The soldier running it, fresh scars pink on his face, looked up from its readout. 'Got an hour or two.' His voice was apologetic and died quickly in the tiny space. 'Filter's only meant for three people.'

Borze did a quick head tally: six. Bodies moved aside to let him and Barsan to the front for the best view of the slate. The way these men moved made a new kind of cold trail its fingers up Borze's spine. It had been a long time since he'd been in a battle, longer still since a war, but their silent ease, each to their position, effortlessly shifting roles and accepting hierarchies without hesitation, that meant they'd fused into the kind of unit that only manifested under conditions of continuous, extreme threat. There was no room for ego, or even a need for names. Some were mercs and others Glimshard men but their faces all had the same intent, near-animal stare. There was survival, or death, and nothing else.

Borze turned his face back to the slate and saw a clear image of the digsite, abandoned. The cone's hatch was shut, unplugged cable lines tangled outside it. Nothing moved there. Barsan's hand glided across the control panel and the image followed his gesture and turned to show the track. Someone stood on it, quite still. Behind him Borze felt the soldiers' tension peak, breath stalling as the image moved in. Borze understood this slate magic even less than the other forms. A spirit brought the visions, he'd been told, by a woman who had looked deeply apologetic for the storybook explanation but all the words of her specifics had failed to make any impression in his mind.

Now the view flew unerringly towards the figure in Glimshard fatigues, rooted to the knee in the rich mud. He was a tall, strong man, his long greyed hair bound up into tight braids that hung down his back in greasy lines.

'It's Ghoriat,' said one of the men, his voice a mix of fear and prurience that Borze couldn't fathom.

'Shut up,' Barsan ordered. The slate shifted. It was a man in a forest, calm, waiting. Then he opened his mouth as the view spun sideways and revealed his ordinary, sweat-covered face, bearded and filthy. A strange hooting sound came out of his mouth, relayed by the same means as the image in faultless reproduction. It wasn't something Borze thought could come out of a human throat and at the same instant he thought that Barsan said, 'He's gone over.'

'What's going on?' Borze demanded, hearing his voice fill the air like a storm of grit, coughing after, the camphor making his eyes water.

'He's calling them,' Barsan said and then glanced at his commander's face and made an equivocal gesture with his shoulders as the man in the slate looked expectantly into the trees. 'You might have noticed a slight discrepancy in the number of people who returned to the city and the number you sent out and what you see here.'

Borze held his gaze over the reeking fumes coming from the scarf. He nodded, even though in that moment he was admitting to a junior oficer that he had been kept misinformed, that someone here was in charge and it wasn't him. Barsan nodded, absorbing the fact too, and his gaze became canny. His eyes moved, looking over the men behind but they flicked fast to Borze again, revealing that all of them were simply focused on the slate, and if they had understood it wasn't stirring them.

'They were reported MIA,' Borze lied, giving Barsan permission to continue.

'They are, in a way,' Barsan said, turning back to the slate's vision. 'But they're not coming back.'

The man who was not Ghoriat hooted again, softly, a greeting sound, and then Borze saw something his mind couldn't reconcile with any reality he knew. Parts of the forest dissolved and reformed into figures, huge and strange, each different but bearing vague resemblances to creatures he knew. In the first moment they were plant, in the second they were animal, insect, bird. Most of them had humanoid characteristics that immediately recalled Tzaban to his mind although the tiger man was much more human than anything that came stalking, prowling, flying to meet the soldier on the path. And smaller. And less likely to make him scream with the sheer impossibility of their existence and the way they had been, a few moments before, nothing but plants growing in a jungle as they should. Now they stalked around Ghoriat and made soft noises in return. He smiled and reached up his hands to them as though they were gigantic pets that he was going to caress. Tentacles and clawed limbs draped around him, touching him in turn as if he was their beloved. His old, lined face, grizzle-bearded, was filled with awe and wonder as he looked into their beaked, fanged faces, their eyes: two, four, eight, a thousand, filled with crystalline light.

They tore him to pieces, throwing him up in a celebrant's joyous exaltation so that his limbs revolved in different directions, bloody guts and muscle painting red against the brilliant greens of the world, the azure cruelty of the sky. They opened their mouths and embraced his return. They sang a song of strange notes, sad and kind, and though Borze didn't see them eat, didn't see what happened exactly, when they parted they were changed and become more like men, grizzle-bearded and dream-eyed, their voices shaping words like those he knew, as if said in foreign ways, half lost by intoxication – 'Stillen koming... all forth... eaten's not deaden... Ghoriatte, Ghoriauten... where diggen... no more. Bad badden. All buried earth etten it. Et it. We culd notta et it but dis eaters etten 'im. Says nay, nay.'

Coming from mouths not made to speak it was a travesty, but Borze listened for his life to it as red ran down beak and fang, was trampled in the mud as they turned to each other, then fell to silent all fours, as dogs, as cats, nothing he knew. They divided like water and ran in both directions, to the portal camp and to the digsite where he, Borze, huddled in his earth hole and watched them come.

'They're getting more coherent,' Barsan said as the soldiers swore. 'We've learned that they take prisoners and use them this way, and other ways. But this is for talking. They have learned to speak, after a fashion. It doesn't always last long for some reason.'

'They knew his name,' Borze said, feeling somehow this was important.

'Yeah, they know everything when they eat you,' Barsan replied bitterly. 'Access codes, passwords, work rotas... Nice way to spy huh?'

Behind him Borze could feel the soldiers' grim, rapt attention as if it were a physical force crawling across his back, filling the air and making it into a stinking, unbreathable solid as they rejected and hated what they saw, and stood in paralysed terror, waiting. In his case the reaction was quite different. A cold, easy clarity came to him, a liquid readiness in all his body and his thoughts took on a smooth perfection. This was his gift.

'What will they do now? How many people have they taken? Do they always sacrifice just one? Do you know if the others are unharmed, wherever they are?'

Barsan looked at him with a moment of surprise at the calm tone of his voice. 'Now they'll come and look for us. They often stay back and try to talk but so far whatever they're trying to say is a load of garbage to our ears. All the people taken and whoever stays out will eventually be, uh, possessed by that smell whatever it is. Some kind of drug in the air, I don't know the details. All the scientists who were good at that kind of thing are gone or dead.' He paused to allow that to sink in but Borze just signalled him impatiently to continue.

'They sometimes bring or get another. One time, there was this linguist, and after they ate her they talked pretty well but all they said was we had to go or we had to stay and be Karoo. Far as anyone knows being Karoo just means they eat you. Whatever it is that's down in this pit is costing about thirty people a week. If it's as big as they claim, full of a city's worth of

stuff ... Well, you can figure it out how long that might take. It can't be extracted in one piece. A lot gets packed and shipped ...'
He stopped as Borze cut him off with a touch on his arm and they both looked at the slate.

The clearing with the pit was empty of human life. To the credit of the team on duty there were few signs of hasty abandonment, nothing dropped, only their scattered footprints in the mud betrayed the speed of their escape. And all led directly to the foxholes.

Two Karoo had come their way. They were big, one bipedal, the other on all fours, and they reminded Borze again of many animals in one although their predatory nature was clear in every sleek or ugly line. They were silent and the forest around them was also unnaturally quiet as they moved together, separating to investigate the hideouts. Tall, beaked, with long arms and powerful hindquarters, clad in green like grass and scales like the iridescent colours of black birds, the nearest to them came stalking directly to their door. To the appalled surprise of Borze he heard its claws scratch the door, and after that its knuckles knock.

'Time to go,' it said, and they could hear it both ways, its rasping voice in the air, through the door, and through the slate's strange magic. The voice was that of the eaten man in cadence. Borze fancied it had a Lowlander's accent. 'No more use cannon ...' But it paused and hissed fiercely then, raging, as they heard the distant, strange sound of a quasi-magical weapon Borze knew as something like a volt gun, but one much bigger than he had encountered before. Barsan touched the panel and the precious view of the monster at the door switched to the portal campsite. The other three Karoo he'd seen were there, in the midst of deserted space that was filled with an inexplicable fury of lightning. It radiated from a metal pole in the centre of the area they had invaded. Tendrils of white light wrapped the creatures around and inside the silvered nets they danced and jolted fiercely, smoking and burning. The discharges stopped, suddenly, and Barsan murmured, 'That's just the half charge. Usually puts them off for a while.' As the strikes vanished. the creatures lay about, twitching and groaning and Borze realised it was indeed only a warning shot. This, he reasoned, was perhaps the storm cannon that he'd heard Alide was testing. In the clear air he saw that the metal pole was one of several positioned strategically about the site.

'You don't have that here.'

'Doesn't work here,' Barsan said with resignation. 'Something about the artefact prevents it.'

The door thudded with a concussion that Borze felt as he heard wood splinter and tear. Then there was coughing and sneezing from the monster and a frenzied assault that ended as suddenly as it had begun. 'Give back. Return!' the voice hissed, slavering wetly as it spoke. On the slate's view the Karoo had regained their feet shakily. The largest, bearlike, with a fur that shifted of its own accord like a rug composed of beetles or one of those gigantic bee swarms that longer summers sometimes produced, reached out with a clawed hand and grasped the metal rod beside it, wrenching it free of its mounts in a single vicious jerk. It held the broken end up before one of its large brown eyes and stared at the twisted metal and the long strings of the wires that hung from the hollowed end. Then, as if they had been signalled, the three as one loped away fast, vanishing into the closest line of trees.

The destruction of their door stopped at the same moment. The slate, when it shifted view, showed an empty site.

'That's usually it,' Barsan said with confidence. 'We'll wait a while before we sound the all clear though.'

Borze straightened up, camphor tears running in cool streaks down to the line of the bandana and soaking into it. He was silent a minute.

'Something the matter?' Barsan was weary now, the survivor of one more by the numbers assault.

'Yeah,' Borze said, feeling a horrible sense of unease. 'I don't understand why you're all not dead yet.'

He reunited with Gau Tam an hour later, and listened to his second's account of the assault at the portal with half an ear as they ate rice and beans in the officers' tent and the heavy afternoon rain hammered on the canvas and drenched the outside world. At his elbow the lists of the missing and the dead lay in a neat stack, curled with damp. When Gau Tam was done he had finished his small meal.

'Has the command here captured any living Karoo?'

Gau Tam frowned at the lack of reaction his story had gained but seeing the expression on Borze's face he shook his head. 'Not so far as I know. They said that they always fight or die. There were some corpses that were shipped back to the city for dissection, but no living captives.'

'I want to see inside that thing, then we're going back,' Borze said. 'But first, I guess Alide isn't here in person but he must have someone dealing with this storm cannon. Bring them here.'

The woman who arrived to his summons was small and he recognised immediately her preoccupied and hunted look as someone who was entirely absorbed in their work and also under pressure from superiors. She introduced herself as Reslyn Frannatin, part of the Defensive Engineers, a research unit run by Alide's ministry that had produced many interesting things for the Empire over the years. Borze's own combat had been taught him in a hand-to-hand age and the majority of it was still bows and swords, though Glimshard magi were renowned for pulling out terrible weapons in times of need; this, and the machineries they had access to were the line that their various harassers had never brought themselves to cross. Reslyn was a typical engineer, he found: once he'd steered her to her pet subject her focus on it was such that she lost her inhibitions and talked at length although she was always careful with her wording.

He gathered that Alide's cannon was still under test, that

there were other machineries in development but as far as he could pick from the scattered motes of interest in her explanations this site was only a testbed, the weaponry of note was not here, it was somewhere else. Because it was not verified fit for field use it remained Alide's sole property and Borze could not requisition it nor expect to be presented with it until it passed testing. Borze thanked her for her fascinating contribution and when she had gone asked Barsan give him a copy of all the shipping manifests from the site since it had been discovered. He left Gau Tam studying that, much to Tam's utter disgust, and then demanded access to the artefact.

He and Barsan walked past the site of Ghoriat's last moments. Bright blood splatters still shone here and there but the rain had washed most of it away, leaving shining mirror prints in the mud in the shape of hooves, three-toed claw feet and enormous paws. They sloshed through these, obliterating them on the way past. A troop of soldiers moved around them in silence, their salutes automatic. The lists of the dead ran through Borze's head. The missing. He didn't understand it.

They came to the pit, descended. The hatch was reopened now, the power cables attached. A woman came out and nearly hit both of them; her head was down and she was rushing, out of breath. The fact they couldn't fit through the hatch together forced her to stop and look up. Borze saw only a mass of gold curly hair above jungle fatigues, and large, wary eyes, preoccupied with the usual gaze he knew for a mage's half trance. She looked at him and stood back, clutching the items she was holding to her chest: a personal slate, something wrapped in a cloth. She looked pale and shocked. He figured she was new.

'General,' she said, after a moment. 'What a surprise.'

'You have me at a disadvantage,' he said as Barsan stood in respectful position, deferring as ever to the woman, particularly because of her mage status and the fact she was under his protection.

'Carlyn Loitrasta,' she said, 'Professor.'

'I wonder if you would be good enough to show me around the inside of this object, Professor,' Borze said. 'An expert eye would be invaluable.'

'I...' He saw her hesitate and think it over but finally she nodded. 'Yes, all right.'

'Barsan, you're free to go,' Borze said, with an affable smile. He didn't miss Barsan's look of wry acquiescence. They exchanged salutes and Barsan had to go back to his duties. Borze turned his professional social smile, least used but he needed the practice for the evening, and saw the professor mirror it with her own. It looked paper thin. 'Did the attack frighten you, Professor?'

'Yes,' she said. She swallowed and her hands gripped and re-gripped her items. 'But it's been the third, so, you know, getting a bit more used to it.'

He noted the repressed hysteria in her voice. 'And how long have you been here?' He stepped through the hatch, expecting her to follow, which she did, his tone conversational, that of a man entirely comfortable and in control. And then, as he saw the interior, the magelights heading off down and then branching out rapidly in long streamers like holiday bunting, their gleams eventually lost by distance, he lost his voice and found himself almost about to fall with a sudden, unexpected vertigo.

Loitrasta was the one who prevented him stumbling to his knees. 'Just two days. Mind the slope,' she said and waited in the dimness for him to adjust his sight. 'I can't show it all to you, only my section really. This way.'

For an hour, that was the last time that Borze felt anything like familiarity. When they re-emerged into the light and the dripping dusk he was a changed man. He understood now why the Empress held on to this at the price she had been willing to pay and the silence, and the rest. But he still didn't understand the most basic part of it. Why they were still alive.

He had seen one Karoo at close quarters, listened to him talk, seen him train soldiers, watched his speed, his ability, his reactions to the humans that surrounded him and he would have given nearly anything for a regiment of those – with that he wouldn't need an army, less still any mercenaries. Everything Tzaban had claimed was true, it seemed. He knew therefore that this harassment was not a fully-fledged Karoo response. It served only to bring an endless smorgasbord of humans southward.

'Will you be returning to Glimshard, General?'

He turned back and found Professor Loitrasta smiling at the expression on his face, which he was reasonably sure resembled that of a stunned rabbit. He recovered, stood tall, smelled the filthy stink of the mud and rot, but no stranger odours. 'Yes, Professor. I am going directly now that I've done all I came to do.'

She nodded. 'I want you to take this back with you please, to Professor Huntingore. Tralane Huntingore of Sircene. I understand she'll be at the ball of course, tonight.' She held out her personal slate. 'Would you? I realise it's cheeky. But you are going there, aren't you?'

He considered her motive in passing it to him rather than use the military post and nodded, took it and slid it to the inside pocket of his damp, camphor-stained uniform.

She looked at him very seriously for a moment and nodded just a fraction, quite a different expression. By intelligence from Mazhd he knew she was Huntingore's closest confidante. He felt a seismic shift within his convictions, another. 'Do you have any particular news I might give the Empress?'

'Not yet.' It began to rain suddenly again. 'I only just got here yesterday but...'

'But?' Water dripped down his collar but he waited.

'Some of the people here, on the science team that I knew from before...' She paused and looked uncomfortable, rain running down all the contours of her upturned face. 'They're not right. It's as if... they don't know what they're doing. Like, they seem to, until you ask a question that's specific. Maybe they've been out here too long?' Her face said she didn't really think so.

'That's what you believe?' he pushed and saw her expression drop to a grim, unhappy weight as she shook her head and curls bounced and fell down into sinking waves, darkening.

'What's your theory then, Professor?'

There was nobody near them and the rain was heavy enough now that it made its own susurrus on the mud and leaves that hid words.

'I can't say for sure but I made a test. It's on the slate. Ask 'Lane. Make her read it for you.' She didn't wait for more but set off through the downpour alone, her cloth wrapped item still held to her chest to keep it dry.

Borze scowled and water ran down his nose from his brow. The rain was so heavy there was no point trying to avoid it. He walked steadily back to the portal site, accepting the guard of four men who came to escort him there with clipped efficiency, exchanging a few words with each until he was reunited with Gau Tam who looked mutinous but was, at least, quite dry under the awning.

'You look like you swallowed a bug,' Tam said, pleased to find he wasn't the only one fed up.

'Might have done,' Borze nodded. 'Find anything?' He glanced at the curling record stacks – plain people's writing tools, for those without mage powers to work slates.

'Defence took a large set of soldiers out to another site as part of the special weapons' unit. It's north of here, away from the treelines. That's all I know.'

'Have them recalled to Glimshard,' Borze said, knowing quite well how that would play out. 'It's time we returned, or you won't have time to get dressed and fuss your hair.'

'How handy that you don't need to,' Gau Tam replied, nearly leaping out of the chair in his eagerness to quit the place. He met Borze's grin with a superior look. 'Just tell them the smell is a new aftershave.'

Borze tried to smile but the slate in his chest pocket felt heavy and strange and it dragged his mouth down. He made departing manoeuvres with Barsan's second and collected his horse from its leaky stable.

'You know what's funny?' Gau Tam said beside him as he led the beast. He looked up at Tam riding correctly, even in the sheeting rain. 'The horses never batted an eyelash during the whole thing, and the officers said they're never taken. I asked why there aren't any left here. He told me they sent them all back through the portal because they were going lame with hoofrot. I suppose a lot of the men decided they'd be better on the Steppe than risk coming back here, took them as peace offerings to the Circle.'

Borze nodded and braced himself for the horrible sensation of being dissolved. For a moment he almost thought it might be preferable to remain that way but the machine set him on his feet into dry, dusky plains air, cooler but infinitely gentler. With the city gleaming before him in all its best decorated majesty he changed his mind. A runner, tabarded, tiny, like a little pixie in her shoes, almost hurled herself into the horse's shoulder before he had a chance to mount up.

'Sir!' she said, her eyes glittering with peculiar excitement. 'The Empress wishes you to attend her immediately, before the ball.'

He nodded, feeling his expectations sink yet further until they might as well have been in a mud pit too. 'I will be there as soon as I am able to change out of these clothes.'

'She has had your uniforms transported to the palace. You are to go directly.'

He heard Tam snicker as he kicked the horse into a canter and left him behind.

CHAPTER SEVENTEEN

ZHARAZIN

Zharazin woke up in an unfamiliar room. Windowed doors were open on to a terrace from which he saw only sky at his pillow position. Gauze curtains lifted on the breeze. He heard paper rustle and turned over. Tralane Huntingore smiled down at him from her seated position. She was wearing a red wrap and breadcrumbs from the roll she was eating with one hand while the other held the day's fresh broadsheet roughly folded up. She was on page two, he noted. He wondered what the time was although he didn't want to find that out too soon as it would probably mean he had to get up and stop looking at her heavy dark brown hair with its slight coil curls cascading in luxurious half circles over her breasts.

'Well well,' she said, letting the hand holding the roll fall on to the coverlet. 'You sleep very soundly for a man with so much in his mind.'

'Must have been tired,' he said, surprised by the soft burr in his voice and the slight tenderness in his throat. He hoped he wasn't getting sick.

'Must have been,' she replied and gave him a look of amusement and warmth – a combination that took his breath away.

He recalled the night before and stretched, finding sore muscles and a growling stomach. 'That was a great dinner by the way.'

'Oh...' She waved her roll at him, 'you must be invited to these things all the time.'

'Yes,' he said honestly. 'But none of them were even half so good.' Part of his mind used to calculating tried to slide away and quickly plan his day's movements, but he silenced it and got up on his elbow, just enough to reach out and bite into the roll held so carelessly at her thigh. Pastry crumbs scattered everywhere. He slumped back, chewing and saw her watching him with that little smile.

'I hope breakfast won't disappoint you then.' She jammed the roll to her own mouth and refolded the newssheet.

'Is this it?' He swallowed and watched her chew in turn before she put the last bite of the roll between her teeth and leant down to him, tossing the paper aside, the wrap falling open.

'Mmn hmm,' she said around her part of the mouthful as he took his, lips brushing hers. Her large dark eyes dared him.

He reached up and slipped the wrap from her shoulders.

TRALANE

'I've brought you tea and a catalogue. You can't wait, you have to choose from whatever's left.' Minnabar's voice snapped Tralane from her doze and sat her bolt upright but she didn't have time to focus before Minna added, 'Oh gods, my eyes! Look, I'm leaving it here on the side. But look at it. You've got about twenty minutes before they close up to start the adjustments and ironing service. Seriously.' The tone was one of utter social despair. Tralane looked about for a shoe to throw but the door was already closing and although there were a few about none were close enough.

She looked at Mazhd, sprawled and only half covered where he'd fallen asleep starfished at her side. Was she meant to believe his story? For now she didn't mind much, she thought, and if only it could all stay here in her room and never have to be revealed in daylight then she'd never mind it either way. She looked long enough to burn him into her retinas and then she reached out for the catalogue and swatted him lightly with it.

'Hey, you. You're good at social stuff. Help me find something to wear.'

He rolled over and sat up, the sheets and cover falling down to his narrow, tight waist and revealing all the muscle she'd had so much fun discovering the night before. He raised an eyebrow and reached out to twitch the catalogue from her hand. 'Chalice and Pearl. Sparing no expense, then?'

Tralane said nothing. It hadn't occurred to her that Minnabar would consider the prices and, obviously, she hadn't. Leaving it so late meant there was no time to fuss. She wondered if her old wardrobe would have anything to offer but a mental inventory said that there was nothing that fitted and was not out of date by several years. 'I hate dressing for impressions. My daughter loves it. Her idea.' Inwardly she quaked at the idea of the price. For one night. For pity's sake! She thought to look at the time then, and groaned. It was already after noon. She had to find more crystals before dusk and by the look of the weather that could prove an interesting task. Alide's threats hung on her worse than the money issue. It was negligible in comparison. Maybe she could sell something later.

Mazhd slapped the catalogue back at her. 'I can't believe you'd give the choice to someone else.' His finger held it open at a particular page. She took it and saw red velvet twisted and pulled and sculpted around an hourglass model. There was a lot of bodice and bone, gold heavy cord lacing and cream bursting unexpectedly from one side of a fishtail hem. Long gloves and a demimask decorated with diamante eyeholes dangled carelessly from the model's fingers, as though she had just stepped out to a balcony for some fresh air and was turned to assess her many suitors.

'You like them over the top, then.'

'It's suitable and it's in stock in your size.'

'What about this one?' She pointed to a plain black and grey up and down kind of dress which fitted her criteria for comfort, practicality and, above all, near-invisibility. It had full sleeves, went nearly to the ankle and could be worn with flight boots.

'You're going to a ball, not cleaning out a shed.' He smiled at her, alarmingly shameless and happy – so much so it quite threw her off her stride. 'Although I've seen you in your shed gear and I'd choose that any time.'

He meant flight leathers, she thought. Well, it could come to that, knowing her luck. She must check the weather and prepare the Flit. Probably she should check up on Isabeau and find out what Minnabar was doing – it wasn't like her to be around the house alone this late in the day. Then she looked back at him and remembered why she was so late. She'd always despised men who buffed themselves to the eyeballs, waxing, oiling, curling, straightening. But looking at his silky belly and the way it narrowed in flat planes of perfect amber to his hipline, broken only by the dark trail of hair that vanished tantalisingly under her ancient coverlet changed her mind. No, she must not. She looked again at her dress choice and felt a pang for the Tralane of two days ago who would never have cared about what she looked like. She flicked to the red dress. It shouted brazenly every ridiculous notion of feminine erotic power. A brilliant woman might wear it but it had nothing to say about first-class minds. She looked at the grey and black shift – it spoke seriously and quietly about thorough professional balance, strategy and composure. It was bland. *But I am bland*, she thought. *I am not out for men, I've got enough trouble. I just want to go, see this*

259

Karoo, shake hands with the Dean of the University to remind her I still exist, and get out without seeing that bloody Minister.

She glanced back at Mazhd, who was grinning mercilessly at her. He would look amazing of course. And that thought suddenly reminded her that he was associated with a lot of women in various high positions, not only at the palace but elsewhere, possibly needing to keep a good face with most of them whether they were actively soliciting him or not. And suddenly that depressed her.

'Lane?' he said, seeing her expression falter.

'Yes, you're right, of course,' she said. 'The red one. Are you um ... Are you going tonight alone?'

'After I've finished what I have to do,' he said. 'I'll be a little late most likely, but I will be there.'

She scoured his tone for any signs of caution, backing off or hesitancy but found nothing. 'I don't have an escort – what?'

His snort had cut her off. 'Of course you don't. That would require forethought.'

She scowled but attempting irritation for her transparent lack of care seemed pointlessly after-the-fact. 'All the most interesting women go alone.'

'I'm free if you change your mind.' He sat up and ran his hands through his hair, flicking the heavy unbound mane of it down his back as he looked around for his clothes.

'Well, but you might be late.'

'You'll be late,' he said confidently, getting up naked and walking around, poking at the bedclothes and slowly gathering the bits and pieces of his understated, elegant tailoring. She watched him disappear into them sadly. A night on the floor didn't seem to have done them any harm. Within minutes he was cutting a dashing, powerful figure about forty times more credible than anything she could achieve in forty days.

'I'm missing a sock,' he said finally, breaking her reverie.

She cast her mind back and then looked up. 'On the light fitting.'

'Of course.' He stood on the bed to retrieve it and a little shower of dust came down with the sock, making him sneeze.

Tralane just sat, realising how incredibly comfortable she felt around him. Just as if he was Carlyn. More so for some reason, despite the fact she didn't and couldn't trust him and that he was the infomancers' man. 'Well I'm sure you must have a lot to do before then.' She got up after a moment of wondering if she really was ready to pad about naked herself and located clean-enough clothing to wear; grey cotton undergarments that were once white, and ancient close-fitted silk flight-liners that covered her from ankle to neck in yellowed bands and made her look a little bit like an exotic grub.

'I will be very busy.' He checked his pockets and smiled, seeming to find everything in order. 'You're going flying?' His look was hard to read. Envy, she thought smugly, and something she wasn't sure about.

'I go every week,' she lied easily. 'And I have experiments to run that need to be done up there. Most of them are just for the weather service.' This last part was true, and had been neglected lately, pushed to the back of her mind thanks to everything else. She closed her eyes briefly and felt the weight of all she had been ignoring for a moment, only because she was under this stupid blackmail. And then there was the dig, and the 'war'. All tied up together. She was a fool to think of romance at a time like this.

She found Mazhd looking knowingly at her. 'Difficult times,' he said, and she remembered his mouth all over her and felt sick and weak with the notion she might never see it in any of those places again. 'Where shall I meet you?'

'I will be outside in a carriage at nine thirty,' he said. 'I'll wait. But I do have business there so if the eleven bell goes I must go with it.'

Eleven was insanely late. She could easily make it before that. 'Thank you. You should probably eat.'

He grinned and eyed her up and down, then bent his head and kissed her on the lips – a lingering, gentle kiss of unexpected sweetness. 'No, that's all right. I had a very big breakfast.'

She showed him out and watched him walk down to the street with a keen sense of unreality. In his long duster raincoat with his hair free he looked darkly sinister, like a knife just taken out and sharpened. Some tether glued to her insides tugged as he stepped on to the paving and she felt it tug more and harder as he got further away, strolling briskly towards whatever appointment he had to keep. She had to rub her belly to get the sensation to stop.

Inside the house, she took the catalogue to the kitchen and found both girls waiting for her at the table. She sat down. They stared at her. 'What?'

'Mooooom!' Minnabar moaned, sliding her arms out between the breakfast plates and stretching across the table as if being tortured, her expression suffering.

Isabeau poured tea very precisely and pushed it towards Tralane in a manner clearly indicating that this was her part of a deal and now it was time for Lane to deliver the other part of the bargain. 'You know who he is, right? I mean...'

Tralane took the tea with a withering look at both of them. 'I know I've spent most of my life up to the elbows in clockwork and engines but yes, I do know who Zharazin Mazhd is, thank you very much.' She tried not to simper, still full of his attentions, and it was surprisingly hard.

Minnabar looked up at her from her place on the table like a mournful dog, 'We thought he might be investigating you, because of the pamphlet, you know?'

She almost choked on the tea. It went everywhere. As she was spluttering and looking around for a cloth, Isabeau added, 'The bank sent a letter. Someone put five hundred credit into your account. Gigawatt Enterprise. They want authority to pay off your outstanding debts with it.'

Tralane scowled at Isabeau, 'What are you doing reading my mail?'

'We wanted to pay for all our dresses, but the account was blocked,' Isabeau said drily as if this entitled them to any kind of actions. 'So choose yours and then we'll be out of your hair, well, figuratively anyway.'

'So who's this Gigawatt?' Minnabar asked, bored, tracing pictures among crumbs with her finger.

'Where's the dress order?' Tralane countered, knowing that Gigawatt Enterprises was Alide's idea of a joke. The money was from the Ministry and it covered her 'expenses' in procuring the crystal. Taking it galled her. Blood money. Once she did there was no more moral high ground to stand on. She was simply an employee. 'And he is not here about the pamphlet.' She hoped. The notion made her scowl. She didn't need to look at statements to know that she couldn't afford to turn that money down, but the alternatives looked bleak. Going to the ball in an old frock was minor stuff compared to losing her home and her daughters. In truth for all her feelings about it she found she didn't dare defy Alide beyond caustic remarks. It was shaming enough that Mazhd knew about the blackmail but what he could do she didn't know either. He was a trader and whatever power he had belonged to his mistress. Tralane had nothing to offer Shrazade that she didn't already know. She had the gun, and that was it.

Minnabar handed her the order paper for the dresses, not counting hers. She looked at the total and at the time and signed it, adding her own. 'As soon as I'm dressed I'll clear this and then I'm going for a flight. I won't be back until late so who's picking you two up?'

'I'm going with Night,' Isabeau said. 'I have to be at her place by six.'

'I'm not sure yet,' Minnabar said, cheek laid on the table, following the wood grain with her finger. 'I just can't decide. Is Mazhd picking you up?'

'Maybe,' Tralane said, suddenly childish. 'But I will be late.'

'Wish I could go late, the first part is so boring,' Minna said, sighing and sitting back up, brushing crumbs off her face. 'All the names and the formal dances. The Empress won't even show her face until gone ten and nothing will happen until after midnight.'

'By happen you mean unwise drunken liaisons and foolish amounts of babble?' Isabeau asked with a withering tone.

'Of course, what's the point of it otherwise?'

'Well for you, nothing, obviously.'

Minna curled her lip at Isabeau contemptuously. 'Like you're there for a higher purpose other than showing off.'

'I don't have a reason to show off. I'm there as my Master's student, because I have to be. None of it interests me in the least.'

'Oh sure, like you don't want to see that tigerman.'

'He's a Karoo. And I already met him.'

Minnabar stared at her, gearing up to denounce the lie but Tralane was faster.

'When?'

'The evening before yesterday. Night was called to a meeting with the Empress. He was there. It was the last thing I did before I came home.' Isabeau gave Minnabar a *so there* stare.

Minna opened her mouth but Tralane waved her hand in front of it, 'Zhzhshhh. What got said at this meeting? Who else was there?'

Minna clamped her mouth shut and glared at both of them but she was too interested to do more.

'The Empress, her guard, Tzaban, General Borze, Parlumi Night and myself.'

Minna cracked with a high-pitched exclamation that bordered

264

on a whine of envy, 'You can't seriously tell me you're getting invited to state meetings?'

Isabeau gave her a contemptuous look. 'I wasn't invited to participate and I'm not allowed to repeat anything. I just say I saw the Karoo. What were you doing? Drinking cocktails and scoring points off empty-headed little heiresses?'

Tralane groaned with annoyance even as part of her marvelled in astonishment at Isabeau's rise and rise to places of power. She got up in search of food and listened to the two of them bicker and bitch while she prepared it, finally interrupting with, 'Minna, put that dress order in or we're all done for. Issa, might I have your help with the Flit in ten minutes before you go?'

Ten minutes later, indigestion at full throttle, Tralane was inside her flight leathers and Isabeau was in her heavy overalls, both of them working on different parts of fixing the Flit's tiny double-stream engine. Isabeau was cutting a new fuel filter pad out of natural sponge. Lane changed the oil and tested the prop shafts for cracks and vibrational inconsistencies. Outside the shed, the sky was a mixture of grey cloud with blue patches and was predicted to clear by evening. Appeals to the University Weather Station had suggested east was her best bet for locating the clashing air fronts that might bear storms but it could be a long flight, at the limit of her range. Winds would be enough, she had reasoned. Alide knew nothing of the workings of what he was gathering and by the time he might discover that the crystals did not contain the same potentials as the ones he had got before it would be much too late for either her or him to worry about it.

'East is flat,' Isabeau said as she worked, her small spanner flashing in the low light. 'And it's tornado season.'

Lane had thought of this too. Tornadoes rarely came as far west as Glimshard and if they did they were weathermanced away from it, but out east they were frequent, resulting in large

265

areas of plain with relatively little human life of any permanency. Nomads and herdsmen dared claim it for themselves, a few farming groups clung to the edges but aside from them and caravans using the roads to cross the lengthy distances between the fertile west and the farther eastern Empire stretches it was a mostly empty place. If she crashed there she wouldn't be going anywhere fast. The risk only sharpened her awareness. Whatever was to come, for the moment she was going to have some fun and later take the pleasure of giving Alide substandard crap.

Isabeau finished the lines and checked the air intakes. Tralane watched her proudly for a moment. It might not be her abiding passion but her daughter had a cool, swift accuracy about her that demonstrated a perfect working knowledge and excellent skills.

'I didn't know you were so familiar with the Flit,' she said, having expected to at least answer a few questions.

'I read the schematic,' Isabeau replied, replacing her tools in their box with exacting care. 'You keep it pretty well maintained. I can't find any real issues with it.'

'Real issues?'

'Well if we had the money and time I think we could make a better one, a much better one, but that would require a significantly larger workshop and testing area, not to mention raw materials and we don't have diddly squat to spend, do we?' Isabeau looked up thoughtfully. 'My internship isn't exactly going to turn any profits I can see either. I think we need to put our family heads together and open a shop.'

Tralane stared at her. 'A shop.'

She nodded, lining up her screwdrivers so that all handles and tips were in a perfectly straight line before closing the case. 'Selling small things that people like to have and need. Like timepieces, and household gadgets and another one, larger, for farming machinery, once we've collected enough finance to open a factory of our own. I looked into the materials' sourcing and it just happens that this region is quite well stocked in the kinds of minerals and ores we need. But I don't think we should finance our own mining company as they already exist and have their own expertise. We could however do a deal with specialised drilling equipment which could get us some very profitable rates.'

Isabeau looked up into the silence, cleaning her fingers on a rag as Tralane stood watching and realised she, Tralane, was an idiot. 'Minna would be good in a shop, selling and bossing people around. She was made for it,' Isabeau added.

'You're right. I never thought of any of that.'

'I know. Why would you? You discover things, you make them work. You're not like me. And you're not like Minna. We're only similar. Mom, you look terrible, what is it?'

'I— This saving our butts thing is supposed to be my job. But all I've done is sit and watch everything fall apart.'

'Not everything. You're kind and you looked after Carlyn and Bestie and the House families who've been with us for donkeys' years, and you took in Minna's web of idiots, and you let me do whatever I wanted even when you thought I was mad. You've written oodles of papers for other disciplines which were all good, and brought lots of machines back to life, and now it's my turn to do something useful.' Isabeau smiled and folded her cloth up. 'I need to get this oil off my hands before I report to Night. We can discuss it after the ball sometime. When you've got a minute.'

Tralane found herself speechless. Isabeau left and she was still speechless as she finally shook herself and pushed the Flit out of the shed and on to the end of the runway. The rig sang in the breeze lightly as she unfolded and braced the wings. After all its treatments the engine started first try. There was that brief, uncertain moment when she opened the throttle and waited for it to shift from purr to roar, wondering if it would still hold, all these years after it was machined into being, older than she was, but it did. The brakes creaked as the power increased and then she let them go. Rattling, quivering like a sensitive aunt, the Flit rolled forwards. Swiftly it flinched from weeds and cracks, then she opened the gas and aether flow nozzles and felt the shimmering change from nervous to smoothly assured as the magery honed the basic works into a perfect, easy fusion of speed and lift. The Flit rose into the air with purpose and turned into the wind. For a few moments she had an unprecedented view of the city. She oriented by the palace's asymmetric towers and took a due east bearing, already so high that to onlookers from the plains ground she would be no bigger than a sparrow. Cloud quickly engulfed her as she rose and she had to put on her mask and breathe bottled air. It was colder in the high airstreams but she didn't mind it. Icy air rushing through the odd chink in her protection reminded her of how precarious every moment was, and filled her with joy.

East she went, for an hour, more or less directly as the flows of the wind let her, noting their increasing strengths. She took her time to look about, making small adjustments on her maps as she matched the human settlements on the land with various geological features. The Flit behaved perfectly, even the usually erratic meteorometer flashing regular updates as it collected data blurts from the ancient weathermasts. These were sturdy bits of kit, basic but robust, located at the trig points where the geological surveyors had left them hundreds of years ago when Glimshard first came to this region under Atsueen. A half Sircene Empress, her obsession with the gathering of scientific knowledge had used up nearly every penny the city and its environs had been able to muster on grand projects. They had paid out for the most part, although now the 'pure' ones, such as the weather listening posts, had been neglected in favour of the profitable benefits of hydroelectricity, aquifer management and geothermal heating.

The meteorometer acted up, blinking warning lights nearly as soon as she reached the tornado corridor marked on her maps with a hashed red border and on the meter's display coloured in orange. Whether this was lucky or unlucky she wasn't sure but at least there were storms ahead, that was certain. She adjusted her flight path accordingly and tightened her safety straps, checking her parachute harness and just playing a little with the controls to feel them working now when it was only bluster before serious weather came to play with her. While she had the time she turned and checked her crystals and the array, tested its aerials and pickups in case something had come loose on the way out, and then put up her lightning hood – a wire cage that surrounded her shoulders and head and connected to the metal cage of the pilot's seat frame and the discharge router, intended to protect her and her instruments from being fried by a strike. She felt better with it there but there was really not much sense of great security in these things: the cockpit was still open and the Flit was undeniably tiny and she was about to do something foolishly dangerous.

She waited, to see if her hands would turn her from it, to feel if she wanted to run away from it, but the overpowering sensation was in the other direction; she felt, contrary to much she might have thought, that she was completely safe and this was what she was meant to be doing. She and the wind, the rain, the cloud, the air, the land – they were all one thing, her body felt this, and felt it in the machine too, it was her, the wind was her, the rain was her, the storms and the gyres of restless airmasses, they were her. She was everywhere and it was purely stupid to think she could be only a tiny creature alone in a lifeless machine inside a chaotic and unpredictable system of massive and indifferent powers. That was simply not true. Her conviction was bone deep and at the same moment she knew there was no way at all she could ever have convinced someone else of this, or even her own mind, if it gripped its principles and its knowledge and started to talk. What she came for, what was up here was this mindless stillness, this experience of one-ness,

269

not alone but at home, always and everywhere at home. Here she knew nothing of fear.

Tralane banked into the direction of the storm. She was so focused on the skies that for a long time she didn't look down or check her maps, and so when she had crossed two thirds of the plain and moved almost as far easterly as she dared the sight that temporarily blotted out thoughts of fuel levels was so surprising that it made her jaw drop. Below her on the sweeping grasslands was a large tented encampment. She saw coloured banners of the Empire and light flashing off something metal or glass.

Bracing the control stick with her knees she fumbled with her goggles to reset their viewing and took a better look over the side. Spire, she thought. That was her symbol of the lit tower on their purple banners. It was no trade group either, but a war force, accompanied by medium weight artillery and at least two separate groups of engineers bearing things in covered wagons, some of them steam operated, others pulled by heavy oxen and horses. Light cavalry was plentiful, and she saw creatures she'd only seen in books before too – the half-reptile, half-bird Vashrapten, armoured and ridden by the archers and crossbow-men, their humanoid hands so bizarre as they held packages or range weapons of their own. All of them had dull plumage, relatively, brown and green. There came the flash of light again, on glass she was sure this time, and she knew herself seen from below. Instinctively, she pulled on the control stick and went higher, though she was already way out of range for any shot.

The Flit bore no markings but its very existence meant she could only have come from Glimshard. She looked up and the magnification of the lenses suddenly brought her face to face with a huge stormfortress of clouds, greenish and grey with their own weight, higher than the Gleaming or any mortal structure. She heard at the same moment the bleeping warning of the meteorometer as it took readings using the delicate sensors on the Flit's nose and wings. It was predicting the formation of tornadoes imminently a short distance ahead, within ten miles, not that Tralane needed a beep to tell her that considering the looks of the sky. There was a clear line of cloud-meet-clear-air and huge, pendulous masses of water at multiple levels in that cloud, lit by flashes of hidden lightning. She banked slowly, staying high, fighting the wind a little as it became stronger – enough to start the strange, deluded song of the crystallograph wires though it was too soon, she thought, to turn the switch yet. Because it might be her only chance she pulled out her bread and cheese and took a few hearty bites, slugging it down with watered juice from her canteen and steering with her knees.

She assumed these were reinforcements for the dig project, sent a long way overland because Spire had no portals, or because until lately Glimshard had had no portals. The distance from Sprianshi, Empress Jagorin's city in the uplands, meant this group had set out weeks before and were finally only days from arrival and that was plausible given that the dig portal had only been tested and verified later than that. If the soldiers had been moving across the plains from Sprianshi's best approach in the north-east, then they had been several days already in this grassland and must realise the dangers of it, but they were horribly vulnerable right now on their present vector which was taking them faultlessly towards Glimshard. She considered warning them, but what good would it do? There was nowhere to go and the paths of such spiral storms were notoriously unpredictable. It suddenly struck her as odd to dare a race straight across when a journey clinging to the hilly ground on either side would have been longer, but far safer.

A shear wind suddenly almost tumbled her out of the sky and she had to throw the remains of her sandwich overboard and grab the stick. She struggled for a while, lost in the elemental fight of machine, mind and weather as she got within a mile of the predicted drop zone and decided that was close enough. The crystallograph was whining, shrieking – she reached to switch it on, then it took all her concentration to flow and glide with the wind, into and out of cloud, hail and rain streaming, as she waited for the instruments in her goggles and on the Flit to tell her yes, that was enough, we are full of storm, we have eaten the readings of its powers and stored its songs, we can go.

She had no doubt that storms were living things or that at least thinking about them as if they were felt more correct than calculating wind and water, heat and cold. A storm lives as a dream, a dream that can be fatal or beautiful or both, it is never more than that, or less. She felt, as she was borne in it, by it, at its whims with which she could not negotiate, only bend herself, that this was true of all things. They were nothing at all, but she dreamed them into being and in so doing made them alive. And the Flit. And herself. These moments were the easiest to remember that; mostly in her life she forgot and went back to being Tralane. But here, when she remembered, she could make anything of the storms that she wished, monstrous devils, glorious angels – anything, and it would be the truest truth, or the baldest lie told with a laugh and a giggle, not true at all. Storms then, were alive, glorious and terrible angels, unknowable and untouchable, so far beyond control or understanding in their essential whimsy they were utterly alien but still familiar and beloved in that wild alien being that had nothing to do with her at all and yet lived only for her.

'I wish I could put that in a crystal and shoot someone with it,' she thought, dully recalling the true purpose of her crazy flight. But if there was a capture method for deeply personal experiences she had never heard of one, save poetry perhaps, and even then that required an attuned listener. Her own efforts at poetry were merely embarrassing. She forgot even that as she struggled to survive against the weather until finally the all clear beep came, the crystallograph's signal for completion. She turned at once for home, her focus altering to returns and the world beyond the clouds, only to see that the promised tornado had nearly concluded formation. There was a broad grey downdraft searching for the earth about two miles from her position, between her and her vector of choice. She knew that to go closer to it was to dance with the angels of hail in a deadly way, and automatically checked the fuel gauge. She saw with a sudden stab of nerves that it was low and flicked the meteorometer to get a prediction. As she waited she saw the massive gyre touch down and draw sudden shadow from the ground. She imagined horses and men caught up in it, banners and gold twisting, screaming, but the sky was so gloomy she couldn't make out any detail.

The next five minutes saw her find a position clear of the rain and hail front. She coasted at about five thousand feet and cued the crystallograph. She had no intention of grabbing anything from the rotator or the supercell, and prayed for a shear-free minute as she adjusted her goggles and looked down again. The camp was abandoned at half rip, and not a second too soon. Banners and tents were in the path of the tornado and already being lifted from the ground a hundred feet ahead of it. Fires went out and leaped to the skies, abandoned heavy wagons shuddered and fell, tipping crates on to the ground. A broad wave of men, women and animals fanned out across the vast grassplain, rushing away from the path of the storm. She saw some keep rough formation but mostly it was panic and rout. Luckily for them the actual tornado itself was shifting slowly, making a stately southwards roll. As long as it didn't change direction and accelerate suddenly they should manage to survive although their heavy gear might not.

She struggled to make it back herself, landing at last on the final choke of the engine as the fuel pump coughed and died on the lees of the emergency reserve tank. Another minute or two and she would have had to crash land outside the city, but she didn't have time to think about that. It was already past nine and she had her rendezvous to take care of below. Wet and cold she had to struggle against her own body's stiffness as she climbed out of the pilot's seat and turned to put the charged crystals into their padded carry bag. There was one spare. She kept that for herself, slipping it into her jacket, and then worked to fold the Flit's wings. Until she tried pushing it to the shed she didn't realise how exhausted she was – fighting the storm had taken a lot more out of her than she'd thought. It was nearly all she could do to close the doors and stand against the fuselage, resting. She made the disconnections and final checks on her own autopilot and then took the bag down the stairs, not stopping to go into the house proper or to change but going directly out the back, through the tangled overgrowth of the brambles infesting the orchard garden, and into the narrow service street.

The carriage did not hold Alide, of course, but a minion this time, who received the bag in silence and merely nodded before signalling the driver. It had turned the corner in a hurry and vanished before she found the energy to turn back and go inside. A light rain was falling and dusk was nearly dark. She trailed into the workshop and undressed there, thinking she'd leave it all until tomorrow, had to leave it. She put the crystal down under her jacket and checked the locks, the covers, the machines and the gun. On an impulse she picked the gun up at the last moment and took it with her to her room. The house was quiet and smelled of flowers, perfume, long baths, recently abandoned rooms. She saw that Minna had left her a note pinned to her door.

'Gone at 6.30 with Best,' it read. 'Bo gone to Night's. Dress on bed. Shoes in box on bed. Underwear in other box.'

Tralane looked at the time. It was nine forty. She went into her room, stashed the gun in the dress box and ran for a shower. By the time she got out and had wrestled her way into the fancy underwear it was nine fifty-five. At this point she discovered one fatal flaw in the dynamite dress plans. The red dress was a nifty mermaid style with a bodice that laced up the back. There was no way to get into it successfully alone.

She yanked it up to the correct height, reached around, pulled and heaved at the laces herself until it felt like it wasn't about to fall off, rammed her feet into the high, ornate shoes and, still standing on one spot, tried to put the gun into the matching bag. A quarter of it would have been too large. There was a roll of engineering tape on the floor near the window. She strode out to reach it and found herself flat on her face on the rug. By the time she had picked herself up, minced to the window, crouched daintily for the tape, returned to the bed at agonising turtle speeds and sat down to tape the gun to the outside of her lower leg where it would be successfully concealed by the huge amount of excess fabric train in the mermaid 'tail' it was ten past ten, she hadn't touched her hair or face and was sweating with a combination of frustration and fury. She grabbed everything she could lay her hands on from where she sat and set off for the door, stuffing the tiny evening bag mercilessly with makeup and a comb.

When she opened the door the road was empty. The rain had turned from a misty drip to a steady patter. Her feet already hurt from the shoes. She thought about calling a cab with the distant understanding that there would be none – everyone was going to the palace or was already there. It was over a mile on foot. She had to go. Just as she was bracing herself to go back inside, find some flat boots and prepare to hike it a carriage drawn by a single black horse came around the corner. It stopped, the door swinging open to a lit interior as the driver pulled it to a halt. She heard Mazhd's languid drawl curl towards her.

'Hurry up.'

She picked up the skirt train, finding a tab on it apparently for the purpose. Hooking it around her wrist she teetered out. Had the driver not flipped a footstool out for her to climb up she would have been foiled, but he did. She got into the warm, softly lit space and met the raised brow and wide eyes of her immaculate and fashionable date.

'Bloody hell,' he said as the door crimped shut and the carriage rocked with the driver's climb to his post.

Tralane opened her mouth to apologise and found herself spun around by his strong hands, then pushed forward over the seat opposite him with her face to the damasked interior wall. She could do no more than catch her balance with her hands as the horse set off at a smart trot. She wondered if he was going to fling her skirts up and have her there and then but with disappointment felt his hands work fast at the knot in the laces instead. He corrected the line of the dress and pulled the cordage back into position twice as hard as she considered right or bearable. Her objection was lost along with her breath as it shot out of her lungs.

'Everyone left before you, huh?' He finished with startling ease, knotting everything precisely and tidying the bows, then turned her around by her waist and sat her firmly down on the seat. Their knees knocked together. Before she could speak he had already opened and was inspecting the contents of her bag. He shook it out beside him.

'Hey,' she said, objecting to his casual appropriation of her belongings but took the comb he held out and began to work on her damp hair with it. 'Why did you come back?'

'I'd circled around six times before you came out,' he said, eyeing the cosmetics and putting all back except her rouge stick. 'You can put this on your lips but whatever you've been doing has been more than enough to put a sparkle in your eye.'

'I hope you're not getting domineering.'

'I'm merely pointing out the facts. You could only ruin the effect.'

She looked at him. He was wearing dark eyeliner, perfectly applied to give his already large eyes emphasis and length, his skin had the unnatural finish of a masterwork painting and there was a hint of gloss about his mouth. 'Did you put lube on your teeth?'

'Of course, and you should. You'll have to smile all night.' He reached into his pocket and showed her a tiny pot of clear glaze she recognised from Minnabar's trunk-sized collection of unguents.

Lane just looked at him, amazed. Her daughters had told her this trick during the makeup class they had foisted on her but she thought it sounded stupid. One thing she had not brought was a mirror. She knew he must have one but she found she didn't want to ask for it. Instead she pulled hair out of the comb and threw it out the small slot of the open side window panel, thankfully facing backwards so no rain came in. 'Are we safe to talk in here?'

He tilted his burnished head and looked at her with narrower eyes. 'I couldn't guarantee it.'

He was right, it was an infomancer carriage. Tralane considered her options and nodded slowly. 'I see. When we get there you'll have your meetings...'

'I will escort you to whomever you need to speak with before I attend those,' he said and smiled at her. 'Introductions first.'

She nodded and tried to catch a glance of herself reflected in the window glass to see what her hair looked like.

'Let me,' he said and, before she could object, leant across and put his hands into the yanked-straight, part curl-ended heavy weight that was stubbornly not drying. He lifted it, shook it and then coiled and curled parts of it with his fingers. She felt ridiculous but the window had already proved it would hardly make matters worse. His warm breath and the cold tips of her hair fell down over her breasts what felt like all the way and she looked down in shock to find she had a significant cleavage on show with the dress neckline – if you could call it that – at least three inches lower than it had been before. Alarmed, she hooked her thumbs into it and tried to haul it up.

'Acchhh,' he said and batted her hands away. 'It's meant to be like that.'

'I'm just not this kind of woman!' Lane snapped at him.

'Well why did you choose this dress then?'

'It looked a lot more elegant on the model!'

He sat back and nodded. 'You'll have to live with it now. We're here.'

Lane grabbed her bag, insulted by not being contradicted and furious with herself for letting her get into this mess. She felt keenly that her dishevelled silliness was about to make him embarrassed, if not for him for her, which was infinitely worse. 'If you want to go in separately—'

'Oh for hell's sake!' He waited until the driver had applied the brake and then opened the door before she could get to it, blocking the way with his leg. 'Rouge,' he said, holding the stick out.

She was tempted to draw on his face but she didn't, used her fingertip instead to apply dabs to her mouth until he took it off her. 'What, no whiter-than-white greasy tooth paste?' she snapped, seeing him looking at her with amusement as the driver came around with his footstool and put it in place.

'Don't worry about that,' he said. 'I sense you're not the kind of woman who smiles that much.'

She would rather have faced Alide than this, she thought as his leg slid back and he preceded her into the damp night beneath the driver's smartly snapped-up umbrella. Moving with the caution she would have given dealing with live wires, she found the wristloop for her train, applied it on the left with her bag and used her right hand on the doorframe to steady herself, only then seeing that her hands were pink from scrubbing and that the short, broken nails were lined in the inevitable black. Dimly she recalled gloves in the bottom of the dress box – they had been the things in the tissue paper she thought were handkerchiefs, although on reflection handkerchiefs made no sense.

Mazhd gave her his hand and she stepped down. They walked the few metres to the awning and the rich purple carpet laid out, squashy with water and the marks of hundreds of past feet. Guards saluted and the last hardy papermen took pictures, of Mazhd at least. Usher girls in brightly coloured sarongs, garlanded with flowers to match the event came to lead them to the correct doorway with a murmured, 'Professor, Infomancer, please, you are welcome and expected.' Fortunately it was the same door for both of them and if Lane looked at all amiss nobody's face betrayed it. She found that almost as comforting as the snug fit of the gun on her right leg.

The interior of the palace, both outer and inner courts was filled with people. Everyone, even beggars, had been let into the gates, and had some provision made for them. Since the start time had been seven o'clock either side of the processional carpets were filled with people already drunk or dancing and high. Many wore fancy dress and masks. The entire galleries of the Manifold Court, usually empty save for a few walking lawyers, were a carpeted and pillowed bordello, shrouded in drifting veils of coloured fabric where they provided a dry and relatively private space for intimate exchanges. Some of them very intimate Tralane noted, feeling almost overdressed as she saw the younger girls and men cavorting about in rain and wine-soaked translucent – well, handkerchiefs really. She was pleased to note that amid the festivity and erotic charges of incense, music and the presence of the Empress, there was no sense of violence in the air, only excitement, sensual repose and pleasure. Whatever her girls were getting up to it felt safe and the many guards present, women and men both, seemed alert and in good spirits.

'The air is enough to get you high,' Tralane said as they

covered the mile of carpet between them and their destination steadily, one hand hidden in Mazhd's arm helping to balance her on the foolish shoes, the other disguised by the golden braid and velvet sash that made her bag's handle. She was, even though she knew it would be a massive event, utterly flabbergasted at how enormous, how lavish, how decadent it was. 'Did something special happen, aside from the Empress's birthday?'

'I fear so,' Mazhd murmured to her.

'Fear?'

'I must meet with Night,' he said, 'and several others. I will tell you what I can later. Rumours will not do.'

Tralane frowned but she already had enough to think about. Somehow she had to pack and leave tomorrow after this was over. 'Mazhd,' she said quietly, following their ushers, hearing others behind them on the long walk. She feared she might not get another moment. 'While I'm gone please would you look in on the girls?' Normally she would have had Carlyn move in but Carlyn was lost and had sent no word back yet, not that she would have had time to do so perhaps.

'Yes of course,' he replied, equally softly, a note of pride in his voice, she fancied.

'My will and other legal documents that are important are in my workshop in the main bench in the bottom drawer.'

He seemed about to object but then he looked at her solemnly and nodded. She was grateful that he didn't say 'you'll be back' or anything like that; he took it like an adult and he didn't sugar things. Beneath the banter there was no hiding some awful undertow, moving through the city and their lives. She knew it and he did too. She kept looking away and praying for angels, but saw now only monsters, concealed in corners; a jowl, a foot, a claw, a hand, a curled lip baring teeth. Mazhd's sudden squeeze on her hand jolted her from the foolish vision. She looked into his dark, acute gaze.

'Stay awake,' he said with a smile and leaned down to kiss

her. It was only brief but the jolt she got from it was electric. She should absolutely not allow this man to charm her. But it was too late.

The rest of the carpet parade could never have been long enough. All too soon they reached the bronzed doors of the inner palace and were ushered to the royal presence atop her dais of gold and purple glory at the centre of the massive ballroom with all its lights and banners. Thankfully, the event was already in full swing and nobody much paid attention, save a few turned faces and voices she heard exclaiming – but their interest was in Mazhd and his choice of date, not in her except as an object of envy. She tried hard to stuff imaginary wool in her ears in case this turned to ridicule but before that could happen she was before the throne and looking at the pale, fragile girl perched on its edge.

The white dress she wore made her look sallow and strained although the purple flowers garlanded on her head and around her neck lifted her a little. Pink roses added reflected colour to cheeks that had none of their own. The shock of her youth hit Tralane hard. This girl was no older than Isabeau, and had the same backbone – a cold iron spine that held her up and radiated its curious power through her grey eyes as she smiled and greeted. 'Professor Huntingore, we are delighted to meet you. We understand you will be travelling to the dig in the morning and are so grateful to be able to wish you luck on your expedition.' That smile and those eyes – they turned the illusion of youthful innocence and vulnerability on its head. The presence, which she had always thought of only as the natural influence of the Empress' personal charisma, was a very different thing at this range and equally at odds with the girl's physical appearance; touching the royal hand was like being touched by divine grace that ran up her nerves as surely as any aetheric current. It filled her being with a sense of pleasure and sensual, erotic power, enhancing her natural possession. Her scattered feelings and thoughts became immediately centred. It lasted only a second, but by the time Tralane was released she felt transformed and serene, as if this, and not the pale sensations of ten minutes ago, were what being a woman was really all about. If this was what the Empress felt all the time... But she had no idea.

'Thank you, your Majesty,' she said, fumbling for the right words. 'I will do my best.' And then she looked up, her attention given leave to wander by Torada's shift to Mazhd, and found herself looking into the amber/orange eyes of the Karoo. At the same moment she heard Mazhd's sharp intake of breath and the smooth tones that the Empress was using on him subtly altered.

The Karoo was a shock at close hand, his physicality and size more than intimidating enough beside most Imperial humans although the Empress' guard Hakka gave him a good run for his money. But it was his coloration and the sheer confusing similarity/alien contrast going on all over him that made her stop and stare helplessly like an idiot. His face was incredibly human although pushed to a masculine extreme so much that it seemed naturally to run into the heavy mane and horsy ears from sheer overload. After a second she realised he was smiling at her, slightly, her reaction amusing him and his head was bowing in a way that suggested he was greeting her though he did not put out his hand and she made no effort to put out hers, feeling very much grateful because her instincts were telling her she would get it bitten off.

'Professor,' he said, his deep, growling tones making her jump. She heard a titter of female contempt from behind her somewhere in the crowd and her awareness of the room came flooding back in a rush of gossipy noise so that she almost missed his next line. 'We will depart at nine bells tomorrow, I understand. I will await your party at the southernmost gate-house.'

'Oh, yes,' she said, trying to bow and curtsey and agree at

282

the same time before giving up and standing straight, which obscurely seemed to please him. Her scientific interest was screaming to ask, to look, but she yanked it back with promises there would be opportunity in the future. The idea of spending any length of time alone with this creature was, on the heels of the Empress' gift, astonishingly disturbing. She stumbled along the carpet at the touch of the usher girl on her hand, making room for Mazhd and the people behind them, and staggered somehow down into a space in the circling crowds without mishap, finding wine given to her and trays of tiny foods offered before she was permitted total escape.

'I see you forgot the gloves,' Isabeau's drawl and a cool hand on her arm brought her around. She looked into her daughter's composed, serious eyes.

'I was in a rush,' Tralane explained. She began to look around to get her bearings.

'You're not expected to look good,' Isabeau said a way that was probably intended to be comforting and with a tilt of her head indicated the tables at the side of the room where Tralane recognised a lot of faces from the University crowd seated or standing talking together. They had mostly managed smartness and order but it was true, they were relatively drab compared to the rest of the room which was a euphony of colour, light, costume, drama and finery. The tables looked like a relatively safe berth at least and some confidence came back to her so that she sighed and smiled at Isabeau. 'You didn't introduce me to your Master, or aren't I allowed?'

Isabeau's glance behind her made her turn and she saw Mazhd at her elbow his face alive with what must be the activation of his particular gifts – she recognised the glow of interest. 'I see you're safe so I'm going to meet my appointments. I will join you later.' He lifted her hand and kissed it formally with a smile and then transferred the expression to Isabeau with a loaded glance, bowing to her. 'Miss Huntingore, please convey my kindest wishes to—'

'Convey them yourself,' said a purring, voluptuous tone from behind them both.

Tralane turned, conscious of Mazhd's unfaltering hold on her fingers still as he also moved and revealed Isabeau's new Master, Parlumi Night. Ah right, she thought, old mistress and old lover, ex-student and new student, and new lover ... She was grateful that she really only cared about Night with regard to Isabeau's welfare because having to face her as competition in some way would have been too much to contemplate. Night was compelling, magnetic. A stab of envy went through her as she saw Isabeau give the woman a quiet, admiring glance of respect.

After the introductions had passed and Mazhd had delivered his wishes with effortless grace and departed Tralane excused herself politely and went to the University tables, hoping that at last she would be able to relax and rest a little. Her legs and arms had started to ache with exhaustion.

She had said hello to her fellow engineers and professors of mathematical sciences and found a seat to rest her agonised feet and relieve herself of the anxiety of walking in the dress and shoes when something happened. She wasn't sure what it was at first. There was a flash of some sort that lit the tablecloth and surprised her. Then the massive hubbub of voices and movement quieted and at the same moment there was a shriek of horror from a woman which sent a boltshot of pain through her own heart so strong she slapped both hands to her chest. Exclamations and a roar of outrage from the centre of the room followed immediately. She turned as one with everyone else, openmouthed, to look towards the throne.

CHAPTER EIGHTEEN

TORADA

Torada found herself on the floor suddenly, a pain in her arm and a heavy weight over her which she realised belatedly in her confusion was the body of Hakka. She both felt and heard his shout, 'Jago, up! Sound the seals!' She tried to see but everything was dark though her eyes were open.

'Hakka, what's happening?' Her voice was so quiet but he heard her, his body tense and vibrant as it suddenly vanished and she felt him kneeling over her, presence still very much there.

'Assassin,' he said to her. 'As you feared.'

She heard the horns of the alarm and then a snarling, horrible growling sound and the rise of voices all shouting stopped and screaming started, fresh shocks trawling her nerves. She remembered a brilliant flash as the growling became a spine-chilling shriek and she felt the draft and flap of wings and a rush of something taking off. She smelled Hakka's sharp sudden sweat and drew herself into focus, travelling quickly to her still place, her spirit home, knowing that the people needed calm, whatever was going on. She must not panic. She was unhurt. With practised determination, trusting Hakka's physical and verbal reaction that immediate threat had gone, she began to spread peace and to require calm.

'Your tiger is an eagle,' Hakka said to her, his hand keeping her down. 'He and Jago pursue. The soldiers present have sealed the palace.'

There was an odd timbre in his voice she didn't recognise but she felt reassured, blinking, seeing that her vision was slowly repairing itself. When it did she wished it gone again. Before her, where he'd fallen to take the shot aimed at her, lay Eth. The front of his white formal chiton over the leather plates of his armour was burned black and punctured, the thick boltshot of the burning quarrel that had killed him sticking out at an angle from his chest. A pool of blood was spreading around him, nearly reaching her splayed fingers on the dais' carpet, but stopped by soaking into the thick wool. His empty hands lay curled. She stretched her arm out and took the one that lay just within reach. It was warm but completely unresponsive as she laced her fingers with it and held tight.

'Eth,' she whispered. But no matter how tightly she gripped he didn't grip back.

She tried very hard not to let her scream of horror out beyond her core and it cost her a great deal of energy, but there was no hiding it from those who were still connected intimately to her through the sisterhood. The other Empresses heard her and swiftly turned to shield her, as training made them do. Three was a strong number. It was not eight, but it was good. The remaining five did not see, did not know, at least, not this way. Meixia and Haru joined her and their conjunction of abilities informed her commands so that she was able to remain alert and in control. She was able to unknit her fingers from Eth and stand up.

The room was in an uproar and half cleared in panic although as she was seen to stand and brush herself down this subsided into a slow round of applause that quickly built to a relieved rush of cheering. She smiled, wanting to kill every one of them if only Eth could live.

Hakka tugged her off the dais rapidly, away from the obvious position, his gaze raking the balconies and the crowd as guards made a way for him but she pulled back against him until he stopped. His dark eyes were fierce, raging as he looked at her with a ruined passion she felt hit her like a blow.

'I cannot leave them,' she said in a whisper to him that nonetheless carried well enough across the noises of the room. 'I must stay.'

'You're not safe.' His reply was a groan, that ferocious stare half rabid already with the need to fight and slay, to avenge and despoil, when all he could do was hold her hand with her permission.

'No, well. That has always been true and it always will be,' she said, finding herself steadied by his hand, though where they touched there was shaking. She didn't know whose. She simply looked at him with soft insistence until finally his eyes glanced down and he nodded in surrender to the necessity. She must stay. Over his shoulder she saw guardswomen covering and gathering up Eth's body. For right or wrong this room had decided that assassins were fled, there was no panic. Or she had made them decide it. She looked at Hakka to be sure, relying on his unerring instincts for danger and his natural resistance to her presence but he confirmed her will. This room, for now, was clear of threat. She moved close up to him, as close as she dared without clinging or showing signs of weakness or odd affection and said with distinct emphasis for his ear only, 'You will not do what he did. That is my command. Do you understand? You will not die for me.'

Hakka glanced at her, just one look that could have been acknowledgement of anything as he pretended to reconnoitre the dais area again. 'That is not yours to command,' he said in his heavily accented murmur and escorted her back to her place, avoiding the glistening black patch on the carpet.

Torada looked about, standing tall. She noted this time whose faces she did not see among those gathered, shakily drinking hard liquors: Borze, Alide, Jago, Tzaban, Shrazade, Mazhd. She beckoned to Night and her student, Huntingore – ah, the professor's daughter, she thought belatedly as if in a far off part of her brain and was astonished to find echoes in the minds of the two Empresses with her. They knew that name too.

'I think I cannot now announce my marriage decision,' Torada said to Night who had come to stand at her shoulder as commanded. Over the feathers of the fan she looked towards the University tables and saw Professor Huntingore moving with purpose, awkwardly, as if her gown was a personal enemy fighting her every step. But her direction was quite clear, she was making a beeline for General Borze who in his own focus was traversing the jabbering gauntlet of everyone between him and the dais, his gaze locking with Torada's for a moment until he reassured himself she lived.

At that moment the room quieted again and froze – shrill screams of horror were distinctly audible coming along the corridors that led to the mezzanine balconies. She hoped that they had apprehended whoever was responsible and dismissed it from her mind for the moment, summoning Borze with renewed insistence so that the people between them parted to let him through. As she stood firm those around her did so too. The conversation reignited. Borze found his way to her side and bowed, to her irritation – she wanted words, not proprieties.

'Majesty...'

'Are we secure?'

'Yes, Majesty. Five arrests have been made. Others are in progress. The palace is sealed and the guard vigilant. Every bit of space is being searched by sight and by instrument for any further evidence or devices. Bombs have gone off in the city at various points and there are casualty numbers coming in. I will keep you as informed as I may.'

She nodded. It had been her intent with this flagrant event

and at Shrazade's suggestions to draw her enemies from the woodwork, and she had succeeded, at least for those sent or provoked by foreign agents. 'Proceed with our plans.' She saw Professor Huntingore approach and hesitate, a look of intensity on her face sufficient to make her beckon quickly to the woman. 'Yes, Professor, you have something you wish to say? Please reveal it as expediently as you may.' She made a sign with her hand to Hakka and he bulldozed a clearance zone around the three of them, though she permitted Night and the junior Huntingore, Isabeau, to remain.

'I flew over the eastern plains beyond Highbrook today,' the professor said. 'There was an army a day's hard march from the Altos pass. They wore the tower colours and sign. I was looking for the general to speak with him personally...'

Torada waved her silent. 'Of course, one could not trust the man blackmailing you or his minions and anyone else in this climate does prove uncertain.'

'You *know* about that?' Huntingore put her hand over her mouth in apology for interrupting.

'I do,' Torada said. 'We let rats run while they may and notice where they bolt to. But this army is news to me. How strong, what have they?'

'I would say about a thousand people. They had heavy weapons and some devices in covered carts that I might be able to identify if I hadn't come straight here. I have a recording.'

'Isabeau,' Torada said. 'Return to your home and bring whatever your mother requires in order to display these records directly to me. Hakka, see that she has a guard cohort and make them ride at all speed.'

She turned back to the professor who had gone paler than before. 'Is there more?'

'Yes. While I was out there a storm came down from the north, a twister. They were forced to abandon their camp when it turned to their direction. I saw them scatter towards the Altos hills. The tornado took the camp's edge. Some of their equipment was surely destroyed.'

'And you have come directly here of course,' Torada said, smiling for a brief moment as her gaze took in Huntingore's windswept face and damp, curling hair. 'Borze, what make you of this?'

'One of the arrested men here bears a tower tattoo,' he said. 'But we take no sign as proof until you question him. Tattoos are easy to make. An army of a thousand... Did you see any others with them, Professor?' He looked at Tralane.

She shook her head. 'If you mean mercenaries or other groups, then no.'

'Shrazade has agents with them,' Torada said. 'I assume that explains their campground being located in a poor position, though it does not explain why no word was sent of their impending arrival. Can we deal with them, Borze?'

'There would be a siege,' he said. 'My emissaries suggest that there have been messengers heading to various points and intercepted messages have been decoded – this army is probably the catalyst for our nearer neighbours to raid or join the assault. It was, alas, only a matter of time.'

'Very well. We will allow until noon tomorrow for recovery from the night's activities. At that point you will sound the recall and ensure the withdrawal of the larger population within the greater wall with all speed. Nobody and nothing is to be left outside. You will inform everyone that Jagorin of the Spire moves treasonously against us.'

'Majesty,' he was startled by the extremity of her actions and the nature of her plan as it became clear to him but she wasn't interested in his objections or whatever he had to say. He might cavil at being kept underinformed but she had not already leapt so far to fall back now.

'Professor,' Torada turned to the woman before her, an easy twenty years her senior and fully accomplished in every way.

'We must expect the worst but try for the best. Tomorrow you will go to the dig. I have sent word ahead that you are to be obeyed absolutely as my voice and presence. You are to gather the research teams and recover, record and obtain as much information about what you find there as you can. I am informed we cannot rely on security and the situation is quite dire. Whatever happens you are not to allow any of that material to fall into other hands. No other hands but mine. At any cost. Are we quite clear?'

Huntingore paused. Torada could see she was not used to this situation. She allowed a moment to pass. 'Professor.'

'I should not preserve the site, if it seems to be taken over?'

'If the takeover is by other humans or magekind, then yes. Lose or destroy it.'

'But...'

Torada waited again, her own patience and conviction enough to push Huntingore into thinking the unthinkable for a woman of her scientific, academic persuasion. Destruction of rare, unfathomable knowledge. She waited and watched, wanting to be sure that her faith in this person was not misplaced. Others had similar instructions but she had less conviction in their abilities to execute the orders, willing or not. 'Obviously if there is any hope of saving it without it being stolen, then you will preserve it.'

'Majesty, do you *know* what is there?'

'I do not understand the details, but I have staked our lives on it,' Torada replied calmly, the decision taken long ago for her. She had known the information stolen from her dreams, plans made by the others, right from the start, years ago. For Huntingore and most people it was all fresh, new, immediate.

She watched the other woman, fascinated as her face reflected states of thought and calm and reasoning in flashes of mercurial change. 'Empress, are you going to move—'

'Yes,' she said firmly, cutting off the rest in case any lipreaders

291

were watching. 'And your daughter will do the honours. Your family is coming into its own, Huntingore. Other cities have Sircene remnants, but nobody has three.'

'You mean Isabeau!'

'She is more than capable, I judge it,' Torada said simply. 'The socialite girl...'

'Minnabar.'

'Will remain as head of your household in your absence.' She didn't necessarily mean this as a threat but she let the implications linger.

'Empress, did you send Mazhd?'

The question momentarily floored her. 'I did not.' She watched that mind reflected in that beautiful face and wondered what it was like to be so attractive; from what she had gathered, Professor Huntingore had no interest in beauty. Like Isabeau, if she saw no use for it then there was no use. Night had laughed with Torada about it when she first took the girl on as student, at the folly of not understanding its power. Send Mazhd. What for? Knowing Huntingore's business was trivial – it was open viewing, as it was with most obsessives and Torada was confident that her intelligence was good.

Borze cleared his throat in the pause and took a personal slate out of his dress jacket inner pocket. 'This may help. Professor Loitrasta asked me to pass it to you.' He held it out to Huntingore but looked at the Empress for permission.

Torada nodded.

'I assume you read it,' Huntingore said, but without much rancour. She took the slate and looked at it in a troubled way.

'Much of what it contains is a mystery,' Borze said. 'Engineering and other technical data. We were unable to understand it.'

The professor held it close in both her hands. 'I must read it immediately then. I— Empress I am so sorry for the loss of your guard.'

Torada bowed her head. 'We must be glad it was no worse here. There are many more dead in the larger city. Let us hope the attack is over. Borze, you must be on full alert for saboteurs now. They will be expecting that army to arrive before long. I wish to be sure we are not here when they do.'

Huntingore stared at her. 'Are we alone now?'

Torada flexed her empty hand, knowing that the professor spoke of the eight cities. 'It is probably best to assume so, for now.'

ZHARAZIN

Mazhd was in one of the mezzanine rooms, secluded, the door closed, in private conference with Horad Alide as he'd been instructed. His lateness had not been noted which he took as the first sign that Shrazade's suspicions and information on the man was correct. They putatively discussed the progression of the dig and portals, the contents of the former so much more than Mazhd had expected that it briefly threw him. Alide spoke confidently about his plans to return and engineer significant projects just using what had already been recovered, although for reasons beyond both their comprehension the majority of the discovery must remain in situ.

'Mages,' Alide said, two glasses of wine down, his manner unable to conceal envy. 'They say these things that make no sense and we must trust them, eh?'

'There is no choice,' Mazhd said in keeping with the official line. 'My mistress sees no reason to doubt those who remain on the project. She has had all of them thoroughly vetted. And their predispositions automatically push them towards honesty and cooperation.' He wondered what Alide's predisposition really was as he watched a secret smile play across the man's bulky face. It was like rocks piled, then cut and roughly sculpted, no two angles entirely in symmetry but overall presenting the impression of a bulwark of stone, massive plated forehead, chin, slab cheeks... He allowed his mind to repaint and reform Alide's face with its own subtler understandings until the Minister no longer looked like a man as much as an earth elemental, his eyes hidden from sight save for glints that shone when the torches and lamps were at the right positions. In contradiction, a long, narrow tongue flickered wetly as he spoke, at odds with the sounds coming from his mouth. Mazhd had had spies painted like this before, snake tongued, but there was no forking, no dual path. This man's business was peculiarly his own.

He heard Shrazade in his mind, felt her presence near along with other agents and the guard who were sufficiently sensitive to hear the infomancers' most powerful commands as whispers of conviction. They were watching twelve people who were not citizens and whose subtler auras and chemistries confirmed their recent arrival; at least nine were hostiles inside the building and there were more than forty more throughout the city, nearly all followed by infomancers. Zharazin had to work hard to keep the tension from manifesting in his body. He sat languidly, the picture of vanity, trusting that to annoy Alide out of noticing anything untoward. His only assigned goal here was to watch Alide's reactions, everything else was simply a play though Alide thought he was there as Shrazade's representative whilst she struggled to master the deluge of data coming from abroad and sifted false from true.

They discussed the dig, Mazhd prying subtly for information, then less subtly as time went on. He knew that Alide had still not officially disclosed his possession of the storm cannon or its actual whereabouts. An agent in the Defence Ministry said the crystals had passed through the portal but after that had lost track of them. The agents who had been at the digsite were dead. This above all worried the Empress and Mazhd as they had studied Tzaban and read the reports from the site. Tzaban showed no signs of eating anyone or playing a wrong step so far, his word was good. Karoo in the south ate and assimilated for their information, and they had eaten a wide menu. Even Mazhd had flinched to see the list and the implications, which he and Night could read, were sobering. They must only hope tha the Karoo, who were long said to be no more than instinctive animals, would not realise the value of what they could know. But then, Tzaban...

'It is a shame we have so few weapons that are useful against the Karoo,' Mazhd said, dilettante with his wine glass, an idle speculator in fine clothes.

'They are the forest,' Alide replied. 'In that the creature is right to warn us against them. I still maintain the object must be extracted or any reliable defence cannot hold but I'm repeatedly informed this is quite impossible. The arrival of the engineers to-morrow should verify that once and for all.' He had abandoned his drink, pushing his glass around the table at his elbow by its stem. 'Whatever is in that site is not worth the loss of so many lives, particularly if, as you claim, the Karoo learn by their ingestion and are able to transmit that knowledge amongst themselves. Surely you can see that, you of all people?'

Mazhd knew he didn't mean because he was part Karoo. Alide did not suspect this of him. He looked much too human and much too like the Steppe ancestors who had beleaguered Alide's city and families for generations. 'I believe I do. But until we leave their territory completely I don't think they will stop. As far as we can gather they have no interest in expansion which is so far the only silver lining to the position.'

'The Empire cities have wandered too far apart,' Alide said, his constant opinion. 'We should regroup more centrally and exert a firmer control over a more united landscape ourselves. Glimshard in particular is too far to the south with acres of warring motley between us and the tower state.'

'The Empresses have disagreed with you.'

'Our Empress has, but the Defences of the Southern circle

are in agreement. This defiance merely makes all our tasks so much more difficult.'

Blahblah. Mazhd drifted off as Alide went into a familiar rant about how the Defensive Council was routinely ignored on Imperial whims based on facts and decisions that were wantonly foolish. He countered with the usual – we have had no wars of note in decades – and Alide wearily riposted with the matter-of-time-and-chance scenario in which the Simple Tribes adapted to learning and cooperation and rose against the city to raid it for its wealth and technologies. Glimshard had been lucky, in Alide's view, in not having to face the enmity that other cities found routinely and this was not the Empress' influence but merely a circumstantial benefit of chance bestowed on a foolish young woman who was so busy satisfying her sensual curiosities that she ignored pragmatic matters.

Mazhd wondered if Alide knew already about her secret marriage. He thought it unlikely, in which case the vitriol being disguised as sagacious concern was curiously ironic. If there was an oversight here it was probably in keeping Alide out of the loop on the real strategy underway here, of which he himself knew only fragments. He gleaned this from leakier vessels of Shrazade's, each of whom had been entrusted only with partial knowledge. Thanks to the earlier priming, Alide was rather careless in talking to Mazhd now. When Mazhd steered him to discuss the digsite his eyes lit up with possessive ardour. Mazhd concluded he did want the materials there, the potential power they represented, though he'd never get anywhere without mages to research, develop and operate any findings. So far as anyone knew. Alide had nothing of that sort lined up here, but that did not mean it was not lined up elsewhere.

The screaming came as a welcome interruption to Mazhd's ears in its way, although it meant the failure of his counterpart outside. It was but a moment after he felt the impulse to get up and move – something was coming. He was looking directly at

Alide at the time and noted a genuine reaction of shock followed by a cold shutdown of emotions, at least any transmitted to his body. He was up out of his chair in moments, Mazhd at his heels, as they rushed to the door and out into the mezzanine balcony.

There was at first only confusion as revellers sought to escape to the walls or along the corridors while guards tried to do the opposite and move towards the apparent source of trouble. In the main room a panic had begun, a huge stir of colour and noise. Then for a moment there was a clear path. Mazhd and Alide both saw quite clearly a tall man in celebrant's robes running towards them. His hand was raised, holding a barrelled device in a manner that suggested it was a weapon though it was nothing Mazhd knew. If the gesture had not been enough his expression certainly was: he would stop at nothing to escape. Instinctively, Mazhd dived to the left, pushing Alide with him.

Alide shook him off, furious and avid. As Mazhd retreated he stepped forwards with a sudden roar of rage and Mazhd saw the other fire his weapon without pausing. The shot went wide, a bolt of searing light which impacted the wall instead, silently, leaving a blistered black scar and the sudden smouldering threat of fire. Alide attempted to trip the running man, there was a brief altercation but momentum won the day, Alide fell back staggering though unhurt and the would-be assassin passed them with a stumble and a surge of sweat-ridden air. Mazhd was watching Alide's face as he was turned and saw only anger and then resignation at the failed effort. Alide pushed away from the wall at Mazhd's side, looking down the way the assassin had come, and over into the heights of the ballroom. Lights were suddenly shadowed and their sightline was blocked: they both stood agape as the orange and lilac stripes of the Karoo filled the gap and then the corridor.

Feathers vibrant with some kind of fierce charge brushed Mazhd's cheek and then they were staring after the Karoo, who landed lightly, boots on carpet soft as paws, vast wings folding closed, shrinking, vanishing until he was a man pursuing another man. Flashes of light. Guards falling, the air shocked by silences between screams, stink of burning flesh and metal. Then emptiness, the corridor wiped clean and still, bodies on the ground like a pile of old linen. Alide's face, whiter now, tinged with grey.

'Did you see that?' Boyish excitement, unable to be contained as he asked Mazhd the obvious.

Mazhd nodded. They both rushed to the rail and saw the Empress standing unhurt. A guard was down.

'At least someone did the right thing,' Alide said with a sneer and Mazhd followed his gaze to the diminutive girl in the white and gold finery with raspberry sashes. He heard from joined minds in the infonet the sudden denoument in the stairwell, saw through other eyes the flashing silent charge of the gun sear the Karoo's arm and then the gun falling down and down the central well alone, the assassin under the Karoo's body. A striped elbow pumped once, the two tumbled down a flight on to a landing decorated with heavy china vases, crashing into one. Smithereens of pottery scattering like snow and then Jago and several other guards running up with rope and drawn weapons. Tzaban's heavy white head came up first from his position on top and dropped suddenly down with a savage lunge. The whites of Jago's eyes flared suddenly stark and huge in his dark, sunblacked face. Tzaban sat up, discarding the prone man like a piece of garbage and for a moment they faced each other down, ready to kill, until Tzaban moved with inhuman speed, darting around Jago's group and away.

At the same moment throughout other rooms infomancers signalled soldiers in civilian celebration clothing to arrest their marked men. In streets and alleys, courts and halls glass shattering, fire blaring in plumes – bombs going off.

Alide's face was excited, grim as well he might be whose defences had failed so well, calculating though he could not yet know the extent of the infiltration and devastation.

'I must go,' Mazhd said, though Alide showed no sign of caring now, signalling to his own officers and marching off quickly. He felt Shrazade's cool, efficient touch in his thoughts.

'Follow him.'

So he did.

TRALANE

Tralane sat at the table, the slate in her hands cool and solid as she stared at the space through which the Karoo had impossibly taken flight. She was no biologist – the real biologists were gibbering at the table behind her – but she knew what she had expected to see in her life, and this was not among them. Wings, speed, ferocity, the change so sudden it was miraculous. Had they always been able to do that? What was it he had even done? Anxiety, the old feeling of not knowing something curious, made her turn and listen but the professors at her back had no explanations.

Frustrated that way, but seeing no more immediate danger, she looked down at what she held and thumbed the slate, beginning to read her friend's words in the hope of finding familiarity in there.

'Lane', it said simply. 'You must see this. You must come. Look.'

She looked, and she fell into an abyss constructed of diagrams, layouts, images, schematics, and did not hear even the third time someone spoke to her until a hand landed on her upper arm and shook her gently. There was a clock chiming the hour: two in the morning. Around her the room had changed into an auditorium, quiet but for one voice.

'Tralane.' It was Mazhd.

She looked up from an undiscovered world of wonders and blinked into unfamiliar light, faces, places, finally focusing on his face and seeing him concerned, a soft smile of amused, loving tolerance on his face that for a moment made him almost unrecognisable to her. She couldn't remember being looked at like that since her father had been alive. The sudden temporal dissonance of the memory shocked her out of her stupor. She would have told him what she knew if she'd had words for it but better for now it lay in the slate along with Carlyn's other note, the one that said, 'There are monsters here. I'm so afraid I'll never see you again.' The pictures of the monsters were nothing like Tzaban. But now even Tzaban was not like Tzaban. Tralane focused hard on Mazhd's coal eyes, seeing the skin around them crinkle slightly into puzzlement at her intensity of attention. She felt safe with him, inexplicably in the circumstances.

The Empress was making an address. Still Tralane could only make out the essentials, her mind tangled in the slate's unfathomable masses, Carlyn's fears, the past. Torada was to be married, to Tzaban, the Karoo emissary. It would unify an alliance it would... She lost the thread as the crowds blundered with celebration and consternation in equal measures, not sure if they agreed, if it was wise, or safe or madness, if it was connected to the attack or not. People had been arrested, there must be an end to revelry and a common effort to regroup and repair. Tralane felt a terrible, bittersweet sense of compassion and union. She looked into Mazhd's eyes and knew it for the presence of the Empress. She stood up and put her arms around him, a hard, warm body, comforting because she trusted him. That was entirely her, and his gentle, careful arms and soft murmured nothing words were entirely him.

She heard a second uproar as news of the bombings came. And for the rest of that night the one embrace she had shared was the only peace anywhere, amid the chatter of disaster and shock, the care of the injured, the questioning of the infiltrators and the merciless, beckoning darkness of the pit and its secrets.

300

CHAPTER NINETEEN

TRALANE

Smoke trickled upwards into the air, making straight pillars of grey and black in the windless warmth of the morning. Tralane sat amid the large, sombre group of revellers on the palace's open terraces where the high hanging gardens formed a background of verdant peace. She was waiting to go home, but everyone had to be questioned before they were permitted to leave, even the most trusted. Meanwhile an endless supply of tea and small cakes circulated via apologetic servants, with fortified spirits for those who wanted to blot out the night's complexities. She wondered if she had been overlooked. It was only six or so, but she was meant to depart, prepared, at nine. She didn't drink the spirits, although she wanted very much to. They would have instantly put her to sleep.

'Professor?'

She looked up, realised she had been dozing. She saw the face and uniform of a female army officer. The woman, looking as smart and polished as a new knife, smiled and sat down opposite her, slate ready. 'I've been looking for you. My apologies. A few formalities and we'll get you on your way. If you're ready?'

The few formalities took half an hour of witness statements, through which Tralane stumbled, realising how little she had paid attention to anything that was not concerned with surviving the wearing of her dress and shoes, talking to the Empress or reading the slate. Truly, as an observer she was utterly disappointing. She had not even seen the weapon or the missile in spite of being right there. She realised belatedly that the weapon must have been a gun of some kind. The gun taped to her leg was a dead weight. Her intention had been purely to preserve it and all she recalled of the moment in question was the shock of the flash, the precious slate clutched in her fingers, wondering what was going on. Fortunately the gown's fishtail had hidden the gun though the gun had bruised her leg.

Isabeau was secure with Night but now that she was out of the palace, Tralane wanted to rush home to look for Minnabar and find out that she was safe. The Infomancy's carriages were all busy elsewhere however; streets were empty here but the city was loud and busy with the sounds of the clear-up of the night's events. She was forced to wait as Mazhd hailed a cab, then more delays as closed streets caused detours round and around. She watched out the windows as they passed sweepers and cleaners. She saw almost no other people but several roads were cratered and stained with dark marks, the sight of each one making her guts twist and shudder as they brought the memories of that scattering army on the plain, running before the tornado. Now they would be regrouped. Mazhd related what he had seen meanwhile.

As they came to her street she turned to him, desperate for some distraction from her fears. 'I don't understand. How does this fit together, or does it? Suppose that army has guns if this was to soften us up?'

'That one is the only one that we saw.'

'Yes but Alide is making massive guns, somewhere,' she said. 'Who for? And this wedding announcement – it is unprecedented, bizarre... A Karoo. To protect this dig?' But she knew the answer to that. Surely to protect it. But the price was looking

302

enormous and she couldn't be the only one to think so. 'The other cities cannot be at war with us over it?'

Zharazin looked at her. He looked at the slate. 'Are you sure?'

The loss of the Empire, the fall of the Eight. She couldn't believe it.

They had halted at her gate. Mazhd paid as she got out and followed her. She was about to protest but then noticed that her door was open an inch, the smoky breeze blowing it a little back and forth on its hinges. She saw then that the lock had been interfered with and the edges of the frame were splintered where crowbars had forced it open. With sick dread in her heart she hurried forwards, all her impulse to run but the dress and shoes wouldn't let her. She kicked the shoes off and left them where they lay on the path. Mazhd caught up with her as she got to the door and slipped in front before she could object. He pushed the door wider and light flooded the empty hall.

'Minna!' She was shouting before she had both feet over the threshold. The quiet that met her voice was unnerving, horrible. She wanted to make noise just to stop it.

Ahead of her, Mazhd paused in the doorway to the kitchen, his body almost enough to stop her ducking under his arm and shoving him out of the way; it was her house, her business. She ignored his word of warning as she hurried through the hall, pausing to stick her head around the kitchen door. It was deserted but otherwise not unusual, she sensed nothing there. Through the far door she could see a figure peep around a corner and recognised Amber Flyght. 'Amber! Where's everyone?'

She heard Zarazhin swear and pass her, lingered only to realise that Amber wasn't going to or couldn't answer and then rushed after him, pushing doors open along the way. Nothing. They paused at the stairfoot and stood in a moment of breathless silence. In that moment Tralane saw Minna's purple silk

303

shoe on the stair and heard a distant grinding clank she knew better than the sound of her own breath.

'The elevator!' She dropped her own shoes and picked up her skirt, starting to run up the flight two at a time, shouting Minna's name. She barely noticed Zharazin pass her and saw the evidence for herself as she reached the door to the stairs that led up to the laboratories – it hung on one hinge and beneath it Best lay unmoving, blood on his face. If there was worse she didn't hesitate to see, stepping over him with an unspoken apology in her soul for being so callous, her voice snapping out to Zharazin to look after him as she pushed the door wide enough to pass and carried on running.

Her legs burned and she cursed herself for becoming complacent and out of shape but her terror carried her up the twists and into the tower base. The laboratory door was matchsticks. They were scattered in the shape of a blast that had been delivered from the landing and shattered it. Some kind of energy weapon or spell she thought dimly as her feet automatically made the turn into the lowest of her dust-ridden antiquity halls. A bright line of carpet showed through the muck – everyone had taken this way – and at the end of it the cage of the elevator shaft glowed wavery yellow, empty but for shivering cables and motes of rust. The squeaking and grinding echoes told her the car was nearly at the top of the rise.

She didn't have the breath left to call even if it had been a worthwhile effort. As she stabbed at the control panel with her fingers, Zharazin arrived. He assessed the situation in a split second and left her, heading for the stairs again, faster than she could have gone. She heard him call out, 'Concussion!' on the way as the bang and rattle of the top cage opening mocked her efforts to stop the car. For a moment that stretched into an eternity she stood staring at the circuits, trying to force her mind to master the uncontrollable, then bent down and ripped the tape off the gun.

Beside the car cage was the closed section of shaft that concealed the passage of the counterweight. She yanked the maintenance panel open and crawled through the hatch, grabbing the cable and setting her bare feet on the cold iron ingots of the counter. She made a short range adjust on the gun grip, put out her arm through one of the air vent partitions into the main shaft and set the gun muzzle against the narrower cord of the brake control cable, pulled the trigger. With a sudden, terrifying jolt and a scream and whinny of vibrating machinery she began to rise with increasing speed. The counter was unstable with her on it and nearly flung her off in the first moment, bashing her against the shaft sides though it could not turn or swing thanks to the tracks it was forced to follow. She passed the falling car in the blink of an eye and she prayed that the emergency brake would work as the car passed the trip switch. If it didn't, her effort to pursue Minna was going to end spectacularly and very soon.

Metal screamed and banged as the trip went off but it was late, and slow. The counterweight jerked and jounced as the cable was pinched tight, groaning like a dying animal. She heard more metal screaming just near her head as she reached the claustrophobic tiny space at the head of the shaft. There was shuddering and the counterweight dropped an inch, then a few more as she tried not to listen and slammed her foot against the shaft wall where the exit hatch was marked in mouldering paint. In her efficiency she had, of course, latched it closed from the outside last time she worked on it in some sunnier, distant year.

Her hammering punctured an ominous quiet, interrupted only by the tocks and, ticks of metal parts straining against gravity. A peculiar vibration in the counterweight cable made her suspect they were losing the bout. With a scream of frustration she aimed the gun at where she though the latch was and fired. A hole the size of her hand appeared in the hatch, then another and another and another, almost silently. She felt heat and heard the pinging of the hatch door as it expanded. Her foot hit it a final time, sending the counterweight and herself back hard. The door flew open and slammed into her as she threw herself at it, trapping her for another few seconds. A few dozen heartbeats later she had wriggled through the hole and was standing up when she heard a crack. One of the wheels started to spin again. The car crashed the last couple of metres into the buffers at the bottom with a tinkling of glass and then there was a massive bang as the counterweight hit the springs at the top of the shaft though she hardly noticed it – she was already running for the open doorway and the harsh grey daylight.

On the weedstrewn deck a Flit of a design she didn't recognise was preparing for takeoff. A figure in purple and black clothing was fighting with Minna, still in her party dress, attempting to force her into a wide door in the craft's flank where other gloved hands waited to pull her in. Minna was bellowing in rage, struggling and kicking out, but her assailant was much taller and stronger. Dodging a punch they wrestled her off the ground, tottered two steps and flung her halfway through the opening.

Tralane lifted the gun, spinning the dials with her free hand. And hesitated in an agony of indecision, sure she might hit Minna even though most of her was blocked from her sight by the body of the kidnapper. The gun was precise on distance, and her mageskill was good for estimates but the gun beam would disperse anything in range. She aimed with determination, wishing she had the goggles. Then she saw Minna's feet disappear inside the craft. The kidnapper's back was to her as they reached for the handgrips either side of the doorway. Tralane closed her hand and suddenly those other hands let go and the figure fell awkwardly to the stone flags, a red blotch blooming suddenly across its left shoulder.

Aboard the craft others saw her as she scanned the fuselage, searching for places to disable it. She heard their shouts but was lost for that moment in searching the flaps, ailerons, cables when something hit her solidly from the side and back and she fell hard, gun skittering out of her hand, her cheek suddenly and painfully in contact with the cold, wet stones. Someone said 'Whuff,' or a similar ridiculous and out of place word, rather quietly, and it almost made her laugh through her frenzy and sadness as she heard the burr of the twin hotburn cylinder engines and the whirring drone of blades slicing air.

'No no nonono!' She scooted forwards on her hands and knees for the gun, a mere metre out of reach, but then the sounds all changed and she looked up to see the aircraft already lifting off. It moved vertically, to her surprise, without a trace of forward motion, magelight streaming around its undercarriage and into vortices that pushed it off the ground. The idea had not occurred to her but it was obviously genius, now she saw it and pictured the hidden internal motors and gears that channelled the air in different directions – the engines were mounted to move which meant they were using metal alloys she didn't have access to and this was a very foreign device, even more so than it first appeared.

It was strange to see this as she strained to get any glimpse of Minna. Bits of stone flicked and bit at her bare legs and the sound of metal bullets ricocheting pierced the drone of the plane. Belatedly she realised someone in the aircraft was shooting at her. She raised the gun but they were already more than ten metres clear and heading north. If she shot them down they could easily end up dropping all the way to the city base. The tilt and turn of the angles prevented more shots coming her way. All she could do was kneel on the stone and watch the peculiar sky-blue machine take her daughter away.

'We have to get them,' a hoarse voice, taut and breathless, said behind her. She turned and saw Zharazin lying on the ground, holding his arm with his hand. Blood was running through his knuckles and he was pale but he jerked his chin in the direction of the fallen kidnapper. 'Find something to tie them with, quickly. Hurry up.' He started to walk across to the body, pausing to bend down and pick up a chunk of loose stone in his good hand.

Tralane knew he was right though she could barely bring herself to stop looking at the receding blob of blue against blue that was rapidly disappearing into the distance. She memorised the bearing – three degrees west of true north – although of course they could turn at any time, and then she ran over to the sheds.

Inside the metallic smelling dark she found a coil of small-link hoist chain and a couple of butterfly bolts. She slipped a screwdriver into her bodice and kept the bolts in her hand, chain on her arm. All the while she thought longingly of the Flit, wanting to push it out and pursue more than she had ever wanted to do anything in her life, but knowing that by the time she was airborne with just a direction as her guide they could be anywhere and with those engines instead of the winds and the magefire they'd be too fast for her to catch. She could waste hours and get nowhere. Staying here made more sense, she told herself, hating every second, feeling numb as she shouldered the chain and gripped the gun firmly before going back outside. Mazhd was standing over the body, rock raised, his bad arm hanging loose by his side, blood dripping from the tips of his slack fingers.

As she jogged across the runway surface she saw him turn the person over with his foot. They rolled heavily but one hand was moving, searching weakly around their waist for something. The glint of a blade flashed the cold grey sky back at her for an instant as she reached them and dropped the whole spool of chain down on that hand before it could manage whatever it intended. Only then did she glance into the face of the kidnapper, lifting the gun at the same time, and saw it was a young woman, not much older than Minna, but bigger and significantly stronger. She had a strange pale face, with the distinctive flat features and smoothly rounded high forehead of the peoples who surrounded Spire's distant city. From a long ago geography class Tralane remembered tribes living on pontoons on the lakes, the city shore-side on the solid earth which they scorned to tread. But this one had trod here, on her earth, taken her daughter.

She pointed the gun into that ashen, angry and defiant face and saw it falter for a moment, staring at her own visage with recognition. Tralane and Minna bore a strong resemblance. The gun's point shook but her voice was loud and steady. 'Who are you and where are you taking my daughter?'

Tralane was vaguely aware of Zharazin getting down on his knees, taking the chain and beginning to tie up the prisoner. She dropped the bolts to him without letting her gaze move a millimetre from the other woman's face.

The prisoner hissed with pain and her accent was strange as she bit out the Imperial words, clipping the ends of them. 'She's insurance. You'll have her back once the Empress is deposed and the Empire united once again.'

The news barely filtered into Tralane's mind. It was nonsense. There was no such thing as a war between the cities, depositions – unthinkable. 'Who are you?'

But now the narrow lips were bitten together, white with strain as Zharazin tugged the chain taut, joining wrists to her waist, his hisses of pain and her grunts of it some ghoulish accompaniment as both were forced to use their damaged limbs. The silence regarding her question made Tralane furious. She felt her arm shaking with the effort of not squeezing more on the trigger.

'If you shoot her we'll never get the answers,' Zharazin said, his voice neutral and almost toneless. She glared at him for a moment and saw dark bands under his eyes, his bronzed skin tarnished. He held the free end of the chain in his good hand. 'I can hold her here. Go get help so we can take her inside.'

His eyes were dulled and distant in the way she had come to understand was him communicating with the Infomancy.

She looked into the sky and saw only clouds. Turning to do as he said was harder than she imagined possible for a simple step and then another, retracing her way back into the house without Minna. The short journey passed in a blur of dislocated moments, her hand fumbling and slipping in the dust on the stair rail and only just saving her from a fall. She nearly trod on Best at the lab door. He was in the act of pushing himself up on to his elbows as her legs bore her unsteadily down, tentacular and unwieldy for their task, jelly instead of bone. She jumped and stumbled to avoid him. As she bent to assist him she marvelled at the callousness of her feelings – it was not care that made her stoop so much as pragmatism in the knowledge he might be able to help her if he could function.

She crouched down and carefully aided him into a sitting position against the wall. He moaned and moved slowly. There was a lump in his hair the size of her fist and blood ran freely down behind his ear. She thought he was lucky to be alive and knew he was not the one to be asking for anything right now, though her mouth said, 'We have to get help,' even as she left him propped there and pushed through the door into the wreckage of the lab.

Fortunately, most of its cluttered mess was simply its natural state, with only a few signs of searching or destruction. She found the device she was looking for on the floor after a panicked minute of forcing herself to look properly and not throw things around any more. She guessed Minna or Best had dropped it as they were attacked. Normally, it lived in a housing on the bench leg. She'd never been more grateful for anything in her life as when she felt its ergonomic shape settle into her hand and flicked it into action with her thumb. She had never had cause to use the emergency communication system before. It was an antique that was maintained as part of city security ordinances and had a working counterpart at the duty officer's post by the palace gate where two hundred patrollers were always ready.

'I need help,' she said, not needing to identify herself as the device did that for her. 'My daughter has been kidnapped. We have a prisoner.' Then she put it down on the desktop, hearing a startled, anxious voice babble questions for a moment before fading away into giving orders.

As she looked about, her sense of numbness melted into a hot, consuming hysteria that faded as fast as it arose to be replaced by a cold, calm precision; terror refined into fuel for her mind. It clicked into gear with an almost physical jolt and her vision became crystal clear.

There was no sign of the goggles. She wondered if Minna had them but unless she found them would be forced to consider them in the hands of the enemy now. A thundering sound, far too soon to be palace guard, made her spin and clutch the desk behind her. It approached from the main house at a great rate, making no effort to be quiet, catching every creaky board on the way so that she could tell its passage was puzzlingly accurate through the winding, twisting ways of the house. It was coming straight for her. She found her hands empty and realised she must have dropped the gun in the stairwell when she almost fell.

Her fingers closed on something smooth and metallic – a spanner – and then dropped that too as the door was suddenly filled entirely by the huge blue, orange and white figure of the Karoo. His disturbing slitted eyes stared at her with alien intensity for a microsecond before sweeping their gaze over the rest of the room and determining it of no interest. His nostrils flared as the gaze came back to her before he straightened and assumed a more human posture so that he seemed a man now and not a beast.

'I'm late,' she said, finally reaching the end of a chain of reasoning that led to him being here at such a coincidental moment.

They were, at this point, meant to be en route to the portal. He must have arrived to collect her after she didn't turn up at their meeting spot by the palace gate. His slight nod confirmed it as he apparently lost interest in her too and turned back to sniff the air in the hall. He ignored Best entirely.

'Go on up to the roof. Zharazin needs your help,' Tralane said and, without a backward look, Tzaban vanished, his feet hammering the rickety steps in just three bounds. Behind him the slack face of an astonished corporal took in the sight of her before looking quickly away and barking a series of commands to fumble-booted persons behind her.

The corporal procured a medic to treat Best and Zharazin and ordered her other two guards to help Tralane collect what she wanted. By the time Tralane had packed her carryall she was much more herself. She gathered from overheard conversations that there was a brief argument about who owned the prisoner first but in order to circumvent it for the sake of speed the corporal ordered all of them into the dining room while her two-man unit searched the rest of the house and made it secure. As they assembled the panic unit from the palace and two infomancers also arrived and so the room was full before Tralane assumed control of the situation. Given that none of the officers present technically held authority over the others her status as householder and senior mage and female gave her the lead.

The prisoner, now given first aid and transferred to the chair at the head of the table paid no attention to any of them. Her wide-eyed stare of horror was fixated irrevocably on Tzaban who had chosen to stand alongside Tralane as if his position as Consort extended to her too for the time being, she being Empress of the room. The prisoner's complexion was ashen and she pressed into the chair in an effort to be as far away from him as possible. She was not the only one who gave the Karoo a wide berth though the Glimmers had mostly mastered their responses and made their fear seem merely respectful by now. Maybe, Tralane thought, this intimidation alone would be persuasive, but she didn't have time to find out. She turned to Zharazin, who had the medic's fingers stuck in his shoulder muscle at that moment although he was looking at her for an instruction.

'Find out what she knows,' Tralane said.

'Mom, that's...'

Tralane recognised Isabeau's voice and closed her eyes in a gush of relief immediately followed by annoyance. 'Against the protocol. I know. Sit down and shut up. Minna's missing. They're from Spire.' She knew that Isabeau at least had a sense of the importance of that, being privy to knowledge of the advancing army where others had not yet been informed.

The slighter of the two infomancers stepped forwards and looked into the prisoner's face. She presented no obvious kind of threat in her neat dark suit with her groomed hair and clean, relaxed features but as she approached the Spire kidnapper shrank back in her chains as far as possible, trembling noticeably. The infomancer's voice was calm and even. 'You may speak freely or I can take the knowledge without your consent, it's up to you. I believe from your reaction that you are familiar with our methods.' As she spoke, she shot her cuffs and flexed her fingers.

She had a perfect manicure, Tralane noted, and the hands of someone who hadn't done more than touch the odd bit of cutlery in an entire lifetime.

'Oh come on,' Tralane muttered, desperate and already annoyed by the drama. Zharazin looked up from his seated place beside her and reached out to touch her hand.

'Shamuit Torada is a threat to the Empire,' the Spire woman hissed, unable to recoil further. Her panic increased as the infomancer laid one delicate hand on her forehead and she struggled pointlessly against the chains. Sweat sheened her face. 'You are all under the mastery of a madwoman. Surrender and mercy will be—' Her voice cut off sharply and her eyes rolled up in her head and began to dart around, up, down, left, right as a thin line of blood formed beneath the infomancer's palm and began to trickle down beside her brow and over her nose.

The infomancer spoke calmly in bursts. 'She knows only to come here and to take the girl away to a rendezvous point on the Eligan Plateau, coordinates... Hmm, there is only a vague placement on a map, this is not the navigator,' the infomancer said, her own eye movements exactly tracking those of her subject. 'Glimshard is not to be infiltrated but attacked by conventional warfare to preserve the city structure if a coup does not succeed from within by the time the army arrives... Ah, she had no idea about the Karoo being here, only that Glimshard is in contact with them at the southern forest... There is a great treasure there which should belong to the whole Empire but Spire believes Torada will try to hold it for herself and... Ah, Spire believes Torada is about to attempt to seize control of the Eight-Limbed and go for godhood... interesting... The city will be secured by joint forces from Spire and Dirt and the Empress will be deposed and replaced with someone who does not share her particular Influence. No other detail.' The woman turned impassively towards the guards who were staring at her, slackjawed. She nodded at them and then looked at Mazhd. 'You are to go to the palace and interrogate Alide immediately. The Empress awaits you.'

'But are they going to harm her? What's going to happen to Minna?' Tralane demanded.

The infomancer's eyes flicked, rapid as arrowshot. 'She will be passed to a second team on the Plateau. After delivery, the kidnap group would be given new orders on site. She believes your daughter is a hostage who would be treated fairly and there is no immediate threat to her life, but, of course, who can say if any of what she knows is true?' The woman withdrew her hand and revealed three red punctures beneath it, small but enough to cause the bleeding and cover her palm in red. As she did so the prisoner lost consciousness and slumped forwards in her chains. The infomancer drew a container from her pocket with her free hand and extracted a damp white cloth with which she carefully cleaned off every trace of blood from herself. She placed the kerchief into a sealed bag and placed that in a second pocket and turned to the guard as if already bored with them. 'That's all. Take her to the dungeons, she is not worth further time for us.'

'What did you do to her?' Isabeau asked in the silence as the guards moved forwards and picked up the prisoner between them, the commander grim-faced.

'I read her,' the infomancer said simply, watching the unconscious body being carried out. 'It can cause brain damage. We won't know until she wakes up. I regret, Huntingore, that there is little we can do at this point until the general and the Empress agree upon orders.' She looked at Tralane and clipped her heels together, chin lowered in a mute gesture that combined respect, indifference and dismissal at the same time.

Mazhd got to his feet, pale and slow, his eyes half glazed with trance communication.

Tralane opened her mouth but the guard corporal beat her to it. 'Professor Huntingore your presence is required at the portal and it cannot wait. You and the Consort must come with me immediately. Your equipment has already been sent ahead.'

'But I can fly after them...' She had a wealth of reasons, all of them, she saw instantly, far too flimsy to justify her delaying. If she did fly after Minna in the Flit then she would go alone and still only have a possibly outdated location to show for it, supposing she were not shot down by the other aircraft. It was impossibly foolish, and she wanted to do it with every burning bone in her body.

'Immediately,' the corporal said.

Tralane turned and seized Isabeau's hand on her way past. 'Come with me.' Her tone was not to be disobeyed and for once Isabeau just did as she was told without a remark.

When they were in Tralane's room and the door closed Tralane stripped off the remains of her dress and underwear and kicked them all away mid-stride to the bed where her going-away clothes of camouflage gear and pack harness had been laid out ready since the day before. She grabbed them up and yanked them on as fast as she could while she talked in a low intent voice, looking at Isabeau all the time to be sure she listened.

'I want you to keep petitioning for Minna's return, any way that you can. I don't know how long I'll be gone but until I get back you are the only Huntingore left to do everything that must be done. You run the house, look after the Flytes and the other families, understand? Make sure that Best recovers and give him the lab and whatever he can take out of the attics. Don't give away anything to anyone but if you can use it, get it working and keep hold of it. I know you have responsibilities to your mentor but this comes first until we're all back in one piece.' She found she was done, clothes on, nothing left to say, almost. She was surprised to find Isabeau staring at her with tear-filled eyes although there was no other sign of emotion about her. 'You're not to say anything to Minna's web other than everything is being done and that Minna is all right. Keep them out of the house. It's bound to be a target if the city is invaded. If that happens you are to evacuate the building immediately with what you can carry and what you can't must be destroyed if they would find it useful.' She straightened and went to seize Isabeau's slight, slow-reacting body with a fierce hug. With her nose in Isabeau's soft hair and the feel of her solid and warm in her arms Tralane never, ever wanted to let go. Thinking of Minna she almost lost her grip on herself but then she straightened up. She whispered in Isabeau's ear, 'Go into the attic and open the spinning wheel seat when I've gone.' Then she let go just as Isabeau clung to her arms and for once looked like an uncertain teenager, scared and unready.

Tralane picked the gun off the bed and paused, then tucked it at her belt where her multitool usually hung. She took a last glance around and bent to tighten the buckles on her heavy boots. The solid grip of the leather on her body helped anchor her in the present moment and gave her a false sense of security she badly wanted. When she straightened, Isabeau was wiping her eyes off on her sleeve, a cool, determined expression in place that set into stone as she watched. She envied that strength of purpose. 'That's my girl.'

Tralane walked out past her without another hesitation and found Tzaban standing at the door waiting for her. She glanced up into his face fearlessly for the first time, feeling that nothing could intimidate her now. Until Minna was home she was in a place of war. To her surprise he seemed no more than a painted man, not remotely beast-like. Behind him, Mazhd waited, his face gone ash white with shock. The medic was hanging on his arm, trying to persuade him to take something she held in a vial but his eyes tracked Tralane instead, delaying his orders until she would speak. She felt more touched by that than anything he had done but a cold resolve had formed in her and she had no smile.

She had no choice but to go, but she would see Minna back safe and sound or someone was going to pay. A tiny voice at the back of her mind was trying to explain the actual probabilities to her but if she paid attention to it she would fall apart so she thanked it politely and told it to shut up. She had the strangest sensation that both Mazhd and Tzaban could see this happen. Their faces were all verticals, hard angles and bleak, unsheltering planes. Necessity must look the same in all faces.

She muttered an 'excuse me' as the Karoo stepped back to let her pass, and faced Zharazin. It was too soon for gushing goodbyes and the wrong time for a simple farewell as if they were mere travellers. She wasn't sure what they were to each other and could not afford to consider that now, but even though she longed to rush away so that the job might be done the sooner and the search for Minna begun, she stopped and hugged him silently. His returning embrace felt strong, one-armed as it was. He gave no sign of pity or concern for her and she was heartened.

'I'll be back soon,' she said firmly to whoever was listening. 'If you find anything out, let me know.'

'I will,' he replied, and she knew he was talking about Minna, and not the Empress or the spy when he added, 'I will pursue her in every way I can.'

She nodded and followed the Karoo, who had assumed matters concluded and was heading out. She didn't seem to breathe out again until they were already halfway down the street, her on horseback, him walking. They glided down silently through the stem's magelit trunk on one of the goods' platforms, then the corporal escorted them to the city gates through crowded streets before surrendering to Tzaban's command and turning back. Tralane assumed he had been accepted by their military somehow, or else this would not have happened, so despite the oddness of it she didn't question it. They paced steadily down the road, flanked on either side by wagons. Families, riders and walkers burdened with heavy loads all trudged steadily in the other direction. Refugees, Tralane realised belatedly, all moving into the protection of the city walls. There was a long stream of them as far as she could see in all directions over the plain, the green tabard dots of the Empress' runners here and there between them, ushering them faster. They looked frightened and weary, even their dogs.

A child riding on top of a wagon tarp stared at her with silent, resentful eyes. She felt a pang, turned in her saddle and looked north, hoping for a glimpse of the plane though there could be none. There was smoke on the horizon at several points. Circle signal fires, she thought with a shiver. They enjoyed a hunter and herder life and had no desire for Imperial things, though they liked looting as an entertainment and the collection of foreign treasures. Whatever they were saying she took it as a given that the Spire army had reached the plains' edge at last. The Circle would join it or be swept away by it – for Glimshard and the Empire it didn't matter which.

'Come on,' Tzaban said, in a grunt she barely understood as words. He made a subtle gesture and without her interference her horse broke into a trot and then a canter, following his easy lope downhill against the tide.

CHAPTER TWENTY

MINNABAR

Minnabar Huntingore felt truly afraid. The ground dropped away in an unnatural angle, the familiar flagstones of the roof quickly obscured by the edge of the flying machine's deck and replaced by other roofs far below. The edge of the upper city wrapped in its bright mageglow slid beneath her, bathing the craft briefly in violet and white light. Blinded by it and still face down on the narrow platform of the flyer she couldn't even see the lower town as they passed over it in a grinding hum through which her mind insisted it could hear the heartbeat of an eight-cylinder engine being driven a touch too hard, one head worn and too much oil in the firing mix giving that strange splutter and clack that was all but drowned in the drone of the propeller blades.

She felt her hands being tied up behind her back, one, two, three quick knots, then she was rolled over and saw that her sense of security in the airframe wasn't at all shared by the other two passengers in the craft's rear section, unless their pasty expressions were fear of something else, but Glimshard had no air defences and neither her mother's Flit nor those of the weather service was a threat to a machine of this size. She looked up into older faces than her own, one man and one

320

woman though they had very similar features, small and neat, their skins a pale olive tending to green and their hair a dark brown, cut uniformly close to their heads. They bent close to her, holding her down on the floor pan with their feet. Her legs were still free but fighting here was dangerous. She had nowhere to go except out the open sides of the flyer into a fatal fall. The pressure of their boots was a security against falling rather than an oppression at that moment. All she could do was catch her breath, swallow the humiliation of her capture and stare at them. Her heart pounded so hard she wondered it didn't burst, but unlike the engine there was no valve weakness there and she had to live, for now.

'Who are you?' she managed after they had all stared at each other a while. Her voice sounded tiny and pathetic, gravely disappointing her. 'Where are we going?'

In return they simply blinked at her and then looked forwards as cold air whipped through the cabin, thin and cruel.

'Put your 'chutes on and get one on her.' The command in strangely accented Imperial came from the front as if it didn't care much either way about what happened. Then the voice added, 'Settle down. We've a long way to go.'

That was all the talking there was for nearly her entire journey. She tried a few more questions but they met with blank gazes of indifference for which she felt grateful in that they were not an immediate harm. They tied a pack to her clumsily, and compensated for their unwillingness to do the job by tightening its straps ferociously across her middle and back. The steady flight, punctuated by turbulent jerks that made her captors yet more green and pale, was so dull that eventually her fear had no fuel remaining and leaked away leaving her to calculate their airspeed and distances covered based on various guesses. She knew from the sun angle that she was going roughly north and from some long forgotten lesson that their green-grey uniforms meant they must be from a region of the world controlled by the Empress known colloquially as Spire. When her calculations ran out she tried to remember what she could of Spire but she'd never paid much attention to what didn't interest her and history and culture were in that category. They had a work ethic they valued over all things, she knew, and which guided their lives in rigid patterns very unlike Glimshard's wandering days. She wondered what they could possibly want with her and guessed it may be to do with the gun her mother had restored, and those storm crystals, and whatever was going on with the Karoo. She wished she had paid attention. She wished for warmth as the icy metal deck temperature ate through her ordinary clothing and made her shiver helplessly there. Eventually, the female guard threw someone's jacket over her but it didn't make a lot of difference.

She held on to the slender hope that the person who had caught her unawares and marched her up to the roof with her arms twisted up her back had been left behind. Her mother had done for them, she thought. They might know things and tell what was going to happen to her. Someone would come for her. It was only a matter of time. Meanwhile her hands, crushed, cold and with restricted circulation, hurt until they went numb.

CHAPTER TWENTY-ONE

BORZE

Borze waited for Gau Tam and his prisoners in the throne room, alone except for the body of the would-be assassin and the Empress' bodyguard, Jago, who had dragged it before the throne. A broad line of blood smeared the paving to mark its passage: Jago had carried it over the carpets but dropped it at the first opportunity here and hauled it by a fist knotted in the body's hair. He stood over it now, face an iron mask that Borze didn't try to read, nor meet his eye. The corpse was a mess, as if it had been scythed by one of the large agricultural machines that worked the lowland flat pastures: the Karoo's doing. Borze was annoyed by it. Bodies didn't talk, at least, not to him. Ordinary palace guard lined the halls and stood at all the entrances, filled the gardens and could even be seen standing watch through the crystal skylights, their gold and rose uniforms fluttering in the sharp wind like fire. Somewhere within her private apartments the Empress also waited. He shucked his heavy dress coat and felt Jago's gaze on him.

Without intending to he made eye contact with the man and saw what he hadn't wanted to see there, the barbarian's gore-soaked hair and streaked face set into a half snarl of resentful rage and the force of grief in him contained into a dark, brooding threat of violence. It wasn't that Borze didn't feel these things. It wasn't that he thought the display of them was a weak sign. He simply knew that to let them out, even as far as his face or the surface of his skin, was futile. What good would it do? Deep inside his chest he felt so many of these things, collected across the years, that he didn't know what would happen if they saw the light of day and he stood patiently with his head down and the smell of blood in his nostrils and met that gaze with silence. Jago was a man of a kind he didn't trust, volatile, the kind of man you couldn't rely on to hear any order to retreat. Like Hakka he was unfit for an army, perfect for a guard dog.

This image made him think of Tzaban. He'd said nothing about the Empress' choice. She was so beyond him that it was merely something to adapt to that he didn't think about. His faith in her was no more shaken than if she'd picked a fine officer or a prince. He thought it should be rattled, but the feeling of it wouldn't come no matter what he pulled to his mind and at moments like these he understood his loyalty wasn't his own. He was hers, like every other subject in the city, and in this he couldn't only not choose but see no choices to perplex him. How much more so for Jago.

A commotion in the outer corridor was stifled by a familiar voice, breaking the obedient quiet – Gau Tam ordering passage for his prisoner. Borze drew himself to attention and was not surprised to see Alide led within, flanked by his second and by the pale and bandaged figure of the infomancer, Mazhd. A second figure, in chains, rattled and shook between grim-faced soldiers behind them – the other assassin. At least they hadn't slung chains on Alide. He doubted such a humiliation would have helped. At the back of them the shrouded sepulchral form of Parlumi Night drifted in a private gloom like somebody's forgotten shadow. There was no sign of the girl who was now her student, Isabeau Huntingore. He'd never forget that name as long as he lived.

'Sir!' He started to find a runner at his elbow, her lanky figure as slight as a banner's edge, her voice raspy as if she'd been shouting all night. 'Spire operatives have kidnapped the daughter of Professor Huntingore. They have got away. Infomancers have taken a prisoner.'

He saw Isabeau's white body bent, naked, indifferent, between two athletes intent... Finding Mazhd's gaze on him, giving him the merest shake of the head. Another daughter, then? He breathed, finding that he hadn't for a while. The runner was already gone when he looked again.

More argument outside brought a face he didn't know into the room – a lawyer judging by her robes though they were carelessly put on. Party clothing peeped between their sombre vertical planes and she wobbled slightly on ribboned platform shoes. Her face held no frivolity however. In her hand she carried a folded document, the stock in trade of deposition and sentence in the purple border colours of the War Court. He only knew it because he'd received a missive on it the day before announcing the Empress' intent to pursue war if she faced continued opposition from Spire and in the south. It was the first time the authorities had admitted that the digsite was more than a skirmish or a single battle. Gau Tam had made a joke about it being a real war now that they had decided to use the purple paper. Alide's hand had signed. Had he known about this assassination plot too, then? It was hard to imagine him a traitor, whatever his personality and how much Borze personally disliked it.

They assembled in a loose half circle before the corpse, the last to arrive a woman in grey hooded robes, a black rope tied around her torso in a criss-cross pattern. She walked with steady intent, the visible lower half of her face quite expressionless. Her hands remained before her hidden in the heavy sleeves. She moved silently to a position just behind Mazhd's right shoulder. He didn't turn to acknowledge her and Borze shivered inwardly, managing to avoid an actual twitch with the exertion of some self-control. It was only the third time in his life he had seen Living Memory and, although there was nothing overt to cause alarm, the notion of what the woman was slid through him like icy knives. He could not quite bring himself to believe that she was nothing but a machine now, personal memories gone, nothing but a meat server. She looked too much like someone. He glanced at Mazhd whose face was too grounded in his own personal pain to reveal a special relationship between him and the thing standing behind him. He must, Borze assumed, know she was there without having to look. Shrazade would have sent her to record the events in every detail. Only Living Memory was able to capture everything within its perception without a flaw. Their recall was faultless no matter how many times they were required to provide it telepathically to other infomancers. The record was processed and studied later by others who still had a mind with which to do it.

The Empress' chamber doors opened and all heads turned in that direction. It was not customary to kneel, although Borze always felt that regardless of how they stood they were all, in fact, prostrated before the presence. Their actual posture was merely an incidental detail. They could feel her before she arrived, like a soft storm in their blood and bones.

Shamuit Torada wore a ceremonial robe and headdress of mourning grey shot with borders and panels of scarlet. Her face was covered in a half veil of translucent grey stitched with silver thread in a design of dragons that weighted it down until the hem brushed her chest. The veil's bridge where it sat across her nose and cheeks was a fine filigree of silver wire. Above this shining line her grey eyes looked out from a painted shroud of much darker grey that ran in a bar across her face from temple to temple. Black liner made those eyes larger, wider, full of rain. Behind her, Hakka bore his polearm in its battle regalia, tasselled and knotted. He was tall enough to look directly over her head and Borze shrank inwardly from the strange, bitter intent of his gaze that stared into the room as if at nothing. For a moment he made eye contact with his counterpart, Jago, and even Borze felt the resentment there drop the atmosphere before the Empress ascended the throne and claimed all awareness for her own.

She glanced down at the corpse below her feet and then around the circle at each person present before her voice, calm and glassy, cut the air up into pieces. 'Minister Alide, you come before Us accused of treason. What say you?'

Alide was calm, from his own conviction or from her command it was hard to tell. He held his hands out, palm forward. 'I am innocent, Majesty.'

'We do not have time for a civilised pursuit of the truth,' Torada said. 'You will remain silent as Lawyer Shan presents her evidence and Mazhd reveals the accusations laid against you and then you will provide a full explanation. Fail to do so immediately and I will insist that the infomancers perform a full reading. Lawyer Shan, proceed with your statement and leave out the preamble. This is a War Court and all common legal protections are hereby suspended at my pleasure.'

The lawyer opened her document and studied it for a moment before she spoke. 'The Ministry of Defence has allowed the infiltration of the city of Glimshard by hostile foreign agents. Minister Alide has personally had contact with several of these agents and has taken receipt of goods from them. Minister Alide has overseen the construction of engineering works at the relic site known as Dig 241 and has failed to protect the information coming from the works. Minister Alide has failed to report military threats exceeding native resistance at Dig 241. The Defence Ministry has extorted and bribed Glimshard citizens in order to develop weapons of mass destruction without the consent or knowledge of the throne for purposes which must therefore be considered against the Reigning Interest. Minister Alide and the Defence Ministry have permitted the access of assassins into the palace and failed to prevent their attack on the Imperial Person knowingly and wantonly in the hopes of obtaining a coup.' She finished and looked up before stepping around the body and presenting her paper to the Empress. 'This is a list of names of all those suspected of collusion in the matters.'

The Empress took the paper and handed it to Hakka without glancing at it. He passed it immediately to Borze who took it dumbly as the Empress spoke to him.

'Arrest and detain all of them if they are not already in custody. Question the foreigners and have them read if they refuse. Those that survive are to be expelled from the city. Citizens may remain silent but they will be imprisoned in isolation unless they prove themselves innocent.'

Borze glanced down and saw the list. It was long. He put the paper into his jacket pocket with his head bowed, thankful for it as he felt the Imperial attention shift to Alide. A sense of grinding inevitability made him want to run out of there even though it wasn't him under that scrutiny. He didn't like Alide but he knew him well enough to pray that he didn't make her prompt him for his explanation. Torada, he had lately come to understand, he didn't know at all. Until now she had been the model of sweet, caring governance of a kind he had never previously imagined. But he had been a fool to think she was not fully an Empress with every bit of ruthless intelligence that implied. They all had been. When he did look up, against his will, he saw that Alide had drawn the same conclusion and was appalled by it. It wasn't blithe ignorance that had allowed events to fall this way, but calculation. He wondered, as Alide opened his mouth, how long Torada had known and laid in wait.

'I am innocent of all charges and of any complicity or acts of omission with regard to this assassination attempt,' Alide said steadily. His face was tightly drawn back. Borze recognised it and thought, 'Backs to the wall, eh?'

At a glance the lawyer almost cut him off with her statement.

'The Empress is already advised of evidence we have uncovered that suggests Defence was ineffective at preventing infiltration of the city in the previous month leading to this attempt. The infomancers in particular have recordings that confirm you have been trading in antihypnotic drugs specifically geared to allowing you to move independently of the Empress' Influence and that these have been provided by Spire agents.' She indicated the grey-robed woman behind Mazhd.

Borze watched as Alide's narrow mouth thinned to a near lipless line. 'My choices began long ago with the refusal of the throne to supply materials and engineers for the storm gun. They were later increased by the arrival and tolerance of the Karoo... Consort. And by the refusal to install military rule across the Steppe as I had advised. In the authority over these acts I counter that it is the Empress herself with her excessive inexperience, her licentious and wanton choices, her frivolous pursuit of everything strange and abominable, who stands in a state of high treason to the Empire. Our present state of secession stands in proof of my statements and all of my actions have been within my role to preserve and protect the Empire.'

The Empress spoke quietly, looking down at the broken body. 'It is not I who overreaches herself in the pursuit of independence and power. And I had my part in your situation. It was my weakness that made Spire think of you when she was looking for someone to use. But it was yours to accept her propositions. However, you leave me in a difficult position. I should kill you now. But then I lose your expertise, which I badly need. Tell me, Minister. If you were me, what would you do to defend Glimshard?'

Alide raised himself a few inches and Borze wondered if he sensed reprieve. For his own part the general felt none of that in the air as everyone hung on the softly spoken words.

'I would offer Spire control of the site in exchange for military support and the immediate withdrawal of hostilities – a return to the status quo the Empire has enjoyed for the last two hundred years. With both armies we could defeat the opportunists, establish a solid control of the Steppes and the south and hold off the Karoo until the site has been fully exploited. Unified with them, whatever one's personal feelings, we are much stronger.'

Whatever her view on this they did not hear it because at that moment a runner appeared, accompanied by a man in Glimshard military regalia, or what was left of it. The runner, incongruously small beside his bloodied and filthy armoured mass, helped him across the smooth tile floor until he was close enough to make his report. The Empress showed no offence; runners were permitted anywhere at anytime as they saw fit.

The soldier saluted Borze and began talking at a babble they could not understand. It took several minutes and a strong drink before he made sense. When he did Borze had to question him closely to prevent him rambling off all the time about monsters and the 'creeping ground' – material that was luridly affecting but in no way useful. They learned then that the tribes on the forest borderlands had seen the thinning of Glimshard forces and had launched a major assault in concert upon the small outpost by the dig and the one holding the area around the portal in an effort to seize control of it. Some of them had carried Spire banners and they had been armed with Imperial crossbows and grenades. To defend themselves the Fourth and Twelfth Units had used the special weapons Alide had been safeguarding there, but something had gone amiss without 'proper' supervision and the devastation that ensued had awoken the wrath of the Karoo, bringing some fatal assault down on all their heads. Both sides of the original conflict were devastated and had fled the field. The portal had been ordered destroyed.

The man sank to the floor, murmuring about the world being on fire.

'Meantime, Majesty, the Spire army is sighted on the Uplands

Pike at Two Birds Pass,' the runner said as the soldier collapsed slowly into a heap and she was forced to let him or fall herself.

Torada looked at Alide from the grey band of her sadness. 'Glimshard is in far greater danger from within the Empire than from without.'

'In that, Majesty, you refer to yourself and the city as one. But that is a temporary and unfortunate union which the righteous Empire itself by nature seeks to correct.'

Borze felt his eyes widen at the other man's presumption.

'I do refer to us as one,' the Empress said. 'Because that is what we are. Much as you are now expendable to me personally I cannot afford to lose your experience and your strategic knowledge. Since I cannot trust you, you will serve General Borze henceforth as his automaton.'

'No!' Alide's sudden cry brought the tip of the polearm's razored blade to his throat so that he froze in place as the Empress' arm came up. For a moment she rested her hand on the side of his face, as if in a tender gesture, and under her touch his terror and repulsion eased and passed away until he was perfectly composed.

Borze swallowed and found his throat resistant and dry. He knew that appearances were deceiving here. Alide, whatever he had been a moment ago, was now much less; his autonomy was gone. He might not be as reduced as Living Memory, but he was not far from it. Borze thought execution would have been far kinder, but it was war. Without a word or a glance of reproach Alide moved to Borze's side.

Torada turned to him and he endeavoured to stand tall and strong under her inspection. 'Go and take personal command of the portal site. Secure it and then do the same for the dig. Recover the storm guns and their materials.' Without a pause she looked towards Zharazin Mazhd.

'I understand the Huntingore girl was kidnapped,' she said. 'I trust your agents will be able to track her progress. Meanwhile you are to shadow the other one in case further Spire operatives are in the city. Go immediately and tell her that the time has come to act on the commands I have already given her. Assist her and give her whatever she needs for the task.' She gave them all a sweeping glance. 'Give the orders throughout the city to batten down. You have at best an hour to perform whatever tasks remain before we depart. Anyone who finds themselves in Alide's position is free to leave the city or suffer a change of heart. As of now treasonous actions are subject to immediate and permanent exile. Borze, you will oversee this, and that includes any mercenaries who find my coin insufficient persuasion.' She turned to Alide. 'What do you say to this?'

Alide responded with pleasant interest, as though he was glad simply to have been asked. The change in him filled Borze with a low-grade nausea. 'You should kill them, Majesty. Arming your enemies makes no sense.'

'And what should I have done with you?'

'Possibly the same. The loyalties of the living are never certain.'

'Mazhd tells me that you and I would never see eye to eye on anything. Our conformation is against it. You are much more suited to a creature like Spire. It is a pity for you that you ended here but you will not be sent to better pastures until your use to me is done. If you do well I will restore you.'

'I have no desire for restoration,' he replied, as calm as a still pool.

She smiled and, Borze thought, suppressed a giggle. 'No, of course you don't. Even so.' Her smile vanished as fast as it had come. 'To your business. runner, ensure the city gates are open until the tolling of the Academy Bells. Mazhd, remain.'

Borze saluted and made to walk out. He was halfway to the door by the time he realised that he was alone. He turned and saw Alide standing exactly where he had left him, the same idiotic peaceable expression on his pinched features. A glance at Mazhd showed no visible communication between him and his grim companion but this would not do for Alide, apparently. Borze would have to shout or backtrack but Gau Tam's propriety saved him, the officer tugging Alide's sleeve and muttering, 'This way. You must accompany the general.'

TORADA

Torada waited for them to leave, watching their backs until the guard outside closed the chamber doors behind Borze, then she turned to the body and stretched out the toe of her slippered foot to touch it, feeling its dull resistance, before looking up at Zharazin Mazhd. 'Eyes of Shrazade, can you read anything out of this?'

She studied him as he approached, feeling only cold interest as one mental adept to another. He was a curiosity – it was rare to find mages outside cities, particularly those with odd or doubled talents. She knew that he read blood as well as mind, had pondered the wisdom of leaving him with Shrazade but eventually allowed it to continue with the understanding that he was not permitted to speak of any blood visions to any except her own trusted advisers. At the moment, she felt inclined to trust none but to alter matters, even to kill him, would have been to broadcast her insecurity and so she merely watched him, her mental awareness reaching out to test his own. Her mind was closed to the Empresses now and in doing so she felt anger at her own eagerness to end the silence and sense of isolation. If Mazhd even noticed her she would have committed a serious failure, of power if not etiquette. But he seemed not to sense her slowly encompass him and she didn't push her luck, stopping as soon as she felt within range to read him.

She felt Mazhd struggle with the pain of his wound as he knelt down to the body and put his hand down to its head.

Repulsion was his major reaction, which she shared, though if he had been able to touch her she felt sure her rage would overpower him and send him into a frenzy of destruction on the corpse in her stead. The idea had its attraction but she preferred to model the simple calculated calm of her new confidante, Isabeau Huntingore. She was grateful at this moment to be able to duplicate the peculiar inner state of the engineer and allow it to run proceedings instead of her natural self, whose desires were only vengeful and shortsighted. She felt the traces of movement within her arm and face as Mazhd's face contorted with effort and distaste and it was all she could do to avoid copying Isabeau's curiosity too and plunging into him to discover how he worked, what he did, what it felt like to connect directly to the flesh of that cold, dead killer.

Without a sound, the grey-robed Memory stepped up beside him and laid her hand on his shoulder, her eyes closed. Torada held herself still, but the woman also showed no awareness of her presence so close and after a moment she went back to watching, not even hearing Mazhd's voice as she saw for herself what came to him through his vision.

In death the activity of the mind had ceased but in the meat the strongest patterns remained printed. Viewing them was like peering through dark glass into deep and muddy water, with fog and smoke in one's nose, mufflers on the ears and sludge in every vein. Her body reacted as Mazhd's did, echoing in every cell the distant horror of the dying moments, shock blocking pain and making everything empty. There was a tiger, the palace turning overhead in a bannered vault of stone – a sense of failure losing its grip in an almost pleasant way. There were people around a fireplace far away, their flattened faces above grey clothing watching the flames and waiting.

Mazhd's voice startled her but she didn't waver, thankfully, and found Hakka at her side holding her elbow. Whatever he did gave him greater acuity than she in this situation.

'A loyal servant of the city. The order was surprising but loyalty is unquestioning. He was disappointed to fail his Empress and he accepted his death. I find no knowledge of anything but his own purpose.'

Who were those people, she wanted to ask, but didn't. She knew already. He would not return to that fireside, as Eth wouldn't return here. She expected to feel justice but felt only waste. Mazhd withdrew his hand as fast as he was able to and shoved it into his pocket, leaving a bloody print on the corpse's temple. Briefly, she wondered how much of that person could be saved in the Living Memory, if they had wanted to. Necromants were rumoured to exist but she had never come across knowledge of one or anything but stories. In any case, she didn't have one nor would she have used one on this. 'Take it away and burn it,' she ordered, knowing the command would be heard without having to direct it. Servants appeared with their usual speed and did her bidding, in silence. She turned her gaze to Mazhd and found him looking at her with his head on one side slightly, the hint of a frown between his brows and she realised he knew – *he knew*.

Dropping all pretence at concealment she addressed him directly and with her full presence, though to other eyes it would appear she merely returned his glance before turning away.

You will never speak of it.

Aloud she said, 'Go.' She looked around the room and saw Jago was missing. A quick check and she found him outside with the pallbearers, reaching between their worrying hands with his huge knife bared and glinting in the cold sunlight. She felt the enormous power of him, his pure, brute strength as he hacked open the corpse and chopped out its heart. It was her hand that held it up, still a little warm, the blood congealed in black jellies that slid from its new mouths. It was her teeth that bit it and she that swallowed it, though Jago did it. He did it for her. For Hakka. For Eth.

In the throne room she pushed away from Hakka's arm and climbed on to the broad seat. She held her arms out before her and pulled up the long, covering sleeves of the robe. In the pale light of the rainclouds a faint pattern of tiger stripes could just be made out against the natural sallowness of her skin as if she had been painted with weak tea. She tasted blood and smiled. When Jago returned, full of grief and needing to fight, he and Hakka would go for each other's throats. Their failure to protect Eth and the fact they had not been the ones to cull the murderer would lash them to the extremes of their nature and their culture. In the past she would have been forced to separate them by exiling Jago, a humiliation from which he would never recover, but now Tzaban's trade would leave her able to rule as Empresses were intended – in a state of domination. How this would change them she didn't know. How it had changed her she would soon find out.

Glimshard was once the city of her predecessor, a city of science, named Crystal for the clarity of progress. Empress' shoes were hard to fill, harder to remodel: let them think she was the Empress of Sensuality, it was close, but mistaken. Glimshard was not just the Rose. She hadn't been able to truly make it her own until now, in this defining act, she declared it the city of Alchemy. Call it the cauldron and make her the witch. She thought of it, and considered she already had the cat and the crazy, and laughed.

Outside they heard the first of the Academy Bells start tolling the call for the gates.

ZHARAZIN

Zharazin didn't hear the bells. He was walking down the halls towards the doors, obeying orders, but his mind remained in a locked room where the Empress had left him. It was such a small space in which to hold the knowledge that had slipped over to him beneath her veils. Though she was a much more powerful telepath than he was she hadn't understood how much of his other talent was down to the helpless transmissions of scent and the taints that always rode the air. He had noticed that she rode him during his reading, but it was through blood and tears, skin and a slip of her exhaustion that had given her away. In the room he knelt looking up at her, a sense of shock paralysing him for a moment as he saw that where she'd been a black tiger snarled and showed him all its teeth. A tiger furled about with shadows and a familiar scent that made him smile and made his heart break all over again.

No, he'd never say anything. She could kill him at a distance without stirring a whisker. That hadn't changed. But before she was a girl at heart, a creature he thought expressed in the city's soft ways and mercies, someone unrelated to anyone he knew. In that moment, in this room, he saw them together, the girl who was Parlumi Night's daughter, and shoulder to shoulder with her, the beast.

He knew too that, though she felt a secret stolen, she thought he saw only Tzaban's wedding gift and didn't realise this final part. Only he knew. How Night had kept it secret – *that* he would give much to find out, though as he passed the closed door of her apartments in the outer court he didn't pause. He left the tiger room and closed that too, shut it off inside himself and, like he had for years, pretended he was someone who didn't know what he knew, who wasn't who he was and didn't feel what he felt.

He saw a woman in black flight leathers tearing off a face-mask and helmet, her dark hair streaming in the wind. He'd been a fool to pursue her. He should have left that particular precious dream alone where it could remain unharmed for the rest of his life. But then, there were always unkind eyes to find it and prise it open before even he knew what it meant. The allure of his fancy revealed itself as he tried to push it back wherever it came from inside his soul.

This is mine alone. She.

He felt cracks on his arms, as if he were made out of plaster and, in spite of the pain increasing, he began to run, hailed the first passing cab on the road beyond the gate and threw himself into the seat, door slamming as he shouted her address.

On the kerb, the Living Memory stood and watched him go with uncaring eyes, then turned to walk the other way.

CHAPTER TWENTY-TWO

ISABEAU

Isabeau watched her mother leave with the guards. She stood in the doorway and found herself suddenly alone there. At her back she heard the quiet gathering of the Flytes and the Highshaws but the house felt empty even so, because Minna wasn't in it and wouldn't be coming back any time soon. She'd never missed her sister. She wouldn't have now if it weren't for the fact that she knew her to be a prisoner of hostile forces. It was a strange feeling, like the discovery of a hole where a tooth should be, where you'd never thought about it twice before. She couldn't stop feeling around its ragged edges and prodding its nagging ache. It didn't bother her nearly as much as the expression on her mother's face however. She'd never seen Tralane look help-less before. Her mother had always known what to do, and why, and when. It was unnatural and, she hated to admit to herself, frightening.

She chewed her lower lip as she watched the Karoo lope alongside her mother's horse. She knew the Empress' gambit and had recommended its boldness and daring with the eager acceptance of someone who had not expected to find herself in the immediate consequences. Now she saw how much Night's glamour and Torada's presence had already affected her mind.

Minna was gone; though she could not be blamed for that it felt as though she was guilty of it by her choice of reckless action. What had seemed brave and important in the council chamber looked less certain in this light. She watched until the bend in the road down city hid the horse and the creature from sight and then turned, before the empty way ate her resolve. Fifteen or so worried faces looked at her from the hall and the kitchen door, and the door to the dining room, silent and expectant – mostly women, some children. Flytes and Tumblebyes and Highshaws and three of Minna's web. It was one of these that stepped forwards, a short, mousy girl dressed fashionably but badly, her nails chewed to the quick.

'Where's Minna? Has she really gone? What are we going to do?'

'You're going to go home,' Isabeau said. 'Taking them with you.' She indicated the other two web members. 'Minna has gone for a while, but she'll be back.'

A tall, lanky, awkward youth she'd presumed to be a hanger-on scowled and stepped forward. 'They say she was kidnapped by the Spire. Is that true? How do you know she'll be back?'

'It is true,' Isabeau said, finding no point in lying. 'And I know because I will go get her back. For now you go home.' She turned her attention to the Huntingore retainers. 'You can just carry on as usual. The bills are paid and everyday things remain the same. Until Mom returns, you can ask me about any problems.' She found the web youth, whatever he was called, gawping at her. 'Yes?'

'How can you be so . . .' he started and trailed off, lost for words as shocked Flytes who were always the quickest to react began to mutter plans and shepherd the rest back into their portions of the house. They had their own businesses, of which she knew only the names. She was confident they could take care of themselves, it wasn't as if Tralane actually did much other than balance the budget.

'So?' She waited for any word at all to drop while mentally calculating how far the Flit could have taken Minna if it were the size and power that she had heard from her mother, and if it ran on similar means. Her mom had said there had been audible engines, something that was maybe eight cylinders each, and propellers with some kind of airjet too, though it was unclear if that was also fan driven. Its fuel stop had to be half its possible range away although it could be carrying fuel...

She realised he was speaking and came to what he was saying part way through a sentence.

'...doing anything!'

Isabeau blinked at him, wondering who he really was and thinking he looked rather like someone Minna had once had an argument with. He wasn't an engineer so at the moment whatever he was didn't interest her. 'The faster you get off my doorstep and start doing something the faster I can do something too.'

His expression as he left gave her no doubt he considered her beneath contempt. She found the mousy girl standing in front of her, half in and half out of the door. Huge grey eyes blinked wetly at her. 'Is there anything I can do to help?'

Isabeau thought for a moment. 'Can you cook?'

The girl nodded mutely.

'Then make me some dinner. I'll be in the lab. It's on the top floor of the main building, top of the stairs, you can't miss it.' Isabeau closed the door and went to lock it, but found the lock broken. 'And start to make a list of everything that needs fixing,' she added, before checking that the door would at least stay closed against the weather. She didn't wait to see what the mousy girl thought, but went straight to Best's room and checked that he hadn't died or anything. He was asleep, breathing at least, on his bed. Must remember to have Mousy check on him regularly too, she thought – and then hurried on up, past the dead and burned-out elevator and into the attic.

The spinning wheel and seat were both coated in a good sheen of dust. She lifted the seat edge with one finger, sneezing in spite of her efforts not to disturb anything. A rolled sheaf of papers sat in the space where spare wool should have been. She took it out and let the lid down again, then opened the covering papers and read the first printed line:

'Schematics and Operational Procedures for the Glimshard City Anchor and Propulsion Systems...'

Then she tucked the papers under her arm in a flat position and followed the cold draught up to the roof area.

The door had been closed by someone unused to its idiosyncrasy and had blown open in the gusts that were bringing more dismal drizzle on to the weeds and slowly watering down the bloody patch where the prisoner had been taken and Mazhd wounded. She could not tell whose blood was whose, it was all mucky brown now. There were no marks on the ground so no clues there about the foreign flyer.

She crossed over to the shed and squeezed through the door. Her mother's Flit was folded up but it seemed in reasonable order. She put the papers into the cockpit as she gave the craft a quick inspection. She'd never been allowed to fly it and nor had anyone else she knew but the theory was something she could learn. Sadly it did not look as though she could carry more than a single passenger or a relatively small cargo. It was really only meant for one person as a jaunting vehicle, though Isabeau felt confident it was robust enough to take a few alterations and bear someone who was not too heavy. There were places on the wing that could be rigged for a harness though there was no way to put in a second seat.

Satisfied with what she'd seen she climbed up into the cockpit, turned on the lamp at the dashboard, and began to study the papers. They were copies, she noted, but the copyist had been careful to make exacting notes of their work, which led her to believe the date cited for the original drawings was correct: five hundred and twenty-two years previously. The engineer who had finalised the plans was Astatuo Mozettin, a grandfather and a Sircene: at that time the crafts and talents were all together in one great house at the service of the Empress when the Empire had been a single city. Glimshard had not been planned as a city but as a folly – a travelling pleasure district, for sightseeing on an epic scale. This purpose was long since vanished under the aspirations of the Empress, or, according to critics, to her hubris and folly. She waited until she was sure that she understood everything she was seeing, and then rolled the papers back up into their binder and hopped down from the cold leather seat. She closed the shed up, fixing the loose door hinge with a wooden chock under that side of the door, and then spent a minute or two finding items to barricade the broken top door shut before following the clear trail through the attics' dust back to the laboratory.

She felt her brows knit into a frown at the shocking state of the place. However, she had enough discipline to know that one woman's mess was another woman's work-in-progress and she knew that it looked worse than it was – the basic apparatus that she had come to find was in its place beneath the workbench. The emergency address system was little used as a matter of protocol. Speedy communications could always be sent over the aether from any mage to another, and that was satisfactory for most purposes, but she couldn't use the messengers for something like this. The situation and her new authority demanded instant action. She picked up the handset and selected the codes for contact to all the civil engineers simultaneously; those in the University and those elsewhere, and she added the code the Empress had given her, to flag her statement with the force of law.

'As of this moment the city is entering vehicular mode. Those not in position must move to their stations immediately. All timing devices are to be set to the Imperial clock time minus ten minutes effective as of the final of ten bells following this message. Final warnings are now automated at all gates. Stem crew, empty and disable all elevators. Remove all cars from the tracks. Warders clear the stem walkways. Prepare for high city de-elevation.'

She clicked off the handset and wondered what this was going to be like as she heard the bells chime down the ten count and set her watch to it.

A chime sounded, followed by a breathy male voice, 'This is Tower 58. Enemy outrunners sighted two miles short of the north gates. Main army follows, half mile behind.'

Isabeau coded again. 'Portal outpost, do you read?'

She tried the line several times but nothing came in return, only static. She called the general to inform him of what he no doubt already knew. His ancillary, Gau Tam, answered for him, his cultured voice that she recalled reeking of self importance now clipped into simple expediency. 'We've lost contact. I'm heading that way myself right now to find out what's going on.'

'We arrive there in four hours and twenty-seven minutes,' Isabeau told him.

'I can't guarantee anything.'

'Understood.'

The line went silent for a moment, then began ringing and ringing – she saw the call list included nearly every engineering station. There was no time to answer them. She checked handset charge and located an empty gear bag, threw that in, along with as many of the toolsets as she could carry, and hurried down the stairs, pausing only to collect her long winter coat. At the kitchen she found the Flytes looking after Best and leaned around the doorpost to face him.

'Make sure nobody goes upstairs for the next hour,' she said. 'And if you hear anything heavy falling, get under the table.'

'I should go with you,' he said, valiantly, though he looked a pasty grey colour.

'You can get up to the lab station and help from there,' she said, hoping the towers would not fall and crash through the roof. 'But there's no need until you hear the all clear.'

Outside, the rise and fall sound of the alert siren wove the air into an urgent chill. Torada's guard, Jago, was waiting for her, his black face above the leather mask that covered his jaw and throat set in an expression grim enough to turn her to stone. He didn't ask questions, but hefted her bag and lifted her on to the champing horse he'd brought. They rode together through the empty streets at a clattering canter broken by thumping as they moved on to the grassed tracks where they could. From windows an assortment of faces peered out at them as they took one turn after another down the hill to the stem elevation station where they stopped and she slid down before she could be moved. Jago came after her, weapons drawn.

The doors into the machine room swung open silently on their hinges and closed after them. Now the alert was replaced by a resonant hum of power moving through metal and crystal filaments. Isabeau moved forward to lead the way along the corridors that led to the control stations for the elevators. At the first station, she entered to find three men garbed in the dark blue and silver of the engineering guild arguing ferociously among themselves, one of them brandishing a book, another gesticulating at the panels. They didn't notice her entry but they turned as one when Jago passed through the door, having to turn slightly sideways to do so, his shoulders and spears both briefly a liability.

'Gentlemen,' Isabeau said into the moment of silence that hung around them, the suspense of it nearly a physical pressure on her head. 'Are the cars at their base positions, cargo offloaded, passengers clear?' She could see from their faces that they had been arguing about her – their expressions varied from outraged to resentful and points in between.

The one with the greyest hair, set in something like a cross between a bush and a bonnet, was the only one to speak, though she felt he summed up their feeling adequately. 'But she's so young. This is ridiculous. Being ordered around by a child!'

Isabeau turned to Jago, towering behind her right shoulder, the sudden sweat smell of him in the confined space almost alarming. 'Can we cut their heads off for treason?'

The huge man gave her a glance over the top of his mask, which, now she noticed it, did make him look as if he had been muzzled. He shoved past her as delicately as possible in the circumstances and punched the only one without spectacles. As he straightened up the other two were already moving hastily towards their stations, leaving a free spot between them which Isabeau took herself with a small, 'Thank you,' as she stepped over the unconscious form of the unlucky good-sighted engineer.

'Cars are stowed,' she said with satisfaction after a further few minutes of busy silent industry had passed. 'Lockout track power below.'

'Track power decoupled!' came the reply from the speaker in her desk. The tension in the voice was enough to let her know that nobody down there had an inkling of what was about to happen next. In theory, they did. In practice nobody had moved this machinery for hundreds of years and several million tons was about to descend on their heads. She was about to make the magical flower stem of Glimshard shrink down to nothing.

A man who had not criticised her looked across to her, whispering shakily, 'Do you know what will happen when the raft reaches the floor and the power isn't required any more?'

'No,' Isabeau said. Power engineering on this scale was nothing that Glimshard engineers knew. As far as she was aware nobody knew the true physics of it, it was simply something that had been used time out of mind and mostly this seemed adequate though the worry here was not without precedence. Large-scale power operations had been known to go wrong in the past. Entire districts of some cities had been blown to smithereens. To her understanding, the flow of particles in the tides that made up the aether should simply stop without a problem once the conduit transmission was closed but *why* this should be was something for theoreticians to work out. She felt, in her bones, they were good, and that was enough for her. If they blew up she would simply consider it an early explosion of the many more about to arrive with the ballistas from the approaching army, supposing she survived it. She pushed the notion aside and followed the sequences she had memorised from the book. 'Initiating descent of the viewing deck. Maintain monitoring of gravitation tolerances and disc balance.' She wondered what gravitation tolerance was, but there was a symbol for it and readouts, and for the time being that was all that she needed.

For a moment there was silence and they all looked at the instruments and each other, then with a crack and a rumble a tremor went through the ground. Vibrations and echoes of the movement sounded through the hollow tubes of the elevator shafts and caught up resonances from other parts of the plating that the viewing deck was made of – reports of stress that Isabeau listened to with her ears trying desperately to read signs in the sounds. To non-engineers it would have been frightening and to her it was disturbing, though she was loath to admit it. She found her hands on the instrument panel, holding it rather than doing anything. Then there was a sharp crack, several rapid retorts and a much more violent tremor that had them all splay-legged as they made to keep their balance. Rumbling and booming noises built up rapidly into a storm of sound all around them. Thundering crashes from various distances led her to suspect that some of the less stable buildings of the high city had already begun to fail. She stared at the readouts, forcing the numbers to change from meaningless signs to information. Graphs of oscillations skipped around. Warnings of various kinds flashed. Her hands moved and did things she barely understood before doing. Behind her she heard Jago hissing his dislike of the situation. To her left and right both men cursed and hammered at their instruments with panicked fingers. She looked at the clock. Only seconds had passed.

'Something's wrong. D-station Ground has not released the dampers,' the older of the two, the man at her left, muttered, cueing the intercom even before Isabeau had time to look for it. 'D-station. D-station. What is your status?'

'Isn't there an override?' Isabeau searched, but the system didn't offer one, it seemed. She couldn't understand such an oversight.

The intercom hissed silent static.

'I'm going down,' Isabeau said, coldly certain there was no time for another choice. 'This suite is functional. I'm putting it on automatic.' She did so and turned to the wide, white eyes of the warrior behind her, his balance on his feet impeccable though everything of his visible expression betrayed loathing of the situation and his helplessness. She had to counter that before it turned bad. 'Jago, you are in charge of my station. Familiarise yourself with the controls. Obey instructions from either of these two. I'm taking the drop chute.' She was already patting her pockets, checking her tools.

'If they fix it before you get there you could be crushed,' the second mate said, tearing his eyes from his own screens for a moment.

'Keep trying to talk to them,' she suggested as another and more severe tremor caused a twist that they could all feel attempting to swing them around to the west: failing, it yawed back east and alarms began to sound. Without a pause she smashed the safety glass over the control of a door in the control room's corner that hadn't been serviced or opened in living memory and pulled the cord. Air hissed and metal clinked as the seals blew. She set her drop zone as D, since all it offered were letters, and then got into the cage of the single person car that hung below a rail in the roof. It swung and creaked. Banging and shrieking came from the tunnel's black mouth. She noted that she was more afraid than she had ever been of anything, even in her wildest imagination. She pressed the master key and a glimmer of magelight swept the outer mesh of the cage as the harness around her snapped so tight she thought it was going to cut her in pieces. Then she fell.

Screaming in the circumstances was only pragmatic. The vibrations she made with the sound effectively counteracted around a third of incoming alarming vibrations from other things. Then the screeching of the cage as it swung, fell, swept around and around drowned her out until she wasn't sure that she was making any noise at all even though her throat felt raw and her lungs full. The terrifying rocking and crashing stopped suddenly, leaving her shaken to bits, aching in shoulders and pelvis where the straps held her to the seat. It was still dark. The harness was still tight. With a sinking feeling she realised she had stalled before reaching her destination. The creaking and groaning of the structure all around her was deafening. She groped in her pocket for a light, found nothing. Both pockets were empty. As if to mock her she heard the tiny skid and tinkle of something small, possibly a screwdriver, slithering past her along the metal chute. She had never figured to close her pockets. They didn't close. They hadn't been designed for being flung around like a cork in a storm. With difficulty she recalled the words for conjuration. Everyone knew some.

'Zirca abbaye,' she said, concerned her voice would not be enough in the groaning but a faint witchlight ball appeared near her, static arcing briefly off it on to the cage.

With its aid she could see that the cage was jammed at a junction point where two chutes crossed. She tried to throw her own weight backwards and forwards to see if that would jar her loose but she was so tightly strapped in that the force wasn't enough. She couldn't see the problem but, as she squinted past the light, she realised she was nearly there anyway. A faint glowing outline of a 'D' was visible in the wall about thirty metres away downtube. If she could get out of the cage she could reach the door.

A loud boom came echoing down towards her and then a crackle from the cage's ancient intercom. She could hear the first engineer's voice gabbling and then a clearer reply.

'This is D station. We had a power out. It's back online. Removing damper arrays.'

'Negative, I mean No! There's an engineer in the chute bay! Repeat—'

'What's that Control? We can't hear you, there's so much interference from the bad links. Array clear.'

Isabeau found herself out of the harness, her fingers turning, slowly turning the wingnuts on the floor pan drop – the only way not blocked by the walls of the chute. She felt a sudden lightness, a rightness in the set of things and the complaints of thousands of tons of material go quiet to be replaced by a mid-toned resonant hum of efficiency. Far above her, but with gathering speed, the clink and slide of telescoping parts, accompanied by the odd crunch of badly aligned plating, began to bang and slam. One nut was off. Another. The noise became a roar and air rushed past her in a sudden wind that whipped her hair around her face, lashing her eyes and nose.

She fell through the hole as the last rusted nut broke free, leaving her coat hanging where it snagged on a raw bolt end. She slowed herself crazily with her boot soles as she shot towards the hatch door only to be blinded with sudden light as it opened. A black half-silhouette looked through. She hit the frame with her foot and arm, was grabbed and hauled inside. The cage shot past a hairsbreadth behind her and struck the buffers with a deafening clang.

She blinked through a haze of dust into the open-mouthed faces of three base station technicians.

'Descent is steady, halfway, Control. Maintain east pressure. East ten point five. Engineer is down safely.'

Isabeau got to her feet. 'We couldn't hear you upstairs,' she said, coughing, barely able to hear herself even though it was relatively quiet in the room over the machine whir. 'The chutes need maintenance.' She couldn't understand why they were all staring at her when the job was only half done. Belatedly she realised they might not know who she was. After all none of them had met her in person. She was nothing but a name on a set of orders. 'Isabeau Huntingore,' she said, holding out her hand and seeing it shake of its own accord. 'Chief Engineer.'

The deck descended without further incident and settled into position within the main city frame with only minor shudders: it amused to her to consider that as she heard the booming reports of it echoing through the corridors from the outside world. An hour ago such things would have been enough to scare most people to death. Now they were minor shudders. Once eighty per cent plate contact was achieved she ordered deck grips in place and when the reports had confirmed all braces were in position she closed her eyes in a moment of relief. 'Transfer power to main engine start and plate cohesion array. Ground anchor points, blow anchors when you are ready.'

She watched readouts which spoke to her directly, and felt the explosive shocks as the screwheads disengaged themselves from their barbed grip in the bedrock and began to spiral back into the gate tower armatures. She felt, as much as saw, the fluctuation in the power grid as the displacement engine started. Then everyone held their breath. From the outside and on the surface she knew firsthand that there was no sign that Glimshard was anything but an ordinary city on the plain, topping a small rise in an otherwise flat landscape of waving grasses and fields. Now a line in the ground was being cut rapidly in a series of tiny explosions as minor bolts blew, matched by a rising sense of pressure in her bones as the engine entered its operational mode.

Without looking, she knew that the total city power supply was lower than one twentieth of its maximum. Having run so long without recharge it was only decades from closedown, and with this flight, more like single figure years. It was the Empress' hope that this artefact in the ground held energy supplies that they could use. If it didn't then its location would be Glimshard's new and permanent home.

A few minutes passed in which sweat trickled down the face of the man beside her as his fingers stumbled over unfamiliar passes on his controls. Isabeau felt the shift as the last of the restraints catastrophically detached them from their ground site. A change in the vibrations running through the floors told her that they were no longer being damped by contact with the land. She supposed she ought to run a check on the proximity of any people but if they were close outside then they were enemies and she could not spare the time to care about their fate. If they were within five metres of the edges, then they were already gone – reports said what was there vanished. Every landing site carved its own depression, and recarved new edges when it left in lines that spirited things away, no matter what they were.

'Ascending,' she said, though there was nothing to feel, not like Mom's elevator in its old cage. The engine thrummed like the hum of distant bees but she could hear the wind outside over it, rattling some loose awnings. 'Ten metres. Fifteen. Twenty. All halt at twenty-five metres.' This was the minimum cruise height for the landscape, any less ran the risk of damaging structures underneath, and more was profligate, a waste of energy. 'Set course, Master Damps. Proceed when ready.'

The transition to forwards motion shook a few loose tiles and sent volleys of settling pigeons back into the air in clouds of applause. Glimshard moved south at a steady five knots, testing itself against the air.

'W-we should see to your hand, Miss Huntingore, I mean, Chief Engineer,' the second officer said.

Isabeau looked down and saw that she had unforgivably covered the station control panel in bloody smears from a cut on her left hand, which she had not felt. It ached now that she looked at it.

'I will be in the control centre,' she said, nodding and stuffing the hand in her pocket to spare more mess. 'Keep me informed.'

She made it to the small, stuffy rooms on the second storey before collapsing into a wing chair. Jago was there already, she saw, bossing someone around who brought her drinks. She looked out of the windows and saw the supremely satisfying sight of fields moving at a stately pace, frozen green waves beneath her bow. She let herself have five minutes while Jago gave her cut hand some militarily fierce first aid, and then she got up and recovered her bag from the viewing deck control room, now conveniently located only a few doors away. She took it back to her seat and extracted her notebook and a pen, watching the bodyguard leave, taking her requests back to Torada.

It was time to redesign the Flit to carry a second person.

CHAPTER TWENTY-THREE

TRALANE

Tralane rode in a state of horrified numbness, through which the pain of riding a horse after so long steadily reasserted itself. She was grateful in a way. Without it the pull within her that demanded she turnabout and fly after that craft, find Minna and protect her, was intolerable agony which no amount of rationalising could banish. Managing the horse occupied her much of the time – Tzaban loping at a steady pace until its cantering started to labour and require much kicking from her heels. Then he would slow to a walk. His own breathing was heavier, she noticed, but he didn't struggle. He also didn't talk and she wished he would, though every time she was about to speak the banality of everything she could ask stopped her.

Before long they were alone on the roads, every traveller vanished as if into thin air. Across the fields she could see houses still with smoke from lit fires and machineries at work here and there as if nothing was happening. Maybe messages had not got through. Or maybe they didn't want to leave, no matter what was coming. She couldn't imagine being stuck out here in this semblance of normality and peace, knowing about the army – though perhaps rumours of the city moving were too odd to be believed, or it didn't matter as they had no intention of moving themselves. She wanted to run up to the houses and scream at them to do something, to run.

Her thoughts were cut short by the distant bark of sirens. Tzaban stopped, the horse snorting to an uneasy halt just in time to let her look back at the city halfway to the horizon. Her eyes scanned desperately for signs of people outside, terrified that there might be some who had not made the gate in time. The faces of the children they had passed on the way haunted her suddenly as she heard the rise and fall wail of the mechanical sound, so strange and eerie across the damp early evening air. The horse stamped. She found herself looking at Tzaban's strange face and saw his nostrils flare with dislike, his attention rapt as hers for a moment or two longer. Then his yellow-amber eyes slid to gaze at hers. Despite being mounted she was only a head taller than he was. She saw at once his intent distaste of the sound, and perhaps all it represented, though whether that was the Empire's culture or its magics and machineries she didn't know but whatever it was she felt suddenly vulnerable and alone. They were foreign to one another and out here with him she was at a near total disadvantage. She felt the gun holster and knew she could never draw it in time if he chose to do something to her. When he spoke, she started with surprise at recognisable words coming out of him.

'We must hurry. All my effort was lost.' He swung around, towing the horse after him, taking her with it in a fumble and curse of sudden complaints from her leg muscles as they went back to their canter. She wondered at his words as she fought to keep her seat steady and relax into the horse's gait against her body's will and kept up her focus by watching his back as he ran. She would have done anything right then for strength, grace and endurance like that. Anything not to be on this bloody horse, wincing and gritting her teeth as every stride took her away from where she longed to be.

'What do you mean?' She fought her way back to balance on

the saddle, the stink of hot horse overriding the scent of mud on the road. Talking was essential for a time, if she was not to notice the dropped belongings that had fallen by the wayside, the pattern of feet and wheels gouged into the softer ground, the sudden abeyance of the distant wail; she could not stand the signs of things falling apart.

His voice was made rough by the depth of his breathing and the puffs he made as his feet padded the ground, two pats to the horse's triple cadence making her feel almost seasick as she watched the white mane of hair shiver and bounce against his shoulders. 'My gifts did not appease her.'

'The Empress?' The politics was beyond her. What could he possibly have to give or want out of Glimshard? And Torada married him so that society would take it as a sign that she meant to treaty for peace with the Karoo. His voice lent no credence to the notion. His body on the other hand she could quite appreciate was worth the gesture, but what he made of it she couldn't begin to imagine. Her curiosity began slowly to overtake her distress.

'Yes.' His reply was late as he slowed down again to accommodate the horse's need to slow down. She wished he would volunteer something but he seemed to see no point in talk so she would have to draw it from him by demand, except her notion of his rank prevented her. She didn't think he minded that she had forgotten to call him Consort so far however, nor any other honorific.

'Why are you the only one?'

For a few moments she watched him, allowing her scientific interest to take over as she waited for his reply. His resemblance to a beast was mostly superficial, physical, she thought. It was hair and colours. His feet were a little different, heels off the ground, and long, the forefoot halfway to a paw, but the rest of him was not more strange than a big man, lean and rugged, heavily muscled – he could have been some lumbering labourer.

The beast was in the way he moved, and in his eyes. He moved like a cat. She was glad he looked the other way. She found his gaze disturbing and not only in the erotic way she had dreamed of when she first saw him in a picture. She put her hand to check the holster's safety cover on the gun.

'It is not easy to answer,' he said finally. 'What is needed is made.' There was a hesitancy to him that made her suspect there was more to this than he wanted or was able to express. She noted it, attempting to wrap her mind around this investigation so that she didn't have to think of the city but just at that moment the distant retorts of explosions cut through the squelch of mud, the chink of harness and the horse's snorting breath.

This time Tzaban did not stop to look back, but Tralane twisted in the saddle, gripping it fore and aft. 'Stop! I must see this!'

In a few strides they halted. Birds nearby whistled and circled in the fading afternoon light. In the middle distance the glowing stem of the city, which had burned blue and bright for her whole lifetime, was shrinking. She'd known it did that, but seeing it was another thing altogether. Her guts churned suddenly with fear, though if anything the sight was smooth and silent as the operation of a well-oiled hydraulic jack. There was no sign of a fault, though she fancied she saw something tiny, like rocks, falling down in a shower from one side. The final moments were missed as Tzaban pulled on the horse again.

'No!' she insisted, hauling on the rein.

'Yes,' he said simply in reply, her tug ineffective as he grasped the bridle. 'Out of your hands now.' They accelerated to a trot and she was nearly bounced out of the saddle as she struggled to look, to see, as if by seeing she could hold the city and balance it, make it safe and guide it with only her will across the miles. She didn't understand how such a momentous, awesome thing could be met with such indifference as he showed it, his back

357

flowing again in motion as hers jolted her head so hard she was forced to turn around and look instead at the encroaching darkness as the road passed into loose woodland.

'You don't understand. I want to see this. I have to see this! The city has never moved in lifetimes, it might not work, it might never happen again...' Her begging fell on deaf ears. More explosions in the background, like soft claps rolling across the fields. It would be the sight of a lifetime and she was seeing it only in juddering bursts. Then as they passed into the treeline and down a small slope she wasn't seeing anything at all.

'It will or it won't,' he said between breaths, so long afterward she felt it was really too late, like he was offering her a kind of apology, though it hurt more not less. 'Whatever it does, it does it without you.'

She wanted to hit him. The trees enveloped them in a kind of quiet made out of the endless blurred sound of wind in the leaves. She strained her ears. The horse jumped as a tremor ran through the ground, and stumbled on a tree root, but after that there was nothing to hear or see. The sky soon became grey as they kept their trot, canter, trot, walk paces until at last it all became walking and she could barely see until they emerged at the other side of the woodland into a shallow valley, at the other distant end of which the portal had been built at the head of the pass into the mountains beyond.

She was jolted out of her miserable reverie a short while later by the peculiar soft whine of something whizzing past her ear. At almost the same moment Tzaban was suddenly half his height and two metres forwards. The horse cringed and reared but it was tired and the movement didn't unseat her as she realised they were being shot at.

Terror bloomed inside her with incredible vivid anticipation of her painful death. She clung to the reins and the saddle, turned around by the panicked horse and then carted off the road and into the woods. Small branches and brush whipped at her. By the time the horse had run out of effort and she had gathered the reins back the woods loomed, almost completely dark in every direction. Then she heard the growling shout of Tzaban's voice calling.

'Engineer, are you with us?'

She wondered who he meant by us, and turned to go that way, trusting the horse's instincts to pick a safe path. He was waiting for her in the last light of the sun, two miserable figures with him, muddy and bloodied. One held a snapped bow. The other hung from Tzaban's grasp, his toes barely on the ground.

'They're ours,' he explained, his tone the most menacing that she had heard. 'They mistook us in the dark.'

This was clearly a lie.

'Are they deserters?' She was too confused to be tactful but they were wearing Imperial livery, with Glimshard badges.

Tzaban's jaw clenched as he shook the one he held, then dropped him. The man buckled to his knees, whimpering. 'They have done their bit for now.' His gaze dared her to say it again and she dared not. Tralane looked again at the two and saw broken creatures, eyes glazed with exhaustion and fear, a starveling desperation in their every movement. She wondered if they were even capable of speech.

Tzaban's nostrils kept flaring. 'The war has taken a new turn. They wanted the horse. Let them go.' At the word both men scrabbled to their feet and began to run, regardless of the dark. She got the impression they couldn't get away fast enough and she was certainly not the cause.

'They wanted to kill you, I think,' she said.

'They have been attacked by the Karoo. It is plausible.' He took the horse's bridle again, and resumed walking as before.

'Now you sound like Isabeau. She never gives a cat's backside what anyone thinks either.' Then she wondered at her choice of words and considered that she had perhaps been spending too much time distracting herself by looking at him. He didn't react to it either way.

'Who is that?'

'My daughter.'

She heard him make an interested kind of grunt and then they stopped again and listened. Others were coming up the path, making lots of noise as people do when they flee near blindly, panting, at the limits of their endurance. More soldiers soon passed them, unarmed for the most part and fumbling in the dark, so fixated that their weary faces barely registered Tzaban and the horse until the last second, and even then did not care. They were almost witless, she thought, and her insides grew cold. When the third set had fled by them into the darkness she couldn't hold it in longer. Whatever he said she needed to hear his voice; anybody's voice.

'What's really going on?'

'We will find out. For now we should rest a few hours. The horse is tired.'

She cursed him for being like Isabeau in the small-talk department as well. Instead she found herself bantering some witless newspaper-fed nonsense about the war as they turned off the road and took shelter in a copse of thick thorn bushes after he hacked a way into the hollow centre with a machete he had brought with him. The horse was given grain and water. To Tralane, who had come with only her toolkits, he gave half a loaf of bread, taking the rest for himself. Though he had surely tried harder she was starving and ate it all. He reacted no more to her silence than he had to her chatter about politics. The ground was cold and damp and she could hear too much noise that she didn't understand to be able to rest; trees, wind, creaking, the sounds of people or things stumbling about a way off. Tzaban remained crouched, eating unaccountably slowly. His white hair shone faintly in the little light that the moon gave; a gigantic, claw-fingered monstrosity. The sight made her shudder. In her mind's eye she saw the view through the telescope of that strange object out near the stars, glinting. She pulled out her oracle and drew up the data from the telescope's autotrack.

She had recalculated its relative position and velocity by the time that he got up and began to pack the blankets back into the saddlebags. Her aching body and freezing arse told her it was not near dawn, more like the earliest hours of the morning. The horse huffed but seemed better when she remounted. Tzaban gave her water, insisting she drink. She delayed them more then by having to relieve herself. Too afraid to go out of sight entirely she closed her eyes and ignored propriety. A woman might do as she pleased, men should avert their gazes. She didn't know if he knew that and the thought put a strange frisson through her that she didn't care for.

They continued, more soldiers coming their way in bursts. One tried to attack Tzaban in a frenzy. The Karoo put him aside with a terrible crunching sound and a wet puff of air leaving with his life. The sudden violence of it, the speed and ferocity, completely silenced her. She swallowed against a lump in her throat. The body lay in the mud and they left it there. She heard Tzaban sneezing.

'They smell of females.'

This meant nothing to Tralane. She bent over the saddle bow. 'What?'

His low voice was hoarse, struggling to be quiet. 'When we are at the other side you must do exactly as I tell you or it is likely we will not live to make mistakes.'

As daylight crawled through the thinning trees they dropped into another long shallow valley and came around a hillock to find a landscape spread beneath them in broad, rolling swathes, the road winding all the way through, riverside, to the distance where the plains rose again to Steppes. Tralane sat up, heartened to find they could see for miles and that the weather was set to be clear. Across the vast acres the smoke of early fires made thin, upright trails into the sky marking camps where soldiers had kept enough of themselves to gather. She could not tell at this distance if they were enemies or allies. The portal encampment, still too young to look anything but ramshackle, lay in an oxbow of the river itself, smokes of greater darkness pluming from it with significant majesty so that she knew they were no cookfires. Thoughts of Minna rose as they must, endlessly, but she pushed them aside, promising herself she would get to that as soon as possible, but now was not possible and therefore she must not let it consume her.

As if reading her mind the Karoo turned, his orange eyes a sudden shock in the pale blues of the dawn. 'To each moment now give all your attention. Give me your scarf.'

Tralane hesitated, wondering, but had no reason to dispute him although his manner made her flare hot with anger. The situation overrode her outrage. She gave him the large cotton sheet of her headscarf, watching its short white tassels play with sudden jollity in a tiny breeze. It unfolded in his hands to its full extent – enough to act as half a bedsheet if it must, so fine that it could wrap a neck or shade a face or be worn as a shirt any number of ways. He refolded it with a peculiar care into a square like a large pocket handkerchief and then to her utter astonishment, undid the front of the soft cloth that lay between his leathered thigh armours, and peed into it with stern deliberation, scrunching it to be sure that it was well soaked. The smell was powerful, even in the cool morning, like a tomcat in full reek that had been fed on burnt apples. Her nose automatically wrinkled in disgust but her curiosity got the better of her and she found herself applying a studiously scientific eye to him as she asked, 'What did you do that for?'

He had a heavy, very human looking penis, she thought as he covered himself up again, though if he had balls that matched she could not see. She thought it was lightly furred at the base, rather than hairy, with that same stripe, but much paler, being part of his ventral side, with skin that strange lilac blue, dark and going darker towards the tip which gleamed. Then at the last moment she saw it drawn inward of its own accord. Like an animal, she thought, and wondered about it as he wrung out her scarf and left only a few dark drips to fall to the ground. The white and grey check was now a grey and pale green check. He didn't give it to her but rolled it and stuffed it down the central channel of the saddle where there was a gap for the horse's spine.

'Maybe won't be water later,' he said. 'Would be harder then.'

'No, I mean why at all?'

'It will mark you as mine. Then we can travel together, through Karoo. Hnn, maybe.' He glanced at her and she saw a quirky smile on his face, uncertainty in it and apology for that.

'Maybe?'

He sighed. 'Empress' touch lingers. Maybe I just die. Maybe you too.' He shrugged and she saw resignation.

'Die how?'

Instead of answering he started to walk and the horse automatically went after him. Tralane thought maybe it didn't matter as she didn't plan to die. She checked the gun in the pack and took it out, keyed the power, set it to the holster on her leg. Once the road had moved them clear of the last trees they left it and began to cut across country in a direct line towards the portal. When they were not jogging along in clear ground she struggled to see the truth of what they were going into but it became clear soon enough as did something more important.

'Tzaban,' she said, leaning forward as she saw his head rise in a sign she had his attention. 'The portal. It's not working.'

The wooden buildings of the site were half torn apart and their pieces made into bonfires. Around these a large gathering of men and some women were milling about. Most wore Imperial livery. Some were seated in rows, heads down – prisoners. As she strained to see she saw a corpse heaved into the flames of one of the fires and then realised the regular pattern of shapes beside the main structure was made of bodies laid out.

Tzaban stopped and she nearly fell off the horse as it stopped with him. They had been seen. A group of four riders had come out on to the track and were moving steadily in their direction. They had Glimshard colours, but came with drawn swords held in their free hands.

'Why?' he said quietly in a grunt aimed at her as one of the approaching officers raised his arm and shouted across – Tzaban was unmistakable so there was no point in not signalling back. He raised his arm and bellowed some military-sounding call in return. 'Gau Tam,' he said to her after, her ears still ringing, as they moved off again. Tralane was tuned enough to their peculiar conversations by now to know he meant why the portal had failed.

'I don't know until I see it,' she said. 'The stanchions are still there in the ground.'

Where the portal had been was easy to see. A churned path of mud, broad as three streets, led up to a straight line between two tall metal posts and ended there, pristine heavy grass beyond. She was busy thinking about how it might work, what power sources it must use, when they were surrounded by the oncoming riders. Before Tzaban she vaguely recognised the face of the man he had hailed – Gau Tam, the general's second or aide or whatever it was. She could never recall the rank names but his familiarity was reassuring. The others, two men and a woman, looked like officers to her too, but all different in some way. Their knuckles, she noticed, were yellow-white, hands pale. Every uniform was covered in blood and filth, rent. One had a bandaged head. The horses were scruffy – not officer horses but regular cavalry mounts, and worn out.

'Sir,' Tzaban said, looking up at Gau Tam. She'd never seen

him so still and apparently relaxed. His voice was quiet. 'I am commanded to bring this engineer to the site.'

'I know you are.' His white cravat lay loosely around his neck in a heavy, stained ring. Two of the others had drawn kerchiefs over their lower faces. Tralane smelled a whiff of naphtha coming off them, and turpentine. She saw their eyes were red and watering above the cloth.

Gau Tam drew a breath, looking at Tzaban as if she didn't exist. 'You'll stay with us. Engineer, the machinery is disabled, you will have to repair it to make passage. I will distract the others as you do so and tell them that you are ensuring it cannot be used.' He paused and swallowed, looked at the others with him but they just exchanged glances and nodded. 'Close it after you. I suggest that you disable it, regardless of any orders you may have to the contrary from the Empress. Leave me to deal with the rest.' At last he turned to look at her with a glance that combined with his treasonous suggestion to tell her all she wanted to know about what lay in store for her. His face was scored with exhaustion but it was his eyes that made her simply nod rather than question him. He looked ineffably fragile, as if a single blow of one finger would snap him.

'Well then,' he said. 'Let's get to it. Engineer. Gentlemen.' He rode forward and let them trail after to display they were no threat but at the sight of Tzaban getting nearer some of the soldiers at the camp got up and began to separate themselves, melting silently into the buildings that remained standing.

Tzaban, now pacing at her horse's side rather than leading it, snarled quietly but Gau Tam waved him down and raised his sword as they came through the gate, shouting in a voice that carried clear across the yards, 'Stand down and stay back. She comes to secure the gates.' He sounded nothing like the way he had looked to Tralane. Power and arrogance shone through his tones. He expected obedience and in any case the men and women she started to pass looked as though they had no heart to resist him or to fight. They didn't look able to do more than they did; sit and shiver like the old in winter.

They passed a long gauntlet of silent stares. Someone in one of the buildings ran a sword along the boards in a slow scrape. Every pair of eyes slid around to fixate on Tzaban wherever he moved. It was the most desperate, empty kind of watching she had ever seen, so at odds with the eager curiosity and speculations of the city. She shrank in the saddle as the horse plodded along, nudging it with her foot towards the outlying column of stone and metal that was the portal's right pillar. Behind her she heard the hoofbeats of at least two of the others and the jingle of their armour and harness.

They stopped at the pillar and she slid out of the saddle, the pain in her legs almost enough to make her cry, she felt so vulnerable and stiff. Instead she undid the saddlebags and equipped her own harness and toolkits. Her fingers undid the safety cover on the gun holster of their own accord in passing, keyed the charge on. She felt the presence of Tzaban close, as if he was radiating heat.

'Do what you must, I will guard you,' he said and his words were followed by the whispering zing of a blade being drawn.

Tralane muttered quietly to him as she walked around the pillar, examining it. 'What's all that facegear and smelly stuff for?'

'To block the hunting scent of the female Karoo,' he replied. 'What I have given you will work better.' He pulled the stinking scarf out from the saddle and handed it to her. 'Put it on now.'

She saw that he and the two men on horseback had formed a rough shield for her, blocking the bonfires, but she didn't think anyone there would have a clue what she was doing; even she didn't. Gritting her teeth against her resentment she tied the heavy, abominable cloth around her neck, arranging it under one arm so it could not be easily pulled off and so that she could use it as a hood if she must. Her own eyes began to tear up.

366

'If only it fuckin' worked,' she heard one of the horsemen mutter as he lifted his kerchief and spat on the ground.

'I thought the fighting was between us and the Mudlanders of the Circle,' Tralane said, clinging to the conversation even as almost all her attention now focused on the formations of the pillar, reading the signs of link and component until she located the access panelling. It was, on inspection, crudely welded shut. At the grass beneath the pillar she saw a microtorch and silver drops of metal amid dark smears of blood and mud. She bent to pick the tool up from the crushed area.

'Was between us and the fuckin' Mudders,' the man said hoarsely, coughing. 'Until someone used a fuckin' mage attack from some blasted machine. Then the Karoo decided to join in. This here is all that's left. An' if you open that fuckin' gate and they come through it then there won't be this either. Won't be nothin'.' Tension in his voice made it crack and his horse shuffled backwards under the pressure of the reins until he kicked and cursed it back to position. 'Speed it up. They want his hide on a post. Won't be long before too many of 'em find their mettle.'

'Sergeant,' Gau Tam's voice was laced with warning. There was no more talk.

Tralane glanced at the camp. Sure enough a loose group was forming by the near gate. She used the torch to burn out the welds, trying to breathe slowly and steadily, the stink of the metal harsh and sudden. She finally broke in and pulled the panel away, dropping it.

The command pane was cracked so badly, a star right across it, that she could barely see the lights in it. She draped her scarf over her head and shrouded herself with it to block out the sunglare. Though she didn't know the pictograms of the object she recognised solid University work when she saw it. The protocols for images and controls were the ones she had seen in other people's lectures and papers. How it worked exactly was beyond her knowledge, science was for people like Carlyn to mine out and deduce. Mastery of method and construction was her business. Fortunately, nothing important had changed since its last use and she assumed the plate welding had been done to try to protect this. She did not think there was more than one other gateway, so she felt confident they would not be catapulted into an unknown space. The only place this had ever been meant to go was to the far southern camp. A power check suggested it had life in it but the startup command – a universal symbol among engineers – did not work. After a moment of stabbing at barely understood glyphs she figured the fault was on the other post.

She looked up and across to it and was staggered to see that they had been surrounded by soldiers while her attention was distracted. Now the officers' horses circled her at the post, shifting nervously as men shouted at one another. Tzaban stood beside her, tulip ears moving as he listened, though his eyes looked at nothing and his body hung relaxed from his shoulders as though he was hearing a faraway music. The white tip of his tail beat from side to side, swishing the few remaining standing stalks of grass.

'I have to get to the other post,' she murmured to him, sliding tools back into their positions at her belt. The gun grip appeared under her palm and she settled it into her hand, drawing it but keeping it pointed to the ground.

At first she didn't think he had heard her. Into the gap the words being spoken over her head and their meaning filtered through to her.

'...filthy piece of Karoo shit is dead we'll settle. You know what's there, Commander. You know it's the only way.'

In response Gau Tam pointed his sabre at the man between them and the far post. 'Move aside. They're going through.'

'An' what if something comes through the other way?'

Back near the fires a woman's voice rose in a sudden

hysterical shrieking, followed by gruff bellows and the sounds of thumping, then silence.

'Then we'll kill it.' Gau Tam made it sound as if this was simply a formality but the iciness of his voice belied its calm tone. He nudged his horse forward and it moved steadily. Tzaban pushed Tralane in the middle of her back and propelled her close after it just to its nearside, using it as a barrier. Her legs shook but she walked, eyes on the protesting soldier. For a moment his gaze met hers and if it weren't for Tzaban's solid pressure she would have stopped.

'If you care at all Ma'am, don't go on,' the soldier said, unmoving as Gau Tam's horse advanced within two metres of him. 'Especially not with that thing. He may be the Empress' choice but she knows nothin' 'bout what it is. She's just a silly child, dreamin'. Nothin'.' He was holding a polearm, the spike at its point was covered in dark stickiness, describing the same juddering tiny circle in the air over and over again. At the last moment he made one step to his left, sabre met wooden stock, and the warhorse shouldered him aside. As if connected by strings the others in the ring loosened their stances and backed off.

'Stand ready, Master Fath,' Gau Tam's voice sliced across the air to his second. 'Engineer, be quick about it, we want no accidental trouble.'

'Be sure not to fuckin' come back,' someone murmured and she felt Tzaban stagger as they covered the final stride to the post.

A roar of rage from Gau Tam, a sudden clack and whirr of a shot right next to her, a steady thock of bolt hitting its mark, a strangled cry and the thump of a body falling but the hand on her back remained where it was. She turned to see but Tzaban pushed her hard and hissed, 'Make your moves, mind your business.'

'Anybody else want to revolt?'

She realised Gau Tam had shot someone with a crossbow. A lever action reloader, handheld but deadly within twenty metres, her mind reliably informed her. This one sounded loose but it had worked well enough. She tugged at the access panel and it fell away at a touch. The fault turned out to be a timed-out power relay. It was the work of only a minute to reset it. She thought that three seconds was more than enough given they were standing right on it and set a countdown.

'Portal in ten,' she said, trying for loud but at least managing to be heard by Tzaban. 'We need to run through. Stand clear. In five, four . . .'

The soldiers ran back, the horses thudded away. There was a buzzing sound of bad connectors fudging a power bridge and the sharp sudden smell of arcane discharges that often heralded major failure, or potential damage. She glanced at her arcmeter and saw a phenomenal reading just as the air next to her sheared with an undescribable sound. Tzaban's hand at her belt propelled her forward with shocking speed and force. She opened her mouth to scream but her feet were faster, already running so she didn't simply fly on to her face in the dirt.

There was a moment of blackness, a perishing cold, then an ocean of heat, light and noise that engulfed her. Someone was screaming, not her. Tzaban's growl beside her turned from rumble to deafening roar. The smell was a thick, fetid miasma of rot overlaid with a sweet perfume that made her head spin. She barely remembered the hood, fallen on her shoulders, her nose dead to it until it was yanked over her face by an unseen hand, then gripped there at the back of her neck so she was held like a puppet She could see through the weave, just, as that hand propelled her. It was a brutal vice that permitted no disputes as it demanded she go this way, that way seemingly at random. Her legs staggered on soft, squishy ground in obedience to its bone-cracking pressure. All over she heard human shrieking and screaming, and the strangest voices shouting, so loudly, things that did not make sense in both Imperial and Swaffish, the lingua franca of the Mudlanders. Suddenly her face was up against a metal post and Tzaban, nearly unrecognisable, snarled, 'Do your work. Finish it.'

'But the city,' she said into her tiny, noxious, chequered world. Visions of explosions, Isabeau, Minna, swam before her eyes.

The hood was yanked off. Tzaban's face was close enough his longer whiskers tickled her cheek. His hard, massive body pressed the length of hers against the dull roundness of the post as he transferred his grip from her neck to her harness. Despite the hood's proximity to her face she was hit by the sharp heat of his sudden stink. Her head reeled. Dimly she realised that all these odours were the codes of systems fighting to control her: a powerhouse of instructions all delivered in the air. One demand was overlaid on another with conflicting commands. She felt acutely sick to her stomach as her body reeled but powering across all that was the crushing force of his weight and the imposition of his body on hers, unasked for and unexplained. The combination made her lightheaded and afraid. As the first seconds passed and she had taken several breaths he let her go. The sudden absence had her sliding to her knees, hands in front of her as she got her bearings though this was only in the service of his order. She scrambled to open the small door, lucky that the lock was broken. Inside, lights flashed errors, warnings, pleas. Even though it was barely useable the portal functioned on the last of its redundancies like a faithful old dog. She felt a moment of kinship with the machine, and then she looked up. It was only for a moment, only to see where he went after she felt the sudden draft of air that signalled his going. She was totally unprepared for what she saw, so much so that it took a while for the shapes and movements to resolve into anything she could understand.

The portal had been erected in a flat area surrounded by scrubby trees, all of which were now flattened or snapped in

371

half. There had been some human-made Imperial tents and huts. These were also flat, some smouldering. For a large distance in all directions the land was destroyed, greenery pounded into mud, huge areas blackened and giving off trickling smokes into the grey air. The smokes compounded in the windless, humid heat to create vast clouds that towered up to the sky. Through these clouds huge creatures moved, and humans – not many – ran and fought in their shadows with lesser beasts. Some were plants, like huge cats made of flowers and vines. Some were flesh and bone, raw golems with many limbs. Some were furred and scaled with features of so many animals she couldn't begin to name them. They were unified in their savagery and the splatter of blood that was everywhere, on everything. Their brutal sounds drowned the human screams, and she saw them speaking with a nonsense of human words, though not human voices. In hoots and yodels they called through the veils of smoke. One was playing with dead bodies as if they were toys, tossing them in the air over and over again; delighted, even as they fell to bits under the treatment.

She shut her mouth when she realised the air and smoke was filled with death. She looked to see where Tzaban was – turned and found him fighting only metres away from her with a strange dark creature half again his size. The claws on his hands had become daggers and the relentless, desperate violence of the struggle as he slammed them in the direction of the beast's shaggy neck told her there was nothing foregone about the results. Possibly she had minutes to live.

The imperative to obey him coupled with the realisation about what was going on and had her turning back to the simple clean emptiness of the machine. Even now she could not bring herself to destroy something others had so painstakingly crafted with skill and ingenuity. She supposed that would not be required in the circumstances anyway, and reached inside it to undo the couplings that held the power unit in place. With a few sharp tugs and curses the unit came out. It was akin to her crystal pieces and not so heavy – the size and measure of a large book.

Behind her she heard Tzaban grunt in pain. She turned and was knocked over, the wind shooting out of her as the creature he had fought came and hit her in a head-on charge. She felt a degree of strange satisfaction that the soldiers who had wished her gone would not have to receive more of this; that Isabeau in the city and Minna, far away, would not have to see these things. She landed on soft muddy ground on her back and lay there, trapped, flailing automatically to try and free herself.

The creature that had tossed her up had hit the post and was standing, stunned, about five metres from her. She stared at it as her mouth gaped and fished for air, pain in every bit of her chest and nothing helping her. She watched from that position as Tzaban appeared suddenly on its back, a military issue sabre in his hands as he hacked at the back of its neck. Wet, crunching noises, muted by the humid stillness of the air, reached her ears and then it slowly toppled over with a huffing sigh almost of relief. It looked rather like a horse once it had laid flat and expired. Atop its ribcage, more red than striped, Tzaban crouched, licking his hands and forearms. He paused, nostrils wide, and then jumped forward, the sabre held carefully at his side.

Before she could object or even draw the first whinnying breath, he had grabbed the front of her gear harness and hauled her back on her feet. Far in the distance an Imperial bugler sounded a retreat. His ears flicked towards it. 'Let's go.'

'My pack...' It was still on the ground where she'd left it, next to the dead thing's muzzle.

He let her go and went back to snatch it, swinging it on to his own shoulders. 'Put hood up.' He was back, helping her again, a constant assault on time and her space, then he was dragging her by the arm at a pace faster than she had ever gone on two legs though she felt light with the desperate need to stay close and safe, if that was possible. It seemed that he was her only hope here. They passed a human, still alive, unidentifiable as man or woman, part mired, part bound in twisting, tightening vines. She slowed but he jerked her onwards and over her protest said, 'No. Can't help them. Too late.' But she felt it hadn't been. A few sabre cuts would have freed them. She was certain.

They tore through the smoke and trees, going wherever the cover was thickest and taking a route away from the path which was busy with activity. She coughed and choked, half blind, her arm almost broken as it was yanked this way and that, her body just a burden in its wake. She ran and when she stumbled he dragged her by main force. This was so painful she always struggled to run again. She would have screamed but she hadn't breath to spare. At one point he kicked her knee out from the back, folding her leg up and pushing her down into some vegetation, then left her without a word. She put her arms over her head and rolled up into a ball. Through the darkness and the pressure she still heard the fight, snarling, screaming, his huffs and grunting booms of pain and surprise when something struck him and made him hollow for a moment, like a drum. She was beyond terror in a strange still place that suggested she should peacefully wait for death except for the nagging pain in her head where something hard was pressing into it. She shifted a little and felt that it was the bulky shape of the gun.

She had no memory of how it had got there but at least now she didn't have to go without a fight of her own. She primed the safety and pulled down the hood, standing up to get the chance of one clear shot.

The opponents spun and struggled, scales and skin, orange and green – she saw Tzaban flung back first into a tree trunk but it was a clear separation. Her hand closed and the lizard thing's top half blew apart into tiny, fleshy bits, spattering the leaves and the ground in a sudden shower of green, pink and red. The

374

gun felt warm and good, like a friend's hand in her hand. It hummed as it recharged. A sense of vital triumph spread like poison through her, seeping from that hand. A giddy lurch of safety and hope made her gasp and the air was fresh suddenly, for that moment.

She walked out of her place slowly, still on guard, ears straining as she covered the ten metres to Tzaban's position. A sweet, citrusy reek alarmed her, and she tugged the scarf's near dry cloth up over her nose again, stuffing it into the neck of her worksuit to hold it in place as she couldn't let go of the gun. Tzaban was moving at least. He leaned forward and fell to his hands and knees, breathing heavily. The sabre was missing and he was bleeding from his right leg but any other injuries were hidden in the coat of gore covering him. Yellow eyes stared at her. 'Good shot. Now you go first. Shoot everything.' But then he hesitated and a darkness came over his face and over his gaze at the same time. Belatedly, she realised it was a shadow as his face changed from agonised to a form of aweful dread. He said, 'Not that though. Don't shoot that.' He was mortally afraid otherwise she wouldn't have been able to hold herself back from turning and doing exactly that. She wanted to. She longed to. She wanted the feeling of being safe and powerful to go on and on, even if she didn't.

'No,' he said, quietly, even his breathing reduced to a whisper. His yellow eyes, sepia in the darkness that had silently grown over them, blinked slowly as they looked up over her head. Her skin felt like it was trying to escape by itself as she froze in place. She stared at Tzaban's face as she'd never stared at anything, like she could cling to him that way. The most minute movement of his nose side to side told her she must not move as his gaze remained huge and glued to a thing that must have been double her height, right behind her.

The gun butt became a hard, painful lump of metal in her hand. She looked only into Tzaban's eyes, the golden yellow of the master, as a tiny piece of her at the back of her mind told her that this was his version of the Empress' magic. The Karoo, of course, were not so different, or the Imperial lines were of similar lineage to them somewhere. She was wearing his collar around her neck, chained to him by the scent magic that sapped her will.

Even if her life now depended on turning around and shooting she could not do it – a greater compulsion made her stay, frozen rabbit stupid, watching his face for his instruction. The cool engineer inside her was charmed, amazed, impressed, marvelling and calculating as the animal part of her lay flat and domesticated entirely in its mortal terror. The bizarre contrast of two such simultaneous experiences was exhilarating in a way she had never experienced anything before, like joy.

She felt a second of immense gratitude to a universe that could contain so much wonder and power and strangeness even as she was completely at its mercy, all her pride and her sense of independence, of mattering, stripped away to reveal only a person in great danger whose hopes and dreams, whose consciousness could at any second be ripped away and made nothing without her permission. Without a warning. She wanted to fall on her knees and cry for the insight and the fear, the perfect feeling that even this was an illusion. She was part of a whole so majestic and strange it didn't even matter if she fell and was gone, because it was going on like a wave rushing in, always rushing on and on. Tumble today here or tomorrow or another time, she was right here and right now aware that she was eternal, only the small brief spark in a gigantic powerhouse fuelling unknown machineries to destinies so far beyond her ken that she could not even dream them in a thousand years of dreaming. She was so happy, and so sad. Happy to have glimpsed it and sad because she would never know its reach or its end.

'Come, child,' said a strange voice over her and behind her.

Tralane remained as she was, anchored by the pain of the gun, as Tzaban got up slowly from his fallen state. His every movement was strange, jerking to the obedience of unseen strings pulling him about. He got to his feet, and she saw that the leg wound was a human bolt shot. He must have taken it before they even went through the portal. Now his blood was dripping on the mud and the leaves, as it had since they had passed through. The red stood out against the brown and green and at that moment she saw that it wasn't blood, but a voice, talking to the mud, to the leaf, to the things it touched that were and were not Karoo. It was like the voice behind her, almost human. All living things talked this way.

She saw herself in her mind's eye rushing to write this down, to begin tests, to look for the grammar and the code, the patterns and the meanings. In her mind's eye she was at home, researching, days and nights passing unnoticed until the puzzle was solved, the mystery undone. All the days of her life in the University, years and breakthroughs, highs and boring lows when nothing seemed to come right and she doubted her sanity in even trying to make her slow, one-way magical brain understand something it could see only from the corner of its blinkered vision. And she would have stripped all the blinkers from them all, to see, to know what others took for granted. If she had been there. If she were not here, watching the magnificent and wounded man stagger in her direction to where he, like she, must obey the one who held him prisoner and who had found him by his blood.

She felt sure that if anything threatened him she would not be able to prevent herself trying to save him. Her loyalty was absolute. Her devotion unwavering. Remembering she didn't know him. Remembering she wasn't devoted to him at all.

He stopped beside her. She could just see him from the corner of her eye. Now he was so close she could feel the tension in him, fighting to resist and remain himself in a battle of wills that was entirely still and silent otherwise. The ties that bound them together were stronger than anything she had ever experienced. No human man, and not even her own children, exerted such a compulsion, nor such a clear two-way communication that took place beneath her understanding, though it was so certain she would have bet her life on it. Through it, she found she could perceive his war, even his opponent; a female of the Karoo, and more, a queen.

It was because of that she realised it was not she in mortal danger at all. She would always be spared, purely because she was as the queen was, female. Tzaban was the quarry and the charm, the bait and the threat. His life hung by silken threads of the blood's voice as it seeped into the queen's demesne and she listened to it through every quivering blade of grass and thirsty root.

The queen advanced a step and Tralane felt her warmth even through the heat of the morning. The shouts and cries of torture, mere metres away, might as well be in another world. Tzaban's scent beside her changed markedly and he cowered. They were engulfed by a primal presence so intense Tralane could only think of the word, 'Mother,' and, remembering her own mother as if she were simply a baby and had never been more, she began to cry silently with the sudden upwelling of love that she felt. All her intellect and the experiences of her life counted nothing in the face of being able to feel an emotion so completely as this. She knew why Tzaban was on all fours. She smelled his submission and adoration.

The engineering voice in her mind made its notes, hoping there would be someone to give them to later. It was the only thing that she felt good about, clinging to the one bit of her that the Mother did not command. She wondered if life was like this for Zharazin, if he could witness these forces at work as though they were simple tools before him, if he felt like she did when he used his abilities. A sense of violation had steered her imagination from dwelling on it, but she found to her total surprise that it was nothing like that, if it was the same. This was much more like dancing than fighting even though she was clearly the subjugated and either of the other two controlled her every move. It was the most inopportune time to think of it but she saw where her hesitancy over the infomancer lay now – in a place she didn't want to admit as her own. She thought of them all as rapists by any other name. An immediate shame came over her and she felt Mother's attention sucked in by it, as sure as a cat at the twitch of a mouse.

'Please, don't,' Tralane heard herself say as she tried to cower smaller, hiding under Tzaban, as if that were possible. Even so she felt him give a little and move in an effort to accommodate her. Tralane clawed the boggy ground, searching for a hole to hide in. Her eyes were squeezed shut so tightly that colours blared in her head. Her last thought as a stinking, body-hot blackness closed over her was that cat and mouse was an apt analogy, as cats had no appreciation of the hunt beyond their own play, but the mouse still went unspared.

CHAPTER TWENTY-FOUR

TZABAN

Tzaban felt the human woman crawl beneath him, moving so he did not crush her as he began the change in response to the queen's command. He tried, for her sake, to cling to his awareness of the outside world, though all of him wanted to surrender. Within the confines of the subtle, where he and the queen met through blood and scent deep beneath his surface, he felt the queen's spark ignite him. Slowly at first, then with accelerating power, he began to burn.

He slid in the mud, falling to his back, arched over the engineer's small form as the queen opened him and he began to bleed out into her sweet, welcoming veins, her blood running back against his tide, stronger, more alive, seeking all his knowledge, all his being. The burning became a fierce, bright pain that consumed him and he leaned into it, every memory incandescent and brilliant before him as it was borne away. The smallest things, held in such light became the veils of the goddess and her handmaids, the angels, beings of such beauty and intensity their presence within him was blinding, terrifying. Wave after exultant wave, they came, the legions of his soul, transcending him as she consumed them. The pleasure, the delight, the joy was beyond expression. Bound with the pain, it was a river of fire that swirled him under and brought him up. Beyond senses he was all that he had ever seen and then, in moments, he was done and no more than a drop of water in the queen's belly, her shimmering light all around him, her contemplation as fierce as the primal hungers that drove her.

He longed never to leave her, for her to carry him or to consume him entire in this warm beauty, a place of peace amid violence. He had been returned to fear's heart and it was divine in the ending of his terror. He never wanted to be let go. Instead take one step further and be ended in it. The bliss of her presence enfolding him was too profound and inside her he was completed, purpose done and passions spent, ferocity sated. But she held him apart and he was compelled to remain in the balance, enough of him to beg her, *Don't let me go,* as her attention turned to the woman below his back.

Somewhere Tralane was bleeding. The queen tasted, and waited. He saw eight rivers and one heart, a scattering of colours like fallen leaves on dry ground, wind blowing them closer together, all making an image he did not understand. The rivers joined. They flowed towards an ocean of green and this he knew – Karoo was green.

Then the swift tides that had brought him there turned. Against his will he was poured back into an agony of sensation, the queen's commands shackling him once more to a body she had re-sculpted. He tried with all his will to resist her but it was as useful as resisting a waterfall you were already immersed in. The shock of the return left him reeling in pain, paralysed by the venom she used to keep him still while she worked.

A final jolt, a final tearing, and he was alone on the mud. He rolled and got to his feet. The engineer was still there, rolled tightly, breathing like a frightened rabbit. Her fear stank so strongly he almost tore her head off on the spot.

Behind him, the queen withdrew and he didn't bother to

watch her form dissolving between the trees. Her interest in him was over and her mercy at an end.

TRALANE

Tralane tasted mud, smelled mud and opened her eyes to find them stinging and watering so much she could barely see. Spitting, she found her mouth was full of mud. Then she remembered why she had passed out and groped around mentally for the overpowering presence of Mother. Nothing.

She pushed herself upright and rubbed her eyes on her sleeves. The fetid cloth around her neck was nearly choking her and she yanked it off, unable to stand the obstruction a moment longer. A gasping breath filled her mouth and nose with horror. She groped blindly for the hood, surprise blocking the things that wanted to pour themselves into her mind: she tasted blood and the sharp tang of vomit, the salty and ill reek of open guts. A low noise, part scream part growl, pushed through her lips and she let it go, wishing that this unending assault of stenches would end. She wondered how she could find in it the traces of herself, and Tzaban, two other dead humans and an avalanche of plant fluids that she would have had to search the University botany log to discover. They were all there and they told her an alchemical story of mixing and mating. She set the kerchief hood in place and breathed inside her collar, finding her own strong scents of fear and sweat dear and sweet in comparison. Little by little, she blinked and cried her eyes clear, wiped her nose, spat her mouth free of grit though nothing got rid of the tastes. And then she was able to look about in the fading light.

The fighting was done and a stillness claimed the land, marked only by her own sounds and the drip of water from leaves overhead. She sat in a small clearing of crushed bush and grasses, trees flattened to make a rough round with her at the centre, and, at the edge of the clearing, the crouched and hulking form of the Karoo, his striped colours darker in the seeping twilight. She blinked and blinked again but she could not resolve what she saw into the shape she remembered. She wondered if he was alive but she saw him rock with breathing. She listened hard but only the patter of a new rain from grey skies sounded. Something had happened to her. Something had happened to him. As the droplets began to fall steadily they ran over her bare arms and she saw that her sleeves were gone, ripped clear off at the seams, and her forearm and underarms were covered in a set of red circular marks like the bites of tiny mouths.

Now that she saw them they stung. On closer examination they were more like rings of tiny needle punctures. Trembling a little with anxiety, she made herself check for any other damage but she was apparently unharmed. She looked about through steadily pattering rain, trying to get her bearings, and saw the cockeyed post of the portal gate to her left, then the other further off in the dimming light. The powerpack was still attached to her bag of tools. Some of these were squashed into the mud. She recovered them with shaking hands, slotting them into their places. It calmed her enough that by the time a few minutes had passed uneventfully and she was done she could get to her feet.

'Tzaban?' she called across the short distance between them, as quietly as she could. She daren't approach him, she found.

He straightened at the sound of his name and a chill ran through her, sending every hair on end. Her skin crawled with unease at the sight of him. He was still recognisable but where he had had deeply animal traits he had lost some of them. His ears were smaller, shorter, his tail gone. The mane was hair proper and his skin was human skin, coloured as it had been but in subtler shades. It was as though he had been diluted one third in the image of her kind.

He was still massive. Unfolding in the ragged remnants of his clothing he must have been at least two feet taller than she was. She found him strangely more alien now than she had before. He turned and faced her, a look of bitter disappointment so strongly written in his features that she almost backed off from it, though she knew it was not concerning her. He gave her his attention without the slightest willingness, even though it was absolutely hers. She saw no resentment, nothing to fear. He was however, in contrast to his former self, another being entirely. She knew then that he was somehow slaved to her and that Mother had done this.

Already even thinking about that thing as 'Mother' felt obscene. Now this was visited on them. To what end? Why was she not dead like the rest?

'Engineer,' he said finally, as if the word would break the deadlock of silence and horror growing between them. 'We should get to the camp before dark.'

Between them the lengthening shadows were already blue and purple. She saw only hints of colour in the world. 'Yes. Do you know the way?' The foggy dampness swallowed her voice, but he heard it.

'Yes. Come.' He waited for her.

She made her way across to him, aware now of her hunger and exhaustion from terror. She had felt so much of it in the last hour she had gone dead to it. A numb pragmatism sat in its place which he seemed to share. As she reached him he turned and set off at a slow pace into the murk between the trees. She trod in his footsteps, with an extra step every third, to catch up. After a time they came to a broad, muddy and rutted lane. Blood darkened the water and reflected the grey starlessness of the sky. He kept to the edges, pausing to turn and drag her up by her arm when she fell, her boot stuck deeply into the sucking boggy ground. As she fell against him she felt how warm and strong he was, and leaned into it for a second. He let her, though there was no care in his grip on her arm beyond what was required to keep her standing.

'Tzaban,' she said. 'How many people did you eat to become as human as you were?'

His yellow eyes, changed, looked down at her. Their pupils were huge in the near darkness, much larger than hers could ever be. His face was grim. After a moment he glanced down at himself and growled in a voice the texture of mud, 'Apparently not enough.'

She looked at him and then found herself laughing. It was partly hysterical, to be sure, but it was still so, so funny, his deadpan voice. Half his face cracked, mud falling off it, as his mouth lifted at one corner into a grudging grin. He turned and kept his hold on her upper arm, pulling her along with him as she sucked in helpless gasping breaths and tears slowly cleared her eyes of the last of the dirt.

She was quiet by the time they saw lights ahead. As they got closer, the burr of the cicadas in the trees was intense but they heard voices through it, unmistakable Imperial tones of guards changing duties. Tralane hesitated but Tzaban pulled her forwards, her arm aching.

'It is really them. Karoo don't use lights.'

Well, she thought, that answers that question. She was nearly too tired to care either way but she mustered enough force to tug at his hand, 'Let me go.'

He did so and she wished she hadn't said it. Walking after him was ten times harder than before. They finally made it to the high wall of broken fencing and she called out, 'Engineer Huntingore, reporting for duties! Hey there! Where is the gate?'

'Say, what?' There was some commotion on the other side as they debated, like she had, the truth of what they were hearing but then an officer's voice came forwards, short on words but forceful in them.

'The Empress' Consort is with me. Don't shoot him,' she

385

added as loudly as she could once they heard the rumble of wood being dragged about and saw movement as a makeshift door was opened in the line of staves and vines.

More orders to stand back, stand down, be ready and then she saw the flash of colours and glint of metal on shoulder studs and a helm.

'Engineer Huntingore, this way.'

She recognised his voice from the ball. 'General Borze.'

They were taken inside a compound with a black mass at its heart which she at once realised must be the pit. Around it a large number of small fires burned, giving off pungent smokes – another effort to curtail the effects of Karoo vapours she thought. The people around them huddled tight together, too much so for ordinary rest. The familiar expressions of horror that had faded to exhaustion were in every lit circle. Glances fixated unstoppably on Tzaban, slid away, returned balefully.

Only Borze appeared to remain his usual self – the only concession to disaster a flattening of his brow and the addition of another line above it. His raking gaze took in both of them. 'Come and take a moment's rest. We've drink and food. City food,' he added after a second, and escorted them with two other men to a battered tent where some chairs were set around a trestle table. Tralane clutched the chair as she sat, not trusting her legs. She was given hot watery wine with sugar in it and dry bread, a piece of hardening cheese set to the side. Borze gave her a look she didn't understand, taking her in perhaps, judging how to say what he had to say but when he spoke he was direct.

'What is the state of the portal?'

'Disabled,' Tralane said, holding up the powerpack for a moment. She thought for a second, watching Tzaban sip the drink given him and then put it aside. 'I could probably fix it, given a few days.'

Borze nodded. 'My orders are very clear. I am to escort you

into the structure and then guard it until you are ready to leave.' He passed a sealed paper to her. 'These are for you.'

Tralane reached for the heavy woven royal sheet and broke the wax sealing it with Torada's stamp. For a moment she was baffled to read Isabeau's regimental handwriting inked across it, then recalled Isabeau saying something about an apprenticeship, administration duties at the palace. Her hand started to shake, making it harder to read so she put it down on the table and flattened it with her dish.

After the declarations it said simply, 'Enter the structure. Assess its total worth and any functionality you are able to. Liaise with all other science officers on site. Prepare removable items for immediate withdrawal. Send an immediate report to me by range transmitter. Use the code enclosed in this letter. If the city cannot arrive to provide support, expect enemy arrival. In the event of becoming overwhelmed you are to employ standard sabotage strategies. The general is to follow your instructions from now on until Our arrival. Be careful.'

She assumed the last words had been added by Isabeau, although there was no way to know for certain. Torada's waywardness was not above personal niceties: her waywardness, Tralane thought, was not above civil war. When does one call that madness?

She looked up into the general's face. 'Do you anticipate this moment of calm will last, General?'

'No,' he said. 'The Karoo were stirred up by the storm gun. When it was used against the Mudlander assault they attacked without warning. None were unable to stand against them. I am sure you can guess it from your own journey here. Minister Alide was killed, as was everyone within a hundred metre radius of the gun itself and it was destroyed. They used fire. A weapon of their own that I cannot get any straight story of from those that witnessed it. I understand ... That is ...' He hesitated. 'You had some responsibility for that gun.'

'Yes. In a way.' She explained the supply chain of the crystals, why she had done it and the fact that she had not had firsthand experience of the actual weapon. 'I assumed it was done by specialised military engineers or, perhaps acquired some other way from another city.'

'The gun you carry on your person, is that the same?'

'I would think it is similar,' she said, glancing down at her leg where the item sat firmly in its holster, crusted with grass and muck. It occurred to her she should offer it to him, and she did so, explaining how it worked, but he handed it back to her.

'I'll stick with what I know. Besides, from what I hear you might need it.'

She swallowed, almost choking on her drink. 'There are enemies inside the artefact?'

'There are Karoo inside it, sometimes. It seems.' He spoke stiffly with the discomfort of one who hates suppositions and has had insufficient evidence. 'Not all of the science officers have returned. There are reports of – noises. Things. I can't send more men in with you. But you'll be all right most likely.' He gave Tzaban a long look and the Karoo lifted his head. 'What happened to you? Whatever it was it's not going to make anyone happier. You should both go now, before we run out of time or someone decides their bow hand is itchy. There's a lot of that around.'

Tralane's heart plunged in her chest with horror but she stood up, absently cleaning the gun off with the end of her scarf. 'How many have you lost here?'

'What you see is what's left. A hundred and ten, some casualties in the med tent.'

She almost didn't think she could have heard him correctly but she daren't ask for a repeat. 'Who is in charge of extracting the items for the city?'

'I am,' he said. 'But I received a message the city will come for them. Guess they won't be that fast given the portal is down.'

'How long can you hold out?'

'When we're down to the last twenty we're coming inside with you,' Borze said. 'The one door will be defensible for a while at least, whatever they do to the outside. The science team inside is forty-one, with some guards and most of the supplies are kept in there. Whatever's inside causing trouble hasn't come out.'

She understood his calm now. He didn't expect to get away from this. He was determined not to concede to Alide's position and call Torada mad, that she had led them here. There were too many dead soldiers on his account for that. He looked across at Tzaban again.

'Are you considered a traitor now then, among them?'

'No.' Tzaban got up too. 'If you stay inside the fences here, you will survive. At least, for now. Everyone wants whatever is in that case.'

Tralane noticed how careful he was to say that the Karoo did not have a way to decipher what was in the case, other than by consuming those that had. Her arms itched. Borze eyed her scratching.

'I don't know where your loyalties lie, Consort.' He managed the word without choking. 'Do I assume that once someone comes out with a discovery that we will be overrun again?'

Tzaban looked at him directly. 'I warned you not to come.'

The general looked down, absorbing this implicit confirmation. 'So you did. And now, do you have any more wise words? Did you, as they say, corrupt the Empress?'

Tzaban considered for a moment. 'I did not. She was already on the way here before I arrived, if you recall. I came to stop her. I was no match for her. Not as an opponent, at least.' He moved to Tralane's side. 'Rest now. There will be a chance to escape when the city arrives. You should send me word when it nears.'

Borze nodded. 'Is there some reason I should trust you?'

'I never lied to you,' Tzaban said. 'And the Queen has bound me to this woman. So whatever happens, my life is tied to hers now.'

'THIS woman?' Borze stared anew at Tralane. 'What for?'

'The Karoo have no engineers,' she said. 'But they can always use someone else's.' She didn't want it spelled out in front of her. Tzaban was guarding the queen's next meal. How far his loyalties went – that would be the taxing question to test next.

'The city should be anywhere but here,' Borze said grimly. 'Come, I'll take you to the door.'

They went with two guards at their backs, more to stop them leaving than help, Tralane thought. Tzaban was tense. In his new skin he was more readable now. His attention was on Borze, waiting for an attack. She saw the sense of it, Borze could use many reasons, all good, to dispose of Tzaban, and no doubt he had thought all of them through. However, even though they had been away for some time. his devotion to the Empress was too powerful. With Tzaban as Consort any idea of getting rid of the cuckoo in the nest was out of the question. They must instead just watch and wait to see what he became. For the first time, Tralane's thought stopped dead in contemplation of the Empress' actions. Normally it was beyond her to consider questioning the Imperial mind either, so far beyond that even to do so was a sacrilege. Her sense of violation was weaker here, however. What had seemed a great romance and a wonderful gesture in Glimshard looked downright odd, verging on the suicidal now. Torada had put Tzaban beyond reach, and so had his own queen. There was more to this than she understood, and she felt the uncomfortable sensation of a mental shiver as she tried to do so – the telltale sign that she was overreaching herself. She let it go, but sensed that she was not untalented for this, only that she had never paid attention to it before.

However the trek down the pit took all her attention. They went by the witchlight she cast and progressed slowly, watched over by archers. The cicadas were their only witnesses however.

At last they came to the thing itself and Tralane looked up at the enormous metal cone. A hatch in its side was tilted at an angle to the already angular ramp – dizzying in combination. She stood with her jaw open looking up at the vast, starless triangle it cut out of the night sky.

TZABAN

Tzaban trod carefully at the side of the engineer. He could smell and feel the tension of the others like a set of weighted sheets winding about him. His mouth still held the tang of the drink they had poisoned. He didn't blame them for that nor was it the first he'd tasted. The toxin made him a little slow and lightheaded.

The attack at the door was expected but even so he was slow to move, almost taking a dagger to the back as he and the guard staggered forward together. He let the man's impetus slam his head into the metal wall, helping just a bit, and straightened with the knife in his hand and an inch deep slash in his side. The engineer screamed as he pushed her behind him. An arrow thunked into the object with a sudden clang that startled everyone, even Borze, drawing his sword but on his back foot as Tzaban thrust the dagger forwards. They froze there at impasse for a few moments, the witchlight flickering weakly and immersing them in moments of darkness.

The woman said something and the general answered her, 'I'm sorry.' He did not stand down however. The guard looked to him for instruction, pale and shaking in intermittent flashes – Tzaban counted him useless, his nerve was gone.

'If you kill me there is no reason for Karoo not to overrun you now,' Tzaban said and the general's shoulders sank a notch in recognition of this truth. He straightened and put his sword away, signalled to his man to pick up the unconscious guard.

He looked beyond Tzaban to the woman. 'It was for the city. For you. She is not here. She doesn't know.' In the next flicker his face was that of a broken man but in the next second that had been replaced so that anyone who did not see it would never have known it was there.

Tzaban knew he had no more to fear from that quarter, turned and found the engineer with her back to the door, staring at them all with wide eyes. She had one hand stretched out towards him and he moved to her until she could grab his arm and use it to pull herself back to her feet proper.

'Let's forget it,' she said, though her wide eyes betrayed her generosity. 'A momentary lapse of judgement under duress. Now, the door.' She did something with her hand and the witchlight died to a tiny glow beside them so that archers would struggle from any distance to see it. She made sure she blocked it with her body.

A man's voice called out of the darkness close by but Borze made a signal for stand down. He did something near the opening and the metal flap opened, rolling silently into the wall beside it. From the interior of the metal cask an odour of long dead air escaped in a sigh, full of the tales of frightened people and their waste. The sounds of the jungle night echoed oddly from it, as if they rebounded, while within the echoes of distant, lost taps and knocks came tremulously out. Tzaban scented Karoo in there, yes, true, but males, not females. He was growling before he knew it until the stifled intake of breath from the engineer told him he was making her afraid.

Borze stood at attention, 'I wish you speed and luck. Empress' fortune with you,' he said, heartfelt with it because he was longing for them to go inside, away, become their own business and not his.

The engineer straightened and turned, went in, dismissing him with her silence. Tzaban melted around her, a protective shadow, finding his new body lighter, smaller, more agile – more suited to the interior universe of the vessel as his mind was more suited to understanding the people.

The door closed behind them with a soft hiss and a thunk that carried from one hard surface to another so that he could see suddenly, as if light had switched on, though there was no light but the witchlight of the engineer. They were on a platform the size of the commander's tent, surrounded by crates and cables, with a single exit leading on to a ramp that led down below the level of the ground outside. It opened into a larger space, and beyond that were warrens and halls that stretched further than he could grasp on that single echo.

There was a sound, a voice of a kind, and then lights came up in long streamers rigged from the walls and hanging from overhead like ropes made of fireflies.

'Hello?' someone called from further down, uncertainly.

'Carlyn? Is that you?' The engineer's voice was hoarse, near desperate as she replied, pushing around Tzaban to go to the edge of the platform where a waist-high rail prevented her moving further.

'Lane?' There was a sudden increase of light and then a hammering of feet on iron stairs. 'Sorry about the lights it's just a precaution.' A small female appeared at the top of the walkway and hurled itself forwards. Tzaban watched the women hug. The new, smaller one was exhausted from terror, he could smell it, and feel her fear as she looked over her friend's shoulder and saw him there. As she went rigid, Tralane noticed and drew back to turn around.

'I guess there's a lot to explain,' she said. 'He's all right.' It was the same voice she had used to reassure the general.

Tzaban felt a new emotion try to take possession of him; shame. He resisted it though it made him want to hunt and kill the other males immediately. Memories of his early days appeared with unpleasant vitality; blood on his hands, bodies hanging in the trees, intestines like liquid wax dripping down to the ground, a pure, puissant feeling of absolute victory in every vein and nowhere to put it so that his pleasure soon turned to frustrated rage and in the absence of further enemies upon whom to vent his wrath he had left to find a new purpose for himself. Instead, with every blood-rich victim, it had found him and led him here. A brief elation in his own mastery had been crushed now by the queen. This fresh denial of his value from the human only highlighted that, much greater, hurt. As the two women stared at him, finding only discomfort from him, he felt he ought to make a submissive gesture but, as ever, he couldn't. He looked back with his own contempt and disappointment in them and was pierced with sad longing for something he couldn't identify.

'There are things...' the other woman began hesitantly.

'He is here to protect us from them,' the engineer said firmly.

'But he is one of...'

'Yes. That doesn't change things. The Empress claimed him.' Her glance told him she knew well that claim was waning with every passing hour away from the presence but she didn't show it to the curly-haired one and the statement had the desired effect of ending the conversation. The one called Carlyn led them down the ramp, down stairs, along walkways, deeper into the structure of the building until they were well below the line at which it protruded from the earth. The grip of the ground muffled the echoes in new ways though where halls opened out into what he had determined to be a central, empty core, sounds travelled far and described areas of ever-increasing size.

Tzaban paid only tangential attention to their conversation, following because he must. They underwent the same uneasy meetings in several large rooms that smelled strange, of things he didn't have names for. All were lit by the strange light ropes, sometimes in the roof, sometimes the walls, sometimes all over the place. A few short fights sorted out those of the guard or the men who didn't want him around. A woman tried to argue for his removal but they were all too convinced by now that he was on their side – the forgotten seal of the Empress on his hand persuaded them. He found it funny, to take a mark like that as a token. The only marks worth considering were scars or those in the scent and taste of a thing. Tralane apologised for him, made peace, though he never did. He remained at her side, ate what she gave him, drank when she gave him water. Few people spoke to him but he spoke to them if they wanted it. He listened and watched. Wherever they went he hunted the other Karoo, but they had gone far into the depths.

That night they were given bunks in a large room where a group called Team B slept and ate, ordered their doings. When they were alone there, setting up the nothing that Tralane had brought with her, she asked him, 'Do you think there are Karoo still in here?'

'Yes,' he said. 'Males only. They have lairs set up where humans do not yet go.'

'Are they – what do they want?'

'They will hunt from there,' he said. 'They are territorial so they will also hunt each other.'

'They hunt us?'

'Your friend said you already lost five here.'

She paused and brushed back her hair. 'Can you find them?'

'Yes,' he said.

He saw her think about it, the dead bodies behind her gaze, the calculation of missed days, names, who.

'Do you want me to?'

'Just guard for now,' she said. 'Guard everyone. Can you?'

'Everyone – maybe.' He went to scout the place and discover what *everyone* meant. He found three 'teams' living in different areas of the interior and most of that he didn't understand except as a series of halls and rooms in a building bigger perhaps than the entire city of Glimshard, which was until now by far the biggest civilisation he had seen. Ancient air there spoke of foreign bodies. The vines of the cables and lightlines were the teams' doing. Sometimes rooms were lit and powered by magic but he had no means of moving this himself and avoided those. A couple of times he came across trails of the other Karoo, one fresh enough to be within the hour. He sat with the scent there a while until he was sure of what he was up against; he wished he had his previous form but instead of his claws he held to the weapons he was given by the humans; spear, swords, daggers, a bow and arrows, a sling though no shot for it. He constantly circled back on himself, patrolling for Tralane, though he rarely revealed his presence to her or any of the others, merely watched their activities as they read, studied, talked and regarded the empty darkness around them with fearful eyes. Thus he did not report the locations of the human remains when he located them. He thought they might try to recover them in a fit of sentiment, and they had been set out in places for ambush.

He came back to her a day later to find her outraged at his long absence. After she had finished shouting at him, growing in confidence as he didn't respond, he said he could not protect the outlying groups unless they all convened together. She said this was impossible and he agreed to patrol and to do his best, but she must accept anyone straying beyond a small range would do so at their own risks. People came up to ask him how they could detect whether or not they were being hunted at any given moment and he stared blankly at them, until at last he realised they thought it was an on and off state of affairs. It pleased him quietly to see them relax more when he appeared now.

A few days later he found a dead male Karoo gutted and bled out, the body hung and stretched out like a sheet across a route he took often. A sign for him. He left it untouched and when he returned to Tralane that night he moved his bed next to hers. She barely noticed until the last moment, she was so absorbed in thought. He saw the surprise in her face. She saw the flat determination in his. He followed her closely for the next forty-eight hours and when he was done watching her meticulous ways, softly spoken conversations and careful, precise methodology with her magical instruments and her intellect he felt himself encompass her, as though he was a room and she was its tenant. He understood this might mean what humans referred to as love. Of all the things he had seen here this was the only promising information.

So began days of burial that turned into weeks.

CHAPTER TWENTY-FIVE

MINNABAR

Minna was taken to the city of Spire on small aircraft with multiple stops in which her guards and the crew were changed. The gave her dry, plain bread she found tasteless and water at two-hourly intervals. At each stop a crew woman took her to wherever the latrines were and gave her two minutes with a turned back in which to do whatever she had to do with her hands chained in front of her. The aircraft were universally cold and she shivered so hard sometimes that her teeth chattered. She slept a few minutes here and there. On the final leg they at last found a seat for her and the bread was supplemented with a piece of cheese. On their arrival at Spire she was taken to a doctor, pronounced fit and well, then stripped, showered and given plain overalls to wear with matching boots and belt. Her hair was cut off to a half inch above her scalp so that she matched every other person she saw. It was the only time she cried, to see the long, coiling brown tresses fall on the rough tiles and be kicked away into a corner. Everything else only made her angry and the anger formed itself up into a cold ball at her frozen core.

They marched her to a small room where a woman and man in white overalls talked to her at length about her life, her mother, her family and Glimshard. They noted all her answers on a recording device that floated in the air like a small disc, a magical thing she'd never seen before. She asked questions about it and they answered with the flat, functional politeness she had learned to expect from them. When she lied they showed no sign of noticing it and she spun a good deal of lies around the few facts she supplied, thinking that they must have some knowledge about her or they wouldn't have bothered daring a raid of that kind. She stuck to the truth when it came to engineering, but she did not mention the goggles. They asked about weapons and caught her out when she tried to lie about the gun.

'Don't lie about your abilities,' the woman said, as though she really could not care less. 'I have a talent for detecting the particular strengths and connections of an individual. We already know you are a Sircene of particular skill in devices and arte-facts. Your mother's fortitude is in complex systems. You have a sister, who is off-the-charts talented at analysis and logical spellcasting. We would rather have captured either of them but you will prove very useful to our military applications division. If you have no further stories to spin about your reprehensible upbringing and immoral social acts then we are recommending you for immediate deployment under armed guard. Any escape attempt will be met with lethal opposition. You will now be taken to see the Empress before you are assigned to your post.'

'Kiss my ass,' Minna said, staring back with her own stub-born expression.

They ignored her. She was marched out of that room and taken in a car that was pulled by people in a chain before it to a low building that matched in every way the regimented streets and typical structures that made up everything she saw of the city. It was built around principles, she saw that immediately, and loathed them. Her head felt light and cool, but when she stepped out into the air for the first time it was warm and humid, like a soft slap of reproof. They took her indoors and she felt the sudden strange certainty of an Empress' presence nearby. It was as cool as the air was hot and to her it had a clammy touch in it and a weight she could not adequately describe. She felt herself pressed down as if she was being impersonally ironed out. She resisted it as best she could but with the horrible recognition that this would not last. The indomitable power of the presence would simply wait for her rebellion to exhaust itself and then replace everywhere in her it had lived with grey uniformity, even temper and bland interests. Spire was named by Glimshard as the Temperate Tropic but she renamed it in her head, the Flat Fetor. It was, she realised, exactly like being mired in her anti-nature. Then she wondered how much of that nature was down to Torada, but she couldn't know and in this minute of confusion she was ushered into the presence itself.

Minna bowed automatically and heard someone snicker. She straightened up and actually looked for the first time, instead of moving on autopilot, and found herself face to face with a well-built middle-aged woman with greying hair cut in the same harsh crop as her own. It bore a severe, intent expression that seemed to be able to bore right into her every thought with disapproval. Spire. For a minute she could not remember the Empress' name, not that it mattered, as she was not of a status to use it.

'We have no hierarchical gestures here, Miss Huntingore.' The Empress' voice was surprisingly pleasant, almost warm. It was rich and cultured, with only fine traces of the accent that otherwise blunted every word at both ends.

Minna looked at her stupidly. She didn't know what 'Miss' meant but in the spirit of dislike for the place she took it as an insult. Since it seemed normal to do so she looked where she liked but was unable to avoid being drawn back to the Empress' face until it was the only face in the world. Grey eyes, like silver discs, with black hearts. A tight pressure inside her skull suddenly made her want to be sick but she made herself stand, closed her jaw and filled her mouth with her tongue so it couldn't happen. She tried to do the same thing with her mind. The world went dark. She heard someone say in a dispassionate tone, 'If you stress her too much she might lose her capacities.'

The pressure ceased and her sight returned. The silver eyes stared into her and the Empress said, 'You work for me now, Engineer.'

Minna nodded, daring nothing more, not even breathing. In the darkness she had felt herself starting to dissolve. The terror of it was only now beginning to hit her but it met the back of her tongue and stayed down.

They sent her to work with the mages and engineers of their military systems unit – a total contrast to her life before. Here she learned that men and women did not exist as she understood it. Their gender was of no significance and any reference to it was erased. Instead they had identities only as drones, or, if they were friends, then they were called 'mates' but nobody was mated to each other. Sexual behaviour was outlawed anywhere other than within the home where they lived in 'caches' of those who had been determined relatively suitable. This was like a web, but one chosen for you, not one you made yourself. It was like a home, but without families or family ties, and the responsibilities of leadership such as were required passed each month to a new member, so long as they were over the age of wisdom. There was no argument, no dispute, no preference save small things or what biology could not be made to surrender, such as sexuality. Minna learned that everyone believed they had done away with structures of control and she smiled at her workstation, because around her all she could see was the covert, subtle work of the bitterness that this regime pressed out of people. It leaked everywhere. And everything that was pushed under by the presence had only taken on another form, which she came to understand, like a foreign language. It said the same things however. If she flirted by a single look or expressed her feelings with a moment too long here, a quicker response there, her signals were picked up. Superficially, they were disliked. Underneath though – underneath she knew it was all the same and this gave her the confidence to keep face with the Spire world's apparent peace.

The Spire talented were divided by their affinities into work-groups. Although they were cared for by the state in a similar way to Glimshard's family-administered systems, they were discouraged absolutely from personal fulfilment outside the group, and from forming relationships other than mateship. Mateship loyalty was, as a result, the only emotional currency worth a damn, Minna found. Group belonged to the state but mates was for you and in spite of whatever silliness was spoken routinely in public about all drones being treasured by the hive or some other metaphor like that she knew it was mere words. Group mattered only where mateship flourished. If they conflicted this was soon arbitrated out of existence with a reshuffle or some other fudge of the rules – they must have learned not to try to live by the letter of the law already.

Minna noted these things only so far as she needed to in order to function as the best possible group member she could for the days she spent there learning their ways. She had already formed the intention of beating this vile Empress at her own game. Loyalty she could have in spades, it meant nothing to Minna. The Empress' creating conformity and obedience via the method of hugely lowered impulses caused her visceral horror. She saw how at odds this was with Torada's regime, and realised well therefore that this was an enemy in truth. Spire could not have been less open to Torada's ways and could only, in analytical terms, assign her as pernicious, a threat and an unbearable challenge. What a meeting between the Empresses could be like she couldn't imagine. It seemed an impossibility.

Meantime she was set to work on parts of blueprints and fragments of machinery. She was under close supervision – they watched her every facial twitch – but she decided not to hold back on what she could see with these, filling in the missing information that the mages had attempted and failed to bridge with invention or guesswork. The tasks themselves were fascinating and working on them a pleasure in itself. However, as she went on she began to understand what it was that she saw, even when they interrupted her flow with other less suited tasks developing spells for use with existing failsafe systems.

She woke in the night two days later, her eyes still full of the dream she had been having in which Spire had created a huge airfleet and had gained total command of the skies. The sound of the engines had been so loud, so real. Her bunkmate's snores slowly gave her a clue as to how that might have come about but as she lay there, unable to go back to sleep, she considered it again and felt sure that these were things she had had her hands on. She could not be sure of course, but the context made sense of what she had examined. Helping them galled her, but she had a faint hope in knowing that so far she had met people who were competent, but none with much vision.

Her hopes on that front were dashed a few days later when she was summoned again to the presence and told she would be sent to the pit site with an elite group of commandos. She was to go on site and recover information for Spire with the team. The only reason to do this was because someone somewhere had domination plans very heavily in mind and whatever she had done lately had been approved of. She was the filler in their gap. That pleased her. It was leverage, though she wasn't sure how to play it. For now her honesty had bought her position.

Minna knew that her mother and even Isabeau might already be there. This filled her with excitement and hope until the moment of departure when she was fitted with a harness and a device she recognised as an explosive. There was enough to blow open a steel door.

The group leader, a man much older than she was, said to

her, 'If you attempt to communicate with the enemy you will be killed. Every member of the unit has a trigger to this and they will use it. Make no mistake. You're group because you're here, but you're nobody's mate.'

Minna felt the brief moments of genuine camaraderie from the previous days vanish as if they'd never been. She glanced around faces that had become known to her across workdesks and calculation tables. Most glanced away, unwilling to meet her eye. She tried to detect shame but she wasn't sure. A couple returned her gaze evenly, with the classic Spire dispassion that said it was nothing personal. She already loathed that look most of all. She returned it with plain contempt. It hurt her to know other engineers could be like this about one of their own. Soldiers, sure, but talentkin? It went against everything she had known in Glimshard. But if it was so, then it was. Mentally she pushed them all off a cliff and out of her consideration. She made a cursory examination of the belt, to be sure that only a deliberate trigger would set it off. Not all explosives were stable or well made. In that at least they had been efficient.

Minna found that the bomb would work. The transmissions spells were ones she had made herself just the day before. She knew they had rigged it so that if she tried to remove it it would explode. She had worked on that too, only at this moment realising what the complex spell had been for with an irony that made her clench her jaw until her teeth hurt. She looked at the others but there was no sign where the triggers might be located. They could be anything from a button to a word. She lifted her head. At least nobody here was trying to sweet talk around the reality. That she could respect and deal with. She was given a water canteen and a food parcel but was manacled for the journey.

They took a larger craft than she had ever seen before. Because of its size it was located outside the city on its own long, flat runway. A large ground crew attended it. As Minna waited she tried to see what they were doing and how it worked. It was nothing like her mother's tiny Flit but she thought that the engine worked on a similar principle although it seemed far bigger, turning fans encased in huge cylindrical mounts. Those on their own looked beyond the reach of what she'd seen in the laboratory. They must have found them, she thought, enviously.

The journey was not as long as she thought it should have been. This led her to think that perhaps her trip to Spire had been less than direct. The reason for that she couldn't understand. The new plane made a terrific roaring sound and was colder than the others. They had put her in heavy overalls, lined and padded, but she was nearly frozen solid by the time the pilot addressed them over the com.

'Landing site in view. Runway strip appears compromised. Taking a flypast to check it out.'

The group commander undid his harness, got out of his seat and went forwards into the room where the cockpit was located. Minna heard a lot of talking, but the noise meant she couldn't make out any words. She gathered from the tones that the commander and the pilot were arguing. Then the commander came back and sat down again. He made some order and the soldiers in the group prepared their weapons.

'Landing will be rough,' the commander said.

'Approaching now,' the pilot sounded tense. 'Expect enemy activity.'

Minna looked around the faces in the row opposite her and saw them, pasty and grey, eyes closed or staring fixedly at something in the hold. She checked her harness – it was rock solid. A sick feeling of intense fear took hold of her – that even if the landing went safely enough some accident could still blow her up. She closed her eyes too, not wanting any last images to be of these people.

What followed was a confusion to her in which she expected every second to be the final moment. The engines started to scream, the plane shuddered violently, bounced, hit the ground hard. All along noises of breaking, snapping outside. Then they spun with a jerk that made her head slam into the rest and continued to slide and spin with a screeching that replaced all the lesser cacophony. Screaming slowly broke through this, and there were more bounces and judders before everything stopped with a sudden, final impact. She gathered they were on the ground and pressed the release catch on her harness.

It took several seconds to get her bearings as she struggled to get up and realised they were listing to the side at about twenty degrees. A few of the other passengers were moving too, but some hung limp in their seats, heads down. To the rear of the craft was a huge hole – the entire back section was gone and three or four seats with it.

'Keep going,' said a voice by her ear. She looked around and saw the pilot – only a few years older than she was. Her face was grim and marked with black streaks, burns and the look of one who won't tolerate any argument. She shoved Minna in front of her, ignoring the rest of the people, and Minna had to get out of the way, which meant going along the aisle to the ripped maw, passing others who were still stuck in their seats, unconscious or stunned, sliding on the sloping floor, until she got to the end where there was a two-metre drop at the end of a long, gouged muddy trail in the ground. Minna sat down on the edge trying to get her nerve up but a heavy shove at the base of her spine sent her out into the air and then face down and winded into thick, lush grass and heavy earth.

When she got to her feet the pilot was already there beside her. Heavier, taller and obviously much better trained than Minna, the woman grabbed Minna's harness and began to haul her along. 'Move, move!'

'But, what about the others?' Minna had all her abilities tested just to keep on her feet as they battered through heavy vegetation, across a sunlit field where the grass was shoulder high and tangled with narrow, clinging weed. She saw the pilot's name stenciled on the back of her flightsuit; Dahn, Flightcrew Captain.

'They've got their orders, I've got mine,' came the reply, followed by a stream of swearing Minna barely understood. She soon realised they were out of sight of the plane.

'No! Wait. They'll kill me. We have to go back!'

'No they won't.' The pilot dragged some object out of her flightsuit and showed it to Minna, then stopped long enough to clip it firmly inside Minna's suit. 'Signal disruptor.'

'Wait. What?' Minna stumbled as she was dragged again.

The pilot made her go further, then sit down, and covered her up with grass. Then she looked firmly at Minna. 'I've got a job to do. You sit tight.'

Minna made a sound, not large enough to be a word, and sat very still. After a short while there was an explosion big enough to shake the ground and it occurred to her that she could go, run now while nobody was looking, if that promise of the signal disruptor was true. But she found she was afraid and she wanted the pilot to come back. Spire had done this, she thought, made her weak, but gunfire came, burst after burst of mechanical ballistic weapons, and she flattened herself even more, feeling water soak slowly into her legs from the ground.

She was sick and moved a few feet away to get from the vomit, crushing weeds that gave off a vile, pungent odour and left little hairs sticking to her clothes and skin where they itched. A scream, and another, and another shook her through the grip her arms had over her head. She could only listen as the sounds of the crew's combat grew sporadic, weak, then silent. She waited, counting seconds to try and guess the time elapsing. After five minutes she wondered why she had faith that the pilot would return at all. Some of the screams had been female, she was certain. She had almost worked up the nerve to try and look over the grass to where pops and bangs suggested the fuselage of the plane was still burning when a rustle closer to hand made her freeze.

Hopefully, she looked up through her fingers and saw the familiar colour and shape of a soldier's overalls part the grass. She was about to speak when she noticed that the man's head was hanging at the wrong angle for any living person and his eyes were rolled to the white. The body moved towards her and then was discarded with a contemptuous gesture by the creature that had carried it there. It sat, a huge, dark brown and purple hairless beast, like a horse that had been remade into a wolf. To her terrified gaze it seemed bone-skinned. Karoo she thought. This must be. It was less human than Tzaban had been, and much less decorative. Its head was the size of a horse's, and the same shape, but narrower, with a toothed muzzle, long whiskers and large, yellow eyes. Blood adorned it freely and ran from a wound in its side. It had huge hands instead of paws at the front. It sniffed the air with nostrils that flared wetly, panting in the muggy heat with its tongue hanging out like a strip of raw meat from the side of its mouth. It sat down on near fleshless hindquarters and stared at her.

She couldn't move her hands from her face. She couldn't move at all but she knew she'd peed her pants. Seconds passed and it sat there, regaining its breath, its huge, ugly ears shifting around, listening though the eyes never stopped looking at her. She didn't understand what it was doing or why it stopped. Then it glanced behind it and shuffled quickly out of the way to let something pass. Minna recoiled, leaning back. Her throat was too tight to breathe and she longed to pass out but she couldn't. She didn't want to know the next part but her fingers wouldn't move to entirely cover her eyes either. What she did see next made no sense.

The pilot, Dahn, walked through the grass towards her. She paid no attention to the creature at all as it scooted out of her way, belly low, shifting out of Minna's tiny slit range of vision. 'Okay, let's go.'

Minna turned her head a fraction. She could not move more. She saw Dahn make a tiny jerk movement with the tip of her nose and the creature vanished into the grass, heading in the direction she had indicated. The pilot turned back to Minna, her dark eyes impatient. 'You get up now. Everything's fine. They won't cause you any trouble. We need to make it to the rendezvous with Glimshard at the burial site.' She crossed the metre to where Minna sat, ashamed and afraid, and put her hand out. 'Come on. It's only a half a day's walk from here. When we get there you'll be safe.'

Minna's mouth tried to form the questions that were zinging around inside her head but then again, she was too frightened for that too – because if Dahn could make that thing obey her then ... Well, she didn't know what then but it was bad even as it was good in its way. Her hesitation was too long for her new helper. The woman, tall and strong, reached down the last inch and took hold of her wrist firmly, prising her hand away from her head and beginning to pull her with a force that suggested she'd be glad to drag her if that's what it took. 'You must move now. We can't stay here. Those ... The animals that did this. They'll come back. I drew them off but they can come anytime.' The last line sounded like a promise.

Minna felt her arm jerked so hard something in her elbow gave for a moment and she shrieked in new alarm. It came out as a faint bleat and then she was on her feet and stumbling after Dahn's confident stride into the grass that stretched up over both their heads.

CHAPTER TWENTY-SIX

TORADA

Torada stood in the unfamiliar confines of the city's flight deck and marvelled at the ease with which the engineers and mages there moved among the architectures of light that surrounded them. She had never had the faintest inkling of how the webs of symbols and shapes that they wore like auras could mean anything. No matter how long she had stared at them they remained pretty lights in the air. That didn't spoil the fascination of watching them change and glow under the grooming hands of the experts now. She revelled in their mastery as if it were her own.

Isabeau Huntingore in particular attracted her attention with a feeling it took her a while to decode until she realised she wished that she were the engineer, moving among the others with such patience, grace and authority. Isabeau was even younger than she was, but already a mistress of her talent. Torada knew she was mistress of her own, although, as she rubbed the itchy rash on the inside of her palms, she wasn't sure if that was changing. It was Isabeau's innocence she envied. What she wouldn't give for five minutes inside that head, experiencing such flow without the guilt and the suspicions that harried her daylong. She indulged herself with the longing for thirty seconds which

410

might plausibly be explained away as fruitful observations and then signalled that she wished to speak.

Isabeau joined her at the helm station. From here, although it was deep within the city's heart, they could see the full vista of the landscape over which they were suspended. On the magepane the city was drawn on to the scene with artistic simplicity, about the size of Torada's hand, and its shadow was displayed upon the ground. Since it was a topdown view at the moment, the sky could not be seen but with a gesture this could be changed to any angle. The dark cut-out of the towered mass blew at a slow, stately creep across the eastern plains, following the line of the old trading road and darkening it and several fields beyond it like a vast stormcloud. Behind them the strange earthen print of the base disc sat in odd symmetry atop the low hill that had given it support for so many years. She was glad there was no sign of damage in their wake, but she deliberately did not look back too far, lest she see people who had not reached the city in time and who now faced the arrival of the Spire army. She must trust in Spire's belligerent attitude to rules and formalities that they would be treated fairly and kindly. For most of them it was unthinkable that one arm of the Empire could turn against another. She was counting on that now.

She turned her head and realised Huntingore was looking at her – rather bold in the circumstances but she was already used to Isabeau's desire to be pragmatic overriding her more social instincts. 'Engineer, please report.'

Isabeau's face was ash white with fatigue but she showed no other sign of it. 'All systems are within functional norms. Structural support fields are stable. The power output remains steady. However, I believe it would be prudent to move higher, although the winds there may push us slightly off course.'

Torada nodded, hearing that things were okay. She knew there had been a few casualties during the take-off but nothing like she had feared. Most were down to walls or furniture falling down and crushing people. Exhilaration filled her again as she revelled in the moment of her daring. After over two centuries of dormancy who would have wanted to consider waking the city again and taking to the air? But she had never doubted she would.

A messenger in her colours squeezed in through the door and curtseyed before her, just to the side, trying not to look at the amazing map of the landscape as she begged Torada's attention.

'Speak.'

'Highness, the portal to the east has been shut down by Engineer . . . by Professor Huntingore. Captain Gau Tam sends word and will take the rest of the journey on foot and horse to the south to meet with you there.'

Torada felt her lips tighten – another tell she must practise eradicating. Too long at peaceful complacence had left her vulnerable in this way. 'Thank you,' she said absently. 'I thought this might be so.' Then she looked pointedly at Isabeau.

'We can change course, but to pass the mountains we would have to gain more than four thousand metres of height and create a shell to protect the city from the cold. The air will be thinner, but it will be manageable.'

'Do it. Move south without delay,' Torada said and hesitated, seeing that Isabeau had more to say.

'We need to create the shell. It should take about twenty or so hours as long as there are no serious problems. We cannot move much higher until then.'

'Do all you can, Engineer. I don't want Spire arriving before us, though I have done all I can to delay them.' She considered if there were more she wanted done, and decided it could wait. For a moment she smiled, seeing Hakka's face rapt as he stared at the image on the pane – the world moved beneath them, so small, as if turned by will alone.

Her moment of pleasure in his awe was spoiled when she realised the time. As the Pantheon of the Empress spread out its mantle in her mind she strangled what was left of her pity, guilt and worry over what she had done. She tilted her head and pretended to enjoy the view, a hand resting on Hakka's arm the only sign to others in the room that she was anything other than properly attentive. Meanwhile, the Pantheon within her expanded until the true and distinct presence of the other Empresses filled her absolutely. They might be at war, but they were still one.

The disharmony was shocking even though she knew to expect it. Within that moment Spire rounded on her and pounced, accurate as an old queen cat. 'You little upstart! There was no consensus on the departure of Glimshard. What about your responsibilities to the Commons? Do you think this is a pleasure cruiser to dispose of at your whim?'

The onslaught of her fury was like a punch in the face, and three others were in cautious alignment with her which only made the blow more penetrating. Torada could do nothing but focus on her own centre and weather the storm of disapproval and, she fancied, loathing. It hurt her deeply and she reflected that they call it excoriation for a reason – these things cut your heart out – and after it's rather strange to go on living; it proves, as Night had taught her, that whatever is having its heart chopped up and hand-delivered to it on a fancy dish is not what you really are. You're not dead.

It still hurt. All deaths must, she fancied, using the moment to muse on it. This step-back from the carnage gained her the required perspective. It was a trick she had grown so used to it was automatic. She found herself in the still and calm centre that nothing touched, even the Eight.

'How small everything looks,' Hakka said, disarmed by the sights in a rare moment of charm.

'Indeed,' she managed, her fingers digging into his solid warmth and borrowing strength. She was grateful for him for the millionth time. To the Pantheon she said, calmly, 'I believe that my best judgement for all has been in action during this unusual time. The terrible losses that my city and I have experienced in our attempts to secure the artefact cannot be sustained at any greater length. Our finances, our spirits, are depleted. To ensure the succession of any powers contained in the artefact we considered it essential to move there as quickly as possible.'

'And marrying that filthy animal?' Spire was again in alignment with five of the rest, their allegiance with her in range from total agreement to uneasy suspicion. 'Can you imagine you are brokering some peace with a petty little warlord like those wretches starving on the Steppelands you have failed to see prosper? Karoo know nothing of civilisation, even so meagre a notion as honour. We counselled you to imprison him. Where then your purpose in this madness?'

All Empresses wished her to answer, their focus so intense that she must, and only hours of preparation permitted her to do it. Speaking in the face of them was as arduous as climbing a mountain.

'I did make a bargain with him, but not a treaty. I bargained for knowledge of the Karoo. The wedding was purely for show to calm the people and show that by embracing what is strange and unknown there can be many benefits...'

The rest of her speech flew out of her head as Spire's conjunction of rage again arrowed in on her. 'Benefits?! What benefits can there be from a breed that has nothing to offer the Empire but death? Although I have heard of your unusual tastes in these matters, Torada, I cannot believe you sate your lust purely to mock the rest of us, whatever trance you have put your people into.'

Torada stood. The impact of their outrage was so enormous that she seriously did wonder what she was doing though it also amused her to find Spire so shaken she was now taking things personally. 'It is the reports from the artefact, and from my general, which have convinced me that the Karoo are open to bargaining with us over the contents of the...'

'I cannot believe you!' Their unity overran her effortlessly, voiced by Spire but she was merely the mouthpiece of the many. 'What could they possibly want with it? It is simply unfortunate that it is within the limits of what they consider their territory.'

'Well it certainly isn't *our* territory,' Torada replied and found, to her surprise, three others in concert with her. They gave her the impetus to continue. 'We need him as a go-between. The Karoo, as he has told me and proven, are relentless, vicious and territorial. Nothing could deter them from defending their territories, so attempting to secure the item by force was a poor decision on our part.' She paused to let the 'our' sink in a little, then continued. 'However, they are open to deals when the deal includes life magic. They are life elementals, at their root, and that is the only currency they understand.'

'Is that what you will call it when they suck the blood from your neck?' Spire said, but her ire was dampened.

'I doubt I will call it anything,' Torada said and briefly found a seven alignment attuned to her dry moment of humour. She used it. 'Since you are already sending your own agents to aid me, *Jagorin*, I feel confident we will manage something together.' The magic word, 'together' gained her at last, an eightfold accord. Even Spire wanted to act in concert more than discord and, as Torada had expected, she also had no intention of disabusing the other Empresses of her true actions within Glimshard. Torada and she had entered into a conspiracy of two with their treachery and Spire must comply now, or face scorn and the retribution of the law for taking arms up against a sister state.

Torada consolidated rapidly. 'The Karoo must face us in unity or we will lose the ground and the artefact to them.'

They agreed and lingered in the eightfold concord a moment, enjoying its relative peace, though a moment later they were asking why she seemed so different and River silently observed that she had matured very rapidly lately and must be congratulated. They swirled, at levels below words, searching out curiosities, and Torada had to remain relaxed and unshielded as they moved around, aware that much as she had trained so hard to place her secrets out of their reach they might stumble across one, as she might find theirs. To discourage such behaviour she did not pry, and this prevented them from being as nosy as they might have been, except for Spire. But Torada knew her ways. She let Spire have a victory – she let her see the truth of what Eth's loss had meant to her. Then, in that private space where she least wanted Spire to be, she said to her, quietly, 'You will pay for this.'

The reply came faster than she anticipated. 'I have found your agents in my city, girl. Don't overstep your place.'

So, Torada thought, we are prepared to fudge things over with each other for the sake of harmony. But that leaves a lot of agents and the agendas of the Infomancy still to consider. She might play games with the Empresses but the infomancers owed their loyalty to the state as a whole and they would not aid any faction warfare, at least not in public.

The Pantheon closed slowly and she found she was still clinging to Hakka's arm, but more like a frightened girl now than an Empress. She made herself let go, rubbing her itching palm against her free hand for a moment before making that stop too. 'That is enough delight for now,' she said, and saw Mazhd enter the room and look about for Huntingore. He noticed her only second, his bow to her rushed and awkward. How peculiar he was so unguarded, she thought, studying him more closely. Perhaps Night is right to suggest using him as a lever to open that very sophisticated can of worms that is the Infomancy. She says he is biddable as long as matters lean in his favoured direction. Let us see.

To Isabeau she said, 'We will leave you to your business. From now on the centre of my command will be located at the

Infomancy.' She pretended not to see the suddenly straightening backs and turning heads at this announcement. 'Mazhd will remain with you since you require expert communications assistance. We will trouble Shrazade Ourselves. Mazhd, you are not to leave Engineer Huntingore's side on any order but mine.'

He looked at her and bowed his head, one second too long. Ah ha, Torada thought. So I am right. They have their own agendas beneath mine and their own little wars. She let him know that she expected his loyalty to her first, using that language of glances that all the mental adepts easily shared. He looked down for a second, allowing his eyelids to do the bowing for him. To the runner, still gawking at the screen, she said sharply, 'Go instruct Night and her retinue to meet me at the Infomancy immediately. And tell her to bring my refreshments.'

This last order was one that Night alone would understand to mean bring more of the potion that she had been taking since her bargains with Tzaban. She had given him an enormous gift of power. She hoped that what he had given her in return would not be the end of her. Her body surged with brief, strange fevers and the itch moved around in damnable endlessness from limb to limb and organ to organ. Only the potion would prevent her becoming a scarlet, scratching fiend. For a split second she wondered at her trust in Night, but her instinct to do so was absolute, in her bones. She hurried as much as one could without looking to hurry, longing for the bitter drink.

As she passed Mazhd, she saw him glance suddenly right at her, his nostrils flared. She recalled his particular talents and realised he must know what she had done in allowing the Karoo to inseminate her with his own genes. She saw an image of a woman giving birth to herself; one she picked up from his mind, and knew with sickly dread that he understood perfectly. If the Infomancy found out they could easily have her deposed. The evidence would be irrefutable – she was becoming the enemy

It would be absolute madness to rely on some hunch of

Night's that Mazhd could keep something so monumental to himself. Her alternative was to kill him immediately. It was the only guarantee – she could do it instantaneously, any other method risked him living long enough to write out his memory cache to the Infomancy. Absolute madness – this was also her path – she reflected as they exchanged the look that said all these things to each other. She saw he expected no mercy. For a split second instead of him she saw a pillar of steel in his place and so she did not strike.

Then she was past him and out of the door into the cold damp air of the low clouds that blew in endless pale grey through the streets. She looked up into Hakka's black eyes. The polearm spike was almost invisible in the threading mists.

'Killing infomancers will make what comes impossible,' she said and he nodded with a look of flat hatred for beings whose danger lay in planes he could not access. Still, he accepted it. 'Hurry. I must arrive at the head of the guard unit.'

He lifted her up into the saddle of the dappled grey horse and for a few cool, blissful minutes, she rode through the streets with him at her side as if they were the only two people in the world.

ISABEAU

Isabeau was too absorbed in her work to notice the Empress' moments of detachment from the world. Once Torada had given her an order she moved to execute it, and that required immersion in a vast complexity of calculations. Working with the other engineers in this task was exhilarating too, so much so that she didn't notice she was tired, or anything else except that her eyes felt so dry and she was finding it hard to look at things.

It was a genuine surprise to find Mazhd at her side. She saw him through a blue-white haze of spell symbols shifting around her in the air and gestured suddenly to freeze them in place, concerned that even speaking to him might cause her to insert an error. With equal surprise she saw that the Empress was gone, and wondered when that had happened.

Mazhd was holding out something. She realised it was food and then what he was saying became intelligible. 'You need to rest.'

She began to protest but he took her by the arm gently and led her to the anteroom – a bare place with a few lounging seats and tables, prints of old schematics decorating the walls. When she sat down she found her legs shaking and a wave of nausea went over her. She picked up the wrapped pasty he had provided and held it, as if she might lose it, while she drained a cup of water. They sat together and he ate with her. The heavy pastry of the case and the solid, congealed meat inside made it slow going. It was a struggle to stay awake and chew after the first couple of bites.

Luckily for her ambition he wanted to talk. They made a few nervous sallies to and fro in a conversation about Tralane, trying to figure out each other's relative levels of intimacy, then Minna. Isabeau considered him strictly temporary boyfriend material so far, and his job lent him inherent untrustworthiness so her replies were stock social niceties and her honest hopes for their survival.

'Minna is too valuable to hurt,' Mazhd said confidently. 'I expect her to appear in the city of Spire, then I will be able to tell you she is well.'

'Through the Infomancy there.'

'Yes.'

'How can you be loyal, in your position, given we're in civil conflict now? How do you decide who deserves to know what?' She held her glass out and he refilled it for her. Whatever he was used to doing he had much greater stamina than she did. Being cared for was nice. She tried to be appreciative and respectful in her questions.

'Everyone must decide for themselves,' he said through a doughy mouthful, prepared to lose manners at eating if she was. 'But mostly the higher you are to the top node, the more power your decisions have.'

'So if I were at the bottom, just a messenger, and I didn't want to tell something, but someone four layers up wanted to know, I couldn't stop them knowing what I know? How would they know to want to know?'

Mazhd coughed as he chuckled. 'The higher level operative would have what we call a "nose" for these things although it's more like having your eye dragged to a certain position because of a movement. A kind of automatic triggering of interest because something moves unexpectedly. You might have a vague awareness of higher nodes, though they often have guards in place, but you would always be able to see lower nodes relatively well. Putting up barriers at that level is not allowed. It would be dismantled and the person would face disciplinary action.'

'And where are you in this?' She made a movement with outspread fingers to indicate tracing lines on a plotted page. 'Shrazade is the city's top node.'

'Yes and I am one lower than that.'

'Is that by talent only?'

'Everyone starts at the bottom. You go as high as talents and permissions allow.'

'So you are vetted by higher nodes?'

'Yes.'

She chewed, pleased it followed logic she understood. 'Who's the top top?' He didn't answer immediately and she looked at him to see if he didn't want to or found it difficult.

'There is some dispute over it. But there does not need to be one person in the top node. There could be many, or none.'

She laughed a little, thinking over it. 'How do you know you're even making up your own mind, then? If you're lower than top?'

He smiled at her. 'Sometimes you don't. You have to assume you have a modicum of control but the opportunity for corruption at high nodes is very great.'

'Sounds like hell,' she said, taking another bite. Half her mind was still filled with equations. She could see the symbols even though they weren't there.

'Did you think that the Sisterhood of the Star were Spire sympathisers?'

This question, gently voiced, made the symbols pause.

'Yes, but they were honest about it. Living here was a form of penance, I think. They were so sure that ideas alone can be proven right that they thought they could come and teach their ways here and that they'd be doing everyone a favour.'

'It was what happened in the Rose that made your mind up.'

She saw no reason not to explain it. It was in the past, and no longer relevant. His interest, even at the time, had not been prurient. 'My encounter with General Borze proved to me that there are processes at work within the individual beyond conscious levels which I could not access to change or deny. The subconscious life of the body has no interest in the world of ideas. Pursuing the body's goals was much more fulfilling than I had been led to believe.' She paused, feeling that she was selling out her erstwhile teachers, but then remembering Minna and not caring so much.

'The sisterhood consider everything must be susceptible to reason and that mind must be made mistress of all lower nodes, as it were. The body has its own reasoning and goals, perfectly obvious ones, however. I tested their theory that one might detach from physical experience. However, I did not feel better or worse for it and what I was doing ceased to have any intellectual meaning at that point. Returning meaning to my actions was infinitely more rewarding so long as the meaning was positive, but my interpretation could go in any direction depending on my mood state, so clearly interpretation is incorrect as an analysis of the meaning of life. It is a creative process entirely. Defining any of the acts bad or good is merely whimsical. Hardly something to base a philosophy on, even a moral one. There was no act in itself more or less meaningful than another. Though some certainly had more energetic and physical response than others.' She paused to swallow and drink. Mazhd was watching her with interest, a hint of a grin on his face. She continued, aware of how primly correct she seemed and not caring.

'The Rose Document suggested that to inhabit the physical world completely, in its own frames of reference, was to enter an altered consciousness in which other realities might be entered by repositioning of the focal point of conscious experience. This was correct. Night was correct. The sisterhood's views were based on deduction and a false assumption of mental supremacy in which events are interpreted rather than created, and they were incorrect as a result. I put my findings in a paper and I was adding to a theory that Empresses are mass focal point controllers, but the Department of Humane Biology refused to read it as it violates the Theory of Hierarchy and Heredity. I considered my research concluded at that point since I have no patience with fools and much else to do in my own expertise. And then Minna was kidnapped and here I am, too busy to return to it.' She had begun to feel much better now, both from the food and from being able to talk and set her ideas out in a methodical way, as if a pressure valve in her head had eased. She yawned and let her head rest on the chair back.

'I'd like to read it sometime,' he said and his face was genuinely interested, no trace of condescension or amusement in it now.

'Of course. I will send it to you as soon as I have a moment. I must say though that there is one person who is much more peculiar even than Empresses. My Master, Night. Her understanding of the instinctual interrelations of all the facets of the individual is remarkable but her magical skill to weave thought-forms and place them, to create ideas and to give them to others, is unparalleled. It must be a very similar kind of talent. And I've never met anyone like her. Don't you and she both have some Karoo in you?'

'Yes,' he said. His expression had altered very suddenly and she assumed he was experiencing discomfort over this reminder. It was not common knowledge and she only knew because Night had confided in her whilst describing the education of her previous acolyte. Surely it was bad enough being marked out as a Steppelander, as people cared so much about these ridiculous things. Abruptly she felt bad because people were so stupid that truths could be taken as offences. It offended her to the core of her being. Still, she remembered her mother's exhaustive explanations on the subject of social cohesion and decided she should probably stop talking.

Mazhd was also quiet after that and they concluded their meal in a comfortable silence, him waiting on her until she was done and then clearing up the wrappers and cups afterwards.

'You ought to nap,' he said. 'Tired minds make mistakes. I'll watch out for you if you like, wake you up in an hour.'

She was nearly asleep anyway. 'Forty minutes,' she said.

'Forty,' he agreed, taking a blanket from the end of the recliner and laying it over her.

She wanted to ask him how he would be sure not to sleep himself but before she could do it sleep stole her away.

ZHARAZIN

Zharazin watched Isabeau as her eyes closed and her lips moved without sound. When they stopped and the blanket moved more slowly over her ribs, he sat back in his own seat and spent a minute listening to the unfamiliar sound of the flight engines.

They were a steady soft background hum that pulsed in waves; a slow ocean bearing them, depth unknown. He felt the resonance through the chair. Everything in Glimshard felt it, he fancied, glasses tinkling in distant cabinets, loose boards creaking now and again, precipitous objects falling unknown in forgotten rooms.

Then he brought his mind back from its butterfly, fanciful circle and let it alight again on Isabeau's last, shocking declaration. Night, like an Empress, only more peculiar.

He got up and followed imagined gossamer wings outside. The streets were quiet, gleaming under the invisible support fields as if lit by a second, much weaker sun in addition to the real one. Double shadows were cast, one strong and one pale across the ground, his own included. They said the magic pulled light around on itself. He watched his feet meet two other pairs as he passed between buildings and along courts, seeming to take a path through three different worlds to the palace as he followed a line and a timing that no guard would bother patrolling. It was harder than he remembered to climb the walls and make his way over roofs and along balconies to the jump that took him on to the corner of Night's gable. He used to take this way when he was in love with her and it was easy then. Belatedly he realised that was more than fifteen years ago and he hadn't slept in two days.

He dropped into her garden courtyard with considerably more weight than a butterfly, hands to the paving as he waited there to see if he was still on the list of people she wouldn't attempt to stop here with her guardian spells. Even the pavers were familiar, every pattern of their cut stone faces a map of a hundred past days. He tore his gaze away to the plant near his face. No point getting lost down those lanes.

Nothing happened and eventually he straightened. She'd know he was here now but that didn't matter, given where she was and what she was about, he figured. In the house of

Shrazade she would need all her wits and he needed his to keep his investigation private from the same woman. Keeping his waking mind to the schooled emptiness of meditation was all that would save him from an interrogation. It was almost impossible. Everywhere he looked he saw keys to memory's gates where in happier times he had stored so much of his knowledge. The immensity of it beckoned but he made himself see them without picking them up, pass them by, when they called to him like sirens.

At last he was where he wanted to be. In her room. On her bed.

He lifted the cover back and pressed his face to the sheet halfway down where the mattress dipped with the shallow imprint of her hip, closed his eyes and breathed.

Something blocked him. His talent for knowing blood normally produced knowledge easily. It swam to the surface of his awareness and confirmed itself with a sure sense in his own bones – like this, like that. But now here he was with his nose, his head full of her and all he could do was tell who she was. This is Night. She has the Karoo in her, about as much as one finger's depth in a standard tall measure of water. She is able to know the blood, like him. More than he can she knows how it flows between generations, across years, across centuries. Time is only another country to her. *And then there is something that he can't access, right there, like a picture that will not come into focus no matter how long he looks.*

He got up, left the bed as it was and returned the way he had come like a golem on its master's path, letting no thought rise and grow. He was a sterile desert as he crossed back harder ways, took a route through dusty rooms and along service corridors until he reached the Legal Promenades. At the entrance to the Halls of Records he used his infomancer's badge to get access to the census from nineteen years ago. The keepers didn't mind his silence and they knew him and had no reason to deny

425

him. He sat down at a magetable and flicked through the pages, letting his eyes see but refusing to let his mind read. He remembered but he didn't register what it meant. Over the vellum he saw once again the Empress' face as she was leaving.

She had seen that he could smell Tzaban in her but she must have seen something else because she allowed him to live and still know it.

His eyes passed over her name. Another, another, another. A signal sprang across a vast distance with an electrical shock that ran down his arms and made him shudder. In a long forgotten, dusty room in his mind something made a tinkling crash as it fell over, an urn full of fortune runes landing on the floor, spelling out a fate that was written entirely in the blood. He could see only two names, written endlessly over and over. Night. Torada. First one. Then the other. Blood.

A thought is a spell. Without words, without images, it is almost uncatchable, so he kept this understanding in that protoform, before thought.

He closed the records and left them as he found them, took the hidden, winding path back to the Engine House and the anteroom where Isabeau was still sleeping as he had left her.

He bent and gently shook her shoulder. 'Isabeau. It is forty minutes.'

He waited until she had got herself up, then escorted her back to her work. As the engineers spun their arrays he stood among them silently, and alone. A feathery trace sent to feel for Shrazade and Night confirmed their attention was distant from him, far enough that he could consider matters so long as they brought up no significant emotions to attract their attention. He cautiously allowed one mote of what he had found after another to fall into his conscious thoughts.

Tzaban might not know why he had come to Glimshard, but Zharazin did. Night had called him. For her daughter.

No doubt that was why he too was here. No accident he

had become her student at all. He had missed far too much about Night, right under his nose which he had never thought to investigate purely because she had once told him that the blankness he found in his knowledge of her was due to the Karoo inheritance and he had believed her because his trust in her was absolute, because his love for her and desire for her had occupied all the space he would have needed to see anything else. He had been her bloodhound, looking out not just for her, but on Torada's behalf, in case anyone threatening came sniffing around.

He knew Torada had no idea that Night was her mother. Why should she? How would he have known it except for his faultless memory? Torada's official mother, Siagnine, was a lesser noble who had never had more children and who had found religion when her daughter Ascended following the death of the old Empress. He had met Siagnine as a matter of course during his studentship, and found her barren. It had never occurred to him that she had been so all her life. Such things happened regularly to women after a certain age. In every other way she did match Torada, she was, plausibly, her mother. They even looked alike.

All he knew now was that Siagnine might have given birth to Torada, but Night was the mother. Leave out any suspect for fatherhood and it was a perfect combination. How she had done it he didn't know but that is how it was. To prevent him finding out Night had blocked him and to maintain that block through the years and ensure he didn't discover it she had kept him close. All his liaisons around the city simply gathered information for her to pick over. He was aghast at the scale of the deception now that he realised how he had been played. And then he was amazed at his own foolishness. It was simply Karoo. What had Tzaban told him? Queens built their empires, guarded their territories, groomed their offsprings. Males collected, provided base material, and then were disposed of.

He wondered what Tzaban had carried south with him to the Karoo at the pit. Torada must have given him something. Whatever Karoo wanted, Zharazin could not begin to know, but whatever it was lay in that muddy hole. He wondered if Night were an emissary too, and what then was he? No wonder Night had tried to keep it from him. If the Infomancy came to the same conclusions they would do everything they could to stop Torada and the city. He knew them well enough to understand that, whatever Empire meant to them, first and foremost it meant human. The Empress reigned, but what she knew was their business. She was at the mercy of their revelations.

He had no way to know how unified higher nodes were in their goals but he would have bet preserving their own power and interests was right at the top of the list.

Just then he felt the Infomancy seethe. Every node shivered as energy surged through it. He sensed Shrazade rebelling against Torada's will, summoning the power to resist an Imperial decree. Without hesitation he concealed all he had been thinking of – hid it quickly, buried it, locked it and hid key after key under layers of irrelevant things.

Mazhd, Shrazade's command was in the centre of his skull. *You should have warned me.*

I couldn't, he replied. *She ordered me not to.*

Then it seems you forget where your loyalties lie. I smell secrets about you. They are like ghosts.

Everyone has them.

Not from me. One day soon your secondment will expire. Think on that.

If you survive what's coming, he thought, feeling his concentration slide away as she used part of his capacity to sustain herself. *I'll think of it then.* He fancied she paused but it could have been for reasons other than him. He wondered at himself, threatening her. It must be the Karoo in him.

CHAPTER TWENTY-SEVEN

TZABAN

Tzaban sat in the dark at the top of a shaft through which air moved in occasional shifts so slight only the tips of his finest fur could detect it. He was perched on a narrow pipe of some tough, slippery material that crossed the shaft from one dark hole twice its diameter to another. It was extremely strong and stiff enough that it had not bowed in the slightest with his weight. His hands gripped it between the points where his feet balanced on their ball, toes curled lightly about the same. He was able to breathe so slowly that he could be relatively sure the air motion did not come from him. Five metres down was a metal gantry of a kind he found everywhere inside the cask, running like insect paths between various kinds of holes and storage areas. It was near the central, empty core of the thing – a place he loathed and had witnessed only once on coming to the sudden open edge of a slipway.

The core was a massive black hole that angled down and down. He had dropped a small chunk of metal down it and heard it hit the side, skid, bounce, slide and stop after a while, though he was sure that was not the bottom. It could be for ever. The air there was stagnant: breathable but as dead as could be. The vastness of the space had upset him and he knew it would be something the other Karoo would want to avoid. The point he had chosen to hide in was near the beckoning depths of it, but close enough inside the walls that its siren lure could comfortably be ignored. He had been up and down the more common parts of the trail he was covering a few times that day, to be sure the other Karoo knew he'd been about and might still be. But this was on the way out of the area, a little-used trip between two stashes, one of water, and the other of plundered kitchen items from the expedition above. The smell of an opened pack of spice was strong enough to blot most of the rotting odours from whatever had been rejected from this.

The outer hairs on his ruff feathered a little and he heard the ping and shiver of a metal cable set to vibrating a way off. He had to work to keep his lips shut against the sudden flow of salty saliva in his mouth. If he had been about to pounce he would have increased the tension, cranked it up now, but instead he relaxed until only pure balance kept him in place. He folded his ears flat and his shoulderblades into his back, unblinking, unbreathing, watching the small area below him until the faint, angular light bleeding across it from a much higher emergency rig was cut off.

He dropped, energy contained so deep the other felt nothing but a breeze and then a hundred kilogrammes of dead weight.

Then tooth and claw, blade and bite. Strike of metal, skin to metal, claw to bone. Bite harder and feel bone break – the sudden give and snap made his eyeballs judder and a fierce joy inside come rising like a tide of hot sugar. This was all there was and all there was to want in the universe.

He rose out of that state a time later, saw his dead opponent under him, felt the warmth of the body against the chill of the cask's natural constant background, dying out. He fed off the energy of it and drained the blood out of it, then dragged the pieces out to the edge of the horrible darkness and tossed them as far out into the emptiness as he could. He watched them turn and turn as they slowly shrank and passed beyond the reach of the lights. He listened and fancied he heard soft thumps, as gentle as the blow of a cat's paw on the side of a vast iron bell. Then he had to go lay up for a while and digest what he had done. He passed the food cache with its stench and wound through rooms of odd devices and some with many things that he almost recognised as chairs or perhaps couches bolted to the floors. The lair itself was in a small dead-end room filled with stolen clothes and some personal items of the expedition team, plus things looted from further afield – symbols and panes, things of interesting shapes or surfaces that looked attractive. He loaded as many of these as he could carry back with him into his pack and then slunk up the long winding ways to the zone where the science team were still working, past their busy rooms where they were too occupied to notice him, to the bunk area and then to the curtained corner where Tralane's bed was.

He emptied the pack and slid the objects under the low army cot and then lay down on top of it and went to sleep. He was hurt and aware of pain that would be worse later, but victory made him content and happy, the taste of the blood in his belly an intensity of joy that warmed every part of his being. He had never felt more powerful.

Sharp voices and screams woke him up. He was alert instantly, then a second later had his ears flattened with exasperation. It was her friend, the curly haired woman she called Carlyn, standing with her hands clutching the curtains behind her for some reason, shrieking at him as if he were a monster.

'Be quiet,' he said. His voice was a growl that was barely intelligible. It surprised him. His mouth felt that same difficulty it had had with words since the queen had changed him, as if he was going to drown on them. Anyway, it had the desired effect. She shut her mouth and stared at him in a way that made him want to reach out and swipe her face off. She must have read the notion in his gaze. She glanced down quickly and he felt the hair on his spine sink down again. He expected to feel the lash of it in his tail, but then felt only the ghost of a tail and a grim disappointment that verged on anger; the queen had pushed him towards them, away from Karoo, and they were weak.

At that moment others came, Tralane among them. He looked at her and was reassured by her. She might be irritated, alarmed and tired but she looked at him with concern and not fear. The others with her grouped behind her, asking questions which didn't interest him. He waited as she got over her grimacing and then sat up, putting his feet on the floor. Only then did he notice how filthy he was, covered in blood; his trousers were stiff with it. He rested, arms on his knees, head hanging, and waited until the initial fuss was over before straightening up to find her sending them away. He didn't know the actual things they said but he felt their fear and hatred of him, their mistrust and loathing, their envy of her. He growled a little, wishing he could kill them too, then she was standing in front of him, holding out two towels and a cake of soap.

'You should clean up before you eat.'

'I don't need to eat,' he said, taking them, finding them suddenly half the size in his hands until he realised that consuming his enemy had made him grow. The towels caught on his claws.

'You need to rest.'

'The men who were taken,' he said, carefully. 'Professor Asynax and Engineer Orblane.'

'You found them?' She sounded so hopeful he hated to reply.

'Get your recorder,' he said, finding the engineer's words flowing quickly into his mouth. 'I will be able to tell you everything they knew, for the next couple of hours, before it's gone.'

'What?'

He looked at her directly. 'I found the one that ate them. I ate him. I know what he knew but after a few hours I will lose the ability to tell it. It will become me, not something I know, something I am. In the flesh but not in my mind. Only a queen would be able to read it.'

She tried to hide her disgust. 'You are – you have the consciousness of the one you killed?'

'And those he consumed. For a little while.' He couldn't help himself smiling. The death was there, the rage, the defeat, the spite of the last moment in which it had hated him so very, very much; an unrelenting ever-hate that he loved to remember again and again. 'But it does not last. The form lasts. My ability to speak knowledge does not last. Hurry if you have questions.'

'Yes. Right.' She started to look for the device under the cot, then stopped. 'What's all this stuff?'

'I found it. It is yours now.'

She pulled things out into the light. They meant nothing to him. Her hands were shaking as she examined them, some of them Orblane's and Asynax's things, others whatever the trove of the dead Karoo had held. He could see by her expression that they meant something to her and that was satisfactory, but when she looked up her face was full of amazement and gratitude and that filled him with a hot fever so he had to look away. In his hand one of the towels tore.

'These things are . . . They're . . . I have to . . . Just wait here! Wait!' She picked them up and ran out with them, calling.

As he heard the commotion and excitement, the horror and the recriminations, all pouring out of them in a mass babble he sat and carved a groove into the soap bar with the claw on his index finger. It was only with the greatest difficulty that he could get it to retract. He had not wanted to eat that Karoo for himself. He had done it for Tralane. Its form was degrading his, pushing him away from human and so away from her. There were others too he would have to consume, though from what he had been able to tell so far he might be better off that way in the end. There were three others left and one of them he didn't

433

like the smell of at all. If he had come across it in ordinary times he would have left it well alone.

Beyond the curtain excitement over his finds overrode revulsion at his deeds. There was almost a heroic moment of support for him. He registered it without interest except to note that humans were like queens in this regard: give them what they valued and they would not care how you got it or what you were.

He gathered up the soap shavings in his hand and went out to the room of water where they had set up places for washing and doing something with their waste that smelled of powerful alchemical stinks. The blood rinsed away in dark rusty runnels but it stained him in places, where his fur was whitest. Afterwards he looked good in human terms. In his terms it made little difference. He could tell his own scent was altering to reflect the changed circumstances – advertising his status so that now the hunt would change for the others – and the true smell of the blood was only dimmed rather than removed by the herbal soap. But humans had no nose for anything.

When he returned they were still arguing about if he could be trusted, though they shut up when they saw him and gave him grudging respect for his title: wasted effort. He could feel how much they hated and feared him. He longed to be away from them but instead he must sit in this tiny place pressed against their every fragile second of terror.

Only Tralane was not afraid. She was sitting on the cot, adjusting something on the square plate he recognised as a device she could record his voice with. He sat patiently on the bed's other end and closed his eyes. After concentrating on her presence and listening to her voice for a while he felt calmer. He let his mouth do the talking necessary – none of what he said meant anything to him other than the facts that the two men had met their ends in the same manner – by being snatched from doorways that opened on to halls near strategic turns (for

434

the Karoo killer, that was) and had put up no significant resistance. They had not known the first thing about how to defend themselves.

They talked for almost an hour and then his recall grew hazy and muddled and they were forced to stop.

'I had no idea you could do that,' she said, packing the device away in some carrying case. 'It was as if you saved them. Well, you saved something about them. Does any of it stick?'

'If it didn't, I would not be able to speak.'

She went quiet after that and spent a while very busy with the things he had brought her. Finally she held up one of them. 'You won't know what this is.'

'No.'

'It's a ...' She paused, drawing out the last sound as she thought about how she could explain it to him. 'It's for calculating the positions of the stars and everything in the sky. You can use it to tell where you are. And you can use it to tell where everything else is. The really interesting thing about it however, is that you could use this anywhere. I mean, it has these old records in it from the person who used it last.' She got up from the floor where she had been sitting and sat beside him, holding it so that he could see a circular pane and inside the pane a lot of bright lights and coloured lines. He recognised the lights as looking like the night sky, except that part of it was blotted out by a large blue and white curve. He watched her finger trace out constellations and name them in the Imperial way though he knew them differently, as points in his body that seemed to ring with faint bells telling him which way he should go when he was abroad in the dark.

'And this ...' She ran her fingertip over the big curved shape that cut the image, a blue glow its edge. She let her finger move into the shaped area and cross a blue and white part, then stop over a green strip. 'This is where we are.'

He was about to say, 'In the sky?' when the last traces of

435

what he had consumed allowed him to understand something so alien to him that the perceiving of it made the whole world come to a stop. She was showing him the world itself, from the outside.

'Tzaban?' Her voice seemed to come from far away. He felt a vast, icy emptiness open up inside him and expand rapidly, pushing everything away to the edges of his awareness. He moved away from her and on to the bed, curled up as small as he was able to and wrapped his imaginary tail around him with his face pushed into the pillow that she used, holding to the scent as he tried to find himself in the sudden new space within.

TRALANE

Tralane put the astrolabe down and reached out carefully to touch the Karoo man's shoulder, but even when she rested her hand there he didn't react. He was still breathing so, after waiting a minute she got up and waited a little more, putting those things she wanted to take back to the laboratory into her pack and putting the rest away under the cot. She didn't blame him for his silence. When she'd realised what it was, she hadn't had a thing to say either. She should take it with her and share this but, instead, a strong inner prompt made her slide it out of sight into the bag with the gun. Given what they had already discovered about the artefact she felt this could wait. She had a terrible suspicion in her mind and she didn't want to share it without proof.

Exhaustion and the revelations of the last few hours made her lightheaded. She went to the rec room and made herself food from the dry stores, though she could barely eat it. Even the smell made her think of what Tzaban had done and its goodness was overridden by the remembered odour of blood. She made herself eat it, breathing through her mouth, and when she was joined by Carlyn and a few others she reviewed their maps.

Tzaban's travels and meals had revealed areas that they were confident they could bring to an active status. The power lines were mostly undamaged in this section and had been closed down by wards and hexes rather than collapses of infrastructure. The language that the artefact's devices used was archaic but sufficiently familiar from previous archaeological explorations that the linguists had been able to produce a work-in-progress iconography that was reliable in all the core symbols. None of them doubted their abilities to waken the deeper layers of the object, they simply didn't know what to expect if they did.

'We need to go down and personally investigate these rooms,' Tralane said, pointing to the most likely looking areas for nexus points. 'Some of them are fire damaged and full of debris but these here, near the central core, are fine.'

'That's where the Karoo are,' one of the power mages said.

'Were,' Tralane corrected. 'The one that used these is dead, remember.'

'So he says.'

Tralane ignored this. She was used to the negativity and she couldn't fault their fear. 'The thing is if they wanted to kill us all, they would have done it already. That's not it.'

Carlyn looked at her and she saw the deep concern etched in her friend's face, kind lines made black with wear and tear. 'How can you be sure what they want?'

'They want us in here doing this for now,' Tralane said. 'The Karoo here are in competition. I ... I don't want to cast aspersions on the dead but the two who died were among the weakest of us in terms of ability. And if the Karoo gain insight by consuming then plausibly they were just like a catchup course in what to look for next.'

'So, what, we should make a list of the dumbest ones?'

'No.' Tralane said firmly, hand down. She wanted to nip that

437

crap in the bud before the grim humour got out of control. 'Everyone is needed now. There aren't enough of us otherwise.'

'To do what? Are we still just researching before we're told to get out?'

'Usually we preserve everything and go slowly but we're running out of time, I think,' Tralane said. 'All being well, re-inforcements should get here in a few days' time. But when they do we should expect another fight so let's consider that the end of the dig. We could lose access to this for ever at that point. I think we should go inwards as far as we can while we have the chance. It's the only time we're going to get. I propose that we set up teams, one to stay here, one to move to this region where we think there might be some central library node and another to this point over here where the majority of the useful objects have been found.'

'You know,' Carlyn said, drinking from her cup slowly. 'One thing keeps bothering me a lot. We've found things. A lot of the power grid is still good. We can even use our own technology to link with what's here, up to a point, but although there are all kinds of things used by people and for people there are no people. No skeletons. Nothing. Not a trace.'

'Magi artefacts are always like that,' a doctor from technical synergy said. 'Nothing new there.'

'I don't really buy the idea that they were put here for us by greater powers,' Carlyn said to him. 'No offence.'

'Everyone has their theories,' he said, shrugging.

'Whatever the reason, we have to move while we can,' Tralane said, trying not to feel the sink in her chest that Carlyn's reservation had produced. 'I will be going to this centre on the hope that it's an information nexus. Doctor Shore, I think you should head the other group and see if this has its own power core we can use. Our batteries are getting too low otherwise. We can operate basic lights and doors but further exploration will be impossible by tomorrow afternoon.'

'What about the Karoo?'

All the faces turned to her.

'I'll take care of that,' she said, as if she was Tzaban's keeper. 'He'll come with me but he knows the way around down there. He'll be able to warn us if anything moves. Take weapons.'

When they had scattered and only Carlyn was left she moved quietly closer and murmured,

'You know it's like you've got your own personal bodyguard and we're all on our own here. If he doesn't eat us first, that is.'

Tralane looked at her. 'I know.'

Carlyn sighed. 'Do you trust him or do you think he's just going to save you till last?'

'I don't know. It's possible.'

Carlyn smiled at her and rested her hand on Tralane's arm. It didn't feel comforting enough.

'Do you have feelings for him, 'Lane?'

'Hm?' She glanced at her friend. 'What do you mean by that?'

'Nobody would be surprised. The big alpha beast, hunting for you, protecting you. Look at what happened when he first came to town. It was like a fiesta. Like he was the missing link between every adult woman and her own happiness. I mean, that could have been the presence and the Empress' teenage dreams having their effect but – who'd say no? Even now, when he's half as big again and twice as ugly. You're the chosen one, 'Lane.'

'He didn't choose me,' Tralane said.

'Yeah. All the same, can I be on your squad? I don't have much faith in Shore's ability to turn soldier.'

Tralane nodded. She felt so glad that Carlyn was there, and at the same time so sad that she was. She didn't want her friend there, mixed up with this. She caught Carlyn's arm, and seeing they were alone said, 'There is a thing. About the Karoo. It's possible that, even if he wanted to guard us, if a queen came he might be turned on us anyway.'

'That's why they're all male in here, isn't it? It makes sense. They might even be competing for other queens, not only for themselves.'

'He's the most human-like Karoo I've ever seen. By a long way.'

'What does that mean though, in the end?'

Tralane shrugged. 'I don't know.'

Carlyn hugged her and Tralane stood there in the embrace and wished it was going to last. She wanted only to be home again, struggling with her own few cache pieces during the day, bothered by minor responsibilities, with Minna and Isabeau safe in the house. But it was too painful to consider that all in the past. She opened her eyes and let go.

'You always were so trusting,' Carlyn said, almost regretfully. 'Be careful, 'Lane.'

'Hm, what does that mean?' Tralane smiled, though she was unsettled.

'Means be careful. I'm going to get some things together.'

'What time is it? We'll go in two hours. I need some sleep. Meet back here.'

They kissed and parted. Tralane took water with her back to her cot. When she got there Tzaban was gone, a few white hairs all that remained. She took her boots off, getting into the cot and finding it still warm. She wrapped herself in the thin quilt, muttered the charm that heated the thin cotton wadding, and closed her eyes, assuming that he had gone on a patrol for lack of information. As she always did in that situation, she reached under the bed and pulled out the gun, set it to a narrow focus, checked the power and safety, and put it under the pillow. As with most magi, she had a good internal time sense and could wake when she wished to. She gave herself the maximum she could. Ten minutes was enough to make ready later. It wasn't as though any of them would be carrying a lot of gear besides basic toolbelts. She hoped he would be back in time.

As it turned out he was back only forty minutes later. She came out of a blank slumber to the sound of his undressing movements and the long shadow of his crossing the curtained wall in the glow of the dim witchlight she had left. Murmurs and voices, scrapes and shuffles told the story of others trying to rest or study at their spots nearby. On the other side of the room heavy breaths and sighs denoted other activity.

Normally he slept on the floor and he was moving her boots aside now to act as a headrest when she reached out of the cot and took hold of his arm, tugging it. There was no hesitation or resistance as he obeyed and got into the bed with her. It was extremely cramped. He had to wrap himself around her completely, spooned, so she rested in the tuck of his body, exactly where she had wanted to be.

'They are not close,' he said, though she hadn't asked him aloud, his voice a murmur, arm under her head and over her as if they did this all the time. 'They have gone down into the depths. I think they are also short on time. Look for something perhaps. Make trail you will follow.'

He was so comforting with his size and warmth. She snuggled backwards into him, giving him her full trust, hearing Carlyn's voice in her mind warning her, though it was far too late for that kind of warning anyway. Carlyn could not have understood why Tralane felt completely secure with him, no more than Tralane could have explained it to her. She felt sure that if there was going to be a turning point – not that she believed that was possible, entirely – it was at least not now, not yet. 'They are leading us?'

'Yes, sure. I think so,' he said and all the comfort in the world could not prevent a sick feeling chilling her from gut to bones. Of course, he wasn't the only one who had eaten a lot of human lately. She realised only now, stupidly, that they could have been listened to all the time but they had assumed the Karoo were animals and unable to understand. They had assumed the Karoo had no interest in the object other than the mere fact of it being stuck in a piece of ground they considered their territory.

'They don't mind dark,' he said. 'Find a lot of things. Wonder.' His hand was linked with hers, fingers through fingers. His thumb rubbed casually over the top of her thumb.

'Mmmn,' she replied, hoping he would stop. She didn't want to know more right then about what else they could do that she hadn't bargained for and knew nobody in the Imperium had thought about even for one minute. So the Karoo research team looked like this, and their interdepartmental rivalry was homicidal. She smiled for a second, thinking of it that way, but the nausea didn't abate. Sleep, longed for, eluded her. Vast gulfs of questions stood between her and it.

'Tzaban,' she said, trying to be quiet enough that they would not be overheard. 'Karoo male and female – are they the same as people, as human sexes. I mean, is it for having children?'

'No,' he said. 'It is for gathering and for making. There's no human word for that.'

'So, are all the males like each other?'

'No. Fit for place, time, business. Made for purpose. Females make, and hm, another kind of Karoo grows. Like plants. It is not like animals walking, talking, doing. It is like grass, growing, sustaining. Has no, uh, no focus, no mind, only energy, good and bad.'

'How human are you. I mean, is it just a look? Do you – that is, do you function like a human male? Is that how Karoo gets into the human population?'

'Touch, bite, that is how usually. If a female wishes, she can make a human a little bit Karoo. They would not know it. That is how it gets in. I cannot make a human baby with a human female. I can only bite or change energy.'

'Do you feel possessive about me?'

'Yes.'

'The queen did that.'

442

'Yes.'

'Why?'

'You are most able to see this thing, learn its secrets.'

'So it's not that you want me?'

'Man does. Karoo not. I understand. I am very like human, enough to feel and know what you are asking. If I was not, how would I be able to translate well?'

She started. 'You're a translator? I mean, that is your purpose?'

'Yes. It took me a long time to realise what my purpose was but it is to translate, to research humans. Yes. Like you research this cask in the ground and other magical things.'

'You didn't do much translating for us. You just warned us off coming here.'

'You didn't ask for translations. You persisted in trespass and I must warn you. And I am not *your* translator. I have said many times, Karoo is this and that, Karoo does not accept this and that. Nobody listens.'

'Tzaban if I were to offer to share with you everything I know, would that mean you didn't have to ... eat me, let's just say, for the sake of argument?'

He paused. 'That needs a lot of trust. Karoo does not trust humanity. They always lie. But the flesh does not lie. Not ever.'

'If you kill me, there won't be others. Not many. Not enough. If you kill me, this channel you have to discovering things you can't know otherwise is gone. Do you understand that? Engineers are rare. My kind doubly so. Once you've eaten us up, that's it. No more knowledge. You've been around. You know it's true.'

Another pause and she actually felt him smile; the change of the air, the sound of his lips and breath, the warmth against her neck. 'Yes, Engineer. That is why I am yours now, and you are mine.'

She wanted to turn and object to this in the strongest terms but, despite the outrageousness of the claim, nothing in her was able to deny it. What did you expect, she thought grimly, the Karoo are writers in blood, not only readers. Her jaw worked as her mouth opened and shut trying to articulate a protest that didn't have a word to its name. What would he say again – I told you not to come. 'You belong to the Empress,' she finally whispered.

'That is a formality that has no weight here,' he returned. 'Humans will take words for truths. So that is what I give them.'

'And what do you want, Tzaban?'

Another of those pauses. 'Your question has no meaning for me,' he said.

She turned around, no mean feat in the bed as there was only enough space for one person and he was already the size of two. She found a way to balance at the edge, her face looking at his, both of them resting on the thin pillow.

At this range, she realised that some of the illusion of his size was in how he moved and commanded space. His head was only a little larger than hers. The lower half of his face projected very slightly, and his mouth contained some alarming teeth though, at close range, she could see them slotted efficiently together, canine points stuck into recesses in the opposite gum, so he didn't look so very different with his long mouth closed. The eyes were alarming at any distance. From twenty centimetres away their nacreous quality was more evident, rainbows on the sheen of the surface over that bright gold and yellow. They were sun-bright though the strip lights gave them a sickly quality. In the dim shaded colours of his face they were so distinct it was difficult not to look at them and be absorbed into their empty black slits.

'All right. What will you do?' She saw old blood still collected at the base of his whiskers. His nose was the delicate dark purple of an opium poppy's heart and she touched it with her finger, surprised to find it velvety, like horse nose, not skin like human.

'What I must.'

She gave up. She could not get to the bottom of her lack of fear – it made no sense. She had heard him reply to questions in dead men's voices and seen the evidence of his behaviours in all other ways. Her head was full of reasons to escape him, get rid of him. She could still feel the bulk of the gun under her side of the pillow. Her body wanted him however, trusted and loved him. She felt like a little girl again when her head touched his shoulder and felt his warmth and heard his heartbeat.

She woke with him patting her gently.

'Time to get up,' he said. He was already dressed and ready, old mud and blood fell in dust off his leather armour as he straightened and checked the position of his daggers.

Tralane got up and put on her outermost set of overalls, tool-belt and the gun. She carried a pack of other items which she wanted with her and went to collect rations and water at the meeting point. The nap was better than nothing but it was the fear of moving out of their safe area that had her nerves running before they had sorted out the communications plans.

Tzaban sat at the edges of these discussions, impassive, as though it didn't matter what they decided. When they were ready he led the way into the dark regions where none of them had gone before. He wouldn't answer questions concerning the whereabouts of the other Karoo and paused at every junction to listen and sniff before progressing. Sometimes they heard sounds in the distance but although these frightened them most he seemed to pay no attention to them. The hike took a while and Tralane had unpleasant time in which to wonder about Minna's fate, and Isabeau with the city. She rather thought about this than what they were doing in the enforced silence of the move.

They stopped and she looked up to find Tzaban holding his hand up at the head of the group. They had come through a series of rooms which led from one to another without many side routes or corridors but now ahead of them lay a long, curved strip about three people wide without doors leading from it. He turned and looked at the eight of them, calculating something.

'Is this where he sells us out?' someone murmured ahead of Tralane, who was taking the back of the group with Carlyn.

He glanced at them and then at Tralane. 'Engineer Huntingore, draw your weapon and defend the back of the line. This corridor runs fifty metres. You can expect something to appear at about thirty to forty. It'll come straight along after or drop out of the missing roof panel at thirty-one. The other one will come at the front. I'll take care of that.'

'But, what?' Carlyn said and turned to look at Tralane.

Tralane felt her mouth drop open, cold horror stealing up her back and rooting her feet to the ground. 'But I can't,' she said, her hand already on the gun grip. 'I mean, I've never. I don't really...'

'I cannot defend both ends of the line. This is an ambush,' he said, as though explaining to a stupid person.

'Are you crazy – why did you lead us into this? He's mad I tell you! We must go back at once!' Engineer Tefa, the power expert said, but not too loudly. He was shaking and sweat was running down both sides of his face. Beside him others huddled close, back to back.

'Noo...' Engineer Shiran moaned softly, trying to look up and down as if she could run out of it. 'This is your fault. You knew they were there and you didn't warn us...' Her voice trailed off into a gasp of panic.

'It was inevitable,' Tzaban said, his gaze flat and certain, so solid that they clung to it as if it was a tangible thing like a wall between them and death. 'I just made sure it happened here and not somewhere else where it would be unpredictable. We go in here, we kill them, we split up and reach our destinations. There will be one left at that point and while you are doing whatever you do he and I will be busy with each other. This way you get what you want and you probably get out.'

'We have to turn back! Ohhh! We have to. Make him, Tralane. Make him do it!' Carlyn clung to Tralane's arm suddenly, dragging her sideways with the force of her terror. She froze as Tzaban's acid gaze turned on her. Someone was crying in the middle of the group.

Tzaban shook his head 'Let's go. If we miss this chance they'll get back upside and have as many free shots as they want later and you'll lose a lot more. Has to be now, here. Tralane, you have the back. Carlyn you keep a hand on her and lead her so she can face that way. We're moving now, stay tight, look at the back of the person in front.' He hauled the sobbing woman to him by the front of her overalls and made her hold a short line attached to his belt which she gripped compulsively, looking at the scrap of rope as if she was losing her mind. Then he turned and set off, grumbling as he had to tow her. She tripped over her own feet until she was moving steadily and the others went mutely along after her as Tralane watched. She knew they had to, because they weren't for fighting and whatever they were good at this was not it and this situation had nothing for them but to follow. More than one was whimpering. She resented the notion of dying here like this. It made her furious. She was as far from tears as she'd ever been.

Carlyn hesitated and Tralane shoved at her firmly. 'Move out. I've got it. It's fine.' The strength of her own voice lifted her and as she felt Carlyn stumble about, hand on her shoulder, she focused on the gun – remove safety, power on, setting maximum. Hm, she thought, it would have made sense to put a safety chain on these things so you can't drop them when you're shitting yourself walking backwards down a narrow corridor waiting for a monster to drop on your head. Had her face not been fixed in position with raw mortal dread that would have made her smile. Then she heard the sound of a rapid patter coming from the direction she faced.

A brindle coloured mass abruptly filled the corridor, yellow-eyed, low and lithe, streaking towards her so fast she didn't have time to draw a breath to scream 'This isn't the thirty mark! This is more like fucking fifteen, you shit!' Though someone said that as her finger turned to a white hot agony and everything in front of her was abruptly blotted out by a grey red fog.

CHAPTER TWENTY-EIGHT

MINNABAR

Minna forgot her fear after a couple of hours had passed. There was no room for it to exist and no energy to fuel it. All she could do was place one foot in front of another and feel the burn of the blisters inside her boots. All she saw was Dahn's back in its muddied white flightsuit with the black harness belt of woven fibre marching ahead of her. The grassland had given way to scrub forest, but here it was on richer ground, squelchy with water. The trees had mangrove roots big enough to trip and slide on even underwater where her feet hit them in shallow mud, and green patches of apparently solid earth were no more than films or mats of grass floating on top of knee-deep holes. She was drenched in water, mud and sweat. Everything rubbed her raw. She had never been more miserable in her life but it paled in comparison to the compulsion she felt to follow Dahn without complaining, no matter how many times she fell. Flies crawled on her like cold, ticklish curiosities and only sometimes bit. She had to blow them off her lips as she breathed so she didn't get them in her mouth but sometimes she still did and then would cough and spit in a panic while Dahn just walked, occasionally pausing to let her catch up or to haul her back to her feet.

The journey seemed to have no effect on the pilot. She gazed around her with ease and made the going seem light. Occasionally, the creature that Minna had come to think of as 'the dog' simply to give it a name that made it seem less terrifying, came back to her and circled around, then continued ahead. She longed to rest, to ask when it would be over but something about Dahn's ease made her want to appear less pathetic than she already was, not more, and so she didn't. She wasn't some stupid little girl who was going to cry and give in. Again. But there came a point when she slumped into a pothole and stuck there, no matter how she tried to climb out. She was aware of herself screaming and hitting the puddle-black water, then Dahn coming back to her and crouching down, crushing some strange plant leaves under her nose and pushing them into her mouth.

After that her awareness was blank, marked by flashes that were curious and seemed to happen to someone else. Dahn walked them to drier land and Minna's footfalls moved exactly where Dahn's did so that she didn't fall. Dahn was reaching up to the trees and fruit fell into her hands from the distant canopy. Minna was eating the fruit, pulpy and juicy, it was sweet and delicious. Her hands shone with a mantle of black flies on the drying residue after. Dahn stopped and let her wash them at a small waterfall. They drank there, cold water, from underground. Minna rode the dog, balanced on its narrow back behind its shoulderblades, smiling because she loved horse-rides. Under her hands the dog's skin was warm and tough, stubbly bits of hair sticking out of it. It was wearing something around its neck and shoulder like a collar, or a trophy. Minna should have known what it was but the knowledge seeped out of her head with the heat. Dahn moved and the forest moved to make way for her. She was a goddess there and Minna was both fearful and adoring of her. Then they stopped and Minna slept in a shaded nook.

The whining of the dog woke her. Dahn was nowhere to be seen. A strange sound was in the air, and a curious dryness like the powdery smell of the most powerful magic. Minna unwound from the tight ball she was in with small cries of dismay as burning pains returned to her. The dog glanced at her and she thought it looked nervous. The sound was a steady hum and it made all the leaves vibrate at a tiny frequency. She saw water droplets bounce off and sparkle in the air. It was nearly sundown but the flies that had bothered and bit her all day were nowhere to be seen. Her head was oddly clear. She stayed away from the dog but it ignored her anyway and went bolting off suddenly. She took a little look about, adjusted the stiff belt and checked the heavy clip of the signal blocker, unclipped it and studied it in a shaft of light coming through from far above.

After a few moments she worked out how to activate it and opened the charm mandala. She saw that it was what Dahn had told her, a signal disruptor. Now that she had moved out of range of the Spire crew the belt should have exploded but the trip-trigger failure was suspended by the closeness of the disruption field. It prevented the belt signalling itself. Then her eyes fell on a set of numbers in the lower section of the mandala and her heart plummeted. The battery was nearly out of power. She calculated quickly how long it had been running, if it had begun at the crash or earlier, likely earlier, if Dahn was prepared – and figured she had only a few hours left before it would run out. She searched her pockets but all she had were a few small tools, the rest were back at the crash site, along with any spare power cells of any kind.

She bit her lips together to prevent herself crying and put the disruptor firmly clipped into her inside pocket. Then she tried to access the belt lock, but it was cued to the trigger switch. Her own spells charmed it closed. They would accept only an access by the master key and she had no idea what that was other than an eight-symbol sequence. Someone else had programmed that. The forest was quiet, aside from the hum which seemed to have settled into her now, almost subdermal in its pervasiveness. She looked down and began to follow Dahn's boot tracks, going slowly, measured, eyes and ears alert. She had gone about twenty metres when she found the white flight suit, the boots and the fabric belt discarded on a tree. Underclothes were left on the ground. The tracks stopped at the boots. Minna looked around, slowly, carefully, silently. Nothing moved in the canopy except water dripping down from earlier rain. In every direction the forest was motionless in itself. She began to wish Dahn back again, even the dog. No, not the dog.

She made herself study the ground. The soft earth was giving way to leaf-covered dirt and harder pack but there were still prints. She saw the dog's marks, and a few barefoot tracks, both pointing in the direction of the hum. She went that way, figuring they could not be angry for her following them – she wasn't trying to escape. The notion tugged at her mind but she knew she would be lost in this forest long before she found the digsite, if that's even where they were. Her only chance was to reach something that could power the disruptor or remove the belt and the only lead she had on that was with Dahn. Fail at that and the forest and the dog or whatever didn't matter.

She had to pause to relieve herself, then she went on, moving only when she was sure of the way. It was so slow. When she looked back in ten minutes she could see the white suit hanging on the tree. A few minutes later she looked again, to check her line and progress and saw nothing. She stopped, holding on to a branch to steady herself, and looked again, certain that the pattern of the trunks and the green against brown markings of the ground pointed her directly at the correct spot. No foliage barred the sightline.

She had decided to retrace her steps and move back to be sure when she heard Dahn's voice from a short distance away to her left, 'Ahoy, Engineer!' She sounded hoarse and breathless.

Minna couldn't bring herself to speak but she moved in the direction of the sound, making a lot of noise. A few moments later the white suit and the pilot inside it came through two bushes and smiled at her with relief. 'There you are. I told you to stick put.'

'I...' Minna began, afraid of Dahn and more afraid of the forest. She clenched her right hand around her belt, feeling the slim packages of explosive compound snugly anchored there. Resentment and anger gave her the fuel to continue. 'The battery on the disruptor is low. I thought it would make more sense to follow you.'

'What?'

She saw immediate concern on Dahn's face as the woman came forward quickly, looking for the item. Minna took it out to show it to her, and at the last moment in a show of perversity, cued the wrong display mandala – the one that showed signal strengths, instead of power life. The sigils on the casing glowed obediently, wavering and flickering as digits altered inside them. She saw Dahn stare at it, her brown eyes at this distance visibly flecked with amber, rather pretty, as the numbers reflected off the surface of her eyeball. Minna saw immediately that Dahn could read it, but she did not know what it meant.

'There's only a few hours left,' she said, the fear in her voice quite real. She didn't want Dahn to know she'd caught her out so she added, to prevent questions, 'At best six hours.'

'Yes, I see.' Dahn looked pensive and Minna took the moment to notice that she seemed tired. 'When we reach the site I am sure there will be more batteries.'

Minna nodded. 'Are we there yet?'

'It is just a quarterstride off. But the city has arrived. It is making a descent.'

That explained the humming sound then, Minna imagined. A flicker of hope rose in her chest.

Dahn looked agitated and for the first time, undecided. 'There are many Karoo very close,' she explained as she saw Minna's

453

gaze on her. 'They are ready to fight. I must think how to pass them.'

Minna glanced about but there was no sign of the dog. 'Isn't the, um, that ... thing – a Karoo? The one that was with you?' She played it stupid, knowing she had that look perfected at least. Hundreds of days of playing the same game in Glimshard for social reasons paid off.

'It is a male,' Dahn said, as if it really was no more remarkable than a dog. 'They are easily controlled once you know how.' She frowned. 'The Spire biomages have captured and studied them.'

A lie if ever Minna had heard one. She knew that too from years of watching other girls blag and brag in efforts to save face or make others lose theirs. She nodded dumbly. 'So, where is it? Won't we need it?'

Dahn had her hand to her head and for a minute she ignored Minna. Then she looked up and drew herself tall. 'Now we go. You come quickly and we will be joining your team and getting you that battery.'

She turned and set off at a deceptively fast pace. Minna followed her, sick to her stomach as if she had eaten lead, not believing a word of it. But she had to find a battery somehow. Regardless of what Dahn was or wanted that was something she clung to as her own personal focus. Your team, she thought. Not our team. Your team.

The war of hope and despair inside her was nauseating but she had nothing to throw up. In any case, the distance passed quickly. They stopped within sight of a large timber barrier, spiked raw ends of posts reaching up into the air at twice Minna's height.

Dahn crouched down, hidden in foliage, and pulled Minna to do the same, unnecessarily as Minna collapsed on to her butt as soon as they had halted. The hum was loud, penetrating enough that she could feel it in her teeth. Over the timbers the sky was visible for a patch where the wood had been cleared and half of that was covered by an immense silhouette with geometrically precise hexagonal edges. It hovered about thirty metres up and Minna did not see it move. She considered that height to be its minimum unless they were going to ground it out. It must be at sky anchor.

She was studying it and just becoming sure it was not descending when there was a second and very sudden sound from behind the barrier itself. After a few seconds Minna determined that it was a kind of warning siren. There was a voice within it speaking words that she knew were not Imperial, although they rather sounded like old Imperial, though she hadn't paid attention enough in those classes to be sure. To her astonishment, however, she found that she did understand some of what it was saying, at least enough to figure out that Dahn had led them true. This was the digsite and the sound was coming from the artefact, whatever it was. She saw Dahn's face screwed up as the woman concentrated, listening with all her being in an effort to understand.

'...main power start.' Minna heard, along with some kind of warnings. '...supply twenty-one per cent... basic functions only... ensure all propulsion systems are disconnected.' There was more, then a pause, then a countdown began. As it was only five seconds she didn't bother saying anything, just crouched down and curled up into a ball again waiting for she didn't know what.

She felt Dahn's grasp on her arms, trying to prise them open. 'What is it?'

Then the ground shook. Minna knew with certainty that her mother was in there, doing this. This was so very much a Tralane kind of thing. She formed herself up into a core around that knowledge as several violent tremors shook them and the trees into a juddering rush of creaking and swishing. Without pause, it was answered by a chorus of enraged hoots, whistles and screams and then she huddled tighter, closer as she heard movement everywhere and the forest itself surged up and over the barricade, all around her. The only constant was Dahn's iron grip on her upper arm.

She was dragged, screaming, through whipping bushes and heavy, sodden ground, moving only because of the pain in her arm as it threatened to break. Green, brown, streaks of crimson, orange, white – the world was a mess of colours in blurred motion that meant nothing to her but most of them seemed to scream and shout with her in all the voices imaginable, some of them human.

She saw Glimshard tabards, fleeing, falling, heard the clash of swords, shields, a roar of fire and the blart of some odd beast in flight that shouldn't fly. Snarls and growls, shrieks, described death in different ways. She saw the dog again, rushing by them, blood streaming out of it like a banner. She was thrown against a heavy, smooth wall and the impact hammered through her skeleton and ended still in the pincer hold on her arm, an undeniable proof of life that made her want to laugh, except it hurt too much and she was crazy, beyond fear, in a place where the whole world was unstitched.

'Open it,' said Dahn's voice, cool and sure, close to her head. A sweet scent of fresh air filled her nose and calmed her, drew her attention to the mageplate before her hands and eyes. The door itself, alight with charms in glowing cartouches, waiting only for her commands. 'We're perfectly safe here. I'm with you. I'm taking you inside to the others. To the science team. To your mother,' Dahn said, relaxed and confident, encouraging. Her hold relented and the pain went away.

Minna cued the mandalas to spin and recognised the lock type. She saw it was only closed, not locked at all. The spells merely held the door in a shut position so that a cue was required, there was no code on it. She turned as she heard shrieking, reeled as a man collapsed virtually in front of her, his tabard awry and body ripped open by a huge thing, like the dog, tearing at him as it in turn was assaulted savagely by their own form of dog, weak but still raking with claws and breaking with its hands. She heard Dahn give it an order, though she couldn't have said what the words were.

Minna pushed the door and it gave way. She fell with it, inwards, and Dahn with her. As the world spun gore and sky to blackness, she felt a sadness like nothing she'd ever known. There was no need to lock the door because nobody outside it knew how to open it anyway, even though they could have run in and saved themselves at any time. She'd never seen an animal butchered, let alone a human torn apart alive. These things combined, image on image, a spell that formed in her mind, cast on them from some master mage that meant they would do these things here, would suffer this way, would die this way, ignorant and isolated in their own worlds when the answers were so close they could be touched but would remain unknown.

She landed on her back on metal flooring as Dahn sprang up and pushed the door closed against the sunlight, the silhouette of the city and the screams of the dying. The dog was left to die out there too, however things took it. Minna came to understand her odd position in things. She was like the dog, good as long as she was useful or until the battery ran out.

'They were Glimshard soldiers,' she said, sitting up, anger too hot to be held down.

'Not many of them,' Dahn said. 'And many too many Karoo. This was our only chance. We would not have survived out there.' She did look shaken and there was a ring of truth to the last words.

'What about the dog?'

'It was just a dog,' Dahn said, uninterested. She looked sleek and full, like a cat well fed in the sun as she put her hand out and pulled Minna to her sore and aching feet.

They stood on a tilted floor inside a small room. Bright light glowed from the lower parts of the walls, illuminating an obvious way through a door on to a ramp and, beyond that and over its rail, more halls and rooms in subtly different earth-toned colours. Long lines of cables, lightrope and stacked cubes of supply crates littered the area and the way as though something had lately gone through them all in a great hurry and left them where they fell. Minna could hear distant, muffled voices that seemed to be talking with animated excitement and fear. She looked at Dahn and saw her also listening, an expression of concentration on her face and her nostrils flared. Air moved slowly around them, strangely dry and scentless after the heat and saturation of the outdoors.

She was taller than Minna, with a greater reach and much better strength and reflexes. Minna didn't think she could outrun her but she glanced around quickly and saw other mage panels near the door. She paused to glance at her battery readout and saw it had shrunk a little.

'All right,' Dahn said. 'You first. Let's go.'

Minna looked around and made a show of studying the inner door panel. She could see this door was some kind of seal and it was broken but others in its area still operated. There was an active major node a few halls down – clearly the source of the voices. She memorised the route and then walked on, her hand out in case she slid or tripped on the sloping panels. Behind her, Dahn was close. Minna went as slowly as she dared – which was not much of a ruse since her legs and feet hurt with every stride and quivered with exhaustion. However, she was really thinking about what she would say or do when she found the Glimshard engineering team – how could she tell them her suspicions about Dahn when she knew Dahn was still wearing a suit with a trigger on it?

After a few turns, and the ever-increasing volume of the chatter, they came to a balcony which overlooked a huge space. At first Minna didn't realise what it was, thinking it a decorated wall, but, as they moved, the parallax and shadows gave away the truth and she stopped, then moved across to the rail where it leaned out, her mouth hanging open.

The structure they were in was huge. She was looking across a space that was at least forty metres wide but as she looked down into it she saw that it grew rapidly much wider until she was staring across some enormous space. On the other side, balconies and walkways, rooms and halls diminished to a point where suddenly the light failed and nothing was visible at all.

This thing was bigger inside than the Square of the Sun. Bigger than the entire University. She thought it was bigger even than Glimshard.

She felt Dahn beside her and looked up to find her sharing the moment of surprise. Dahn's face was mostly blank save for a hint of bafflement around the edges and she turned her head to look from different angles as if she didn't believe what she saw. She might have spoken but at that moment they heard footsteps in the way behind them and turned together to find the Glimshard engineering team approaching them, waving and talking loudly all at once.

The sight was so relieving and uplifting, or it could have been, except Minna knew that all this safety that was being offered to her now wasn't real and could never be as long as Dahn was there, and this belt was on her. It was the most cruel joke instead, that she must play along with or risk them all being blown to pieces when Dahn lost her patience in the weird game she was playing.

In spite of all her determination to get out of Dahn whatever there was to be had from her in payback for that, Minna found herself crying, so there was fresh humiliation to add to the total of the horrors. For some reason, it was the worst of them; to see so much in such a short time, to have colluded in the fabrication of your own death, to make it through the forest, to face the dog, to see what happened outside and to see it again and again as if it was etched in plain sight – to somehow survive all that and still function – and then this personal betrayal of the self.

Hate and rage filled her until she felt nothing but their consuming burn. She missed the first few lines of conversational exchange that Dahn managed with the others, explaining the lies of their lucky escape from the mysteriously downed plane, their ordeal in the forest at the mercy of the wild Karoo and then their salvation with Minna's heroic pushing open of an already open door. The replies were full of hope about power supplies and requests for news of the outside camp which Dahn skilfully avoided answering except to mention fighting.

Minna didn't hear her mother's voice anywhere. 'Hey, where's Tralane Huntingore?'

Her question broke through the chatter – having seen her and now identified her they were pleased to accept Dahn's story. Minna knew they wouldn't see her harness' true nature unless they really looked. She decided that for this moment Dahn was better controlled by letting her carry on into the deception. If she told otherwise then they would all immediately have to dispose of her – killing Minna – or become prisoners alongside her. For now, let everyone keep what they've got. She looked at faces, saw excitement and fear.

'She went down into the Print Room,' one of the engineers said. He was an average height man, stocky and given to frowning, which he did now. She thought she'd seen him before and his name might be Rofelo. 'It's a walk from here. There's another group at the Loom.'

Minna didn't know those words but it hardly mattered. Fine, there was a print room and a loom. They were far off. 'Is she all right?'

'She is. The Empress' Consort was with her ... She, you can talk to her on the links. Come this way.' Rofelo beckoned, his face full of the cheer he wanted to give her after the ordeal, and she went without a backward look, wondering what Dahn was going to do about it, if anything. So long as her mother was alive she felt there was some kind of chance.

In the end everyone went, Dahn among them as if she was a woman with her job completed, like she said – 'just waiting for the rest of the city to arrive now.'

Minna was sat in one of the only decent chairs while the others brought her water and ration food. She took the disruptor out and looked at it, against her will – four hours. Then she caught the arm of Engineer Micklas as the woman bent to refill her cup. 'I need a battery, for this.'

Micklas, a strong woman with a lined face and lips thinned both by age and compression in thought, lofted her eyebrows and hunkered down to take a look at the device. Her overalls badge told Minna she was a weaver mage – someone who could fit devices and spells together. Micklas tried to take the small item but Minna held on to it, knuckles white. The older woman read the mandala slowly and then looked up into Minna's face, her own expression gone from friendly to serious. Then her gaze roved slowly over Minna, taking in the flight suit and then the harness belt. She let go of the disruptor and her fingers carefully touched the harness and then turned part of it over so she could see underneath. Wires and thin lozenges showed for a moment.

'It was so I didn't escape,' Minna said. 'It won't open. I already tried that.' She could hardly stop herself from breaking down as Micklas stared at her with hollow eyes and then glanced around. 'Dahn knows but don't tell the others. They might try to get it off.'

Micklas' voice was whispered as she replied, 'You can't wear it for ever.'

'I might be able to work out a way,' Minna said. 'But I need time. It's on a double failsafe. If this signal stops it will go off. Can you find me something?'

Micklas took a small multitool out of her pocket and gently took the inspection plate of the blocker off, looking at the nested crystalline battery inside it. 'Disconnecting this looks bugged too. We could recharge the crystal maybe without cutting the energy flow. Best bet. Wait here and rest, I'll look for the right parts. Power's not something we're short of right now.' She gave a smile, strong and confident, and replaced the plate exactly as it had been with great care. 'You should speak to your mother. I'll check and see if Rofelo has the pane set up.'

'Don't tell her about this,' Minna said, still gripping Micklas' wrist. 'Please.' She couldn't stand it if anyone knew, especially Tralane. She didn't want to worry her when there was so much going on.

Micklas nodded after a moment's hesitation and then Minna let her go. She tried to eat but she felt so tight inside that nothing would go down except the first meagre bite. Her guts were twisted in a huge, hot knot that filled every bit of space. She pretended to cut up the food as she watched Dahn, who drank also but didn't eat. Dahn glanced at her across the room but Minna couldn't read the information in the long look they shared and she broke it first, afraid that she'd already given her hate away.

Dahn reached up to her collar and brushed her thumb to the spot that the Spire officer had indicated – the detonator point. Minna realised she could have fixed that when she found the flightsuit hanging on the tree, if she'd had any brains, but the chance was gone now. Would the pilot have one? She didn't know and had to assume so. Would it override the disruptor? Again, no way to know for sure. Let's say so, to be on the safe side, she thought and the phrase made her mouth smile all on its own.

Dahn frowned and turned to stare at what the engineers were doing, the huge arrays of spell lights that filled the room like turning star systems in the air, the crystal panes of foggy colours that tried to display places that weren't connected, or never had been.

Minna's eyes automatically read what she saw. Slowly she put down her plate and cup and although her legs screamed at her not to she stood up and went to see the smaller of the three panes, where a diagram was laid out, with markings in arcane, ancient hieroglyphs; a schematic. Here they were – she put her finger on the glowing spot, saw the flow of energy in the conduits there. And here was another lit room, something to do with weave – it must mean loom, this cartouche, she realised. Where everything was put together. And this other room then, that was makings or perhaps something like production or growing –what they had called the print room. Her mother was in the print room. Where she was, and the loom and the print room were all in the first third of the whole – but she could see that this in turn was only a small section of something much larger.

She found herself reading the edges of the schematic until she found the symbols that looked correct for moving out into a larger view. She touched them and then thought she had made a mistake, went back, went out again. Engineer Micklas came up as she was flicking through the change and looked over her shoulder. 'Now, child, are you sure you can read that... Ah, of course, Sircene, you can read it all, I should have thought... What are you looking at?'

'I think this must be broken,' Minna said. 'But—' She held her hand still over the pane.

'Ah, yes, we thought that too,' Micklas agreed.

Minna turned to her. 'Nothing is that big. This is the size of the whole of Hadirath, or more.' She couldn't imagine a device the size of an entire country. 'And this would be like some tiny piece.' She looked at the schematic which put her in one of twenty different lesser sections arranged around the much larger central spine of whatever it was. Most of it was displayed in flat grey with only the portions she had seen in lit up white characters. 'All this.' She sketched the grey mass.

'All that is lost, gone. This bit—' Micklas cued the original back. 'Is all that remains, and in fact we think most of this is gone too, only the very bright parts with the yellowed star marks are whole and functional. You can see why we wanted it so badly now though. You almost never find anything as good as this. Nothing like as good as this. If this is correct we could potentially fit all our archaeology for the last two centuries somewhere into this map.'

Minna was aware of Dahn loitering near them, watching. 'I don't believe it.' She did. Her mind was buzzing with it, her nerves electrified with the excitement of what she had seen and what it meant.

'Well, it will take a lot of studying,' Micklas said and held out the small boxed kit towards her. 'Can you work this out for yourself or do you want help with it?'

Minna opened the case and looked. 'I can manage it. Thank you.'

Micklas smiled warmly, 'You're welcome. We nearly have connection to the print room too. A minute or two should sort it. If you have any trouble, I'm right over here.' She pointed to her station.

Her confidence was touching. Minna saw her turn and her expression fall however. Who could blame anyone for that in the circumstances? She thought it best if she limit the potential for disaster and made some excuse about going where there was better light. Dahn followed her out of the room and back towards the balcony. The light was worse if anything. Minna sat down and opened the kit out carefully, saying nothing as Dahn lounged at the rail, looking at the astonishing view.

'Can you fix it?' Dahn asked, when they were quite alone.

Minna opened the back of the disruptor box. It had occurred to her that it might be a fake, or the belt was a fake, or everything was a hoax. But she pretended not. How could she know? She didn't know an explosive from mud. Anyone could be fooled with so little. 'I might be able to.' She deliberately didn't look up. She had lost interest in Dahn for the time being. She concentrated instead on locating connectors and trying to match the resonance of the Spire power crystal to the assorted battery components Micklas had found from the Glimshard supplies. She wondered if Dahn had been fooled by her too, if she had read Minna's real anger and resentment and tantrums and thought they were all due to the circumstances and that as far as Minna was concerned Dahn really was nothing other than a good Glimshard agent doing her job. After all, there was no reason to think that Tzaban had not given special information out about Karoo, that dogs were merely – controllable things. Only, if they were, why was everyone outside so very dead?

'How did you get this anyway?' she asked, holding up the disruptor. 'How did you know they'd do that to me?'

'It's a standard Spire tactic when they use anyone who isn't in their elite forces,' Dahn said. 'The unit captain had the disruptor on him. They always carry them.'

Minna scowled, working on building a circuit up. That sounded true to her, and plausible. She had to keep remembering the dog. With the kit open, she began to see other possibilities beyond a simple recharge. Her fingers worked steadily, clipping, trimming wire, soldering, spellsmithing the components with symbols and cues that any engineer could use.

Dahn watched her and sighed. 'I see nothing in these things.'

'Minnabar! The pane is connected. Come, come, your mother is waiting!'

It was Micklas. Minna packed up the kit and went obediently, slipping the slender box into the long leg pocket of her flight suit and sealing it there.

CHAPTER TWENTY-NINE

TRALANE

Tralane stood, surrounded on all sides by the intricate astral light glyphs of a machine so intricately manufactured, so beautifully spellbound, she was at a loss for anything but awe. Awe had to be smothered however, to speed the interpretation and reading of what she had called up after the power had been restored by the weavers. As before, the language of the glyphs was both familiar and new to her, not only filled with archaisms but formulations she had never seen before and which she had to puzzle out one radical at a time until she was able to make educated guesses of the meaning and the function. In her hand, her small, worn magepane felt as if it too was struggling to cope with the influx. She had not been able to form any working connection between it and this incredible room so she had to copy the symbols by hand into it and the going was slow. It was so absorbing, however, that she soon lost track of everything else around her as she delved into one spell after another, each a phrase or melody fragment of a vast concert. Gradually, things began to form into sense, but the more she saw the more of a chill she felt. Around her, she was vaguely aware of Carlyn and the other two mages for a time, until they too ceased to register and only the white language of the starlight remained. It was like swimming in a new ocean of unimagined vastness, limitless potential. She forgot everything but the rapture of discovery.

A voice, harsh and tired, broke her from it. Stopping was almost painful, as if her mind was meshed with the spells and separation physically pulled it apart. She found herself aching, exhausted, blinking with dry eyes as Carlyn stood, hand on Tralane's arm firmly, pale face concerned. "Lane, where did he go?'

'Who?' Her head was swimming with marks. Those suspended around her stopped and fixed themselves in place as she looked through them to her friend. They lay on Caryln's skin like snowflakes, writing out their plans.

'Tzaban.' She said the name with dislike, but also worry. 'He was lying on the floor until just now when he suddenly got up. He was listening. Then he went out. That way.' She pointed at the door they had entered by and back the way they had come.

Tralane looked where she was directed, and then back at the spot where he had been against the wall. A large patch of smeared blood marked it. There was no telling whose blood it was. Tzaban hadn't spoken since the fight, nor did anyone want him to. He had changed during it in a way none of them were prepared for, including Tralane who had seen him do it before. This time it had been different. This time he had turned into a monster. There was plenty of vomit not far away after they had been forced to witness the two Karoo fight each other. She still couldn't quite believe his transformation or witnessing him desecrate the corpse of his opponent in what she assumed Carlyn would understand as a way that was all too human. She swallowed on a sour taste and felt weak. She took some horrible dried biscuit from her personal pocketful of the things and made herself eat. 'Did he say anything?' She could see sickly relief in Carlyn's face as her friend shook her head.

'Started sniffing, sat up, got up, went out.'

'There was one left, he said.' Tralane started to come out

of her study haze. She took the water Carlyn offered her and drank, then looked around. 'Maybe that's where he went.'

'Soros says the main door opened five minutes ago.'

Tralane started – another thing she hadn't noticed. She looked through the astral display to the other shifting clouds that surrounded Soros and Fa'su, the other engineers. 'Can you track movements on that?'

Soros shook his head. 'I should be able to but for some reason it doesn't activate. I think there's a lot of disruption here. A lot of things are broken and jumbled up. Even if I can tell what things do, I can't make most of it operate. Lot of protection spells in place that would take a better mathematician than me to get rid of.' He sighed and Tralane watched him pop a pill out of a packet and drink it down. 'I gotta stay awake here,' Soros said, guilty, and then sighed. 'You know some of it, I think, is down to the shot you made. I'm not saying it's your fault.'

Tralane's stomach clenched and she thought she might be sick again. The shot had been much too wide, taking out not only the Karoo but also one wall, a section of ceiling and most of the floor. There was now a tiny walkway at one side of the hall for two metres, instead of ordinary floor, and beside it a drop into the dark rooms below. The walls and fittings were coated in blood and dust, the only remains. When she'd recovered from the surprise of that she'd altered the gun setting radically. Rather late. Now that she looked down she noticed her hands and the front of her were coated in fine grey and red films. She dropped the biscuit on the floor. She might well have destroyed a great deal of valuable research potential, there was no denying it. At the same time, not much of any ancient thing worked first time, even hundredth time.

'I don't think that's likely,' Carlyn said. 'So much of this whole place is a mess.'

'Are you getting much out of it?' Tralane asked her, trying for water again.

'Yes. I think that the people who made this were here less than ten thousand years ago. I found some bones and dated them. Later I can see if we can get any blood traces out of them. It's actually a terrific find. We've had bone before but only fragments.' She smiled and some of her old fire came back with the thoughts of returning to research. 'If we get out of here I'll have enough for a lifetime's work.'

'Don't say that. We're going soon. The city should be here any time.'

'I think it is already here,' Soros said. 'I have a line in from the top. They are reporting fights, engine noise . . . It's garbled. Wait. Tralane. They say your daughter's there.'

'Isabeau is here?' Tralane moved eagerly towards Soros and the pane she was struggling to operate. Bits of image flickered in it within the moss-coloured mist it seemed to prefer displaying. Parts of them were undoubtedly the entrance room they had first opened up and parts of the people she knew very well by now. 'Can I talk to her?'

'I can't get the sound to come,' Soros said. 'We're just noting . . . Wait, not Isabeau. Minnabar.'

Tralane had to resist the impulse to push Soros out of the way. Instead, she stared at the pane and tried to see through the flickering bursts. Then Soros made a small surprised noise and the picture and the sound cleared. Tralane saw Minna standing there among the survivors of the doorside team, some kind of grey overalls on her. She looked terrible and strangely tiny without her hair. But she was alive. Tralane's fierce joy couldn't be contained. 'Min! You're here! How? Why?'

Minna's face was painted with dirt and exhaustion but through it Tralane saw an edgy wariness that sounded every alarm bell in her body.

'Minna?'

'I'm okay, Mom. It's a long story. Better left for later. I'm okay. Everything's fine.'

Now Tralane was sure it was very far from fine but something in Minna's face pushed her to be quiet about it – a thing which only turned her initial joy to dread quicker. She searched the rest of the image of the upper room and saw a face she didn't know. Micklas was there though, and Tralane had learned to rely on her.

'Mick, how are things?'

'We're all right. No sign of any more of those things. There was fighting outside though. Um, the agent who brought Minna back says that she thinks the crew outside didn't make it.' She paused and then carried on. 'We have engine sound outside so we can confirm the city is here, at least close. We're prepping for an exit within an hour or two. There's some signals coming that we think are from Glimshard. Just need to refine a few frequencies and order a few spheres.'

Tralane looked at the strange face. That woman. The Glimshard agent. She returned Minna, but Minna stood apart from her, wan, shy, almost cringing in a way that Tralane had never seen before. She didn't look a bit rescued.

Tralane was still looking at her, puzzled, when she realised the silence waited for her to reply. 'Um, well, since you're here now, Minna, I think I could really use your help down here for the last hour or two. There's so much to do, so much to gather and some of it is definitely your special area. I can't even figure out the first thing about it.' She had begun to gabble, she realised, and shut up.

'But what about the, um, the thing,' Micklas said, swallowing nervously.

'Well Tzaban should be back soon from . . .' Tralane's hopeful plan was cut short by a sudden huge commotion at the other end. She saw the room's tableau break up suddenly and heard a cacophony that the poor transmission couldn't make sound like anything other than crashing, banging and snarls. She gripped the projection console as she saw Minna shrink and back out

470

of the picture, matched by others also fleeing the doorway. The noise was intense and terrible. She recognised Tzaban's voice in it, at least his vocal sounds, as there weren't any words. But what stood out to her as she shouted pointlessly at the glass, was the image of the strange agent, still standing in the middle of the room where she had always been. She alone of all the people there was peering around the doorframe with interest, her face alight with a kind of fascinated rapture Tralane had never seen before, lips parted, hands poised as if to snatch something incredible out of the air.

It was exactly at that moment she became sure that what she was looking at was not human. At the same moment she saw the reason why she had not understood the half of the spells in the room. She had assumed they were as written. But they had been corrupted and that was why things didn't seem to fit as expected. They hadn't generated impossibilities, the faults had passed the fitness test of syntax for spellcasting. They parsed out – they simply didn't say anything that made sense to her. She turned to go back to them, but then turned to the pane again, equally unable to tear herself from that sight.

Then the agent moved. With decisive speed she darted to where Minna had gone and in a second she was back, dragging Minna with her by her collar and one arm behind her back. A knife was visible in the collar hand and, as she shoved Minna towards the pane, it moved to her throat. Minna gasped. Tralane stared.

'What the . . .' Soros began but the agent was already speaking.

'Call off your male. Call it off! Or the girl dies.'

'Mmom, Mom, she means Tzaban, Tzaban!' Minna spluttered in a high, terrified voice.

Tralane froze for as long as it took to process what she saw and heard. She opened her mouth, shouted at the pane. 'Stop it! Tzaban, come back, come back!' Her own voice cracked at the top of the call which she hoped was good enough because she had nothing else. She leaned over, stared into the pane as though that way she'd reach the people in it. 'Don't hurt her! I don't know what else to do! I don't understand! Please. Don't hurt her.'

The next few seconds passed like years. She looked for the other engineers, cowering, some of them reaching for tools but too frightened to move now, plastered back against whatever furniture was near them. The agent didn't waver but her attention clearly moved back towards the door for a moment and then a creature walked through it which Tralane assumed was the unaccounted-for Karoo male.

It was much less human looking than Tzaban, lithe and sinewy like a giant cat with an elongated head, it was covered in scales that changed in the light so that it mimicked the background exactly as it moved across it, rendering it visible as if it were made of transparent liquid crystal. Its eyes were crystal too, save for black pitted centres, though its mouth was red inside and blood described the curve of its jaws and chin, the long teeth that it displayed in a strange deferential yawn as it approached the agent and cowered beside her.

Tralane glanced back at Minna who was staring at her through the pane as if the force of her stare could transmit information on its own. Behind the fear, her brain clicked pieces together. This woman must be Karoo or else used as Tralane had been. But why would she be here, and how? They had come from Glimshard, so she had been in position far in advance of this day whereas nothing that had happened to Tralane had felt orchestrated at all.

The knife blade was removed, though Tralane watched it go with the thought that maybe she had fallen for a bluff. If Minna, she and the others died, who was left to go through this and tell anyone what it was? There was a hard limit on how much you could eat without leaving yourself nothing at all. Unhappy thinking as it was to do she had to admit the ones who had been culled from the groups were the weakest of all, able to follow others' leaps of thought and remember them, but people who rarely made original work of their own.

She made a kind of nod with a blink and a small move of her head to show Minna she was still there, still thinking. Minna looked wretched still and Tralane knew there was something important she was missing. But Minna was safe. The woman stood relaxed and let her go, pushing her towards the Karoo. Tralane tensed, but the creature did nothing except lie down, licking at its shoulder and foreleg where it was wounded. Minna held on to the belt at her waist and where it went over her shoulder. Her stare at the pane was miserable and furious. She mouthed a word that might have been 'Mom' but then Tralane thought it was 'bomb' and looked at the belt again. Again.

A strange reaction then: as it seemed all the blood drained out of her from head to foot leaving ice in its wake. She felt Carlyn come close beside her.

''Laney,' she said, to show solidarity, and Tralane nodded to show she heard. Around her the others were waking from their stunned reaction.

Tralane looked into the pane. 'I need her down here,' she said. 'She has the skills necessary to fix this stuff and read it. I don't care which... who brings her. Just bring her.'

The nonhuman woman looked back at her for a long moment, her face idiotic in its blankness. Now there was no more Glimshard charade to keep up and she was revealed as a spy. Tralane didn't know what her priorities were, but this seemed as good a way of finding out as any. She didn't underestimate the value of being what she was now. 'Without us you know nothing. If she doesn't come here then this entire project will be a big waste of time.'

A lie, but what would they know to contradict it? Half the

473

things they had discovered already they hadn't had time to document or even speak to each other about.

A sound from outside came through the speakers and everyone in the room, except the Karoo, turned to look at the door automatically. Tralane guessed that Glimshard's greater forces had arrived on the doorstep.

'If she's not here in ten minutes we're out of here. We have to meet the incoming recovery team,' she said and reached out, slicing the link spell and breaking the connection. The pane became grey mist.

'Are you sure that was Glimshard?' Carlyn said, a shred of hope in her voice for the first time in days.

Tralane pointed to a spiralling cartouche a few feet to her left, filled with tiny characters flickering so fast in their changes that they looked like fairy dust. 'That's them connecting threads with the loom, or trying to. Filaments are incoming. I'd bet they're on the ground outside now.'

'Or more of those things are trying to get in,' Soros said glumly and shrugged when she looked at him, as if he was only saying what everyone was thinking. 'Why did you shut off the link?'

'So she had to make a decision,' Tralane said. 'If Minna isn't here in ten minutes' time then we leave everything here and go up to the surface by the safest route. I suggest we bypass the top team altogether.'

'What about the Karoo?' Soros insisted. 'It will find us, even if she doesn't. We're better off waiting here for the guard to take charge up there and then come get us.' He folded his arms and then used one hand to rub his eyes, hard.

Tralane saw his exhaustion telling, but they were all tired. It didn't mean they were useless. 'Either my daughter comes here to me or I will go get her. You do what you like.'

'All this politics,' Soros moaned, as if it was personally directed at him. 'I am sick of it. Where is the Empire when you need it? One woman from Spire, is that what they send? One filthy Karoo, that's what we get to defend us?'

Tralane let his misery pass her by. She turned as she heard the quiet step and drag of feet coming along the hall outside. Carlyn moved back and Tralane went forward to meet Tzaban as he came in, limping, his face full of baleful misgiving aimed at her as he arrived. He opened his mouth to speak but a red bolt spat out from his right shoulder and smothered the wall behind him. He looked surprised, gaze passing her, and then the words became a long groan stopped by a thud as his knees hit the floor and he collapsed into a slumped seated position, hand going to the entry point of the bolt.

Tralane turned and saw Carlyn standing, the gun in her outstretched hand, its muzzle falling slowly as she tried to lift it back up again and take aim. It seemed her arm wouldn't let her. At her hip the empty holster felt light as Tralane automatically checked it. Her shock at the action was matched by the cut of the betrayal. She saw the hurt and confusion on her friend's face, the fear and the sickly relief of having done something about it, at last.

'You idiot,' she said, moving to take the gun. She was shaking with rage and didn't trust herself to say any more.

Carlyn gave it up without a protest, her mouth opening and shutting with a soft 'pop pop' sound. 'He's one of them,' she said quietly.

'He's one of us too,' Tralane said. She disabled the gun, restored it to her side, and looked at the rest of them, standing where surprise had left them. 'Get me the medical kit and pray he's not going to die or we really are screwed.'

Tzaban was cold and shaking. The shot had punched a hole right out of him but although it had left a huge bloody debris in its wake it had cauterized its path and the wound only seeped rather than bled. It was an addition to an already considerable list, however, and when she tried to examine him he snarled and told her to stay back, he was having trouble with the pain. She sat down where she was, arm's reach away, and handed him a sachet of water which he tore open and drank before dropping it from his mouth.

His yellow eyes fixed on hers. 'That woman up there is a Karoo queen. In here to get all you know for herself. Use it to rise over others, claim this as her own.'

'Use it how?' Tralane offered him more water but he turned it down.

'Not to use this.' He looked around, indicating the entire artefact. 'But it is new, unusual, powerful, and full of magic. The Karoo don't do magic like you, but they want to. Whatever's here she uses to gain advantage. But she has rivals. Outside. Big rivals.'

'The one who changed us.'

'Yes,' he groaned and moved to sit upright. 'You should know I had to give her all I had. The Empress traded her, something. Now she and this new one fight.'

'The Empress?' Carlyn said.

Tzaban glanced at her. 'Torada had faith in paying. Doesn't listen. It was in my blood.'

'Tzaban,' Tralane said firmly and his attention slid directly to her. 'How is it that this new one is so human looking? How is it that she speaks, knows?'

'I don't know,' he said. 'Never saw female do that before, but... hm, how you say, she is a half half, not female or male, both. Can do both things. Sometimes made that way, accident.' He sighed in a bubbling breath. 'She knew trouble here when couldn't make me serve her. Then she grabbed your girl.'

'Does she understand we must stay alive if anything is to come out of here?'

'Yes but, hn, law of diminish returns soon. Only look human. Only sound human. Not caring about these things.' He closed his eyes and slid down to the floor where he lay with one arm under his head, breathing in a laboured way, making a hnnn-hnn sound to himself.

'Tzaban?'

'Rest,' he said. 'Soon she comes. Torada close. Dahn closer.'

Tralane looked around at Carlyn. 'You're the people person – what do you guess?'

Carlyn looked at Tzaban, her face white. 'It was a mistake,' she said quietly.

'Forget that for now,' Tralane said sternly. 'I need you to consider what the Empress was thinking with all this. Where it could go. I need you to concentrate on that. Soros, is the line to Glimshard open?'

'Minute or so maybe,' Soros said.

'We have to warn them what's going on in here.'

'And what is going on in here?' Carlyn asked. She had her arms folded and was trying not to shake. The other engineers had returned to their stations but kept looking back and to the door.

'If we don't get out of here very soon there is a good chance we won't get out at all,' Tralane said. 'We need to disable that other Karoo male or kill it, and we need to get hold of that other one. Dahn. Tzaban, can you kill her?'

'No,' he said. 'Never kill females.'

'Well, can I kill her?'

'Will die same as you, likely.'

'What are you asking him for, he's finished,' Soros said. 'Line's up by the way.'

They all paused to listen. Across a hiss of static interference Isabeau's voice came through, unemotional but clear. 'Artefact team, stay at your station away from the door. The area outside is to be cleared. A rescue team will come for you once that is done. Stand fast.'

'What does she mean, cleared?' Carlyn said.

'The city has weapons of its own,' Tralane said. 'I think she means razed to the ground. With fire.'

Tzaban groaned. 'No. Tell Torada to talk. Talk to the forest. Night knows how.'

Tralane got up and relayed his message. She knew Isabeau would know her voice, as she was comforted by hearing Issa's. There was a pause and then a hesitant, 'All right, Mom.' Then the line closed. It clicked back on. 'We're still clearing around you. Wait for update.'

Tzaban groaned again and tried to get to his feet.

'Sit,' Tralane said to him but he shook his head and looked up at her.

'Listen to me. I ate enough human and smelt enough Karoo to know something I didn't know before. Karoo brought you here, whole city, as trophy pile. Understand? I did not know, now I do. Figured it out.' He smiled briefly at her, shy pride in the look that made her heart go out to him. Then pain made him speak faster and more urgently. 'Karoo eat you enough, become like you, no more need for you. They used me to help bring you. You smart humans, can't let any buried thing alone. Karoo found this thing. Brought you here. Thousands of you. It was not my will. Know that, Tralane Huntingore.'

'I believe you,' she said, more afraid now that he was going to die and leave them defenceless.

'But the city is here now,' Carlyn said. 'Karoo can't take that. They have no chance.' She sounded more hopeful than convinced.

'Not by assault,' Tzaban said. His breathing was laboured and the purple depths around his eyes had become pale lilac. 'But you will stay to study this. You will always come. Maybe you will think you fight Karoo back a little to a distance. You will come.'

'This Dahn queen. What does she gain if – if she has us?'

'She needs you alive,' Tzaban said. 'But not all of you. Needs

478

you to feed herself until she becomes like you. Then she has no more need of you. It will take time. She knows there is none, now the city is here, and outside is the other queen who took the Empress' gift.'

'So she might do anything. To win?'

'Eat or be eaten. Karoo way,' Tzaban said with a deep sigh that ended as a groan. 'I think Torada gave gift to help talk. Make talk. I don't know. I can't see these things.' He smiled very briefly again. 'Was a good gift. Or we would be dead.' He made a huge effort to get to his feet and got them under him. By the time he made it upright Tralane had helped him there and he stared at her, reluctantly grateful, as she supported his weakened side. 'Let go.'

'Really?' she said, exasperated now. 'And what are you going to do?'

'Go back, kill other male. Queen does not come, won't send her. Your girl.'

'Forgive my scepticism,' she said, not letting go. He swayed. She wasn't sure he could even make it up there alone. 'Anyway, there's another problem you're not aware of with regard to that.' She told them all about the suspected bomb.

'Now, what?' Soros asked. 'The top team are signalling for a link.'

'In twenty seconds you will open the comm, and say that Carlyn has used a human weapon to disable Tzaban, show him. You will say I have been taken ill with stress and have been given a sedative. You will then conduct with them whatever business must be done as if this is true.'

'And what about you?' Soros said, weaving the link spell around his fingers.

'I'm going to sort it out by myself,' Tralane said. 'They're all there together, they won't expect me to come alone.' She helped Tzaban closer to Soros and then left him, gingerly, as if

479

he were a house of cards, and said to him, 'When you see them, fall down.'

"Lane, it's too dangerous,' Carlyn said. Her face was white, her hands gripped together in front of her.

Tralane felt a burst of irritation that bordered on hatred. 'You stay there and don't do anything,' she said. For a moment they shared a glance. She knew Carlyn had only acted, as she was about to act, from the necessity of fear. She understood it, having seen what the Karoo had done. She could not find it in herself to forgive the particulars of the cowardice however and turned to go before her heart hardened further. 'Don't say a word. I'll see you later.'

Nobody tried to stop her.

CHAPTER THIRTY

ISABEAU

Isabeau stood on the edge of the pit under the beating noon sun and looked down into its cracked, scorched mud where the magefire had touched down. The edge of its swathe made a perfect circle just inside the hole. Piles of ash tried to lift in the slight breeze but failed. The humidity had already made the fragile flakes too heavy to rise. At the centre of the destruction the angled thorn spike of the artefact jutted upwards, coated in a patina of black. She wondered if it had always looked like that.

Behind her she heard the shouts and cries of dismay as the guards located the bodies of more Glimshard soldiers in the wreckage of the small fort which had sat atop the bank. The search had been going on for more than ten minutes and she had been held back with a couple of assistant engineers and a few personal guards while it went on. She gathered from the shouts and the silences between them that what she had glimpsed of dismembered bodies and blood was only a prelude to the rest. What surprised her most was that the jungle stank. Mud, blood, plants, rot, water and flowers of a peculiar sickly sweetness left telltales in air as thick as syrup. It clung to her face and her clothes hung heavy with it. Nearby she heard Night and the Empress talking in hushed tones. She still felt it wrong but

Torada had insisted she descend to the site herself. Isabeau was grateful in a way – the presence was comforting. She finished her inspection of the city's work on the ground and lifted her gaze to the green wall of forest on the far side of the pit.

The trees at the edge here were small and the spaces between very narrow. Bushes and vines filled up the gaps quickly so that she could see only a few spindly uprights between splashes of green, and beyond those a blurred darkness that seemed to have a still, attentive quality focused enough that it seemed to watch her in return. She stared, trying to see who was there. People ran behind her, voices highly charged rushed back and forth, but she paid no attention.

A touch at her shoulder from one guard made her turn away. 'Engineer. The Empress requests your company through the camp.'

Turning her back seemed imprudent but she went, following Torada and Night as they in turn followed a cadre of guards. Alongside her, the small, grey figure of Shrazade the infomancer strode with grim determination, not giving her a glance. Shrazade was an unwilling visitor here, more used to minions doing footwork, and her anger was palpable.

Isabeau looked cautiously to left and right as they went, driven by curiosity. The bodies had been ordered and covered up here in the early part, but then they were laid in lines as they neared the centre of the camp – nothing left to cover them. Where the bodies were not whole they were also laid in line in the flat grass. Flies clustered on them in the bright sun, black carapaces sparkling.

They reached the only standing structure left – a ragged tent with loose, flapping sides that was open to the front. Guards parted before them. The smell of the flowers was even sweeter here, though Isabeau didn't see any.

Shrazade's sudden hiss startled her so that she looked at the woman, and then followed the line of her gaze between Torada and Night's heads to a figure seated in a chair by a small table, just visible inside the tent's shade. She moved forwards and saw General Borze, his uniform stained and ruined with red, green and brown. His short hair was crusted in filth and his scabbard hung at his hip, empty. A bandana hung in his fingers where his hand was fallen at his side, quivering with a bizarre nervous tension that also opened his eyes and animated his face. His wide eyes did not recognise her, but stared glassily at the Empress. A foam had collected at one corner of his mouth.

A sensation of slow prickling cold ran over her from toes and fingers, up her arms, up her spine, as if her skin tried to shed itself. At the same moment a horrible, unexpected opening happened inside her chest and belly as if her guts were sliced open and spilled out, all warmth gushing with them towards him. She recalled all her words, all her papers. She saw his face in the steam room, his hand on her wrist, water rolling on his face like sweat rolled on it now. All empty. All worthless. The Empress spoke and he replied like a dreamer who walks in their sleep and can be talked to as if they wake, but are not awake.

No, she thought, watching him, her face stone as her body's energy drained away through her open centre like water down a gutter. Don't wake.

The Empress spoke. 'I am Torada, Empress of the Imperia Aethera. I come to deal with you for peace and mutual gain.'

He replied in a slow, laboured drawl, the words pulled carelessly out of his mouth as if on a string. There was no sign of anyone else in the tent, or the camp, or the forest. 'Your offer is accepted. For now.'

Isabeau stood in shock, frozen to the point that whatever they said meant nothing to her. She hadn't known that a person could be undone this way. She'd thought that because it was only bodies it didn't matter. Now all that kept her standing was the fact that her body was emptied out and couldn't move. Had she been in love with him? How could that be and she not notice it? She hadn't believed in it but it was still true, discovered inside her after all this time.

She remembered throwing the book into the garbage bin. It had never occurred to her that the mind had its worlds – a billion planes – but the body had only one, and they did not necessarily ever meet. What could they say to one another when they were from different realities? She had written off her body as merely her vehicle and now it was mortally wounded and all her realities wanted to die.

Beside her, Shrazade touched her arm and she looked down into the shorter woman's eyes and saw a peculiar compassion there. It was so unexpected she nearly recoiled. Then she realised that the telepath was reading her. She was reading everyone. Until this moment Isabeau had never given a thought to what that kind of ability meant or the power it gave the person who was able to use it at will. Now she knew why Torada demanded she stay close – only proximity would give the Empress' presence enough leverage to remain in command of Shrazade: which meant that what happened here was against Imperial will. And it meant that Torada was withstanding the force of the other Empresses. She filed this away for future reference, noting that her mind operated, clickety clack, unhindered by her heart. For the first time in her life this disgusted her and she tried to make herself look back at what had become of her abandoned lover.

As he talked and moved listlessly, twitching, jerking at the commands of the unseen queen she knew that Borze was no more. She was looking at a body that looked like someone she once knew. The horror remained but it was dulled. She looked back at Shrazade and noted the haunted expression, the gaunt face, the tired eyes. Infomancers did this to one another too, until they figured out who was strongest, the Unassailable. Shrazade's face slowly deformed as the conversation plodded remorselessly to its conclusion, becoming a mask of loathing. She feared possession, Isabeau saw, and looked across at Mazhd, standing on her other side. A rigor of self-command kept him from anything but sadness. He was resigned to it, she thought. She determined that his was the best course of action, and that she would take it now: resign herself to reality and move on. Then she glanced at her new Master, Night, and saw there calculation, as cool and precise as the revolving tumblers of a lock. She leaned, just a little, towards Torada.

On the breeze, the smell of sweet flowers could not disguise the odour of decomposing flesh. It eddied around, both scents together, while they concluded arrangements and formed the ingress party. Isabeau was left to herself for a few minutes as last-moment decisions were made. She moved as far away from the tent and its dreadful effigy as she could. From her bag she took out the goggles that her mother had so liked to tinker with. She had kept them with her since Tralane left the house, thinking she would find a use for them although now she knew it was as a way of staying in contact even though she hadn't tried to use them for that purpose. There hadn't been any free time since she'd been up to the lab and dropped them into the kit, even to look at them herself. Now that she did, she found they were fascinating.

'Time to go!'

Mazhd surprised her – she had become so lost in the intricacies and the unexpected compactness of the mass of spells that were crammed into such a small device. 'Just a minute!' She sniffed, blotting tears from her nose with her sleeve, and quickly opened a part of the weave up in the goggles' peripheral weft, writing a message quickly in summary of all that she could that seemed important. Then, as she was stitching it up again, she noticed a blinking signal in the viewer. She put the goggles to her eyes to see what it was.

It drew her up to look at a point in the sky, covered by the heavy clouds of a traditional jungle afternoon. Tiny readouts kept attempting to unfold some kind of pictogram, but failing.

She let it go and shut the device down – there wasn't time to figure it out now. It was probably something her mother had been working on and she should leave it anywhere, or risk spoiling it perhaps.

Mazhd was still waiting for her. Instead of moving straight off to join the crew he hesitated and held on to her arm, looking into her face. He got a lot into three words, 'Are you okay?'

'I will be,' she said and pushed the goggles against his chest, as much to get him to let her out of his spotlight as to hand them over. 'Here. These are Mom's. Give them to her when you go inside. She might need them.'

He nodded and secured them inside his jacket pocket, holding his hand over them. 'Will do. Try to go back to the city. I'm sure they'll take you up if you ask.'

She looked to the other side of the sky where Glimshard itself hung, impossible and vast. That it was her doing seemed ludicrous, but it strengthened her. 'No, I'm going to wait until you both come out, thanks all the same.'

'If there is any trouble promise me you will go straight back,' he said, flinching as he did so. Behind him, a distance away, Isabeau could see Shrazade, impatient.

'I will,' she said.

He nodded and turned obediently to go. She watched him join the guards, engineers and Shrazade and then walked over to do her part, following them down the ramp into the pit. At the door she pushed aside the warped shape of the access panel and activated the door cartouche.

'S'open.' After all that it seemed funny. She nearly smiled, until she glanced guiltily back up at the tent on the rise. She pushed and the pressure-close released. The door swung silently inwards.

'Signal them that we are coming,' Shrazade said. 'Your methods will be preferred to mine I am sure.'

Isabeau nodded dumbly and began to do as she asked.

Shrazade nodded and Mazhd went first into the opening, followed one at a time by the rest. 'Wait!' she said, hearing a voice from the door com. 'Someone's coming up.'

TRALANE

Tralane allowed herself to pause only once on the journey back up to the top. She sat for a moment on the lip of the hole she had shot in the structure and looked at the neat shear line it cut through the thick metal. It clearly had a range limit – on the far side of the hole beneath there was only a circular smear effect visible now that the lighting had come on and illuminated patches of the structure in yellow brilliance. She checked the aperture setting on the gun's barrel lens and widened it out, then made a reduction in what she thought, from reading the sigils, was the penetration depth of the beam. Then she got up and moved along.

As she had expected, once she got within a reasonable hearing range of the top team camp the male Karoo came out to see what was going on. He came by himself, not invisible, but very strange to see nonetheless. What would have been superb camouflage in the thick forest was not much help in the regulated geometries and flat expanses of colour inside the artefact. She could see him perfectly well. He didn't take any evasive action during his accelerating approach as she stood and took aim. She had bargained on that, since he had no idea what the gun was. She breathed out, held her breath and pulled the trigger.

There was a soft whooshing noise, brief and gentle, a thump as one unvaporised leg fell over on to the floor and then a gentle patter of a few larger pieces descending. A foul mist began to slowly drop towards the ground. Tralane pulled up her neckerchief over her mouth and nose as she walked around it and into the team room. She wasn't noticed for the first couple of strides – everyone was looking at the pane where Soros was talking insistently, Tzaban visible in the background on the floor.

Tralane walked directly to the Karoo queen and took hold of her by the high collar at the back of the flightsuit just as she began to turn around. She put the gun's cold barrel against the side of the dark head. 'I killed your champion with this weapon and I will kill you too if you don't do exactly as I say. Stand still and shut up. If you move I will kill you.' Her voice left no room for doubts.

The queen stood still. Tralane smelled the first sweet tint of something like violets. 'Stop that immediately. I'm counting to three and when I do you better not smell of more than sweat. One, two, three.'

The smell had stopped getting stronger. Even so Tralane felt her resolve wander for a moment and her hand on the collar loosened a fraction. How could she threaten someone so vulnerable? She forced her grip to tighten.

'Don't hurt her!' Minna said. It was the first thing out of her mouth as she turned around too, slower to react and then struggling for a second with the shock of seeing her mother in such a position.

The other engineers stood aghast by this turn of events though Micklas said, ''Laney, are you sure about this?' and because she was first and most trusted they waited on the answer.

'She's mind controlling you with this smell,' Tralane said. 'I'm sure. Minna, come here and let me look at that belt. Everyone else move away from your stations, hands in your pockets, sit on the floor. Do it now.' To forestall any discussions she shifted the gun barrel for a moment fractionally and shot past the queen's face into the pane. A hole appeared next to Soros and smoke and a vile stink of chemical burning followed. The barrel was back in place before the queen felt it go.

'They put it on me in Spire,' Minna said, tears forming in her eyes as she put her thumbs under the belt and showed it. 'I think she has a detonation switch. I've been using a disruptor but I don't know how much longer it will work.'

'Micklas come here,' Tralane said as the others slowly crept forwards, their loyalties and feelings still torn. She knew she was only moments from a mutiny if she was not careful. 'Can you find some connection threads and get it off without breaking the round?'

'I think so,' the older woman nodded after a moment's study. Within moments she had organised the others into the tasks necessary. Obeying her was the easiest thing for them – it was a job, a problem, they could solve it and it helped one of their own – in any war of loyalties for them, that was a winning condition.

The Karoo queen took the moment to say, 'I am open to a bargain. There's no need to be hasty. We have nothing like this weapon. I am unarmed. But not without influence.'

'Don't talk,' Tralane said. 'I have no power to deal with and no interest in a bargain. Where is the switch you carry?'

'I believe it is on my front right under the collar of the suit – a squeeze thing attached to the fabric, covered in a plate of something hard.' The queen's voice was even, but a measured kind, about as regulated as Tralane's was. In the pane, Soros had stopped talking and was only observing. Behind him she saw Carlyn bending over Tzaban.

'Minna,' Tralane said, looking at her daughter. 'Reach in and take it out, see if it is.'

Minna obeyed her and after a moment of difficulty held up the item.

'Go throw it down the big hole off the balcony,' Tralane said.
'But...'

'Now.' She had her most severe voice on, the one she had, to her shame, used to crush rebellions of any kind when they were at home. Minna was proud but Tralane's rage could ruin her composure.

She went to obey.

'Micklas, search her for more.' Tralane concentrated on reading the queen's body language as the search went on but there was no resistance, no telltale relaxations. Maybe the threat of having your head vaporised and Tralane's own state were enough to stop it until this Dahn had some better idea, but Tralane dreaded that better idea.

Micklas found nothing. She stepped back and Tralane hit Dahn as hard as she could in the side of the head with the butt of the gun. The woman went down and out in a moment.

'You said you wouldn't hurt her,' Micklas said, though not objecting.

'I said I wouldn't kill her,' Tralane corrected. 'Bring some of that spare cable and let's tie her up.'

They finished securing her as Minna arrived back, pale and nervous. As she explained how she had been fooled into making the spell locks Tralane and the others determined that even if they couldn't undo the closure, they could expand the belt by weaving in extended threads on to the warp holding everything together so that the flow of symbols would not be broken. The technicalities of doing this with the belt tightly fastened on to Minna were awkward but not impossible. After about twenty minutes of splicing, soldering and tinkering they had a good solid set of connections and then it was only a matter of moments to cut through the original wefts and the belt's physical structure before removing it.

'Over here,' Tralane said, and put it on to Dahn instead. She passed the disruption unit to Micklas. 'Now you're going to take her up and out of here, all of you. If the team from Glimshard are at the door you hand her over and if they're not then you put her outside and shut the door. Mick you'll hang the disruptor over the door higher than she can reach it and use the internal connection to tell the Glimshard guard what you've done.'

'What if she wakes up?'

'If she does you tell her what's going on. If she doesn't, it doesn't matter. Minna, you come with me and help me gather up the things from below. We'll wait for the Glimshard crew there. It's safe now. No more Karoo around.'

'Wh-what about Tzaban?' Minna said.

'Aunt Carlyn shot him,' Tralane said. She waited until she was sure all the crew were on their way to the door, bearing the heavy, awkward Dahn with them. Then she looked down into her daughter's face and snatched her into a bonecrushing hug.

After a few moments they let go of each other but Tralane held Minna's hand and Minna clung on to it as they went down again, beginning to talk of the artefact as neither of them could bear to speak of anything else.

As they reached the print room Soros had established a speaking connection to the outside world. They could hear him exchanging information with Isabeau and Micklas too, attempting to explain the situation with the Karoo queen at the door. Both of them rushed up to add their voices, if only to hear Isabeau speak and to let her know they were there. Tralane imposed order on the connection by flipping the signal tone in the engineer's emergency code, which gave her the right of speech and thought nothing of leaning past Soros to take over.

'Issa, it's so good to hear you!'

'And you, Mom.'

'Minna's here. But listen, the woman at the door is our prisoner, she is Karoo and cannot be trusted.' She explained exactly all she had learned of the way that the queen would attempt to gain control of any human she was near, and how to forestall this with the bomb threat, if need be. Then she added, 'Isabeau, I need you to study some schematics I have found as a matter of urgency. Thread your pane into the loop and as soon as you are done I want you to signal me with your report. We are all preparing to exit immediately unless we receive counter

491

orders but Carlyn and Tzaban must go now and we need medical support.'

Once she had dealt with all the necessary matters she turned, still holding Minna's hand, and crossed to where Carlyn sat down next to Tzaban.

'I think he's dead,' Carlyn said. She looked up at Tralane, then Minna, hopeful for forgiveness. Minna rushed into her arms and she was left looking at Tralane over Minna's shoulder.

Tralane put her hand to Tzaban's neck and felt the faint movement of a pulse. 'He's not dead yet.' He was unconscious, however, his breathing so shallow it was all but invisible. She knew there was nothing she could do for him except hope that the Empress sent a healer quickly. It seemed inadequate, after all he had done for her. She sat back on her heels and met Carlyn's eye.

'Don't look at me like that! Like you're so – disappointed,' Carlyn said.

'I am disappointed,' Tralane said.

'You weren't here the last weeks. You don't know what those things did,' Carlyn said. She let Minna go reluctantly with a shaky smile that thanked her beyond measure for the hug. 'They turned people against each other. They ate us. Their whole behaviour system lets you befriend them. It makes you. How could I be sure it wasn't like that and he wasn't going to kill us all?'

Tralane thought it over. 'You couldn't,' she said, and got up.

'But you're still acting like I'm the one who did wrong!'

'If he'd ever...'

'How can you take the high ground? How *dare* you take it! Like you had a special insight or like it makes you better. You had the gun, and that's what you have now. That's what you got. Don't think this is your superior knowledge because it isn't. It's just the gun talking.'

Minna shrieked over the last of Carlyn's words, 'Stop it! Stop

492

it! They're winning when we fight each other. Whoever they are. Whatever they want. Stop.'

Tralane felt furious but she did stop, in that no more words came out of her. She felt the gun under her hand. 'What if I throw it away and it's all that stops them? Don't you think that's why Alide wanted those cannons here? Whatever else we do has no impact at all.' She heard the irony in the silence that followed her.

'So now the pacifist asks for weapons?'

'Should I put them down and let us be consumed until there are no more of us left, then?' Tralane asked. She didn't know the answer. Once she would have said, yes, let it be then, let us move on into other forms and be ended rather than clash and prolong the hatred, but in those days she had lived in Glimshard in a house that nobody bothered with.

'Nobody is suggesting that as the alternative, I hope,' Soros said. He and the other engineers were all looking on now.

Tralane looked at all of them. 'We've been here for hours now,' she said, gesturing at the room. 'We've had a good look at this. Does anyone have anything to say about it?'

Glances flashed between people, knowing, wary.

'A lot of the spells I've seen here are corrupted,' Soros said. 'They seem to be part of a larger whole...'

'A whole system of related instructions or schematics for making or printing. The words are hard to understand but...'

'...for making living things out of some base material. Always the same substrate, the same alchemical start ingredients, these white basalt, black camphoric, scarlet rye... And other things which are treated like dyes, colours in a factory...'

'...a huge number, a huge variety of things. There are all these references to cauldrons though where they are I don't know – cauldrons of making and cauldrons of brewing...'

'...some of the things look like people. Like it was making people. But how could that be?'

493

Minna looked up then from Tralane's pane which she had been using while the engineers all spoke. 'This is a ship,' she said.

They turned to look at her, six heads as one.

'Look, it's a piece of this much larger whole. It has propulsion systems, sixty different kinds of engines but basically it's an airship, only without a balloon.'

'How could it be that big? It's more than two klicks long.' But Soros sounded all too sure, excitement rising.

'This is only one part,' Tralane said. 'Where's the rest?'

'What if that stuff we pick up all over the continent is the rest?'

'The bits are too small to be sure. They could be anything, not necessarily fragments of one object. And if it is as you say, why don't any of us remember such things or have any records of them?'

'Any records of what?'

The new voice made them all start and turn, guiltily, as if caught in a conspiracy. Zharazin Mazhd stood in the doorway. He hesitated a moment, catching Tralane's eye and a smile flickered on his face. Then he moved aside and two medics and a group of armed guards moved past him into the room. They made Tralane and Carlyn step back as they took over Tzaban's care and began to strap him to a stretcher.

'I'm afraid to tell you that all your work is confiscated by the Infomancy as of this moment,' Mazhd said in a businesslike tone. 'I am sure that once an initial assessment has been made you will have it all returned to you for further research, some of you at least.' Now he definitely didn't catch Tralane's eye or anybody else's. 'Please give your personal recording devices to my assistants, making sure each is easily recognisable for its swift return.'

Even Tralane wanted to protest but Soros said it for them as he folded his arms and glowered. 'You fuckers think you're above everyone else don't you? Well good luck with reading it.

494

I hope your eyes fall out.' He shoved his tablet at the downcast assistant – a grey-robed neophyte, pale and sickly with nerves – and then set about gathering his tools.

'Professor Huntingore if you would be so kind as to close down the devices as for now,' Mazhd added, as if he didn't know her. Tralane wondered at it and stared at him, feeling a pang as Tzaban's shrouded body was hauled out of the room, the stretcher-bearers already puffing and complaining under his weight. The assistant infomancer arrived before Minna and looked up at her.

'I don't have anything!' she snapped, shaking, her arms crossed. 'Can't you see I've been kidnapped and everything? Nnnhhh...'

They were of an age, Tralane smiled for a second as the boy cringed and had then to step in front of her. 'Here you go,' she said, in as kind a voice as she could muster. He took her tablet and placed it with extreme reverence into his carryall. She wondered if she'd ever see it again.

'And the gun,' Mazhd added, as the boy was about to move on.

No! Tralane's gaze said as she flashed a look at him, furious.

Yes, his cool reply in kind said, though there was an edge to his expression that was almost pleading with her to obey, as if he had a lot more to say but couldn't.

She knew the Infomancy could bury whatever they wanted if they thought it compromised Imperial benefit. They could kill without weapons. It wasn't as if they were going to start carrying guns themselves. Even so, it felt wrong as her fingers unclipped the holster and slid the gun out. She turned it off, applied the safety warding, and then put it into the sack, keeping her eye contact with him all the while.

'And now, if you have all gathered your personal belongings, we will adjourn to the surface and the city directly. You will be debriefed at the palace.'

He needed say no more. The notion of safety, shelter and a return home, albeit a moved home, was too much for them. They couldn't get out fast enough. Only Carlyn lingered as Mazhd waited for Tralane and Minna, neither of whom had moved.

'You go on with Aunt Carlyn,' Tralane said to Minna, giving her a push. 'I'll be with you in a minute.'

Minna looked surprised, raised an eyebrow and then pulled a face as if to say – oh not at a time like this! She looked thoroughly disgusted and shook her head, sullen as she went to Carlyn's side. Once they had gone, Tralane looked back at Mazhd.

'How much can you remember?'

Mazhd's pretty face became arch although his tone was wry. 'I take it you're not referring to our evening? No. Well then. I remember everything I witness.' He seemed patient, his hands folded in front of him, still playing his role.

'I'm going to show you each of these devices in turn,' she said. 'Prior to turning them off. I want you to look at everything I show you very carefully. Do you understand?' She was praying that now he'd be her memory bank, one she needed, if not entirely trusted. 'Doing your duty by the Empire most thoroughly.'

'Yes Professor, I understand very well.'

'Get over here.'

She kissed him first and when she felt better she showed him everything she could pull out of the weave. She didn't know how long they had, so she went at random without trying to get anything in particular, screen after screen, watching his eyes track across the symbols, the minute nod of his head when he was confident of each batch. At last his face began to fall in its expression, a chaos overtaking it like shadow and she knew that even he had had enough. Without looking at how much she had left out, she closed it down.

'Oh, I nearly forgot.' He smiled charmingly at her, the room

496

darker now and the sense of their isolation almost complete. He opened a high pocket inside his jacket and drew out – her goggles.

'Ahh,' she said with delighted surprise, taking them from him and checking if they worked.

'Isabeau was most insistent that I give them to you personally.'

Tralane put them on and cued the message she saw waiting. When she had read it, her smile had gone, though it tried to come back as she glanced at him through the strange lenses and saw his expression.

'Very adventuresome,' he said, meaning how they looked.

'You have no idea,' she said and took them off her head, and then put them on to his head, adjusting the eyepieces to the right places. 'Stand here and look up where the arrows want to lead you.'

She watched his head swing through the arc until she knew that he was looking at what she had just looked at, through iron and steel, through miles of sky, through clouds and rain and whatever in between to a star that was not a star over them in the sky. 'I'll translate for you. That object is like a magestone, high up above the world. These symbols running around it are the stone talking. It is talking to the ship that we are standing in. The ship has been talking to it ever since we put the power on. And these other symbols to the left, floating, the ones that change, that look like old character writing, those are a message that the stone is sending down here.'

'Who from?' He put his hand to the lenses, as if he could help things resolve for him, though she knew it wouldn't make a difference. Isabeau hadn't read it. He couldn't read it, but she could.

'It's from whoever picked up the signal,' she said. 'They say they have received our distress signal and they are on their way.'

He tore the goggles off his head, rounding on her so fast she took a step back. 'It what?!'

She took them back carefully and glanced again though she needn't have. She would never forget what it said. 'It says they're coming.'

She watched as he looked at her, incredulous, wondering if he were able to believe her or not. From trouble in a land war where the sky was only sky it was a long leap out into the edge of the world and beyond. Muscles in his face worked several times as if he'd speak. Finally, acceptance smoothed the deep lines out of his forehead and his wry, self-mocking grin returned. His eyes bore the deep, dark fire of passionate interest that sprung from the soul – like her, he could not resist the mystery, the scale, the romance, the danger. 'Is this one of those glorious angels you were telling me about?'

'The bolts from the blue, forces of nature, that kick you sideways out of all your best laid plans? Yes.' She couldn't help but smile in return, glad of it in this private moment they shared, before anyone else knew and took away all the decisions about what must be done.

He nodded and handed the goggles back to her before embracing her tightly and holding her there.

He hesitated. 'Does it say anything about when they will arrive?'

'No, but supposing the signal travels at the speed of aether consistently and taking the start point here as the power-up time, assuming a small delay for receipt and composition of a reply, I still have no idea because we know nothing about the propulsion engines. If the schematics here are correct those parts of this machine have never been found. I could extrapolate from the systems that power the city but there's no telling if that would be appropriate. All I can say is that wherever "they" are, aetheric signals take approximately two days to get there and two days to get back.'

'There's nothing to stop us talking to them more?'

'Theoretically, no. Politically, I would think this is Infomancy work. But Isabeau mentioned that she thinks Torada is truly rogue and yet the Karoo seem to speak with her and prepare to negotiate. But that, fortunately, is no concern of mine.' She caressed his face, finding it dear to her, the impossible smile that found humour in the situation still there.

'I fear my concerns are only beginning,' he said.

'Let's delay them a little while longer.' She unfastened the front of the thin jacket he wore, knowing he was right. 'They won't send anyone to look for us if you play your cards right, will they?'

He pretended to frown and shook his head. 'No, no. It is my duty to be sure everything is secured and it is no lie that there is so very much to see here before that can be determined.'

He unmeshed the front of her overalls. 'I am ashamed to admit I find these hideous clothes unbearably attractive on you.'

'You know I'm only using you for your body. I know the Infomancy sent you to spy on me don't forget, Agent Mazhd.' She stepped out of them and rid herself of her underwear.

'Recent developments have rendered you of insufficient interest to be a candidate for seduction and infiltration, Professor. I'm sorry to inform you that my interest is purely personal from here on in.'

She put her arms around him and took a deep breath close to his skin. He smelled glorious, divine. 'My interest is purely professional. You have all my notes.'

'The beauty of it is you'll never know exactly what I have. Nor will anyone else. I fear you have put me in a compromising position – as a pair we have exclusive power, alone nothing.'

'What do you propose we do about that?'

'I'm open to a deal.'

They negotiated the deal on the cold, angled floor among their discarded clothes. Afterwards she lay and looked through the goggles as he rested with his head on her shoulder, legs entwined, inside the starship that lay buried in the mud.

'Do you suppose anyone wants to hear a theory about how we were created by a dead Master Magus who got all his spells mixed up?' Tralane asked. The signals fluttered steadily, repeating, from shore to star to shore.

'Oh no, I don't think anybody wants to hear that,' Zharazin said.

'Time to go before we're missed.' Tralane stood and offered him her hand. 'What will you say?'

'I'll tell the truth, that the stars are coming to see what they have made.'

They got up and dressed themselves again, then she led the way back to the surface.

POSTSCRIPT

Greetings Prime Node Mazhd from Living Memory #51
Access Path Whitebirch, authorisation nodes 1,2
Diary Pages: Huntingore, Isabeau.

1. Vexation. Another thing I don't get – why are the humans outside the Empire so very different? Saying they're badly educated and don't eat well doesn't cut it. Lots of people here are poor, stupid and addicted to all kinds of crap but they still manage magic, even if it's only working the elevators and summoning the mail. Nobody outside does those things. And even if we're not using this power to take everything while they get nothing, even if we're just sitting here, trading and setting a 'beneficent hegemonic example' I don't think any of them feel it inspiring. They just think we're frightening, and weird, and they probably hate us. I would.

2. Sister Auchie was explaining 'the birds and the bees', as if we all don't know everything already – but afterward she said that not every City in the Empire is like ours and they see us as rebellious and 'ill considered' because our Empress rules with 'velvet gloves'. They did not say what the other Empresses ruled with, although an iron fist was mentioned, and a Sleight Hand.

3. The velvet gloves, whatever they are, seem to be bad because they are somehow obvious and unsophisticated, manipulative and indirect, whereas much more respect is accorded to an Empress like Dirt who has a Work Ethic and Rules with a system based on cultivation and communal labour. When I asked what kind of gloves Dirt wore Sister Auchie looked at me as if I was stupid and then said, 'I suppose they're work gloves, dear.' Genius.

4. So, it seems that it's considered better to be ruled through exhausting yourself industriously than to be ruled by being petted nicely with a soft glove. I fail to see the link. Especially after today's work in the lab grinding samples. Given the choice I would rather the latter, unless the former benefited me enormously, but then I wouldn't need gloves at all, would I?

5. The Sorority line on why our Empress is weaker than the others goes something like this. Reason 1: women are the natural rulers of men because they bear the children and all the responsibility, therefore they must also have the power and authority. Our Empress has no children so far, so she is too ignorant.

6. Reason 2 : Men's natures make them territorial, possessive, argumentative, violent and antisocial. They can be used successfully for military power and for labour, and must be kept occupied each within his own field, in order to maintain a discipline among them and to turn their inclinations into mild and profitable enterprises. Our Empress does not keep discipline; here they do as they like. Ergo, her men are running wild and some kind of disaster is implied.

7. Reason 3: Men must be ordered by natural qualities preferentially, before being considered as potential fathers of one's children or indeed any children. Men of unsuitable temper and type must be prevented from reproducing. Our Empress has no visible selection methodology and does not matchmake. She risks dissolving the bloodlines and ruining the talents. Apparently.

8. If one remains in the Sorority one must produce a worthwhile thesis on the subject of motherhood before progressing to the act accordingly. Meantime one might dally as one likes with whatever men, women or whoever the Sorority deem socially appropriate. Have seen list. Ick. Gloom.

8.5. Our Empress' aptitude dictates much for us in Glimshard: harmonious companionship. There is an adequate and variable supply of every kind of person. Yet the Sorority considers it second class for our Empress to exert her authority via pleasing men, even if this is a by-product of pleasing women. Nobody can speak directly about this. When I ask about it I'm told to stop wittering about matters I'm too young to understand. It is understood that men are not to be gratified as if this is not a viable route to power. Instead they are to be kept in a state of instability through partial gratification. As this has proven time and again to foment both addiction and resentment it cannot be sensible to pursue it yet that is exactly what the Sorority suggests as its best course. What is wrong with these people? (Note, since they are so keen to shut me up clearly there is more to be got out of this. A flick through the Spire Court Proceedings of the last five years reveals increasing numbers of violent crimes against persons and their chattels within the city. Austerity has been imposed at higher levels in response. Crimes of Indiscipline have altered away from persons and into group-based aggressions since.) An outlet for aggression is clearly required.

9. Boring lesson on gender. The Sorority consider the eight existing pronouns in Glimshard Imperial make language matters too awkward and our poetry despicable, want to return to the Spire form of just three. 'Why must one constantly advertise one's preferences if one is only asking for the price of fruit?' An oddly chosen example given a previous lesson on metaphor. I am beginning to suspect Sister Auchie of having a sense of humour at times. Or perhaps no sense of irony.

10. I decided to ask what considerations the Sorority recommended for locating a mate, if we were to do away with the pronouns. Sister Auchie said it must be first the good health, then the Talent combination and its possible outcomes, after that the looks of the male (she assumed breeding-mate you see as I did not use the correct pronoun to indicate a loving partner of any suited gender), for beauty generally indicates a strong and robust constitution, after that his friends, since he may be judged well by those whose company he seeks and maintains: after that his character and after that his charisma and latent 'appeal'. *His* gender only has bearing insofar as it may or may not impede said breeding. I said, fine, that covers Empire men. What about the rest? She looked blank. Finally she said, 'One does not breed outside the Empire. What would be the point?'

11. It occurs to me that the Sorority has entirely missed the point sociologically. Surely the point is desire, which is the only impulse one does anything for? A walk behind my sister (a block behind, but she's easy to follow as she

never pays any attention to anyone except herself) puts a spanner in the cogs of the very notion that the desire for sex has its point anywhere near the Sorority Rulebook. There are enough foreigners from the barracks creeping back in the early hours after midnight to prove that. I don't think everyone is filling out forms and pursuing a rigorous algorithm of selection – unless they are doing that unconsciously, of course. If so, it is not an algorithm that the Sorority has heard of. An algorithm for desire would be so very useful! Although I might have to expand on the notation re the genders issue. I will ask Sister Auchie why it is that the inbuilt process for selection of mates is insufficient and they have attempted to impose another.

11.5. Cross. Idea of Algorithm of Desire met with derision. Auchie mentioned Night's Student, called him a halfbreed bloodmancing monstrosity and made the sign of Annasward though there were no trace presences about. She said he would know it if noses could talk. I don't know what she means by that but her expression indicated she was having some kind of intestinal problem so I didn't ask.

12. I find most of the Sorority's statements outside the rigors of mathematics to be vague and highly scientifically unsatisfactory. It is not what I expected when I first came to learn here although once they have alchemical science in their sights they are without peer. But when I pursued Sister Auchie about these 'rules of social and political conduct' and how they came to be she said only that they were agreed by the original collective which had taken root in Spire a century ago. These tenets were now considered canonical. I suggested they were in need of revision, scientifically, but she said that tradition was more important than factual correctness as human social mores derive their strength and

usefulness from collective conscious concurrence, which is what elevates us above creatures like the Karoo.

Speechless.

13. For the Canon and the attendant nonsense the Sorority clings to in the mistaken belief that such stuff is the glue of civilisation I award a further demerit to an already dis-piriting list. Their application to the biological and social sciences is nearly entirely reliant on subjective opinion. I am taking all information set out on these subjects with a large pinch of salt and have moved my files on them into the 'Reservations' section of my studies. Nonetheless I must remain here until I complete the entirety of their physics and astrology teachings though I fear their lens on history will be somewhat fish-eyed to say the least. Gloom. NB It appears my mother has discovered a gun. Checked it this evening with Minna when she was out. I wonder what else is in the attic.

*

Do you require further memories, Prime?

Thank you for sharing your memory of reviewing this material. A cache of your subjective state appreciation of this material has been remembered for you. Would you like to re-interpret any of your previous readings?

Would you like to send any memories to the Angel Node?

Would you like to grant access to the Infomancy's Memory to the Angel Node?

Would you like to access the memory of the Angel Node?

Please respond, Prime.

Thank you, Prime. Here are the last memories of Shrazade, Prime Node of Glimshard.

Mind Poison, Mazhd? Really? After all this time I thought we were friends. Like friends. Something like that. Was it the Diary? You saw it too. Of course you did. It's because of that thing you wouldn't show me. That thing about Night. You can't hide what you know but you could hide what you didn't know. And you do the same with the Huntingore woman. It is futile.

When did you discover Angel Node? Was it before the jungle? No, it must have been after. It must have been inside the ship. You could read some of the ship memory, because everyone was there and there was blood everywhere. I couldn't stop her sending you. Yes, Night, of course. She knew you would always belong to her as I have always belonged to the Empire.

It wasn't easy to keep Angel Node a secret. Will you keep it a secret? I'm sad that I will not see its arrival. I did not dare to look and see what it knew. Will you dare that? Will you do it straight away, or will you wait? Will you tell them, or will you see what the information can do for you? Don't hold it too long, Mazhd. Like me, it has an expiration date.

'Much will be asked of you.'

Ah, I see it was asked of you. And you have not disappointed them. Or me. You were a good student.

Hold my hands. I'd hoped for better. I wanted to know so much ... goodbye. Ah I thought it would be so different ... diffe ... d

*

Would you like to keep the memory of your visit to that memory
    as an official record, Prime?
As you wish.